T0162692

The Dean Is Dead Again

The Dean Is Dead Again

#3 in the Briarpatch College Series

William Urban
2009

iUniverse, Inc.

New York   Bloomington

The Dean Is Dead Again
#3 in the Briarpatch College Series

iUniverse books may be ordered through booksellers or by contacting:

iUniverse
1663 Liberty Drive
Bloomington, IN 47403
www.iuniverse.com
1-800-Authors (1-800-288-4677)

ISBN: 978-1-4401-1552-3 (sc)
ISBN: 978-1-4401-1553-0 (ebk)

Printed in the United States of America

iUniverse rev. date: 01/22/2009

Foreword

This series of novels started December 11, 2000, as a play based on a concept from the early 1970s. I had thought that the success of the play I wrote for my college's Sesquicentennial, "Founders Days," could be duplicated. However, since this play lacked whatever it was that directors were looking for, I turned into a murder mystery in 2003 and published it in 2007; the second play was begun in 2003, turned into a murder mystery in 2004 and published in 2008. This novel was begun in September of 2003. My thanks to Bill French and Ed Miller (who are not models for Smith and Jones) for allowing me the use of their pseudo-paper in Chapter One; also to Mary Bruce, my colleague in English, who read early drafts and shared the experience she had garnered from workshops and from writing her own novels; and to Lee McGaan, whose insightful comments led to some significant improvements in the final text. My thanks also to administrators and faculty members across the country for providing me with never-ending inspiration. This was at its most creative in the Nineties—whenever one thought that their idiocy could not get worse, they would come up with something new. God bless them!

It helped that I have largely worked in small colleges, where the good and the bad are more easily observed than in large institutions where genius and incompetence are obscured by the many distractions of intellectual and social life and by the sheer numbers of faculty, staff and students. This reduced circle of acquaintances has allowed me to get to know individual students and colleagues in other departments well, and also deans. A large institution has so many deans that none of them are particularly important, and none would be particularly missed. If a few million bucks disappeared, some alumnus would contribute that amount or more—as long as the football and basketball teams were doing well. At a small college the dean is involved in everything, every dollar counts, and more students are on teams, in plays, and in musical performances than in the stands. It might be noted that my relationships with a long series of academic and student deans have been good, especially so with those possessing a sufficient sense of the absurd to appreciate the more bizarre aspects of modern higher education.

The situations and personalities are universal in higher education (except maybe having undergraduates become academic deans). They should not be understood to refer to actual living or recently deceased individuals.

Cast of Characters
from *The Dean Is Still Dead*

DO Donahue—former detective, now assistant professor of Sociology in his second year

Mary C—assistant professor of Spanish, still working on the publication required for tenure

John Justice Biggs—Middleville chief of police, nearing retirement, looking forward to it

Lill—professor of theater, formerly acting-president of Briarpatch College

Lily—professor of theater, formerly acting-dean of Briarpatch College

Molly—adjunct instructor (part-time) in English, formerly married to the late Dean Wooda, close to becoming engaged to Sal

Salvatore Iva—former chemistry professor, former lover of Flo Boater, imprisoned for conspiracy to murder Dean Wooda, but expected to be released on parole

Jenny—adjunct instructor in Music, closely attached to Hiram Jason Bird

Jay Bird—former janitor, pled guilty to assault on Dean C. Wooda, now back on the job

C. Wooda—late academic dean of Briarpatch College; still dead, but not forgotten

Stanley Wooda—current academic dean of Briarpatch College, young and ambitious

Floyd Boater—late president of Briarpatch College

Flora Boater—widow of above, now president of Briarpatch College

Maximilian Stout—head of the English department, with ambitions to advance

The Creep—head of the History department, with similar ambitions

Miss Efficiency—the president's secretary

Windy Burg—Athletic Director and football coach

Choir director—professor with a single-minded dedication to music

Dean of Students—a practical administrator: "If we didn't see it, it didn't happen."

Ms. Gates—the librarian

Miss Fox—professor emerita of Spanish, house-bound by age, eager to see visitors

Luci May Mankiller—president of Arcadia Junior College, Briarpatch's main rival

Smith (Smitty) and Jones (JJ)—students too busy to study, but with nothing to do

Ellie (L.E.)—transfer student from Arcadia; bright but bored out of her mind

The Briarpatch College motto: *Hic jam etiam sumus!*

If the 1996 enrollment numbers can be sustained,
the motto may become *Vivat et floreat!*

Chapter One

Act One: the Diner

DO Donahue was studying his half-empty coffee cup, musing over the recently resolved deaths of the academic dean and the president of Briarpatch College, wondering if *resolved* meant *solved*. Or did mean *re-solved*? "Did Chief Biggs and I really solve the same crime twice?" He thought he knew why the two cases of the past year had resulted in only one conviction—the confession of a chemist who apparently was guilty of nothing but an overactive conscience: "The evidence... the evidence was so... so *contradictory*. And the law... was so difficult to apply." Then he smiled at the irony of his situation: the person he held responsible for both deaths had been found "not guilty" and was now his boss—the president of Briarpatch College, Flora Boater, the late president's widow.

"How'd we mess up?" he asked himself. Then he laughed, thinking, "A month later O. J. Simpson was found 'not guilty.' The prosecutor there was even more sure than we were that the case was open and shut. Goes to show, you can't second-guess a jury." The trial had been at the start of the spring semester of 1996, almost nine months earlier, but it seemed both longer ago and more recent. He felt much older, probably because he wasn't getting enough exercise. He should have done better during the summer. But life got in the way of good intentions.

He looked up from his cold coffee, having promised himself that he would not have a second cup until Chief Biggs appeared. Not that the waitress would fail to fill his cup—"warm up," she would say— but the Old Doc had warned him about too much caffeine. "Hard," he said to himself, "to break the habits of a lifetime." He sighed and looked longingly at the half-empty cup. A slight motion demanded his attention, but it was only the waitress. "No, not yet, thanks." He glanced toward the door—only two farmers and a... somebody, a bank

1

employee he guessed. Nothing significant, hardly enough to keep his mind sharp. He looked again, to see if the stranger was behaving oddly. No. Not at all. Just another customer. Or was he even a stranger? While Donahue did not know everyone in town, he recognized most people who came into the Diner regularly. The waitress, however, seemed to know the fellow. Did that mean he'd lost his edge, that ability to sense trouble? He had it when he'd been a cop, when he had been so welcome in coffee shops, not because people liked him particularly—though he made many friends—but his presence, or that of his uniform, was... what's the right word?... reassuring? That changed when he became a detective—no uniform—except to proprietors who knew that he carried a weapon. Strange, he reflected. He had never used it, but people felt reassured knowing that someone was armed. Not as well armed as the bad guys, but armed, and trained to use it. How different from Briarpatch College, where some students must have weapons in their pickups, but several members of the faculty believed that the police—even Chief Biggs—were a greater threat than... than what? Anybody, he guessed. Fortunately, in Middleville the greatest criminal activity was stealing hubcaps, and faculty cars did not have hubcaps worth removing. "How many believed policemen were dangerous?" Not that many, probably. More were interested in the golf course. Golf... he'd not seen the course, but he understood that one really had to love the game to tolerate it. That's why some drove to Arcadia, where the course had eighteen holes. Less challenging, but... what did he know? Arcadia Junior College was there, too, which under Luci May Mankiller was becoming more culturally radical. He smiled to himself, trying to imagine what she thought of golf.

How many of his colleagues understood as little about sociology and politics as he did of golf? And how could they believe so deeply in their various causes? They might ridicule religion, but their own "belief systems" were pretty superficial, too. No matter what they said, they didn't deviate much from the rest of society. Classes and family came first. Not for all of them, but most. They often believed in zero population growth, but still had families, and from what he heard, his colleagues were proud of what they were doing. They might put comments about politics into lectures, but never at the cost of explaining carbon rings.

Education may have been partly a method of advancing political goals, but it was still education. "Oh, well," he sighed. "One generation's radicals are the next generation's conservatives. Or," he added with a smile, "the next generation's professors." He had seen too much of real life to be optimistic about either bringing about change or resisting it, but he was not ready to be depressed by it.

Donahue's mild conservatism was not resented by his colleagues. Small colleges tended to have polite faculties. "Why not, anyway?" he asked himself. "When everyone seems to be against you—the town, colleagues at the universities looking down at you, newspapers not considering you for interviews, and grants hard to get—you might as well be polite, even to those whose ideas...." As he mentally formed an appropriate end to the sentence, he smiled wryly—"whose ideas cannot be found in the *New York Times*, not even one delivered three days late."

Not seeing the chief yet, Donahue realized that such thoughts would eventually ruin his day. Surely, there was something else to think about. Maybe something for a publication? Something on golf, maybe; perhaps on why most people don't play golf. That would be different. Maybe bowling. The research would be easier—everyone all together and most of the time sitting down, not scattered over the fairways, walking all the time. Not a scholarly publication necessarily, but something worth saying. At that, his thoughts drifted back to Briarpatch College. He tried to form the first lines of an essay: "From time to time a mystery appears at every small college. Most resolve themselves quickly and quietly."

That's as far as he got. What came next? Could he say, "Only rarely do they surprise or shock the faculty and staff or the students who are not following soap operas and baseball?" He had not decided before he was surprised, then mildly shocked, himself. The chief entered, spotted him and sat down quickly without giving the waitress his usual signal for coffee. That was the surprise. The shock came in the chief's report that Miss Purdy, the financial officer of Briarpatch College, had told her co-workers that something was amiss, then disappeared. It looked like another case of "foul play."

Act Two: Briarpatch College

Foul play was almost unknown on the campus until the past year, 1995; even news of crime elsewhere rarely reached campus. The internet was still practically unknown; that is, there was one person on line at this isolated, under-funded liberal arts college—the Computer Center Director, who had been so reluctant to share his treasure with anyone but majors and the late dean that colleagues in the science building had gleefully refused him permission to expand into a larger office where he could provide them access to the Net. The local radio station carried mostly country music and sports, the newspaper was a weekly, with little news from outside the county; the college newspaper considered Middleville a foreign nation—even though most students came from towns much like Middleville or smaller; and the college radio station broadcast only in the Student Center, where the lunchtime noise was too great for anyone to hear. The movie theater had just closed, leaving yet another vacant building on the square, and the only real dance hall was populated largely by high school kids. There was more gossip than sales items in the stores, and most city problems were minor, imaginary or too expensive to fix. But occasionally a serious matter arose, as appeared to be the case now, at least in the mind of Chief Biggs. Had Biggs's story been written by a real writer (Mickey Spillane said that a real writer was someone who sold books), his narrative would have been longer. However, because Donahue was an academic, that is, someone who was paid for teaching (or, at better places than Briarpatch, for writing books that almost nobody read), the chief didn't even have to set the matter in context. While most persons who heard of a missing Vice President for Financial Affairs might merely have wondered where she could be or what she did, the chief knew that Donahue would understand his concern instantly—might there be a connection to the recent deaths? Indeed, as Donahue listened, he saw so many concentric rings to the story that he began to imagine a target. What he could not help imagining at the center of all this was a woman—Flo Boater, the president of Briarpatch College.

Briarpatch was a small liberal arts college forgotten by much of the world, certainly by the state department of highways, and by most of those few alumni who had done better in the world than their talents or education suggested would occur. But in the minds of many who taught and studied there, it was not isolated. No living person could remember the true isolation of frontier days, when the Briarpatch was a small meadow in a vast forest, and few could remember life before electricity and flush toilets, when visitors were rarities and news came via a crackling radio or the *Middleville Moderate*, a daily paper until the arrival of fuzzy television reception in the mid-Fifties. Consequently, no matter what comments outsiders might make—especially visiting speakers from the state university at Zenith and recently arrived faculty (who often viewed their stay at Briarpatch as only temporary or a ghastly joke of fate)—students and their parents believed they were very much a part of the modern world. Some went even farther, quite the opposite of feeling isolated, to think of Briarpatch as the center of the universe.

This was not entirely foolishness. Everyone knew that the sun was the center of the solar system, and, if asked what the center of the universe was, most would wrinkle their brows, realize that this was a trick question, then admit that they really didn't know, nor did they particularly care. The physicist (at Briarpatch College that was singular, not plural) would, of course, delight in explaining why astronomers believed the solar system was rather more toward the edge of the universe than the center, and excitedly add that we were living in a great era, that we might even come to understand the greatest mysteries of all time; as his words poured forth, faster and faster, non-physicists would roll their eyes, then look for someone to rescue them from the detailed explanation they knew was coming. Lill and Lily, two seasoned professors of theater, had once been so uncharitable as to whisper to Donahue, that it was a greater mystery why so many faculty members considered the *New York Times* essential daily reading. He had smiled and nodded agreement, because the newspaper was most highly prized by those who denounced the destruction of the forests by capitalist profiteers out to make a buck out of trees.

Local hunters, who read this statement in a letter to the editor of *The Middleville Moderate,* laughed that the trick was to find a buck *in* the trees. In reality, however, that was not too difficult in Middleville's neighborhood. The number of deer was far larger than it had been when Native Americans roamed the region each summer, stopping briefly in the Briarpatch to pick berries before returning to their distant fields and winter quarters; in fact, local hunters shot several thousand every year—and that was only in Milledgeville County; even more were "harvested" over in Arcadia County, the home of Arcadia Junior College. The deer were not exactly defenseless, however. Every long-time resident had a story of a friend or relative who had been "attacked" by deer. There was a kernel of truth to many of these stories, but the local sense of humor (which newcomers rarely understood) was more important. At its core was a realization than anyone who believed the *New York Times* or the *Zenith Apex* were infallible, or whose view of nature had been formed by Walt Disney, was also likely to believe in "killer deer" (or, in the age of Jimmy Carter, "killer rabbits"). This joke became all the more delightful as victims tried to square this new information with cartoon stereotypes that made even carnivores into vegetarians, or how they struggled with the idea that dangerous stags possessed of full racks could hide in the grove behind the Gym. Yes, it was overgrown, but it was only a hundred yards square and hadn't other new friends warned them to stay away from the "unkempt copse" only because poison ivy grew on every tree? What, anyway, was an *unkempt copse*? Why hadn't they been told of the "killer deer" before? And what should they do if they encountered a beast on its way to drive cars off the highways? The joke was especially fun when the victim was named Bambi.

It may have seemed funny to some that the missing person was named Miss Bambi P. Purdy—some joked that she was Purdy big for a fawn. But not to Chief Biggs. Not at this moment, and not because he thought the local sense of humor was cruel. It was because of her that he had made the appointment with Donahue, and her disappearance was the reason he was late.

Act Three: the Characters

It was not *ignorance* that made some give undue importance to this little college. At least not among the faculty. The students, of course, individually and collectively believed that the world revolved around them, but students are by definition uneducated. If they weren't naïve and ill-informed, what would be the point of the college existing at all? What the faculty offered, when not engaged in the business of preparing students for a world of work, was *wisdom*. Of course, there was sharing the right political opinions, which for some was the main point, having been taught since Kindergarten that sharing was good. Whether political education was essential or not largely depended on what individual professors taught. If students had to master material sufficiently to do well in the next course of the sequence, students' attitudes toward the political fads of the moment were less important than in subjects where it didn't matter if the instructor finished the syllabus or not (or even had one). Modern Languages was often an exception to this—understanding why Latin Americans had legitimate complaints against the US being more important than being able to talk with them—but at Briarpatch this was not always the case. The chair never appeared on campus in daylight, and Mary C, whose politics were far to the left, trusted students to be smart enough to make up their own minds without her aid. Mary's non-interventionist attitude was one reason that Donahue continued to hope that there was yet a possibility that their minds might meet on a non-political basis. That is, romance.

Retired professors, such as Miss Fox in Spanish (a legendary teacher whom Mary intended to get to know someday) could see the many ironies in the changing faculty enthusiasms, but for those still actively involved in class work and committees, everything was deadly serious. Some saw in Miss Fox's laughter the wisdom of age.

This attitude was not shared by those self-selected groups of professors and instructors who had enough in common—age, rank, political opinions, and marital status—to see themselves as the saving elite of the institution. Only they, they believed, had the insights and wisdom to guide the college through the difficult days to come.

This subject, in fact, was being discussed that moment, in early in September of 1996, by Lill and Lily, who had reasons to be somewhat cynical right then.

"I get so discouraged sometimes," Lill said during their morning walk. "And it's not Flo Boater as much as our colleagues." Flo Boater had grounds to hate the two doyennes of the thespian arts. *Doyenne* was a word Lily had picked up recently from a French teacher, who was using it to describe her own job—it sounded so much better than *instructor*. Not as good as *doyen*, which was masculine, but, as Lily joked, "French is just another language that favors the patriarchy."

Lill continued, "I know how petty people can be, but why do they have to be *so* mean-spirited?" Lill was a veteran of many faculty disputes, but she had never been treated badly before she had accepted the acting-presidency of the college the previous year. Yes, "acting" was appropriate for a theater professor, but not "acting-president."

"Ah, forget about'em," Lily responded with a wave of the hand. "The mayor and citizens are behind us." With a further wave, she urged her friend to pick up the pace a bit. A good walk could wear off despondency, she knew, but not if one dawdled.

Lill, with a sigh, moved forward more quickly. It was not easy. She was a "substantial" woman and she would have preferred sitting around a table with students in the Japanese coffee house to doing anything healthy. "Damn, why do you like this so much?" she groused. Getting no response from her friend beyond a wide smile, she added, "Our colleagues don't give a damn about the citizens, but without them we'll never get anywhere with the trustees."

Lily turned her head to respond, "The trustees think the faculty are all idiots, and since the faculty don't consider the citizens of Middleville likely to have an idea worth discussing, the trustees are more likely to trust the citizens." Lily loved little jokes, but in her efforts at humor one usually found something worthy of further reflection.

"Come again?" Lill asked.

This worried Lily, because Lill was usually very sharp indeed, very quick to pick up on whatever she was saying. But, as was Lily's wont, she never went back to review a subject; instead, she plunged on, "The faculty's irresponsibility is one more proof that professors are all former students. And," she added after a pause, "that some have never gotten over graduate school."

At this Lill laughed, and the walk became less a strain. The conversation drifted to speculations on why so many of their colleagues disliked Briarpatch and what enlightened administrators might do to change that attitude.

Lill's spirits fell again as they discussed how easily Flo Boater was keeping the trustees tied up in irrelevant discussions—especially planning sessions for the future, ambitious cloud dreams for which no money was likely to be available. Yes, there was the insurance money on the late dean and president, which had not come in yet, but paying off debts would swallow most of it up. "Besides, ten million dollars isn't what it used to be."

"Ah, some planning is necessary, Lill," Lily said.

"Of course, but it shouldn't be used to cut the trustees off from faculty and staff, and alums. And they never meet with townies anyway."

Lily snorted, "Are you really sure, in your present mood, that you want them talking with our colleagues?"

Lill didn't say much during the rest of their walk.

There were a handful of professors who actually enjoyed working at Briarpatch College. Some liked the small college atmosphere, the small town life, and the freedom from publish-or-perish stress. What price should they put on the ability to walk to work, to let children play outside safely, and to not worry about finding a parking place? They understood colleagues who were unhappy at being identified with a college that not only lacked prestige but barely had an endowment. Their spirits would pick up whenever they talked with retired colleagues like Miss Fox, who could remember when times really were tough, but were also proud of what they had been able to accomplish with some very unpromising, but hard-working, young people.

There were a few professors who, while they would rather have been elsewhere, were pleased to have a job, any job, anywhere, as long as it was in higher education—even Briarpatch College would do. Donahue was in that number. A professor in graduate school had told him, with evident enjoyment, that an ex-cop wouldn't be hired anywhere except "to teach remedial courses to flatfeet." Donahue had thought that the professor himself could hardly boast of being at a university of Ivy League caliber, but he had been wise enough to keep that insight to himself—unhappiness came in all sorts of forms and it often came to the surface in the form of cruel comments. With a shake of his head he wondered why it was considered demeaning to train policemen to be better at their jobs. Still, since he himself was happy to have escaped that fate, he must have more in common with his former professor than he wanted to admit. In his own defense, he thought, his principal concern had been, primarily, that if he had been at a junior college, where so many of the programs for police training existed, his students wouldn't stay around long enough for him to get to know whether he was really helping them or not. Also, college students were young, still forming their "value systems" (i.e., doing what their parents should have done, or their schools and churches, or testing out what they had learned almost from birth), and curious; he might make more of a difference. Maybe that's what the professor had meant, though he didn't think so. His tormentor would hardly be impressed by Briarpatch, but at least he was teaching Sociology and Anthropology, and it was a four year program. Even if most students were mediocre and barely interested, there were a few who quietly signed up for more advanced courses. Enjoying the job came later—it was an acquired taste, Lill and Lily explained, but once you got it, like Mary C, you could never get enough. Enough, at least till exam time came. At such moments even this handful had their doubts.

Donahue taught more courses per semester than the national average, with more students per class than was common in liberal arts colleges, and he was paid below regional averages. But there were compensations. One was the town and its people. Assertion of this odd belief was rare, because it was sure to provoke sneers from more sophisticated colleagues, sneers that would only become louder should he or his friends suggest that Briarpatch students had real potential.

Lill and Lily were prominent among the most hardy and thick-skinned optimists (almost all of whom were, like them, "older faculty").

Some younger colleagues scoffed, "What else could one expect of *theatre people?*" Aside from the fact that many "theater people"—like Hollywood actors and musicians—were disgruntled about politics and society, and saw little likelihood that the world would take a turn for the better, Lill and Lily had, in fact, for a short period the previous year traded in their faculty status for administration, but their efforts at revising the faculty's negative attitudes toward themselves and the students were mocked behind their ample backs and posteriors; then Flo Boater persuaded the trustees to transfer the acting-presidency to her. "Back to her," she said. This was the cynics' moment—proof that the power structure would never relinquish its authority, and certainly not to two women known informally as "the Leather Lesbians." This phrase had originally referred to their motorcycle gear, but it was picked up by those who wished to believe that they practiced, well, you can imagine! Among themselves the cynics had mocked the LL's for accepting power; now they mocked them for having believed they could ever exercise it.

When Lily had first heard that thesis, not presented in a noticeably friendly way, by one of the more radical feminists, who quickly thereafter moved on (and, by her standards, *up*, to newscaster—actually, to become the Zenith "weathergirl"), that their accepting administrative positions was equivalent to *selling out*; she had asked, "I thought Flo Boater was a woman, too, and—some say—a rather attractive one." Not her type, of course. Beauty is more than skin deep, no matter how many moisturizing oils one uses.

Lill had gone even more directly to the heart of the problem, "If women who accept responsible jobs are 'selling out,' how to you ever expect women to rise to positions of authority?" It wasn't a question. It also made no impression.

Indeed, Lill's comment had threatened to undermine the foundations of an entire ideological edifice, that of powerless women trapped in an exploitative society—locally, nationally, and, to fit the new era's wider vision of its responsibilities, globally. Ignoring the comment, the cynics changed the topic to the campus and campus life, even suggesting that it was time for the "older generation" to get out of the way.

Lily, who had heard this too often to ignore it, retorted, "And perhaps we should also die, so that you don't have to pay Social Security taxes?" The dark humor was lost. Satire was long dead in *Academe*, as professors were now referring to their supra-institutional affiliation when they were not insisting that their primary allegiance was to their departments and to those who taught the same subjects all across the nation and beyond. They stated that all professors were equal, and none could be the subject of ridicule—except perhaps the occasional religious conservative or Republican. Lily was neither of the above, but she had committed the unforgivable sin of joking about Bill Clinton and his girlfriends. This was understandable to her friends, who understood that Lily couldn't pass up a quip on any subject unless her friend Lill was there to intervene, and that she actually admired Bill Clinton and intended to vote for him. (Lill *might* vote for Bob Dole.) To those who did not know Lily—and while it may seem odd that on such a small campus that such individuals could exist, faculty turn-over ensured that most instructors were new—those who did not know her well considered her either merely "bizarre" or having been "co-opted." Those who believed that the wide variety of human beings contained in *Academe* all thought exactly like them wondered if she were insane. But Lily had tenure—thanks to a questionable deal with Flo Boater that still haunted her in the still hours of the night; hence, she could not be dismissed without a good cause. As the late President Floyd Boater had repeatedly explained to alums and trustees, "Ah, yes, faculty members are, one might say, *different*. But they are different in so many ways, and the *creative* mind cannot always be restrained in the ways that, shall we say, are customary in the rest of society; but it is this ability to make students *understand* difference, and *appreciate* it—that is the creative heart of our vital enterprise. Moreover, we must *tolerate* those few, that small handful, who go *over the top*, I believe that is the phrase, in order to avoid intimidating those who remain firmly within the bounds of good taste and moderate expression from *pushing the envelope*, as I believe one commonly says, doing so in ways that are models for the young scholars who are in our charge, those who are the future for our college and our society. (Pause for breath and, hopefully, applause.) While experimentation and change are necessary and desirable, as well as inevitable, in a quality educational institution, I assure you, nothing *illegal* or *immoral* will be tolerated on the Briarpatch campus. As is appropriate to our ancient Christian, and Jeffersonian heritage. Indeed, to the humanist component of our thought and belief, which match our spiritual and ethical journey, all of which our generous donors make possible." Floyd Boater was, alas, deceased, and his level of rhetorical obfuscation could not be matched by his widow, Flora. Such eloquence was a gift, a gift which could be enhanced, but never simply acquired.

It was not unusual for community outsiders to see individuals like Lill and Lily as leftist extremists, while campus insiders thought of them as hopeless conservatives. Such was the world of 1996, when one could be all things to all people without attempting to do so. The new generation of instructors, seeing themselves as the embodiment of the "Left" (always in capital letters), felt it necessary to label the older generation as "subtly Right Wing" (also usually in caps) in order to edge it out of power. This consternated that handful of senior faculty members who had actually been in Chicago in 1968 (or, more likely, had seen it on television) and had campaigned for McGovern in 1972 (usually at faculty dinners and coffee hours), but soon enough they found that it was easier to plan for their retirement years than to fight a hopeless battle in faculty meetings. The spiritual home of the new radicals was (as was true in most colleges and universities) in the English department, where the political infighting between the generations had ended with the expulsion of Shakespeare even to the extent of removing his bust (and Chaucer's) from the secretary's office, where they had stood for perhaps seven decades. The busts had been copies from an earlier golden age of literature—real marble and a bit of craftsmanship—but no one knew what had become of them. It was briefly suspected that they had been acquired by the Art department, but that department's chair denied the accusation by reminding everyone that this was modern times, and modern times needed modern art. The English department agreed—it gave gracious retirement parties for the aggrieved traditionalists, then privately celebrated their departure with a reading of post-modern poetry stressing the hermeneutic imperative of understanding others' viewpoints.

The English Department, despite the presence of Lill's friend, Molly, was the center of "contemporary concepts." That is, all the new ideas expressed elsewhere in Academe quickly appeared in its classes, particularly in those of the chair, Max Stout. (Lily detested Stout, whose name she always elided into "maxed out." She knew that this annoyed him, which caused others to adopt the pronunciation.) Emboldened by the change to an anti-Theatre administration, Stout had snorted, to an audience that did not include *theatre people*, "Yes, the students might be able to act, a bit, but as for *serious* matters, such as free verse poetry or literary theory, they are not equal to the demands of the times." He then renewed his appeal to make his unofficial honors program the center of the college's academic life—and to introduce all students to Derrida and Foucault in order to determine which ones might profit from the attention of the "best professors" on campus. This served to remind the philosophically-minded that life is not fair, and that the least fair treatment comes from those who put feelings paramount. That is, the feelings of distant strangers, that is, folks one is unlikely to ever meet. But such was life in Academe in that distant era. Equally true was the fact that, just as every society has individuals who can find pleasure in life wherever they are, Briarpatch College, like its more affluent peers across the country, had a hardy core of dedicated "teachers" who were happy there. These had to ignore their unhappy peers' mocking reference to their employer as BRARpetch Co-ledge, but ignorance is where you find it, and those who believe themselves most sophisticated can be among the most ignorant.

The English Department was extremely frustrated at being housed in Old Main. Its traditional architecture seemed to imply traditional styles of teaching, and every professor and instructor in the department (except part-timers like Molly) mocked traditional teaching styles and the historical "canon," meaning poets and writers their parents would have recognized. Ideas, not literature, paved the yellow brick road... a reference that their students would have recognized only from television—and every year fewer could, since *the Wizard of Oz* was no longer an annual family viewing event.

Stout had recently shown Lill a student paper—part of the application process for the honors program. She took it carefully, trying not to seem as if she were afraid of contracting an infectious disease. She almost smiled as she read the first paragraphs, sensing that her worry was valid—for Professor Stout.

I. Introduction

Since the development of quantum mechanics, all perceptions of cultural hegemony must be distinct from relativistically absolutist views of monoculture and geoculture. While it is true that Space-Time compression is spacial, let us never forget that it is also temporal.

The metafunctionalist stenographic methodology of non-euclidian geometry has politicized ahistorical historiography. Following Long's agonistic systems model, "the nexus of hypersubjectivity which takes numerological informatics as its object, assumes the tropes of cryptozoology, thereby sustaining precambrian hegemony.

Taking all of this into account, one must come to the conclusion that philatelic critiques of the macroeconomic paradigm of the modern world-system are inversely proportional, and yet isomorphic, to hypno-gynecological cosmetics. Using liturgical network theory, we will map the proto-substrate of the advanced chronological practices of precorpuscular diagnostics."

"A bit dense," she commented.

"Oh, but all good thoughts have to be puzzled out nowadays," he retorted. "Read a bit more. No, not there. From the next chapter. It will be clearer."

Lill, raising an eyebrow at his overly enthusiastic help, allowed him to assist her in finding the right page:

II. Prestructuralist vehicular dialectics on pseudo-democratic autophagy

"In the context of unconditional autocannibalism, Marxist simulacra are unable to provide an adequate spectacle for the macro-constructionist modus operandi that has permeated the subtextual landscape of post-Incan Latin America. Immediately an objection arises: if prereflexive ontological narratives are unable to penetrate this hermeneutic alphabetical soup, as Lyotardian vehicular orientalists would have us believe, then are we not interrogating semiotic geology rather than post-positivist accounts of astro-psychological apoptosis?

Clearly, if we have learned anything from extra-solar mammalian geocultures, then it would be necessary to resort to Kondratieff's theory of moral incontinence, in which "lethargic truisms become truths and monothetic trapezoids overrun our supercycles of overproduction, clogging our moral compass with pederastic excretions."

"Who wrote this?" she asked. "Ellie?"

Stout laughed, "Close enough, perhaps. I sense her fine sense of style for post-modernism. But you'd never guess." His smile echoed his laugh—more contempt than mirth—but it helped explain why he'd never been married. Some women are desperate, but there are limits. He then puffed his chest up slightly, a gesture that rarely failed to intimidate opponents on the tennis court. Noticing that Lill, not being a tennis player, had ignored him in order to concentrate on the essay, he deflated with a slight sigh.

To herself, Lill said, "JJ," but she only asked, "No, I guess I wouldn't. Let me read the rest." That proved impossible—he took the essay from her, smiled broadly, skipped to the next chapter, and promised that "this passage will be especially good." When he handed the essay back, she read aloud:

III. Postcapitalist Patriarchialism

Section III is highly classified, but we can tell you that most of it is about the migratory patterns of llamas within the desert of the Real.

Lill turned to the next page, but found it blank. Looking back at section III, she said, "Apparently a reference to something I haven't read." After a pause, she added,."And a bit short."

Stout started to reply, but she had already started to read aloud:

IV. Conclusion

Pre-didactic models of communication are purely superstructural to the freudian microphysical ramblings of trans-atlantic aquacultures, since even Derrida understood that salmon are, and must always remain, bi-cyclical.

At that she stopped and read the entire essay over again, this time silently, hence quickly. She brightened, and smiled. "I guess you got me," she said.

"Oh, no," he exclaimed, "it's very clear."

"Clear?"

"It's about change, predictable change, life and death, meaning and…" He paused to grasp for a word. Theatrical gestures were one of his well-practiced gifts.

Lill, however, was a professor of theater—she was hard to impress. Taking advantage of the opening, she asked, "Who wrote it?"

Stout frowned momentarily at having his explanation interrupted, but quickly smiled again. "Smith! Perhaps with some help from Jimmy Jones, who sent in a similar essay."

"Smith! His grades aren't anywhere near honors!"

"Ah, but that's the beauty of the program." He smiled again and almost laughed. So simple it was. "We look for bright students, not for the grade grinders. Smith and Jones are so obviously unchallenged that the honors program is exactly what they need!"

Lill thought, "So unchallenged that they need to buy grades." Well, they won't need to put out any more cash now. Then she asked, "Are you going to accept them?"

Stout frowned, "No. I made a mistake earlier, setting the requirements so high that students on academic probation could not get in. I'll have to change that." He paused to think, "So it would be next semester at the earliest. Maybe then."

Lill thought, "If they are still around."

"Actually, I've let them in… as Audit students. To see…" He paused to grasp for the right word, looking toward the heavens and waving his right hand in front of his hand as if to summon Athenian birds to bring him inspiration. This technique, which usually worked wonders, led to disappointment again—Lily, joining the group, unobserved, interrupted his thought by asking, "To see if they might become intellectuals?"

Stout changed the topic, commenting sourly, "There's no place in today's society for a true public intellectual!" Meaning himself, apparently. "Someone who thinks independently, without regard for the consequences."

Lill had listened, wondering where this was leading, "I thought President Clinton was open to intellectuals."

"Ha!" he replied, "He has a few from his Oxford days, but right now it's all identity politics."

She thought a moment, putting a foot on Lily's before she could speak, then said, "So, identity politics doesn't attract intellectuals?"

"Ha! Only small gauge ones." He paused to see if there was dissent. Not discerning any, he continued, "I mean *public* intellectuals, the kind who take on big issues, who can point out the connections between issues, among people… you know, the kind of statesmanship of the mind that Oswald Jacoby wrote about a decade or so ago, pointing out their demise."

"Well," Lill protested quietly, "there's always Arthur Schlesinger Jr."

"Ha! Exactly my point, exactly Jacoby's point, that nobody jumps to mind except the Old Guard who don't realize that we've moved past the New Deal, nobody who can express the ideas that we deal with in my honors courses."

"Hell, Max," Lily broke in. "It's still only an 'unofficial' honors program, and I haven't seen anybody particularly exciting among the authors you're studying."

Stout reddened momentarily, then burst out, "Exactly my point, there is nobody worth reading nowadays. How can I run a properly exciting program without new thought!"

"There's always Chomsky," Lily put in, knowing that Stout could not tolerate him.

"He's just an anarchist! And nobody in my classes can read him anyway."

At that Lill nodded agreement, "He does tend to put one to sleep."

To which Lily added, "Not what one wants in a classroom assignment."

Stout twisted his mouth, then retorted, "Ellie understands him."

Lill rolled her eyes. She had heard the Ellie had transferred last spring from Arcadia Junior College in mid-semester—with help from Stanley Wooda, who became the academic dean shortly afterward. She had wondered which classes she had taken then, which she was taking this fall. Now she knew at least one—Stout's classes had no tests, required no papers, but was heavy on discussions that reflected Stout's viewpoints. Stout must have been overjoyed to get such a radical thinker, only to discover that she was more radical than he was. And that she understood Chomsky, or believed she did.

Stout persisted, "She finds him exciting."

"And Jones and Smith, too?"

Stout pouted, "I'm not sure. They don't attend class."

Act Four: the Problem

The president and academic dean, Flo Boater and Stanley Wooda, ignored this conflict of values... and as many others as they dared. They saw nothing in campus politics but a potential for bad publicity, nasty quarrels that might reflect poorly on their leadership skills. Their ambitions lay in the greater world, but the possibility of their escaping the intense gravity of Briarpatch's black hole seemed as dim as the light which it gave off to the rest of the academic universe. Although the college's name—the joke of academic rivals and townsfolk—had become a badge of pride (much like the name of the college's athletic teams, the Pricks), to them it was a constant reminder of their own failure to rise in the world of books, degrees and cocktail parties. The name Briarpatch could invoke images of Brer Rabbit, but Flo Boater and Stanley Wooda were not acquainted with Southern folklore. They were Yankees through and through, much out of place among what they called "the morons of the midlands." Stanley Wooda may have born in the Caribbean, but mentally he was a Yankee—quick-minded, superior, judgmental and sharp-tongued. In short, the perfect dean.

They lacked only one attribute of the true Yankee—money. The college was barely paying its bills. The former courthouse that was now the administrative building was a beautiful structure, and the president's office on the second floor was everything one would expect of a large courtroom—airy, filled with light, and impossible to furnish properly. It was also a perfect sieve—just as it let winter drafts in, it let money out. When people began sweating from an overactive furnace, they knew it would be an hour or two before the thermostat turned down the heat; thus, they had the choice of waiting or opening a window. They usually did what seemed most necessary at the moment, often not bothering to dial down the thermostat, then forgetting to shut the window when they left. The president and dean had been discussing the cost of heating when Flo Boater glanced out a large window and observed two figures coming out of the distant Japanese coffee house. "DO and Mary?" she asked. Observing out of the corner of her eye her colleague's shrug, she snorted, "Should have gotten rid of them!"

"We tried," he replied, carefully avoiding any suggestion that her effort had failed before she made him dean.

Under her breath she snarled, "That damned detective and Nancy Drew."

"I don't think that's them," he responded, "but they're a long way off."

"Why don't you think so?" This was more a challenge than a question. Only moments before he had taken a step to one side when she had attempted to drape an arm lightly across his shoulder. She was slightly taller than him, which made such "motherly" gestures seem natural to her. Not having children of her own, nor husband or lover (at the moment), she saw Stanley as possibly filling at least one of those roles.

He ignored the tone in her voice, "They're holding hands."

"I've seen DO and Mary hold hands."

"Not recently. They've had a spat."

"A spat? Over what?"

He gazed out the window a moment, "As I heard it, she quoted Edward Said favorably."

"So? Don't we all?"

Stanley glanced sideways at her. He knew that she had a tendency to read *about* people rather than to read them, and in this case probably had heard about it only from Professor Stout. "Well, DO supposedly joked that *Anti-Occidentalism* was overblown."

"What's wrong with that?" She paused to give him a sideways look, then asked, "Occidentalism?" Had she misheard him?

"Well," he replied, "the theory is *Orientalism*." Seeing that she was struggling to formulate a response, he continued, "The basic idea is that the American and European scholars who taught us about the Middle East saw Islamic and other eastern cultures through western eyes."

"Okay," she answered, more coolly than she intended. "How else were they to see it?"

"Ah, you're on to the central point. A jump ahead of Stout already." There was an air of approval in his voice.

There was also an air of superiority in that voice. Male superiority. And that crack about Professor Stout, who was one of her most loyal supporters! Unnecessary male antler rattling. But she suppressed a desire to correct him, "So, what happened?"

"She said that he was a Sociologist, so he ought to be aware of how his upbringing and his culture disqualified him for making such a comment about 'the other.'" Observing her discomfort, he explained, "The *other* is everything you are not—that is, in his case, she said, female, lower class, out of the power structure, in another culture."

She responded, "Yes, go on." But what she thought was that if she were seated at a desk, she would be drumming her fingers. "Why do I have to listen," she thought, "to such twaddle."

"DO retorted that he may not be female, but his mother and sister were, his family was lower class economically and were certainly not in the power structure, and that Irish was at the very least an important ethnic subculture."

"Yes?" Her left eyebrow arched. This was an argument that might work well with the trustees, with her own biography carefully woven into it. She frowned momentarily, remembering the *faux pas* of one recent presidential aspirant in borrowing a working-class life story, one that didn't quite fit his middle-class upbringing, then smiled when she realized that nobody would ever know what her father had actually done or that Donahue had said it first.

Stanley Wooda took this as encouragement. "So, he asked how could she say anything about what *he* was?" He paused before continuing, "He might, in fact, have gifts of which she could know little. Family jewels, for example."

"He actually said that?" she asked, turning to see if Stanley was joking.

"Oh, yes. And more. He asked if Orientalism meant that we had to rely on representatives of the culture to tell us about themselves? She, of course, said yes."

President Boater nodded, "Makes sense."

"If so, he asked, what do we do when two of them disagree?" He paused for a moment, "He said, if I understood correctly, that if we can't rely on our own observations, or on the natives themselves… Yes, he used that word. They would either disagree with each other from time to time or they wouldn't be human, and if we can't rely on our own judgment as to which informant was most accurate—because that would require us to filter the conflicting statements through a western lens—what do we do? Under those circumstances knowledge was impossible. Or at least education was useless, because we could not transmit what we learned to others; or, if we were only allowed to parrot what the 'natives' said, we could not analyze their ideas. Moreover, it implied that since moral values are all culturally determined, there was no absolute right or wrong."

"No right or wrong?"

"Yes, that's *exactly* what Mary asked. And can you imagine, he said it was even more complicated, that when it came to Islam—Edward's Said's own religion—not even he was allowed to question what the foundations were, why some things were right, others were wrong. So Said could say all sorts of things about the West, on which he was a *foreign* expert—an "Occidentalist"—but was limited as what he could say about things about which he had a native's understanding. Therefore, only Orientalists, with western traditions regarding inquiry and scholarship, could ask penetrating questions."

"What did she say to that?"

"Nothing, apparently. She stomped off. Yes, stormed right off. And she has hardly spoken to him since." After a pause he added, "I'm sure he was joking."

"So they wouldn't be holding hands. Anyway, that couple clearly aren't them. Students maybe?"

"They're not students. Dressed too well, and a bit older."

"Mary dresses better than that."

He glanced over at her. Was it pride or envy he heard in Flo's voice? But he only said, "Sometimes." When Mary was angry at Donahue, she wore academic grunge.

She squinted at the approaching couple, "Not parents, however. Not old enough."

"Alums, I'd say. They're still holding hands. Maybe five to ten years since graduation."

She nodded, "Probably so. Before your time. Before the mid-life crisis, too. We'll see soon. They're almost at the sidewalk."

"Probably headed for the Campus Crawl. All the alums go there."

"I wouldn't know," she responded. "So bourgeois!"

"Middle class sells."

"Yes," she sniffed. "Our students have such pedestrian goals in life."

The dean smiled to himself as he imagined Lily saying, "No, they'd rather have a car." His smile widened at remembering recent student complaints about parking. But he was wise enough not to say anything, and astute enough to erase the smile before it became a grin and she asked what he was thinking about.

As they watched the strangers pass out of sight around the corner of the building, headed toward the square, Stanley shrugged and said, "Told you so."

But she had espied something more interesting. On a nearby hillock, actually hardly more than a rise above the slowly winding sidewalk and sometimes believed to be an Indian mound, were two seniors lounging on the grass, enjoying the last days of summer warmth before the beginning of their long winter of discontent. At least everyone thought they were seniors. Only the registrar knew for sure.

"Smith and Jones," President Boater guessed. "Who else has hair that long?"

"Girls," Stanley suggested. "But they wash it more often and trim it better." He checked to see whether she would smile at his little joke.

Flo Boater gave him a smirk, then started to turn back toward her desk, but stopped suddenly and took a longer look at the distant pair, squinting slightly because she refused to wear glasses and thought that contact lens were too much trouble to wear—as they usually were, for her limited needs. Her face flushed as she recalled their most recent escapades—two weeks into the semester and already they had a handful of parking tickets ('How had they gotten them?" she had asked. "They don't have cars."), several reports of noisy behavior in the dorm, and one possible incident of graffiti ("How much Wooda would a woodchuck chuck up, if a Wooda would chuck up?"). She had tried to reproach them, but discovered that they thrived on scorn. They had actually laughed at her. Called her a "harpist," or was it "haughtist?" Did it really matter? They were jerks in any case.

"Yes, it seems to be," Dean Wooda replied. "What are they doing up this early?"

"Up? To me it looks like they're down." She sighed, "God, I wish we could get rid of them."

"Certainly they aren't in class."

"Never are, from what I hear." With that she returned to the discouraging mound of correspondence that had come in with the morning's mail. Flo Boater believed in a clean desk. A very clean desk. Fortunately, her secretary, Miss Efficiency, had cut open every letter and sorted all of them by category as best she could without reading them, indicating which ones had to be given priority. This was not a perfect system, but Flo Boater had insisted that every communication with the president was "confidential," and that was the way Miss Efficiency did it.

Stanley Wooda sighed as he watched Flo glance through the ones considered "urgent" and "important" quickly, flipping them into new piles, then pushing him the largest stack. She kept only two or three for herself, then pitched the rest, unread, into the trash. "Not summer any more, is it?" he observed.

"No," she grunted. "This place is a lot easier to manage when the students and faculty are gone."

"Don't you think," he suggested, with a gesture toward the trash can, "that I should look at the notes from faculty?"

"Don't be silly. If they have something important to say, they can make an appointment."

"But you told them to send us their ideas in writing. 'More efficient and usually more clearly stated.' Don't you remember? The last faculty meeting."

She starred at him.

"Just throwing them away?" he asked, "How'll you know what they want?"

She starred at him again before answering, "What do I have to give?" Briarpatch's sorry finances were notorious.

His mouth slowly opened, but nothing came out. There was the money from the insurance settlements, and the late dean's bank accounts. Not available now, but perhaps any day.

"What would I give them if I had the ability?"

"Nothing, I guess," he confessed.

"You are beginning to learn, Stanley," she jested, giving him the slightest of smiles. "You are beginning to learn."

Chapter Two

Donahue was ready to believe in *déjà vu*. It was the next morning and he was sitting in the Diner again, nursing his cooling coffee. When Chief Biggs finally appeared, he seemed older than usual. He apologized for being late, "Had a talk with Flo." He turned to order coffee, only to discover the waitress was ready to pour it already. "Like you suggested."

"Yes?" Donahue asked as soon as the waitress left.

"Couldn't get her yesterday. She said she was too busy to talk, but to come to her office in the morning—today. I think it was a "power trip" or whatever they call it—just to put me in my place—but her excuse was that she wanted to look into it herself. That seemed reasonable, but it was her tone.... That would have put anyone off. Anyway, she said not to worry about Ms. Purdy. It was common for staff to take off. They usually leave her a note."

"Yes?"

"She said to let it rest for a few days. Probably just an overly-excited staff person."

"She never misses work, I'm told."

"Probably just some unfinished summer plans, she said, or a project she's working on."

Donahue, who was still laboring on his own lesson plans, nodded that he understood. Not an enthusiastic nod, but a nod.

Smith and Jones, with their usual lack of enthusiasm for resuming the supposedly regimented ordeal of life in a dormitory, were bemoaning the end of summer vacation. They did this quietly, often not leaving their beds until past the lunch period that would have provided them breakfast. They did not answer letters or phone messages from parents, deans or anyone else not young and of the opposite sex. Only hope of such a message made them flip through the mail at all or skip through the answering machine, but except for their "male magazines" there was only disappointment waiting for them. They had never yet allowed the calendar to dictate either their moods or their occasional preparations for post-college life. Among their fellow students Smith was famed for his ability to organize a party more swiftly and imaginatively than anyone else, while Jones, though once famed for being able to "jimmy" any lock, was now better known for being able to assemble almost instantly demonstrators to protest the latest administrative initiative, whatever that might be. This limited the time available for study or attending classes, at least it had in the spring, the last great moment for protests and one of the most memorable—though, to tell the truth, neither Smith nor Jones remembered much about those events. The beer bust they remembered. The coffee house had been locked, but somehow Stan Wooda had gotten into the Gym and somehow barrels of beer—cold beer, no less, something Smith couldn't always guarantee—had been waiting for them.

Smith and Jones were a local legend—in their own way, of course. Their peers imagined their lives to be one enjoyable adventure after another, one long *Ferris Bueller's Day Off*, an image they were not going to destroy by admitting that neither had been able get a date all summer—their efforts having been self-sabotaged by fear of rejection— and neither was willing to confess how unhappy this made him. Their mental horizons were bounded solely by the hope of escape, but they were not eager to go out into the wider world. For them Briarpatch was a safe and secure environment—non-threatening and non-challenging, but not boring. Even though Middleville lacked the professional entertainment available in the big cities where they had grown up (actually suburbs and private schools), Smith had become adept in the skills of renting rooms, buying beer for minors and developing party-themes. Both appreciated Briarpatch's laid back approach to student life—paying off the dorm counselor (usually by inviting him to the party) was relatively cheap and the dean of students was terrified that any student might leave—and a college party was all the better without the annoying presence of parents, who were likely to come in at the most awkward times. In short, Smith and Jones loved Briarpatch with a depth of feeling that few of their peers at elite colleges could understand. Not pride, but something akin to love.

Theirs, of course, was not a total college experience. They understood, vaguely, that classes had a purpose, and that there was a "the life of the mind;" moreover, they believed that one day they would look into education more deeply. But meanwhile, they were so deeply immersed in planning their evening hours that they even imagined the cafeteria meals would be good—though their daytime "schedule" was so irregular that it was easier for them to go off campus for fast food (such little as Middleville offered). Rarely did they ever find themselves, as now, outside, on a hillside, soaking up the sun. "Pleasant here," Smith said. "We ought to do this more often."

"Yeah," Jones responded. "But there's no sand, no babes, and the grass itches."

"Those are chiggers," Smith responded.

"Oh," Jones said, then lapsed into silence, wondering if Smitty had made an uncharacteristic racial slur.

Known universally as Smith and Jones, only the registrar and two or three admissions councilors were aware of their birth names. Most friends could not have guessed at their first names and most instructors were puzzled when their unfamiliar last names appeared on the grade lists at the end of the semester. That had helped them from time to time, when they appeared in the instructor's office to explain that the instructor's "error" had been responsible for their having seemed to miss so many classes. But what had kept them "in school" was the college's unresolved financial crisis, which had caused the late president Floyd Boater to encourage the committee responsible for determining which students were working toward graduation and which were hopelessly behind, to be "generous" in allowing "each student to march toward their (sic) degree at his or her own pace." The college was, after all, "a place for experimentation and self-examination," not a "factory of knowledge." "Nuts and bolts education" was suitable for arch-rival Arcadia Junior College, but not for Briarpatch. Actually, Arcadia was on the way to "cutting-edge relevance" much faster than Briarpatch, "cutting-edge" meaning teaching nothing that might help a student get and hold a job, and contributing to society meant, not doing providing useful and profitable services or products, but offering snide criticisms. That was what many heard President Luci May Mankiller to mean, though her exact words were, "those who offer necessary criticisms are those who best demonstrate true love of society." When one critic suggested, half in humor, that "necessary criticisms" lead to divorces, she informed him, first, that marriage was an outdated institution, second, later, that his relationship with Arcadia College was being terminated immediately. There was a lawsuit, of course, which the plaintiff easily won. The amount awarded was kept secret, but it was sufficient to delay the building of a new "center for intercultural and non-traditional values." All that Smith and Jones knew of this was rumors that the center was supposed to have plans to distribute medicinal pot, but since they did not have cars, that attraction was as irrelevant as the fact that the center would not break ground before they graduated. If they graduated.

For these reasons, though President Flo Boater hated Smith and Jones passionately, she knew that she could not afford to kick them out—her husband's dean had created an inventively high tuition program to maximize federal and state grants and loans that had only two drawbacks, 1) although the exorbitant tuition had been the envy of everyone Floyd Boater had met at conferences (high cost being considered a mark of high quality), the figure discouraged students from inquiring into Briarpatch's very generous scholarship program—actual cash outlays by students were roughly at the level of Zenith University. Thus, the regional state institution's recruiters were able to obtain a significant advantage simply by showing parents all competitors' tuition charges. Parents, once they had stilled their heart flutters, crossed Briarpatch off their list of places to visit and either wrote a deposit check to Zenith or drove over to Arcadia Junior College; 2) the program's legality was questionable unless a few students actually paid the full amount in hard cash. At the moment Smith and Jones were the only ones who did so. Thus, they were as safe in the Briarpatch as any canny rabbit ever could be. Moreover, last spring they had made a friend of Stanley Wooda, who was almost their contemporary in age and, therefore, had been able to talk them into almost anything except studying.

"Academic probation again," Smith moaned.

"Me, too," Jones echoed. "Dad's after me to attend more classes."

"Yeah, know what you mean. Threatened to cut my...." He hesitated. He wanted to say, "my allowance," since that is what his parents called it. But it sounded so childish.

"Uh, maybe we can get into the honors program."

"Oh, I don't know. You're supposed to read books."

Jones snorted, "You're supposed *to talk* like you've read books. We do that all the time. It works with the girls. Prenuperal sensitation."

Smith thought about this, wondered when Jones had last impressed a girl, but what he asked was, "Is it true that Stout only gives A's?"

"True, though I've heard some only get B's. The ones who don't attend class."

Smith smiled, "That's us. And a B is good enough for me."

Jones reflected on this, then asked, "Didn't we apply for the program already?"

"Damn," Flo Boater said to herself, "when can I get rid of those two slackers!?" But she knew the answer, and kicked half-heartedly at the rug after silently reviewing the unlikely prospects for reducing the mountain of debt left over from her late husband's administration. The good enrollment figures had just given her some hope, but then her new acting-Superintendent of Buildings and Grounds, Jay Bird, reported that many structures were in disastrous condition. There had been similar reports by previous superintendents, but they had always been modified by an unwritten order to "be positive." This year, however, the insurance company, angry about millions it was expected to pay on the policies insuring the late President Floyd Boater and Dean C. Wooda, had announced it would send an inspection team to campus, to check all the buildings carefully. Flo Boater, seeing this as a first step toward the company canceling the college's remaining policies, had hurriedly ordered Jay to give her an analysis of what the inspectors were likely to find when they went through the campus.

Over the years Jay had worked on every problem the college had; therefore, all he had to do was dictate a report to Jenny. This was done on their free time, since Jay had no secretary and it was a relatively enjoyable way to spend an evening—Jay not liking any activity that required him to sit still, and Jenny putting a limit on walks around the campus (which seemed to involve more picking up litter than walking). They had delayed marriage partly because neither was young and both were set in their ways, but more because they were worried about a rumored new policy that would discriminate against married couples working on campus. Nobody was better informed on college affairs than Jay, and although he could find no conclusive proof that Flo Boater was about to propose this new policy, he had heard her quoted as saying that the medical insurance plan would be cheaper if the college had a higher percentage of unmarried faculty, and also that finding replacements was such a bother—Middleville didn't have many people who could take over classes when female employees wanted time off for childbirth and child care. He was also fairly confident that, once a policy of not hiring married couples was announced, it would make no difference that both he and Jenny were past the age for childbearing.

Flo Boater had no children. By choice, she told herself. She did not believe that professional women should be distracted from their careers—if they had children, their husbands should stay home and take care of them. Her first career had been to promote her husband's career. What a mistake that had been! Look at what little he had been able to accomplish! She looked at Jay's report, read through it quickly, then almost crumpled it in her hands before she remembered he was watching.

Jenny's summary of Jay's remarks was discouraging, especially the conditions of the buildings, maintenance having been deferred so long that roofs were leaking, mold was growing in walls, and foundations were crumbling. Jay's oral summary was blunter, "Noth'en been done so long, the place is going to hell."

Flo Boater, not expecting coarse language from him, of all people, had actually jumped slightly, "What do you mean?"

"Rain coming in, walls is green, bricks coming out."

She peered toward him, his report in her hands, wishing that she had her glasses, but wanting to preserve the illusion that her eyesight was still excellent. "Thank you," she responded with a slight tremor in her voice, "I'll read this later. I'm sure it's excellent." And it was.

Jay had recommended that attention be focused on two critical structures: the Music building, most of its rooms already long locked, should be totally and permanently closed for asbestos abatement, and the Gym was far too small for the number of athletes who had enrolled this fall. Flo Boater dismissed the music program—the college could always use some church for concerts, and if the building was "self-insured" (that is, not insured), it made little difference. But why had Jay said that the mold problem was exaggerated? Hadn't that been a long-time problem? The Gym represented a more serious situation, even though the insurance company would have little interest in its size. She had already been both encouraged and alarmed by the number of women who had signed up for sports. This would be the salvation of the basketball and track teams, but locker facilities and practice areas were now inadequate. She had spoken to Stanley Wooda about the problem: "I never imagined that track was so expensive."

"Neither did I."

"Well, how could you? You were overseas for your entire baccalaureate program." There was a slight sneer in her voice.

This grated on her young dean, who responded, "That reminds me, shouldn't I be awarded my BA now?" He paused before adding, "quietly, of course." Another pause, "Just enter it in my transcript. No publicity."

Flo Boater rolled her eyes, "Let's stay on track."

"Of course," he responded, "the track program."

"Now, what's this all about?" she asked, "Overnight stays at big meets, improvements on the track, assistant coaches?"

"I did some calling around. It's pretty standard."

"Windy's not putting something over on us?"

"Actually, no. Other schools are spending more... some much more."

She rolled her eyes again. She detested references to the college as a "school." She smiled ruefully, thinking how affordable a failing program had been! Ah, thank goodness, she almost said aloud, she could blame it all on Stanley, who would blame it on the Athletic Director; and he could explain it to the trustees. "Tell Windy that he can do anything necessary as long as it does not involve money."

Stanley hesitated, "There will be *some* money involved." He paused before adding, "Motel rooms, assistant coaches, buses."

"Well, try to get alums to put them up, maybe in churches. Something. Keep the expenses within reason."

Stanley hesitated again, "A good program... Windy says, 'can't be got on the cheap.' He says he needs every penny."

She sighed, "Okay. Just tell him to keep receipts."

As Stanley left, Flo wondered if perhaps he could handle the problems indicated in Jay's report, or at least deflect them. After all, Stanley had labored through the summer to resolve some equally challenging problems, and she had come to admire her protégé's talents. He had organized new faculty committees, persuaded the members to meet through the hottest days and through their normal vacations, and, more amazing, he had come up with reasonable plans for dealing with specific academic problems—among which was a blue ribbon committee to study the curriculum (he had chosen Professor Stout to be chair, a move that won acclaim from the loudest of the faculty factions, that wanting brighter students). Though other solutions owed much to Stanley Wooda, she understood that many suggestions for improvements came from faculty who normally never raised their voice or sent her ideas. At least, she didn't remember reading any notes from them. The best ideas, truth be told, came indirectly from Lill and Lily, the recently replaced acting-president and acting-dean, who had been rigorously excluded from the dean's committees, but who could not be prevented from talking with some of the members. That was, of course, strictly, hush-hush, but Stanley Wooda had sized up the committee members quickly and accurately and could recognize when their proposals reflected wisdom and experience beyond what they possessed.

Stanley thrived on challenges, but he enjoyed getting around problems more than he reveled in resolving them. In this he was an unusual dean. Normally administrators prefer to put off decisions. Since every plan of action is likely either to cost money or make somebody angry, it is often wisest to do nothing. Stanley Wooda liked to make problems disappear, even if it meant persuading everyone that the problem was less troublesome than the difficulties which would arise in its place. In addition, in an era when it was rare for an academic dean not to have a Ph.D. in hand before assuming what is often a killing schedule of meetings with individual faculty members and committees, counseling students and resolving "misunderstandings" over academic dishonesty (cheating), collecting data and writing lengthy reports, directing applications for grants, and consulting with the president and trustees, Stanley did not have an earned degree of any kind. "TBCW," some said, "The Briarpatch College Way." But he used this potentially fatal handicap as an excuse to pass off the duller aspects of the job to others, especially to the emaciated chair of the history department, who was hungry for advancement. That acted as a lightning rod for faculty discontent. Stanley had promised to name him associate dean someday, but he put that off on Flo's principle that carrots should only be dispensed as needed; meanwhile, he named "the poor duffer" to several committees, the most important of which heard all applications for tenure and promotion. Although Professor Stout had wanted to be chair of that committee, too, Stanley had named the Creep. "Play enemies against one another," he told the president. That much statecraft he had learned from Machiavelli. Amazing how well it worked on a college campus.

Stanley also realized that Stout's newfound enthusiasm for administrative duties might dampen with overwork. Too many duties created burnout even in faculty members who had none of the usual distractions of family life. Stout hired locals to take the burdens of household ownership from his shoulders—student maids twice a week, a professional gardener twice a week, and a laundry service every Monday; students from his unofficial honors program assisted at dinners and parties; and shopping was supervised by the departmental secretary. For taxes he had an accountant in Zenith.

Flo Boater, once she learned of all this, suggested that Stanley use that knowledge to obtain his "cooperation," but Stanley chose instead to give Stout hope of becoming the director of a real Honors Program—promises worked better than threats with most people, especially those proud of their reputation of being proud. In this case, the Honors Program already existed "unofficially" by Stout's having declared his classes such (and thus shutting out weaker students who were a chore to teach). Stout was, he often asserted, a "scholar," not a "teacher." He hadn't published, but only because being a true scholar left no time for writing.

This had led to a memorable exchange with Lill when she was acting president. He had confronted her at a faculty meeting by challenging her assertion that their primary duty was teaching: "I don't think you can make such a statement. It runs contrary to everything implied in Academic Freedom."

Lill had responded, "Academic freedom means that there should be minimal restrictions on what you think and say regarding your teaching and publishing, not whether you are obliged to teach or not."

"No, academic freedom has to be regarded in the broadest possible context, because there is no gray area between freedom and slavery, and we cannot operate effectively in circumstances that circumscribe the choices we make between good and better. Therefore, if I know that it is better that I concentrate on writing, it is incumbent on you to recognize my right to make that decision."

Lill thought a moment before answering. "Professor Stout," she had begun, passing over the inclination to call him Max, "it is true that there are institutions which proclaim themselves to be primarily interested in scholarship. In such universities much of the teaching of undergraduates is left to graduate students—an arrangement that most of us are familiar with. However, Briarpatch College has specifically said in its Mission Statement that its primary purpose for existence is undergraduate teaching. I don't see how you can decide to opt out."

"The Mission Statement," he retorted, "is nothing more than some trustee's power-point presentation." He then glanced around to be sure that his colleagues understood, because power-point was not available yet in classrooms. "We can't let the trustees get in the way of our primary mission, and we, the faculty, have to decide what that primary mission is."

"Max," Lill had shot back, forgetting to hold her temper, "we may not agree with the trustees in every matter, but the college charter, granted by the state legislature, makes them responsible for the operation of the college. We are, I grant you, not exactly employees in the business sense of the word, but the faculty have to recognize that the trustees have an essential role in the..."

He cut her off, "The trustees should send us their money and shut up."

In spite of such occasional rudeness, Stout was uniformly polite to trustees, even deferential on those occasions when they appeared on campus. He invited them for wine and cheese at his elegant home, and asked questions about stocks—his independent wealth was based on investments wisely chosen by his long-deceased parents. He was looking forward to an opportunity to chat with trustees about the need for a new dean—himself.

Trustees who raised questions regarding the "musical chairs" in the academic deanship were told by Flo Boater that Stanley's being dean was not only taking advantage of his obvious talents, but it was also marvelous publicity. When they asked Stanley himself, he explained that even negative publicity was better than no publicity. Besides, "I do not intend to remain in this office long. I have other ambitions." Some trustees believed him, and eagerly anticipated the flood of government money which would flow the college's way once he reached a position of real power (something called "earmarks" that they were unfamiliar with, but willing to take); others were willing to tolerate the "experiment" for a year or two; and others only wanted to know what he could do for the football team.

They especially wanted him to deal with Professor Stout, who had recently proposed that the football team be renamed *the Briarpatch Rabbits*. Little did they know that this was a joke inspired by Stanley Wooda himself.

As he related it to Flo Boater, Stout first shouted, "My God, Stan, isn't there anything you can do to prevent this college from turning into a football factory? Those idiotic athletes are ruining my classes! Some are in the Pre-Honors section!"

"I responded, 'I'm sorry, Mr Stout'—you know, Flo, how he hates to be called 'Mr'—'but they all met the admissions standards.'"

"Stout persisted, 'Stan'—he knows how I hate that name—'anybody can meet our admissions standards. We've got to tighten up.'"

"I responded, 'It's out of my hands. The trustees won't change anything until we pay off the accumulated debt.'"

"I don't want to be associated with a football factory."

"To which I remarked, 'The season hasn't even begun! And last year's record was miserable.' That really made him angry. Stout was really steaming, sputtering, 'No, but look at all the athletes we've recruited! They're ruining the college.'"

"I remained calm, 'Recruitment was good this year, and by my count, only fifty or sixty are on the football team.' I had a hard time not smiling."

"That made him yell again, 'That's too many!'"

"I just gave him a blank, 'I don't understand'—I really acted dumb, Flo, and he bought it—'you don't teach any freshman classes, and most of your load is Honors. How does this affect you?'"

"They're underfoot all over the place. They're teeming like rabbits!"

"…and that's where I slipped it in, Flo—'The only way you can stop it is if the football team *plays like rabbits*!'—at that I paused before adding—'and I don't see any likelihood that the faculty would change the name of the team.' You should have seen the gears start to turn in his head. He spun on his heels and stomped off, muttering about rabbits."

Flo Boater clapped her hands. She would have hugged him, if he hadn't taken a step backward. "That was brilliant, Stanley. He obviously took the hint." She was about to say more, when she stopped, her mouth half open. Then she asked, "Can the faculty change the name of the football team?"

"No, that's a trustee decision, or should be, because it is never popular with rich alums. But Stout thinks that the faculty *is* the college, and whatever the faculty wants, should be done."

Flo Boater chuckled, then told him about some recent "fund raising" adventures. What she didn't tell him was how little ready money had come in, and some of the gifts were bequests in the form of insurance policies that would pay off in thirty years or more. But they looked good in the financial report for the trustees. It would be more accurate to say, as she sometimes did, that she had been laying the foundations for a future fund drive. She had gotten some interesting offers to perform construction work "at cost." God knows that Briarpatch buildings needed work, and the donors, who were in a slack period anyway, were happy for any business that would save them from letting good workers go. She had picked up these names from the Athletic Director's contacts; consequently, there was more work done on the Gym and the football stadium than in the academic buildings. "Also, Stanley, there were also some hints that money might be contributed if the football team had a successful season."

The dean nodded, indicating that he understood.

"And one or two stronger suggestions that substantial generosity depended on beating Arcadia College." That was a feat no Briarpatch team had ever achieved. "Until then, all we can do is bring in a little money here and make a little cut there; together that might amount to what the trustees would accept as *progress*."

A couple drops of perspiration appeared on Stanley's brow, "Do you think the joke on Stout could backfire?"

"No, no, not at all Stanley." She smiled broadly, "You've got to understand, you can't *stop* people like Stout from making trouble, but you can *control* them, *direct* them. Moreover, if the trustees concentrate on him, they won't pay much attention to our real problems." She paused before adding, "Those we inherited from Lill and Lily."

Only insiders would have understood the implications of that statement. The budget had been left "in the pink" by Lill and Lily, who, in contrast to Smith and Jones, seemingly had no last names. Even the local paper, the *Middleville Moderate*, always referred to Dean Lily and President Lill. Their administration had been "informal," and though they had resolved several serious financial problems, their efforts to move from red ink to black had gotten no farther than "pink." Their real problem had been with the trustees, who had assumed that "pink" had deeper connotations than a summary of the fiscal situation.

Flo Boater, after being found "not guilty" of conspiring to murder the late Dean C. Wooda, had successfully used her long-established relationship with the trustees to play on their latent homophobia. That was not the only reason that the trustees replaced the "Leather Lesbians" with Flo Boater and her young protégé, but it tipped the balance at a crucial moment.

This thought caused Flo Boater to wonder what Miss Purdy might have to suggest, some plan to balance the budget, or make it appear to be balanced. More students had meant more than more income—it also meant more spending. The loans and grants fund was overdrawn—more students meant more of both, and Flo Boater had found it necessary to go hat in hand to the local banker. She knew that eventually the increased numbers would pay off, but she ground her teeth at the memory of her humiliation—the college's credit rating did not qualify it for a low interest rate. The freshmen wouldn't graduate for four years, if they stayed—and if enrollment dipped again, the financial situation would be as bad as ever. Oh, if only they could graduate faster, make tons of money, and write big checks to the college. But they were still young; in fact, even the seniors looked more youthful than they used to. This led her to another thought, one she could indulge now that the dean had left the room. "How young Stan Wooda is," she said to herself. "And attractive, damn it. Embarrassing, too, when every other academic dean has a Ph.D. and Stan hadn't finished his B.A. Moreover, he is clearly making no progress whatsoever toward graduation. Damn, it would be embarrassing to have him enrolled in classes, but unless he earns credits, how can I give him a degree? I can't try to slip it by. The faculty has to vote on all degrees. That's in the damn charter, so I can't go through the trustees. Someone, probably Stout, would spot his name and I'd never hear the end of it." Nevertheless, she knew that Stanley ("Got to stop thinking of him as *Stan*, that's unprofessional") was indispensable. Once she had persuaded the trustees that she had found a youthful genius, there was no way she could admit to having made a mistake. At the very least, he had been able to bring an end to the demonstrations that were making the college a regional laughing stock.

The question was, she ruminated, what means, fair or foul, dared they employ to resolve the financial crisis before the trustees' good will ran out? The late dean, C. Wooda, had persuaded them to invest in an imaginative insurance scam of which her husband, the late Floyd Boater, *might* have been aware. Probably not, but still maybe—and the large monthly payments on the policies might pay off big time now that both C. Wooda and F. Boater were dead. The policies would go far to paying off the college's debts and repairing roofs—but that was not the end of the late dean's inventiveness. C. Wooda had also sold off some or much of the anthropology collection and pocketed the money. Not that what remained of the collection was likely to be displayed soon, since the construction of a proper museum was well down the list of air castles that exist on every campus, and no one had ever seen more than the few items that Dean C. Wooda had displayed once at a party. No one knew what the secretive chief administrators had in mind now, but those who cared to think about the matter were certain that they would come up with something. Flo and Stanley were too ambitious to imagine spending the rest of their lives in Middleville, and unless they came up with a workable scheme, they might not even survive in Briarpatch. No one who knew them well ever talked about "plans," but about "schemes."

This is where the goals of Smith and Jones crossed paths with those of Boater and Wooda. They had a scheme.

Chapter Three

The boys' scheme involved grades. Smith had complained that his parents had said that one only got what one wanted by earning it or buying it. "Damn," Jones said, tossing his hair with one hand, "I can't believe it."

"What can't you believe?" Smith retorted. "That they expect *me* to work?"

"No—that they'd tell you a better way to get the grades."

"Huh?"

"Buy them."

Also looking for a scheme, or at least a plan, was DO Donahue. His courtship of Mary C was going nowhere. The only time she seemed attracted to him, he reflected glumly, was when he was solving a campus murder. "But, hell," he said to himself, "all I really did was assist Biggs." That was twice now, and he could not count on a murder every semester! Short of another unexplained death, he saw no way to move their relationship along. Mary seemed more than content to remain "friends." Maybe even less.

He shook his head rapidly, trying to rid himself of the idea that the disappearance of Miss Purdy might have a good side.

"Sometimes he thinks he's still a cop," Mary said.

Lill smiled and observed, "That's going over well with the students."

"Role-playing works," Lily added, smacking her lips for emphasis. "Our students aren't always easy to reach."

"Then he carries it too far! I just can't stand it sometimes."

"Tell him."

"I have. He stops for a while, then he reads something in the paper or hears something that Stout said."

41

"Don't talk campus politics," Lill suggested, one eyebrow rising higher than the other.

Mary had wondered about this characteristic of hers, because Lill, in contrast to the rest of the human race, would vary the eyebrow. She should have become accustomed to this, but she had developed a habit of trying to guess which one Lill would choose. Mary shook her head, trying to fling the thought out so that she could concentrate on the conversation. The gesture, however, was misinterpreted as disagreement. She might have corrected this instantly, but she was too busy berating herself doing something that she objected to when DO did it.

"Try something more physical," Lily offered, then responded to Lill's kick by amending her suggestion to, "Maybe dancing."

Mary reflected for a moment before confiding, "He's a bit *dull* when he's not talking about *important things*."

"I think he's funny," Lily said.

"Maybe, about some things. But he never just, well, just relaxes."

"Too tense?" Lill asked.

"No… not exactly. Just, well, I can't put my finger on it, but it bothers me."

"Never silly enough?" Lill suggested.

"The way you put it, it sounds, well, silly. But you're about right. I'd prefer, well, I don't know what exactly I'd prefer, but I know what I don't prefer."

"Maybe you'd prefer Stout."

"Uggh," she replied with a shiver.

Professor Stout was looking for a workable scheme, too, but he was more interested in ideas than romance. He was senior to Donahue, but since Donahue was only in his second year, practically everyone was senior to him, and Stout, with several additional years at Briarpatch behind him, felt that this was the time for him to become the intellectual and moral leader of the faculty, to position himself for advancement to Academic Dean when Stanley Wooda moved on—or, more importantly, Flo Boater. Who knew what the trustees might do, or her successor? To do this, he would have to somehow supplant Lill and

Lily, who were now back in the Theater department. He was assisted in this by Dean Wooda's numerous efforts at inflicting petty humiliations on those rivals; Stanley Wooda often attached job advertisements from professional journals to his notes refusing already budgeted funds for the production of plays. By forcing them to improvise in making sets and costumes, he hoped to limit the time available for entertaining the college's brightest students in the coffee house, and he was pleased to see how well this worked. These students, for lack of interaction with other faculty, began to drift into Stout's Honors program—which was still "informal" due to lack of faculty action. Thus, Stout's interests and those of the president and dean ran perfectly parallel. Or close enough for Briarpatch.

Stout's plans intertwined with those of Smith and Jones. But they were not identical. Or even similar.

If Stout had been anxious only to rise in *Academe* (as professors called their business, making it seem more Plato-like and less an enjoyable way of making a living), he would have been satisfied with his rise in the administration's favor. He could envision being an assistant or associate dean, but shrank back from suggesting that. Those positions implied work, daily work… dull work—the kind of work that deans didn't want to do themselves. It was better to aim at the top job, then pass those tasks off to newly hired assistant deans or even to committees. Besides, he would have had to abandon his beloved role as chief faculty rebel, the role that so charmed most of the new colleagues who joined the faculty this fall—until he suddenly became too involved in committee work to speak out forcefully. Co-opted, that was his worry. Had he been?

Briarpatch had hired several new instructors and assistant professors to teach the large number of freshmen who had enrolled after visiting the campus to see the murder scenes from the previous year. Most were already tired of teaching freshman courses, even though the semester had barely started—that's what they had done in graduate school or their previous places of employment. Truth be told, most of them had not starred at either. Briarpatch salaries could not attract the best and the brightest, though that was the way they thought of themselves—

good people steered by an evil star onto Boater's academic vessel rather than to an opportunity to change the course of the world.

Stout's real desire was to affect the way the state and the nation conducted affairs. The fall of 1996 was, after all, an election year. Stout had been cultivating friendships with local Democrats. At first, they had been suspicious of him—after all, he was an outsider and he had never shown an interest in mainstream politics before. But once he made it clear that he had no desire to occupy the offices available locally, they welcomed him as a valuable ally, one who could recruit students to go door to door with literature or who would drive ailing voters to the polls; he could also afford to provide free beer for strategy sessions. Stout's major problem was that the relationship of the local political leaders and the faculty had long been strained. Local Democrats were absolutely practical in their policies, and their interests were rigorously local, while the faculty was almost exclusively interested in national and international politics. The two groups rarely met to discuss their common interest—electoral victory. Good thing, too, since each group had members who ridiculed the other, and moreover, each group had splinter groups who preferred third-parties candidates—"townies" tending to veer toward the right, "gownies" toward the left.

Town-gown splits had existed since the Middle Ages. At the heart of each quarrel were students. Town businesses welcomed students, and therefore, so did most citizens—as long as they didn't make noise, drink too much, make fun of their small-town manners, fill up the bars on weekends, take up all the parking and generally just be there. Citizens wanted their quiet little city, with five Fridays of home high school football games every fall, a 4th of July celebration, and the Christmas tour of homes; happily, students were away on almost all of those occasions, and the campus was also almost empty from Friday noon until late Sunday night. There were friends of the college, too, but most were graduates of Briarpatch or related to the many people who were employed to cook, clean, copy, etc., etc.

In these circumstances the faculty tended to be protective of students. They could criticize them, ridicule them, etc., etc., themselves, but they firmly believed that only they had the right to do that; not even the staff were permitted much beyond echoing professors' sentiments, despite their being better informed about what went on in the town and on campus. Moreover, the younger faculty members, knowing almost no townspeople (who could be encountered only in the local churches, stores, social clubs and veterans' organizations, etc., etc.), assumed that most townies were escapees from a Hollywood satire of small town mores.

Stout's plan was to bridge this gap. Somehow he would bring the town and gown together, though he had to remind himself not to use this term—whenever he referred to college people as "gown," Middleville citizens would smile and nudge one another in the ribs. Nobody in Middleville wore a gown after 7 AM, and only women wore one before then. But they suspected that there were some whose sexuality was a bit… "different." One of the local bars was becoming a bit… "uncomfortable" for straight guys, and the women who went there had even stronger instincts for that sort of thing than did the men. Younger faculty, in contrast, felt themselves obliged to frequent that bar, to demonstrate that they were not the sort of people who had… prejudices. That they were different from the regressive churchgoers of the community.

Stout's principal problem was his inability to persuade anyone that the election was going to be close. Both groups would have to worry enough about the outcome to agree to work together under his leadership, otherwise everyone would stay home. There was considerable sympathy for Bob Dole in the community, especially among those old enough to remember THE WAR, and this group despised Bill Clinton for not having served in THAT WAR. It was exactly the opposite among the faculty, some of whom were, the truth be told, were too young even to remember THAT WAR, and a few even believed that there was still a draft. This was a misunderstanding principally among females, who never had to go through the process of registering, but Stout had persuaded a few of the younger males that they would have to move to Canada if the election came out wrong. He assured them that Canadian universities were discriminating against American applicants, so they would have to find some manual labor job, and that the winters were harsher than they ever imagined. (Actually, he did not say "Americans." He had tried to say "United Stateseans," but, bobbling the pronunciation, he ended up with "people like us.") As for the election campaign, the issues under discussion were so inconsequential that Stout had great difficulty in persuading anyone off campus that a Dole victory would bring about immediate war with somebody, economic collapse and probably the triumph of fascism. Nor could he persuade his colleagues to join in a campus get-out-the-vote campaign. He did not have good arguments for those who believed, a) that most students wouldn't vote anyway, and, b) those who did, might turn out to be Republicans. From time to time, he saw that his colleagues were not so far removed from being students themselves, only, Thank the Powers of Nature, few of them were Republicans.

The only person willing to disagree with him publicly was Donahue, who debated him once, right at the start of the academic year, before a tightly-packed crowd in one of the college's smallest classrooms. Stout had argued that this was a pivotal moment in American history, to which Donahue had countered that elections were usually won by the man with the shortest name (though he conceded that this had not been the case in 1992). It was a battle of H's—hyperbole versus humor. By the end, Donahue had won over a few listeners—including some who disagreed with his political philosophy—persuading them that, no matter who won, the 1996 election was not going to change American history significantly. Besides, it was obvious that it was colder in Canada than in Middleville; and the Canadian protectionist policy limiting the number of American professors had nothing to with American politics.

Stout told everyone who would listen that he had trounced the newcomer. The usual response was a question—"Why did you have this debate now, in September? The conventions were barely over."

Donahue learned quite a bit from the experience. Not only did a debate take more preparation time than he expected, but he was told that, "You are upsetting our happy family." Shaking his head at being called an outside troublemaker, he thereafter declined to debate again. He told Mary that he could either write or debate, but not both, and writing might get him tenure eventually. Mary did not understand this. She disagreed with his liking Bob Dole, but she was appalled that he did not see the long-lasting significance of the ideological confrontation, and that he would publicly suggest that Dole would be a good president. Donahue tried to explain that it was not a lack of concern for the fate of the country that caused him to refuse a second debate—"First of all, I'm uncomfortable using the implied authority of my degree to advance a political agenda. Secondly, I believe that Stout is his own worse enemy, and that there was nothing I can do to make him look worse than to let him speak, and that more publicity would reflect badly on the college. Lastly, this leaves it up to Stout alone to drum up an audience—and the fewer people who hear him, the better it will be for the Republic." Trying to explain to Mary that tongue-in-cheek humor was a perfectly good way to get past the pseudo-seriousness of the pseudo-intellectualism of academic partisanship only made matters worse. She did not speak with him for days. Instead, she went out of her way to congratulate Stout on his courage.

Stout was thus encouraged to persevere. His original plan had centered on forcing Donahue into a confrontation over the election, thereby stirring up local enthusiasm. But his plan could have succeeded only if their debate had resulted in Donahue's humiliation. In this he had failed. So far.

His second plan was to force Lill and Lily to abandon their neutral political posture. If he could undermine their reputation, especially with the more radical members of the faculty and student body, he would ingratiate himself with the dean and president no matter how the debate turned out. Victory was not in how many young voters he swayed, but in "unmasking" the enemies of progressive thought. He found young Smith a willing acolyte, and even Jones stayed awake through the first meeting of the pre-honors class. This was considered quite an achievement, since Smith had never been excited by any idea he had encountered. Except sex, which still remained, for him, more an idea than an accomplishment.

For Smith the challenge had been trying to write down the four-letter words—as instructed for the next day's vocabulary quiz—which he did as best he could until Stout reminded everyone that there were no formal grades, just educational challenges. Jones survived by recording with iiii and / the number of times Stout said "I." He began recording "uhs" after Stout noticed what he was doing.

Stout's plan to expose his foes' presumed arch-conservative views failed to take into considerable the political views of the trustees, most of whom had earned both money and respect by careful planning, hard work and taking risks. He felt he could ignore their views because he despised everyone who held them, and he could despise them all the better because he thought he knew them very, very well.

Stout's father had been an entrepreneur. He had really missed THE WAR, but, having been in basic training at the very end, he had qualified for the educational opportunities that became available for veterans. Discharged quickly along with millions of other men, his service consisted of little more than a few months guarding Fort Hood in Texas—fortunately in the fall, not the summer. He attended a small liberal arts college near his home, earning a degree in Business Administration and meeting his future wife, and then went abroad to work for what was later called a multi-national corporation until he knew enough to start a business of his own. Being away from home for long periods of time, he arranged for his wife to join him as often as possible. But since he was often working in areas known for violence and disease, he was uncomfortable taking along his young son, Maximilian. Stout, therefore, grew up largely under the supervision of nannies and grandparents. Once, when his grades were too low to qualify him for a well-known prep school, he even had a private tutor who instructed him in writing and math. Then his parents were killed in a highway accident on a primitive road, en route to some plant or mine deep in the interior of Africa or South America—he believed that it was the former, but he hadn't cared enough to remember exactly. On the whole, he thought of himself as a Dickens' character—abandoned by his family and loved only by the simple but hard-working poor folk who took him in. His grandparents were not rich, but they were well-to-do. When they died, too, he felt he had been abandoned again.

A summer or two in the care of distant relatives who lived near a tough neighborhood made him aware of the economic inequalities in society—and his guardian, a banker friend of his father's from his college days, carefully invested his inheritance so that it continued to grow through those very days when he believed he could have put it to better use himself—on himself. In vain Stout had tried to persuade his guardian to ignore a clause in the will establishing a fellowship at his parents' *alma mater*. His allowance was sufficient to earn him the respect of acquaintances, but inadequate to afford the vices that could have ruined him, and far from sufficient to correct the ills of society that he saw all around him—and whenever a friend suggested that he exaggerated, he dropped him.

Stout's prep school days remained shrouded in mystery, though, truth be told, few cared enough to enquire into them. He did not name the school on his *Vita* when he applied at Briarpatch, and he politely changed the subject whenever "high-school" experiences came up in conversation. Today a few strokes on the computer could probably get the desired information, but the internet was not yet available in Briarpatch when he arrived and the library holdings on prep schools were practically non-existent. His Ivy League education, BA, *cum laude* in English, though just short of *Phi Beta Kappa*, got him into graduate school. Into three, in fact. The last was not a well-known name, but he only mentioned the first in conversation. Possession of a Ph.D. guaranteed him an offer from Briarpatch, which rarely saw applications from anyone who had attended an IVY LEAGUE university. It helped that he was now independently wealthy—the guardianship ended at age twenty-six, and he had spent summers in his guardian's investment firm—so the slender salary offer that Briarpatch had made (quietly bumped up a notch to attract his attention) was completely unimportant.

No one ever asked why his interviews at other colleges and universities had not resulted in an offer, or why he had not gone to work on Wall Street. It was just one of those unexplained strokes of luck that occasionally came Briarpatch's way.

Lill had once asked him, "Max, you denounce capitalism all the time. But I understand that you hold stocks and bonds, and you have a lovely house."

"Thank you," he had replied. "But money is the root of all evil, and in our dualistic universe, there is really no difference between good and evil. Therefore, one should use evil against evil, employing their natural magnetic mutual repulsion to achieve those goals that superior minds understand are what the destiny of mankind must be."

Lill had smiled, "Nothing in common with the college's religious foundation, then?"

"Briarpatch College has no religious affiliation worth discussing, and Christian beliefs are essentially irrelevant in the world of today. Floyd Boater can talk about morality all he wants, but the trustees will still only invest in the football program."

Lill noted that the football program had not flourished in recent years. "Thank God," he had replied.

In contrast to the football coach's career, Stout's upward progress at Briarpatch had been spectacular—moving quickly to the chairmanship of the English department, then to the chair of numerous committees. He was the confidant of the late president (less so of the late dean, there being some indications of mutual jealously there), and seemed to always be away at a convention. His name figured prominently in various national organizations and would have been even more prominent if he had ever published.

Stout had once sought to be published, but his brief flirtation with Automatic Writing had not been well-received, nor had his advocacy of Anarcho-Primitivism. His problem, he had decided, was that he had been unwisely attracted by the great ideas of the past; the solution was to embrace those of the future. Unhappily, one could not see where the future lay unless one worked at a cutting edge university—the ideas that were so excitedly discussed over coffee or fine wines there were out of date by the time anyone at a small semi-rural college could read about them. "Publishing is such a poor method of disseminating ideas," he had said many times in advocating more travel money. "Attending conferences is so much more important."

The ordinary frustrations of life were thus multiplied for Max Stout, who could at best "imitate" cutting-edge concepts and couture—in his conversation and clothes one could see that he aspired to something better and more worthy…. What this was… was… not clear, but it was clearly something superior. And thanks to inherited wealth, he could afford to demonstrate his superiority to the ordinary.

Lill had asked him, "Max, ever think of going into administration."

He had been mildly affronted. "No, the world of details and committee meetings is incompatible with the life of the mind. Now, mark you well, at the right college or university, at the right time of life, with the distractions of routine removed, one could do a great deal of good—or evil, if one can tell the difference. But first of all, one must put oneself forward...."

Lill had half-forgotten this advice until those days following the death of Dean Wooda, when Flo Boater had been charged with conspiracy to commit murder and Floyd Boater had taken a leave of absence. She did not push herself forward in any obvious way, but she had seized the opportunity to assist the trustees when they asked for volunteers to serve on study committees. Nor had she anticipated their inviting her to be acting-president, but once the offer was extended, she remembered Max's words—and she accepted.

She had either forgotten or not heard the conclusion of his statement, "but such an ambition will certainly end badly. Ambition is an aspect of competitiveness, and competitiveness, like capitalism, will destroy you." She remembered vaguely his saying something about "There may be no difference between good and evil except what we think of them."

"What's the point of life, then," she had asked.

"Enjoyment. First for oneself, then for the rest of mankind."

"No friends in between?" she had joked.

"Friends? We really only have acquaintances, and those only for short moments. Our obligation is to great ends, not to friends."

"Family?"

"A scholar should not have a family."

Mary had been briefly attracted to Stout. Despite the difference in their ages and his unfortunate name, she realized that they shared many of the currently fashionable ideas and interests. One date brought an end to that. Fortunately, he never asked her out again. He seemed to have no interest in women (or men, either, for that matter). That would not have been a barrier to a close friendship, she thought, until she heard that he had referred to her as "infatuated" and then said that, "one doesn't screw where one works." The vulgar summary of her sentiments as something appropriate to pre-teens spending their baby-sitting money on movie magazines had repelled her immediately, but the more she thought about it, the less pleased she was. Why would he think that her interest in him was only a desire to "screw?" And why, even if he thought that, would he say it to anyone else?

Besides, he had a habit of *touching*....

In such a mini-universe—such as we each live in—there is little reason to worry about the schemes of lesser folk. Lesser folk like undergraduates. As if they had the imagination to work up anything worthy of the title *scheme*.

In such a universe a missing Miss Purdy was easily lost. Her co-workers were becoming concerned, but theirs was such a minor galaxy that virtually no one outside the Finance office saw it.

Chapter Four

It was still the beginning of the fall semester, Donahue's second year of teaching. In contrast to the previous late summer, when he had worked himself almost to exhaustion to prepare his introductory lectures, he was now relaxed. He had spent much of this summer with his mother. This free time, without the usual distractions of food and laundry, enabled him to write several long essays that were quickly snapped up by editors of popular magazines. This provided some welcome additional income, but he knew that such publications would not help him win tenure, that guarantee of continued employment which so obsessed Mary. The Personnel and Promotion Committee would be impressed only by books and articles that specialists in each discipline read (and no one else). But that critical moment in every academic's life lay years ahead, approximately five years; moreover, because he had already made so many career changes, each time going in a dramatically different direction, that he was not worrying about one more. In five years anything could happen. Maybe Briarpatch would have a P&P committee that was not intent on improving the college's standing in the *US News* survey. Who reads to the bottom of the list, anyway?

He was also more relaxed this year because he had discovered that teaching was not only fun, but that undergraduates were a very different audience than graduate school professors. He did not have to be ready to defend every statement with a long list of citations. The students didn't care about citations; they wanted information to be understandable and relevant. Whether two people they had never heard of disagreed as to what the information meant, was unimportant; moreover, while some of them might be interested in the ideas, they couldn't care less about their names—he learned quickly to restrict memorization to the "classic" names that had withstood the test of time. Donahue may have been a beginning instructor, but his academic career had stretched back almost two decades, back to 1975-6, interrupted by two years in the

53

military and ten as a cop and homicide detective. He had noticed in graduate school that names praised by his instructors when he was a freshman were now mocked by his professors. The intellectual world had changed much in the years between those experiences; it had come as a surprise that the fads in education were much like those in fashion. He remembered having been told that, but it was still unexpected. He was even more astonished that his brightest students had reached that same conclusion already, and most of the rest had somehow learned to ignore the trendy stuff—they had already developed a "BS Nose"—or they had switched to an English major, where "cutting edge scholarship" was replacing the "canon," the traditional books and essays unfortunately written by "dead white men." Donahue occasionally commented that they weren't dead when they were writing, but he rarely got a smile from his hearers—subtlety is not often found among American college students, sometimes not even in the faculty. He was certain that if he had stayed in college past age nineteen, he would not have noticed the importance of intellectual fads by age twenty-two. Perhaps everything moved more slowly in the Seventies. But more likely, he confessed, he wouldn't have known enough to know what was conventional and what was new. Everything is new when one is young.

Observing his students' equally rapid progress in their love lives, he was increasingly aware of a similar generation gap—his courtship of Mary C was going very slowly. The telephone conversations over the summer had been few and short, and though she had greeted him warmly on their first meeting back on campus, they had soon quarreled. He gathered that there had been some pressure from *her* mother, which he had unwisely suggested might be worth listening to. Then there was Edward Said, whom he had been reading and, unwisely, thinking about. That incident had passed, but his tendency to espouse heretical attitudes got in the way of his efforts to espouse Mary. Donahue's colleagues called him DO, from DOA (dead on arrival), a reference to his passing skills as a freshman quarterback in a short-lived athletic career. Now they might as well call him DIW. Dead in the Water. Of course, someone might confuse the order of the initials, thinking he had a drinking problem. Which he didn't. At least, not yet—though Mary's stand-offish attitude was moving him in that direction, and the open hostility from President Boater and Dean Wooda was pushing him down the road to perdition, too.

Then he had spoken with Chief Biggs. Afterward he was not sure whether a missing Miss Purdy was good or bad news. Would her disappearance have a negative effect on the college's finances? Did she run away with the money? Or was there something more sinister? Biggs had intimated fears of the worse. Or would this be an opportunity to draw closer once again to Mary?

Only the day before Lill had asked, "What do you and Mary talk about?"

"Books, movies—though I don't go to many, since the theater closed—college politics, students, the usual sort of things."

"Politics?"

"Now and then. Well, fairly often. But we don't agree on much."

"Do you both enjoy those discussions?"

"I think so. She's holding her own now. She likes winning a point now and then."

Lill smiled at this, since Mary's politics were based more on emotion than logic, "Ever talk about the future?"

"Not often. Mary says she's not ready for the future yet?"

"Talk about your families much?"

"Mine a bit. She's a bit more private."

"Forgive me from probing, DO, but there are other young women out there."

"What other women?" It was more a statement than an inquiry.

Lill thought for a moment, then changed the subject, "What exactly do you see in her that you don't in the others?"

"She's nice to be with. You know that."

"That's not a good answer."

"I just enjoy being with her. We're more alike than she knows. We'd be a good pair."

Donahue was thinking about this conversation when an image of Chief Biggs came to him. Not realizing it was his imagination, he asked, "Any news about Miss Purdy?" Almost instantly he snapped out of his daydream, looked around, and saw Flo Boater and Stanley

Wooda at the counter, getting cups of coffee. At that his eyes narrowed. He whispered to himself, "What is it about Briarpatch now? I get suspicious at every little thing out of the ordinary." Relaxing only when they went out onto the patio, he thought, "Strange that they'd be down here. That's unusual." Then he persuaded himself that he was being suspicious of nothing. Perhaps they were only imitating Lill's practice of walking the campus—going into buildings to see how things were going. He smiled at himself, "Probably not…." But if not, then what? He shook the thought off.

On the positive side, Donahue now had a good command of his class material. The previous year he had been organizing his lectures only a day or two before giving them, praying that he not get sick or his eyes give out. But somehow he had made it, and when he described his experiences to Lill, who had been acting-president at the time, she shared a few of her secrets to academic survival. She had told him to plan out the semester, assigning one topic or idea to each class period. At most, two. Make sure that everything was included in the forty-five hours of class time available—lectures, reviews, exams, and most important, a review of the exam results. When possible, she said, he should spend the last five minutes asking students to repeat the important points from the lecture. He had not found any of these suggestions easy to apply at first, but once he got the method down, he revised all his class preparations. The students responded better, and he was almost selected teacher of the year. Had he made the switch the first semester instead of the second, who knows? Surely this year he could beat out "the Creep," as the emaciated senior historian was universally known. How had the Creep won? Nobody took his classes, and those who did, got miserable grades. Was there some manipulation? Something underhanded by Dean Wooda?

Probably. Or, as Lily put it, "You have any doubts!? It was his payoff for being a snitch!"

Anyway, in any fair process of selection, nobody was going to edge out Lily this year. She had not been eligible last year, when she had been either acting-dean or fighting to get her job back. Her sparkling classes in theater were always packed. The junior partner of "the Leather Lesbians" had a style that was as unbelievable as it was indescribable.

She uttered no sentence that was not a joke, and sometimes she could hardly get to the important points because the class was laughing so hard. She did not follow Lill's strategy of careful planning, but somehow she covered all the material and did so effectively. As she said, quoting what she claimed was "some pop philosopher"—"I gotta be me."

The only obstacle might be their half-year replacements' anger. Flo had found full-time part-time work for them, teaching Freshperson speech sections. There they mounted a relentless campaign against the Theater Department. "Oh, well," Donahue yawned. "There are feuds everywhere in Higher Education. Can't avoid them." Then he smiled, "Maybe it keeps them out of real politics... probably Bob Dole's only chance locally... unless their arguments would get angry Republicans to turn out."

Jones was telling Smith that the scheme sounded good, but there were some tricky details, like, "Where do we buy grades?" He was usually the practical one.

"Where'd we get them before?"

"Hell, he's dead." After a pause to wait for Smith to think, he added, "I don't even remember much about that."

Smith laughed, "I don't either, but we got to be sophomores."

Jones was not moved to similar hilarity. "Maybe we should attend the pre-honors class, that's a guaranteed B."

"Get up for a 10 AM class! You gotta be kidding."

Jones acknowledged that this time Smith was the practical one— they rarely got up before noon. If they started making ten o'clock classes, they might end up studying. But there was that nagging question, "Where do we buy them?"

"Hey," Smith suggested, "maybe we should just ask around."

Jones made a reply half-way between a snort and a guffaw, "You betcha, you'd get turned into the dean so fast!"

Smith hardly had to think about that at all, "Maybe he's the person to talk to first."

Donahue was crossing the campus when he saw a familiar figure. He called out, "Chief Biggs... Chief Biggs!" Several students turned to look at him, but after watching him trot over to a man in uniform, an elderly man as far as eighteen-year-olds are concerned, though the chief of police was barely into his sixties; they went back to more important business—themselves.

The chief, hearing his name, turned around, and walked back to greet the friend hurrying toward him, "Hi, DO, What's up?" Then, before Donahue could say anything, he added, "I haven't heard anything new about Miss Purdy."

Donahue, puffing slightly, said to himself that he needed to get more exercise. Since he had stopped swimming, actually since the day he had found the dean floating in the college pool, he had done little except walk to work and back. Mary had early morning runs around the campus, but he no longer had the knees for jogging. Too many days walking on pavement, a couple of jumps from rooftops in hot pursuit. One story buildings, but afterward running was something he did only when he had to. "Nothing really, I guess..." he said. "Not about Miss Purdy anyway."

"Then isn't it about time you called me 'Jus'? That is my name, or my dad's version of it. Or, if you prefer, Justice."

"Lazy, I guess. When I'm around others, I don't have to remember which name to use." He didn't mention how strange it would sound to be running, well, walking fast across campus, yelling, "Justice, Justice."

"Okay, I can live with that. Anyway, something's up. Something worth running for. Or do I imagine that you're out of breath." The chief knew all about not being in shape, though he could still probably do the hundred in fifteen seconds... or twenty.

"I guess I need to get into shape. Being a teacher has its downsides." He had already fallen into the students' habit of calling professors teachers.

Biggs kidded him, "The downside seems to be the chest slipping onto the stomach."

Looking ruefully at his belly, and still puffing, Donahue said, "I do need to work on that." He also remembered how much Mary disliked fat men. Another incentive. But was it worth the effort? "Home cooking. All summer."

"That's not why you called to me," Biggs guessed.

"No. Not really," Donahue gasped, more in need of air than he had realized, "Something else."

"Out with it!" Biggs was joking, but he was also impatient.

"I need some advice about Mary."

This made Biggs laugh, "A former cop needs advice about women!"

Donahue answered with a joke, "Women I understand. It's Mary who confuses me."

"How so?" he asked, pointing to a bench where they could sit.

By now Donahue had ceased puffing, "Well, in that business, you know, Dean Wooda's death, then President Boater's, we got pretty close."

"I'd say everyone expected you two to get married any day."

"Yes. I thought so, too. At least, perhaps."

"But?"

"She can't seem to make up her mind."

"How so?"

"She finds it hard to explain, but she gave me this book to read." With that he slipped a paperback out of his coat pocket and handed it to the chief.

"*The Bell Jar*," Biggs said, reading the title. He opened it at page one and read a paragraph, then flipped back a few pages. "Surprisingly, I'm familiar with it."

It was Donahue's turn to say, "How so?"

"My wife liked Plath's poetry." Then he asked Donahue, "Have you read it yet?"

"I've tried. It's pretty depressing."

"My wife thought so, too. She knew enough about Plath's marriage to wonder why she was complaining so much. What's his name, her husband, seemed like the perfect guy for her. Took care of the kids, all that sort of thing."

Donahue did not hurry in his response, but he finally said what he was thinking, "A lot like the way you took care of your wife." Not everyone even knew how long the chief's late wife had been an invalid.

Biggs's response was as close to a blush as Donahue had ever seen, but he brushed away the compliment, saying, "Mental illness is harder to deal with than physical."

"I don't know if Mary knows about that," Donahue sighed. "She just says that marriage and scholarship are not compatible, at least not for a woman."

Biggs thought for a second. He reflected back on his own marriage. The issue had never come up. But then his wife had been ill for so long, and now she had been dead for years. When their daughter had been young, she had the time to spend with her, but by the time the child was in school, she was too weak. He himself had neglected their daughter, too, or so hindsight now told him. He was paying for it now, too. So, he asked himself, what *was* compatible with marriage? With a career? He was lucky, in many ways, that he lived in a small community and could arrange a somewhat flexible schedule. A bit awkward sometimes, when on duty, but usually it was possible to stop by every hour or two to see how she was doing. Their families had problems of their own; they could help for emergencies, but not on a daily basis. What advice did he have to offer to somebody whose concern was merely a job? On the other hand, how could he judge another's priorities?

His daughter had been closer to his parents, but now that they were gone he rarely heard from her. Realizing with a start that he was ignoring his friend, he shook his head and said to himself, "What does that have to do with Mary?" Turning back to Donahue, he asked cautiously, "So she still puts her career first?" He paused to think, "Not unusual nowadays." He looked at Donahue, but when he saw that he was going to wait for more advice, he continued, "Many marriages don't work out. A woman has to have a job to fall back on." After another pause, he observed, "Children don't take up an entire lifetime, either." And after yet another moment of silence, he continued, "Also, many women love their jobs." He looked at Donahue again, "Mary loves to teach."

"All true," Donahue agreed. "And for Mary all that hangs on getting tenure."

"Tenure?" Biggs asked, "Isn't that where they can't fire you for being incompetent?"

Donahue had to smile at the truth buried in this popular misconception, "It's more to protect people like Mary from people like Flo Boater."

Biggs was surprised, "What's the problem? I understood that when Mary published her research paper, the one you call 'Crime in Rural South America,' she would qualify easily." Seeing Donahue's mouth move toward a frown, he asked, "Has something come up?" Getting no immediate answer, Biggs looked at his watch and indicated that they should move along.

Only as they stood up did Donahue speak, "No. No problem with that paper. At least not with the topic. Two editors have expressed an interest in publishing it. Once she writes it, of course. Good journals, too. Not trendy ones, though, like the ones the committee wants to see."

They slowly began to walk in the direction Biggs had been going, though Donahue had not asked where that would be. Biggs said, "I'm not sure what you mean by trendy, but... if the paper's not the problem, what is?"

"There are people here who don't believe that married couples should work at the same college."

Biggs was surprised. "That was true, sort of, I guess, when I went to college briefly, how many years ago? Almost forty years now, but I thought that was ancient history. Who would bring that back?"

"That Creep, the historian."

"Ah, yes. The Creep. He's single. Besides, what business is it of his?"

"He'd like to be dean." And Donahue thought to himself, so would half the faculty, if the job wasn't so much work. "'This could save on medical insurance premiums,' he says, and bring 'new blood' into the classrooms."

"He doesn't have any talent. He'd be a terrible dean."

"Many deans don't, either—at least, that's the joke—or don't know how to apply it," Donahue observed, thinking to himself that Stout might be more qualified for the job. When he saw that the chief didn't understand, perhaps thinking this was an observation of Lily's failure as acting-dean—the only time in his life that Biggs had paid any attention to the activities of any administrator other than the Dean of Students—Donahue continued, "That's why so many professors believe they could do as good a job, or better, than their dean does."

Biggs nodded, "And why is he picking on Mary? Why not Dean Wooda?"

"Mary is just an issue. The Creep wants to be heard on every issue. He has to have something to talk about."

"Like some policemen I've known, he wants to be feared."

"Exactly," said Donahue, as several half-forgotten examples crossed his mind.

"So he's picked Mary as a target."

"It fits right into Flo Boater's agenda."

"To get rid of all her enemies." That was quite a task, Biggs reflected, since so many people were involved in her trial for conspiracy to commit murder, that is, the death of the first Dean Wooda by poisoning, and the suspicious circumstances surrounding the demise of her husband, President Boater.

"Yes." Donahue's mind was running down the same list, with himself and Chief Biggs as her foremost foes. Donahue had been the one to find the dean's body floating in the college pool, and Mary had been among the faculty present when Floyd Boater dropped dead. Actually, though, he knew the president had not died from the small amount of curare on the Amazonian dart tip, but from a heart attack precipitated by panic. Everyone in that group—Lill, Lily, Jenny, Molly and Mary—would be on her list. Almost everyone he liked, he thought, except Jay, whose loyalties she thought she had bought; and Sal, who was still in prison for conspiracy to murder the dean—a conspiracy with Flo Boater, his lover at that weak moment in his life.

"Let me see if I understand this. The Creep is arguing that couples... who probably meet in graduate school... and both want to teach... should work at different colleges?" He knew that the nearest university was hours drive away, in Zenith. Arcadia hardly counted.

"Yes. Jay says that he also wants a clause in the contracts requiring anyone marrying a faculty member to resign."

Biggs saw how impractical this would be on a campus where potential mates were so rare that utterly implausible marriages resulted. "Nepotism?" he asked.

"Apparently not," Donahue remarked, "or not nepotism in its usual sense of hiring a relative who did no work, or working under the spouse's supervision."

"Favoritism in hiring?"

"That's more a problem, though Middleville doesn't offer much competition for part-time jobs." Donahue thought a moment, "It's all still rumor, so we don't really know…."

Biggs saw the point, "One of you would have to resign!" He didn't add, "If you could persuade Mary to take you."

Donahue nodded, "Yes. Then he could decide which one to keep."

Almost laughing, the chief asked, "This is the only college for miles! Where would *you* work?" He emphasized his point by a friendly elbow in the ribs.

Donahue smiled in return, then explained. "In effect, he would be letting both of us go. Most often, people marry in order to live together, and so they would move to some university town where one could teach (the students' word again) and the other find a suitable job, hopefully at a nearby university or college."

"That's terrible." He paused before asking, "He wants couples to just live together?"

"No, the board is opposed to 'immoral cohabitation' and they would never stand for the woman becoming pregnant."

"Huh," the chief snorted. "Damned if you do… Not very practical. Not many jobs in Middleville."

"He doesn't care about the practicality of the situation, he says. It's the principle."

"It sounds like Flo Boater is very practical about it all." Biggs saw right through the plot to the grey eminence behind the Creep. He wondered if the historian was willing to eat bugs, too.

Donahue explained, "There is a principle to it. A practical problem. If *one* doesn't work out… doesn't get tenure…"

"They let him go."

"Or *her*. *Her*, too often. At least that is the belief." He paused, looking up to see if Biggs was following his argument, "Or they give the weak one tenure in order to keep the one they want."

"But once both have tenure," Biggs inquired, almost with a twinkle in his eye, "they can get married?" He was actually thinking about Lill and Lily, and the immoral cohabitation clause, but both of them had tenure, and unmarried female faculty had lived together forever. So had men, for that matter, and in his experience most were absolutely straight. Today, of course… but he shook that thought off.

"If it's not in the contract. Anyway, I'm a long way from tenure myself."

Biggs raised his eyebrows, "Is it that hard to get good people here?"

That got a laugh out of Donahue, "Here, yes. This college isn't exactly the center of American higher education!"

"Then why stay?"

"It's not always easy to move, and it's very hard for a couple. Many academic couples work hundreds of miles apart, or one has to drive from one part-time job to another. Often they see each other only once or twice a month. And they are often too exhausted to be pleasant. Mary doesn't want that."

"What about children?" Biggs asked.

"Ah, another complication," Donahue conceded. "There is certainly no consensus about that. Some colleges allow one to stay home—usually the mother—and teach part-time until the youngest child is in school; others insist that part-time work is degrading, so the couple's decision is 'all or nothing'… usually nothing. Around here there is a problem finding child care. At least, I'm told there is."

"I gather you and Mary have talked about this?"

"Not really," Donahue confessed. "It would be more correct to say that we've touched on the problems now and then. She is absolutely persuaded that the stress would be too much for her."

The chief, who knew something about stress, believed that Mary was stronger than she believed she was. Most women were. "What she needs is a model, someone she can talk to."

Donahue agreed, but all their friends were either unmarried or childless. Lill and Lily were unmarried, except in a sense to each other; Molly and Jenny were divorcees and, given their ages, even if they married Sal and Jay, they wouldn't have children. Miss Fox was too old, and even if Mary had been willing to get to know her better, she was *Miss* Fox. There were younger faculty with children, sure, but most of them were men and Mary felt awkward among their wives—she was an academic and usually somewhat older; they wanted to talk babies, and she was interested in linguistics. In their company she felt like an old woman.

Biggs shrugged, "I'm not sure that I know what to suggest."

More earnestly than he meant to, Donahue said, "You are a practical man. I trust your instincts."

Looking ahead, Biggs smiled and pointed to two well-known figures, "Here come Lill and Lily. They think like women, but understand the male point of view. Why don't you ask them?"

Donahue nodded, "Maybe Lily thinks like a woman, most of the time, but Lill thinks as *vertically*—Mary's word for it—as any man I know. But they're awfully good friends and this is kinda personal. I don't know." He thought about his recent conversation with Lill, then decided that there was insufficient time to explain it.

As the Leather Lesbians came up, Biggs greeted them and said, "Girls, DO has an interesting question." But before they could inquire what it was, Donahue had started to move, going in the opposite direction so that there would be no question of their walking together, "It's nothing we have to resolve right now." He turned after a few steps, "I'll work it out. See you all later." He turned and added irrelatively, "Got to run."

Lill, half-laughing, asked the chief, "A *Mary* problem?" When he nodded, Lily observed, "It's really a *marry* problem."

A big smile on his face, Biggs watched Donahue disappear from sight, as did Lill and Lily, then asked them, "How are my favorite administrators doing?"

"Ex-administrators now," Lill said.

Lily took a deep breath—it being an unusually cool day for the season, it felt good—flexed her biceps, stretched and then commented, "Lill hasn't accepted it yet, but I'm rather glad to be just to be myself again. More time for the motorcycle."

Lill apologized, "She goes on like this, as if she doesn't care." To which Lily retorted, "Oh, don't exaggerate."

"She enjoyed being a dean," Lill explained, to which Lily made a face, exclaiming, "Not the meetings! Not the *endless* committee meetings!"

Quietly Biggs inquired, "I thought you didn't hold many meetings."

Lill laughed, "We didn't. We learned long ago that ten faculty members…"

"….Can figure out any problem," Lily responded, "in ten minutes…."

"….over lunch."

"But put them in a committee room…."

"…and they will talk for hours…"

"…without getting anything done." This was a familiar routine, one of the leathered twins' most admired skills. They had often reduced crowds of students to teary fits of laughter. Not for what they said, but how they said it.

In the mood for banter, Biggs suggested, "Like the city council."

Lily pointed her finger at him for emphasis, something she had seen in a pro football game, and said, "Exactly!" Lill sometimes wondered if she had invented the gesture rather than copied it.

"Or the faculty union," Lily suggested. She had served on the steering committee often and, because she was a big woman with a loud voice, she was often chosen to speak for the union, toothless though it was.

"You may actually have it worse than we do," Lill agreed. "Mayors and councilmen are always thinking of the next election. Our professors have a lifetime contract."

"…if they behave," Lily countered.

At that, Lill became more serious, "Actually, it was more demanding than I had expected. Not just the meetings, but planning for them. Even when we were relaxing, the brain continued to work."

Picking up on the more serious turn, Biggs asked as he led them down the walk, "Speaking of that, how is Flo Boater doing?"

"As president?" Lill asked.

To which Lily added, "Or as widow?"

Biggs paused reflectively before saying, "Both."

"She's a spider."

"Don't sit down beside her."

As Biggs walked on silently, thinking, Lill asked, "What was that about DO?"

"DO, oh, he's worried about Mary."

"What's up with Mary?" Lill inquired, but Lily almost instantly said, "Here she comes. Why not ask?" The encounter was something that reminded Lill of a play: Actor Mr exits stage left, Actress Ms enters stage right. She had to smile at the artificial nature of the encounter, but on a small campus with one central walkway such encounters were not unusual. Mary was indeed approaching on a cross walk and appeared to be going in their direction.

They waited for her to reach them, but Lily cut through any preliminary formalities to blurt out, "Mary, we've just been wondering? What's going on between DO and you?" Lill tried to stop her, but Canute had better luck with the tide. Lily was just plain blunt at times. Fortunately, it didn't matter now. Mary took it as a question of no consequence, and replied while continuing to walk, the others joining her, "Oh, we just had a quarrel. Nothing big."

"Nothing big," Lily started to say, until Lill poked her in the ribs.

"Just the usual thing," Mary continued. "Politics."

"Oh, that's nothing," Lill interjected. "Friends shouldn't let politics get between them." She paused till Mary's raised eyebrows went back down (this was not the first time Lill had said this), then continued, "No, I mean, what's the problem?"

Mary stopped to face them, then sighed, "Oh, it's just... just..." Then she burst out, "DO just lacks patience."

"You've asked him to... what?"

"Nothing like that. I'm trying to work with that little Dweeb, Dean Wooda the Lesser."

Lill laughed, "I like that name!"

Lily would have made a joke here, but Biggs had already begun to speak, "I assume that Dean Wooda... the Greater, is the late Dean Wooda."

As the others nodded, Lily, as dryly as she could manage, opined, "No one is great until they're safely dead. The deader, the greater."

Lill opined, "Dead white men." That got a brief smile from the others, but did not deflect the conversation from the Wooda dynasty.

Mary, starting back down the walk, followed by the others, said, "His nephew or whatever he is, has taken his place, and *is his head swollen!*"

Lill agreed, "A real jerk."

To this Lily could think of nothing more original than, "A real young jerk." Such restraint was unusual for Lily, who made up for her reticence by flexing her muscles as if warming up for a strangulation.

After a moment Biggs asked, "How is the tenure decision coming?"

Mary answered quietly, "Oh, okay." Then she stopped, and as they stopped, too, she looked them in the face to admit, "Okay, it's not okay." She paused for a moment before continuing, "There are personalities involved, and... issues."

As Lill and Lily looked at one another, Biggs asked, "What kind of personalities?"

"The chair of the tenure committee...."

"The historian," said Lill, which Lily amended to "the Creep," and Biggs revised to "the would-be dean."

Mary looked at them skeptically, "I think *you* already know as much about this as *I* do."

Lill confessed, "Well, we know a bit." But Lily took the edge off the issues by saying, "But we'd like your take on it."

Not interested in the faculty politics, Biggs asked, "How does DO fit into it?"

Mary, reluctant to talk about him, nervously started to walk again, a bit too fast, before stopping again and turning to them, "DO wants to get married." Two passing students heard the key words and turned to look as they walked past, but they were soon out of earshot.

Three pairs of eyes were on her, and three pairs of lips asked, "Yes...?"

She almost pouted, "But I'm just not ready yet." She refrained from saying that her mother was ready, which was another reason for saying no.

Biggs asked encouragingly, "You like DO, don't you?" She nodded reluctantly.

Lill asked, "There isn't another unmarried man here equal to him? Is there?" When Mary hesitated, she continued, "Surely not Stout." Mary slowly shook her head. Lill then repeated her question, whether DO wasn't the best prospect around.

It was Lily's turn, time for the killer question. But, instead, she ruined the moment by commenting, "He's a hunk."

The spell was broken. Whatever adjectives a coed might apply to Donahue, "hunk" was not in the top ten. Mary started off again, saying, "I just can't make a decision like this in a hurry."

Biggs followed along, trying to keep up with her pace, "No rush. No rush."

Lill gasped out, the short sprint having caught her in mid-breath, "We are just all concerned. We are your friends, friends of you both."

Catching up with Mary, Lily said, "We only want you to be as happy as we are." At this Mary stopped, caught her in her arms and gave her a big hug. She then turned to all of them, "Thanks. Thanks for being concerned." After a pause, she added, "When I make a decision, I'll let you know." Then she started out.

Lily called out, "Before you tell DO?"

Mary waved back, rather half-heartedly, then said, "You *always* know things before DO does."

Lill stood still for a moment, wondering if Mary realized what she had just said, and whether it meant what she thought it did.

Chapter Five

Flo Boater was sitting at the large table at the far end of her office, her feet uncomfortably not reaching the floor, looking out the high corner windows of the former courtroom. The chair was uncomfortable, but it enabled her to look sideways out over the campus. She thought of getting up to pace around, but she had tried that and it hadn't helped—not only was the room in the process of renovation, so that her desk was momentarily under a paint cloth again, but she had been conversing with the senior historian for at least ten wearying minutes. Studying the campus was an acceptable alternatively to looking into his sad eyes. Talking with him was never a pleasant task, even though he was her most valuable source for campus gossip and almost as valuable as chair of the Personnel and Promotions committee, or "whatever it is called this year." At times it was difficult to remember to call him by his name, so common was the practice of calling him "the Creep," but she managed. Since her close encounter with the law the previous fall, she had learned to keep a stone face under the most severe provocations. She turned when the distant door to the office opened and Stanley Wooda's young face appeared, "Good morning, President Boater. Good morning, Sir."

She stood up to return the greeting, signaling him to stay where he was. Indicating that the historian should sit and, legs dangling, wait for her, she walked over to her young dean and spoke softly, "Don't close the door yet, just go join the… join our friend." She then stepped out to speak to Miss Efficiency, to say that there should be no interruptions, then suggested that, since there were no appointments scheduled, this would be a good time to take her coffee break. She loitered at the door until the secretary had scurried off, then shut the door behind her and threw the paint cloth off her desk and the nearest chairs and signaled the men to join her. She stood, looking down on her guests. She had considered taking a slightly less dominant place in the charmed circle of

70

comfortable chairs that were reserved for special guests, but she sensed that her young dean was thinking himself too much her equal. Time to put him in his place, even if that were only on the wrong side of the "desk of power;" besides, the historian was there, and she definitely did not want him to believe that either one of them had risen above his customary humble station. The office was so large that entire areas could be devoted to arrangements of tables, chairs, desks and display cases, but her eye fell on the empty space where a display case containing her late husband's book, *Agamemnon at Bay*, had once stood. The memory made her smile. She was remaking the entire office in her image. As she looked farther back at the massive table, she frowned, uncertain how to remove the carcass of that unsightly and unwieldy monster from her cave. But if she did, how could she look out onto the campus without standing up? And how else could she make unwelcome guests so uncomfortable that they would leave quickly?

Stanley Wooda, standing up and coming over to her, asked in a whisper why she had sent her secretary away, she answered that she suspected her of still being more loyal to Lill than to her, and that this conversation needed to be completely private. When the historian cleared his throat noisily, she sat down, separated from the visitors by her huge oak desk, immaculately polished and without a paper upon it.

"If you don't trust her, why do you keep her?" the dean asked, ignoring the historian's presence.

Flo was becoming very accomplished at her late husband's most effective technique of answering questions, which was to number off the points, "First of all, she's very good. She was trained at ..." Her memory failed her, but she remembered being impressed when Lill had hired her. "Second, I can leave all the details to her."

Stanley Wooda asked suspiciously, "I thought details were a dean's job." And he glanced over at the historian, who sat up straighter and stared back, not sure what to say. The historian finally nodded in agreement with the president, because he hoped to be dean some day himself, and he knew that as long as Stanley Wooda's performance was adequate, his own chances were too small to measure. At that Stanley Wooda shrugged, a gesture that indicated acquiescence rather than agreement, and which caused a slight frown to cross the president's face. "Sometimes," she seemed to say, "He's still a child." Then a smile indicated that he was a very good looking child. Dancer's legs, good hair. She frowned slightly as she added mentally, "But no initiative in… important matters." Then back to business with a forced smile at the historian.

"I need deans for thinking," Flo Boater commented, "not paper shuffling." Apparently, Miss Efficiency could shuffle enough papers for both of them; or perhaps faculty committees; or trustees' meetings. Not to mention the State Board of Higher Education. Now was the time, she said, to announce her intention of hiring an assistant dean who would do nothing but deal with that bureaucracy, and Briarpatch was a *private* college, not a state university or junior college. No, she had not decided whether it would be an internal hire or a regional search. Certainly not national.

Her brief explanation was good enough for Stanley, who merely asked why she had called him in.

"It's about your idea," she said. Turning to the historian, she explained, "Dean Wooda thinks that we have a magnificent opportunity for moving this college ahead." When the historian nodded, she asked the dean to explain.

"Yes, the first five million dollar insurance settlement, when it comes in, soon we hope, will be a tremendous shot in the arm for our fund campaign."

"Obviously," the historian agreed. But what fund campaign? He hadn't heard about one, and he was the best informed person on campus. At least, he believed he was. Any information that made its way into town would be picked up almost instantly by his mother. Anything on campus, he would garner. Neither had heard anything beyond vague expectations that the insurance companies would have to pay up eventually.

Flo Boater exulted, "It could be two settlements in less than a year!" That would be ten million dollars! The historian was impressed.

Stanley Wooda was equally enthusiastic, "I wish we could arrange for that more often." As the others looked at him, questioningly, he realized what he said and apologized. "I'm sorry, I didn't mean it the way it sounded. I do respect your feelings, having lost your husband accidentally to… the heart attack in that way." He stumbled over his words trying to avoid mentioning poison.

Flo accepted the apology. It wasn't often she had the advantage over her very bright junior partner, "No problem. It would have been much worse if my husband had not been so well insured, both for the college and for myself."

"And the former dean," Stanley Wooda added.

"Yes, Dean Wooda's insurance will be even more important than my husband's, coming as it will after the financial crunch is overcome." She hesitated before continuing, "Once we settle the lawsuits." After a pause, she added, "The first insurance payment will persuade our creditors to give us more time; the second will clear up all remaining debts so that we can use our resources to move ahead."

The historian broke in here, wheezing, "I'm sure he would have appreciated how he could serve the college even in death."

This was the opportunity the president had been waiting for. "You are absolutely right; and what I would like you to do is to spread the word that this college is going to move ahead quickly once the money is available… and that will mean some *significant* changes."

Stanley Wooda suggested, "A stronger faculty, for example."

The president was not quite pleased at the interruption, but she conceded, "Yes, we will have to attract better people."

"Good people," the historian amended, intimating that "better" could still be pretty poor.

Stanley Wooda pressed on, referring to the visitor's main committee assignment, "And tighten up on tenure decisions."

The historian smiled at this. He nodded to indicate that he understood and approved. However, when the dean asked what he thought of Professor Stout, the smile disappeared momentarily. It reappeared, only slightly distorted, as he said, "I think we agree on some important issues." At that he paused to think.. "But there are some points of concern. For example, Max's current effort to place campaign posters on every faculty office door." He stopped to observe the administrators' reaction. He saw only a faint smile on Stanley Wooda's face and mild surprise (he thought that was what it was) on Flo Boater's. "The problem, as I see it, is that Max is not asking individuals if they agree or not." Seeing puzzlement on the president's face, he hastened to explain, "It's not that I disagree with his choice among the candidates, but if we allow faculty members to begin organizing for causes we think are worthwhile, we will soon see them organizing for those we abhor." He visibly relaxed as he saw Flo Boater's wide smile of agreement. "This, I think, is why we have to put Max on the list of professors in line for future replacement or early retirement. It is not the specific action that is wrong, if you follow what I mean, but the principle."

The president started to say that Professor Stout was years away from eligibility, but she was cut off by Dean Wooda's noting that Stout had tenure. He was about to say more when Flo Boater gave a "Harrumph," and looked directly at the historian, "Yes, Those are very good points. The question of 'politicizing the faculty,' as the *Chronicle of Higher Education* puts it, is not important here. I imagine that some of our employees were quite willing to have their doors covered and that others agreed as long as they were not expected to do anything more." She smiled again at the historian, who wanly smiled back, wondering if he were now only an "employee." She took this for encouragement, "I certainly cannot disapprove of his actions because my political beliefs lie elsewhere, because they don't...." Here she smiled again at the historian, whose mouth was now frozen in a mask, "but because if the trustees heard of it, they might suggest that a faculty member should exercise private rights privately; some would suggest that political opinions, outside of appropriate and rare situations, should be kept out of the classroom. In fact, I can imagine one or two who follow campus politics nationally will be aware of the catch-words of our time and argue that Stout's actions constitute an 'abuse of power.'" She paused briefly, then added, "This is a situation we must approach indirectly, not by confrontation, and naturally we will welcome further examples and suggestions how to apply these principles across the curriculum and the campus." After a pause, she added, "As for early retirement, that is a possibility. But Max is still relatively young, and he is independently wealthy, so there is no inducement we could offer that would persuade him to devote the rest of his life to other occupations... if he has any."

The historian, overwhelmed by the torrent of ideas, slumped mutely in his chair. He nodded his head almost imperceptibly as she elaborated on her beliefs concerning the necessity to balance "conflicting goods"—how to encourage Stout to continue his efforts to awaken the students' social consciousness and to elect the right persons to power, but without stirring up those who think destructively to emulate his methods.

Stanley Wooda broke her soliloquy by asking it she agreed that the historian and Stout should work together now to tighten up on tenure?

A bit irritated, the president looked at her dean and reluctantly agreed, "Yes, tighten up on tenure." She turned back to the historian and spoke more positively, somewhat seductively, "We need the faculty to understand how important these coming months will be, and how important it is for everyone to trust us." She stood up and began to walk around the desk to escort the visitor from the room, but stopped when Stanley Wooda interjected, "We can't reveal exactly what the trustees are saying. Their support is vital, and they would be displeased if confidential information was made public."

Again irritated, Flo Boater reluctantly concurred, "Yes, the faculty has to be tolerant until the trustees buy into our proposals." She then touched the historian on the shoulder, seductively, "We won't forget who our friends were in these critical moments. You will help, won't you?"

The historian shook head in agreement, not quite certain of what he had agreed to do. But he could not formulate a question before she had taken his hand and escorted him to the door. When she got back to her desk, she opened a drawer for a facial tissue and wiped her hands off carefully.

The dean leaned back in his chair, "Thank goodness he's gone. That creep gets on my nerves."

"He only wants your job." She smiled after she said it—one of those sweet "gotcha" smiles. She was sure she had.

Stanley Wooda slowly countered, "I think he wants yours."

That was a new thought for her, but after reflection, she said only, "Most deans are that way." She allowed Stanley to think about this before adding, "The late Dean Wooda was." She didn't say how she knew this was so.

"I really didn't know him."

The president sat back down after depositing the tissue in a trash basket, then asked, almost off-hand, "How was it again, that you were related to him?"

Stanley Wooda was evasive, "It was fairly distant."

"How distant?"

"I'm not exactly sure. My late Aunt Emeline kept track of all the relatives. She said that all Woodas were related."

Flo looked at him for a moment, wondering where she had lived and when she had died, and why Stanley was so evasive. "I thought you said once you were related to someone in town?"

"Oh, I was too young then to pay much attention. I wish she was still around to talk to. And she may have meant someone on my mother's side. She was my mother's sister-in-law."

"What was your mother's maiden name?"

"Chu, I think, but she was married several times, like her mother, so I get them all mixed up."

"Chinese?"

"Do I look Chinese?"

She paused for only a moment, "And your father?"

"Never saw him, really, but Aunt Emeline said that he had no relatives. None close enough to name. She wasn't even sure how he made a living." He paused, shrugged his shoulders and said only, "I don't even know when he died, or how. I've been pretty much on my own since grade school."

"Who paid for the academy?"

"The academy? Oh, Aunt Emeline left some money, and my grandmother. Then scholarships. A bit of summer work."

"How could you afford our off-campus programs?"

"Oh, I owe a lot of money. A *lot* of money."

This alarmed his listener enough to make him explain, "I've been given some nice gifts, too, people who liked me. And my salary as dean, together with my student spending habits, is allowing me to pay the loans off. I could be clear in a year or two."

This satisfied the president, who saw that she wasn't going to get any more out of him, and who didn't believe even what he had just told her, "I suppose that if we don't mention it, everyone will assume that you are a nephew."

"I'm certainly not his son!"

"Just as well," the president agreed. "But with his reputation, you would imagine that a few children could be hiding here or there."

"There are sure to be some woodpile jokes." He clearly hadn't intended this to be funny, but he drew a smile from Flo Boater, who thereby reminded him of his early claims to be Black rather than West Indian.

She grinned at his discomfiture and suggested, half jokingly, "Might not be bad. Nepotism charges would distract people from your youth and inexperience." This was unusual for her. She usually saw humor as a form of weakness and was one reason she disliked Lill and Lily so intensely—they were welcomed everywhere because they were so funny.

"Youth, maybe," Stanley Wooda conceded, "but I've had more experience than many who are far older."

"How many countries did you say you studied in?"

"Four to a dozen, depending on what you count, but I only spent a full year in France and in Brazil."

"That's why you speak fluent French and Portuguese." She said it as a fact rather than a question, though she was unsure about his claims to fluency.

Stanley Wooda responded, "The French helped in the months I traveled in Africa."

"You were in Japan, too?" she asked.

"Not long enough to learn more than basic vocabulary," he said. She, however, remembered reading that he had traveled too much to practice the language. It was tempting to reveal that knowledge, but she said only, "Enough to greet visitors. If we should have any."

He agreed, "Visitors from Japan will be surprised to find anyone who can pronounce hello properly."

She nodded, "I can see that you will be very useful. I have some plans to contact alumni in Japan."

Stanley Wooda was surprised to learn that any Japanese had ever found their way to Briarpatch, but he immediately understood that the unusual coffee house might be connected to that. "I would like to see what I can do for the fund drive. There is some money out there. I have some personal contacts in Japan and Nigeria."

"We will have a fund drive someday, but right now, can you get us some full-paying students?" She did not say that she had met with some diversity-minded faculty, a collection that Stout had brought together, and had promised to make a greater effort to bring foreign students to what one had called the whitest campus in the state. They had left the room imagining exotic students from the third world, but Flo was thinking about parents with well-padded checkbooks. She winced slightly at the prospect of having more kids like Smith and Jones—although their parents had promised to "be very generous" if they managed to graduate, she wished that the promise had been more specific, a skepticism based on a suspicion that the family money would go to better schools attended by the parents' other children.

She smiled slightly, remembering something the late Dean Wooda had told her as pillow talk, that Smith's parents had not only promised to be generous, but had suggested that they had ties to the Mafia. The faculty member in charge of reviewing student eligibility to return the next semester had taken the hint. Only it wasn't clear now which Mafia he meant, or even if it was Jones's parents, not Smith's. Or someone else.

Not knowing what her smile meant, Stanley Wooda gave a thoughtful answer, "I imagine I can, though it's not as easy as it used to be. The competition is getting tougher, and we might have to offer some scholarship aid or work-study opportunities. However, I might look for foundation money to cover part of the tuition, or, better yet, for a new dormitory to house foreign students." He was thinking out loud, but as usual he made sense.

Very pleased with the way the conversation had turned out, Flo Boater stood up, led the way out and said, "Dean Wooda, I think we are going to get along very well indeed!" She almost touched his shoulder, but held back at the last instant.

Stanley, pleased to have his title used so respectfully, responded enthusiastically, "I hope so, President Boater."

She paused at the door, closing it again so that her comments would remain private, in case anyone had come into the secretary's office, "Before we move ahead on the fund drive, we have some internal house-keeping to do right here."

Stanley Wooda was ahead of her, "I think I already know what you mean."

"The malcontents on the faculty."

"The Leather Lesbians," he said.

"Lill and Lily, yes." There was something in her voice that suggested they were not numbers one and two on her list.

Stanley Wooda, picking up on this, suggested, "But first Donahue, in Anthropology."

"Sociology, actually. He's not tenured yet. Can we find some excuse or other to give him a terminal contract?"

Stanley Wooda thought for a moment, "It does make sense to get him first. He has a nose for trouble, and there is enough potential trouble around."

Suspiciously, the president asked, "What do you mean?"

"There is a smell in every area of the administration, and in some departments. Nothing specific. Just a lot of carpets to check under." Awkwardly, he had hit upon one of the reasons for the renovation— dry mold in the ancient carpeting. It was not the initial reason, but it was enough to persuade the trustees, and she could not stop with redoing her own office. She had begun removing all the carpet, starting with the finance office, to see if the original marble floor there was still attractive; in her mind's eye, she could imagine her prize porcelains reflecting in the marble. Since her own office had oak flooring, it might be necessary to move people about. Her plans were interrupted by an unpleasant thought. Stanley Wooda had been frustratingly vague, but he did not sound like he was guessing. Moreover, it was bothersome that he spoke up so boldly. What if he said this to a trustee? What if the trustee asked himself, or herself, what Flo Boater had been doing in those years? But she did not reveal her thoughts. Instead, she raised her hands in the air and exclaimed, "You are right. My idiot husband and his crooked dean. We don't even know how much damage they did, and we can't afford to have it exposed at this time. Not with the trustees so suspicious."

Stanley Wooda suggested that they should get rid of everyone who could uncover the scandals and embarrass them, but he said that this had to be done "just so."

"Donahue, then Lill and Lily."

With a bit of a leer, he asked, "Isn't there someone else?"

"Mary C. I had to promise her a fair chance at tenure...." The name came quickly, as did his confirming nod, but she didn't anticipate the connection he was making.

Stanley Wooda played it coy, "Why would we want to get rid of her?" It was not a question of why, but the why of the why.

She wasn't in the mood for games, "Not the time to talk about it now. But if we could get rid of her, we'd probably be rid of Donahue, too."

He wasn't so sure. Their relationship was not progressing, and relationships were like riding a bicycle—either you move forward or you fall over. He reminded his boss that Mary C was fond of the quote about fish and bicycles, and therefore was unlikely to marry Donahue. No relationship, no connection between Mary's tenure and Donahue's staying.

Flo Boater was having none of it. "Many men are romantics, and Donahue is among the worst. If Mary went to a distant city, he would find some way to go there, too." If he had a job offer from a better college—as his publications seemed to make likely—he wouldn't go without her. Fortunately, there was no chance that Mary could find employment in Middleville, or they would have Donahue around their necks forever—and even the likelihood that he would publish, they wouldn't be able to deny him tenure; and, in any case, "Can we afford to wait six years?"

"Why not just give him a terminal contract now?"

She explained that their relationship with the trustees was good, but it was not deep. It could be undermined completely by evidence that they were abusing their authority by sacking personal enemies. "Imagine what Lill and Lily could do if we fired the one faculty member who was publishing?" Even if the publications weren't very scholarly. Whatever they did, had to be strictly by the book. At least, for a while yet.

"We could say that he isn't that good a teacher," Stanley Wooda offered.

But Flo Boater retorted, "Compared to what? I've looked into the student evaluations." Then she added hastily, "As have you."

"You're right," he conceded. "Nobody comes close to Lily, except Mary. I guess he's a long way from the bottom anyway."

She grimaced at this, then said, "If only Lill hadn't restarted the alumni magazine! That article on new faculty. Every trustee has told me how pleased they were with new crop, small as it was, and most mentioned DO by name." She paused for a moment so that this could soak in, then continued, "They liked his 'rags to riches' story."

Stanley Wooda snorted "How anyone could think of a Briarpatch salary as riches?"

She dismissed the comment, reminding him that the central story was a working class boy with a widowed mother who managed to put himself through college and graduate school and now promised to become a well-known scholar.

"Being well-known in Middleville is hardly a national reputation!"

"Granted, but the trustees also like his politics. They've long thought it was high time to get some intellectual balance on the faculty."

"Balance?"

"Yes, balance. One trustee actually said that if the faculty was a bird, it could only fly clockwise."

"He meant Stout?" Stanley Wooda asked. He smiled as he asked, "Only a left-wing?"

"More than Stout, of course. But Stout and company we deal with later. Right now we have to concentrate on Donahue, and, obviously, we can't deal with him head-on."

Stanley Wooda reflected on this, then agreed. "So," he said, "If we want to get rid of Donahue, we start with Mary C."

"How can we do that," she asked. "She is one of our best instructors, and she has a good research paper almost finished." She paused before correcting herself, "At least started."

"It can be done," he said, "Do you want me to do it?"

She nodded, "Think of something. Something non-controversial. I don't want a scandal. I don't want the AAUP on campus." She turned back toward her desk, but sat down in the first chair she came to. She waved for him to sit down, too.

He was quickly ready with a plan, "Okay, we go for Mary first." After a pause to see if she was following him, he asked, "Now how do we deny her tenure? How do we explain it? Uncooperative?"

Flo Boater thought for a moment, "No. She does everything we ask, sometimes more."

"Not prepared, maybe?"

"Her syllabi are models. She's a perfectionist."

The dean laughed, "Not like Stout's."

"Speaking of which, did you resolve that problem?"

"Yes, I spoke to him. He said that he just can't write out a detailed syllabus.... It would inhibit spontaneity; distort the natural rhythm of the class."

She snorted, "You believe that?"

He laughed again, "Yes, I guess I do... considering it's him. I doubt he could stick to a plan for an entire semester. Between us, I thinks that's what he likes about post-modern liberation theory, that it allows him to do anything he wants... night classes, movies, anything."

Her eyebrows tightened, "I gather he isn't going to cooperate."

The dean's throat bulged slightly, then he swallowed before explaining, "Well, I put him in charge of seeing that everyone else turned in a syllabus, then...." He swallowed again before continuing, "And checking on their following it."

Flo Boater frowned slightly, "And what did you promise him for that?"

The dean blanched at the thought that she had read him so correctly, but he recovered quickly, "I, uh, I suggested that this would be good experience in case, uh, in case he ever thought of moving into academic administration." Seeing her frown again, "No promises, of course, but I thought it was a way of killing two birds with one stone, so to speak—it avoids a confrontation over his, his refusal to comply, it deflects criticism away from us, and it gives him a reason to cooperate in other matters."

She thought about this for a minute, then shook her head in agreement, "Good idea, good idea." She shook her head again, then asked, "Now, what about Mary?"

He thought for a moment, "Too few publications?"

It was her turn to think, "Maybe. She only needs the one, and she's started on it."

"What's left?" he asked.

"A temporary financial crisis might work better," she suggested. "Cash flow."

"You mean use the delay on the insurance money as an excuse to reduce staff in non-critical departments?"

"Why not?" she said. "What's *less* critical than Modern Languages?"

He was a bit annoyed, "I studied Modern Languages."

"But you went abroad. That's the best way to learn any language."

Stanley Wooda thought for a minute, "The Vice President for Financial Affairs might not cooperate."

"She's new."

"You mean Miss Purdy might not be on top of things yet?" He doubted that she didn't know. Looking at anticipated incomes and expenditures for the coming year would have been her highest priority. She looked more competent than her predecessor, but he wasn't sure how to say this.

Flo Boater came to his rescue, "I mean she might take a hint seriously."

Stanley Wooda was not sure, "I thought she looked pretty tough. Like she knew who she was." Besides, anyone who had replaced her first name, Bambi, with the second name, Prudence, was likely to be a stickler on matters of honesty; moreover, Miss Purdy had returned unopened his first letter inviting her to an interview. She had crossed through the "Ms" and put "Miss" in its place in block letters. His second letter she had answered, but there was that hand-written comment that she had not used the name Bambi since the fifth grade, and that she had made it very clear in her interview that she was to be addressed as Prudence.

The president was more hopeful, "In a year, maybe. Right now we might get her to go along, and once she's gone along this time, the next time will be easier." Corruption as a habit. Then she remembered—Miss Purdy hadn't shown up for work. She asked her dean about this.

Stanley Wooda, after saying that he didn't have any information, indicated that he still preferred the publications ploy, but that he'd go along with her wishes now, "Mary, then Donahue, then Lill and Lily. Anyone else?"

"Take another look at Stout. The Creep might be right. Max is thinking himself too important. Find out what you can. I hear he is talking about making the faculty union effective."

"We still have a faculty union?" Stanley Wooda asked. "I thought it was dead."

"It hasn't been active for some time, and while Lill was president it almost went out of business."

"Oh?" he asked. "What was Lill offering? She didn't have any money." He was still thinking like Machiavelli, or how he thought Machiavelli would have thought.

"Good insight! She couldn't offer the faculty much in the way of money, but she took care of minor needs promptly."

Stanley Wooda made a mental note to do the same himself. "I'll do that," he promised. "Shouldn't be hard. At least now and then." Then he asked again, "Anyone else?"

"Chief Biggs! He almost sent me to prison. Is there a way to persuade the mayor to fire him?"

"I will find out," he said. "I have some contacts in the 'city'." He didn't remind her that the mayor was the chief's cousin.

"Also," she said, pausing before speaking further, "our 'friend' says that a couple of students are asking some strange questions."

"About what?"

"I didn't want to know," she said peremptorily. "Some old scandal, I think. Anyway, you talk to him alone, find out what is going on and handle it."

"No problem," he said before asking, "He didn't say which students?" Knowing this now would eliminate one link in any possible chain of evidence should this backfire.

"I said that I didn't want to know." And that was that!

He shrugged and smiled, "It is as good as done." He was still smiling as he rose from his chair and started toward the door.

She stopped him with a quick command, "Stanley." When he half-turned to face her, she added, "Jay. See that he's made permanent Superintendent of Buildings and Grounds."

He nodded without asking why, "Done." He was learning quickly. Follow orders without asking why. She rewarded him by providing the explanation, "With enough increase in salary to insure his loyalty."

Stanley Wooda frowned, "You have doubts about him?"

"He needs to be watched. His girlfriend, Jenny, is a friend of Mary's."

"Why give him a promotion now, then?"

She explained, "We can't take on everyone at once. Divide and rule."

He liked it. "Now is the moment to divide." It was not quite a question, but definitely a request for instructions.

"Yes," she said. "Think of some more ways to split that coalition up." Then she indicated he could go.

As he stood, he promised, "Will do." But as his hand reached for the doorknob, he turned, "Just one question, President Boater."

"What is it?"

"Your trash cans are full. What is it you've been throwing away?"

"You were with me this, morning. Faculty memos."

"Those couldn't fill one trash can."

"Right you are, right you are. Very observant, Stanley." She paused before answering, "Just junk from old files. Not worth reading."

"Oh! I understand." And he did. The old way of doing business, of keeping records that might be embarrassing, was in the trash bin of history. Still, there was that nagging memory of how important records had been thrown out before, only to end up in Donahue's hands. How had that happened?

Chapter Six

As Stanley Wooda left the president's office, he began mulling over a problem, or rather a person, that had been nagging all week. Max Stout had been calling him every day to demand that more minority faculty be hired. Stout wasn't supposed to be causing trouble—hadn't he bought him off? But there it was—Stout was acting like he was smarter than the dean. "Older, yes, but hardly smarter," the dean told himself. "When I'm his age, I'm going to be somebody. Not an English professor without even a single significant publication, without a national reputation for... anything." At that he smiled.

Stanley Wooda had explained that the budgetary situation was such that he wasn't hiring *anybody,* but Stout had sidetracked the conversation onto the difficulty of attracting talented people (other than himself) to Middleville; there wasn't even a Mexican restaurant, much less a French one (or any eatery that pretended to be worth three stars). Middleville barely had fast food, and that only if one didn't expect *fast* to mean *swift.* Stanley Wooda had snorted, "Can any Academic Dean remedy that?" But Max Stout wouldn't listen to that argument. As far as he was concerned, not having *any* minority faculty was proof that the college was racist. This accusation made Stanley Wooda angry enough to ask, "Don't I count for something?" But Stout had only responded that Stanley was really just an Asian Indian, and that minority didn't count because their SAT scores were always so high. "In fact," he said—ignoring the dean's efforts to explain that he was West Indian—"You might as well be Chinese, and Briarpatch once had rather more of them than we needed." The conversation was awkward in several ways, but especially because Stout had become so accustomed to translating "Indian" to "Native American" that he found it difficult to say "Asian Indian." When Stanley Wooda pointed out that there was a Cuban teaching Modern Languages, Stout responded that the individual in question was totally white, male and an anti-Castro fanatic. Stanley Wooda couldn't remember that individual having ever said anything about politics, but since he couldn't remember him having said anything about anything, he let it pass—the guy was close to retiring, anyway. He similarly let the crack about Chinese pass, because he was unsure of the facts. He believed that his predecessor had hired some Chinese ABDs (all but dissertations) to teach science, but they had left as soon as they had gotten their Ph.D.'s and their English improved sufficiently to make a good impression at interviews. But he wasn't sure. He'd have to ask Miss Efficiency. She might know, even though she, too, was new.

As he reflected on the conversation, an idea came to him. Max Stout was on the Personnel and Promotions Committee; he was not the chair, but he still dominated its sessions. If he mentioned to him that *if* there an opening appeared in a department, say Modern Languages… If someone there failed to get tenure—he was careful not to mention Mary's name—perhaps… perhaps… something could be done. Perhaps he could put Max in charge of the search committee. That is, leave the Creep the title of committee chair, but let Max do the interviews, so that if someone suitable appeared, Stanley would get the credit for reaching out to underrepresented groups in our society.

It would be awkward to fire Mary, but that just might be the way to get rid of Donahue… and Stout would get the blame.

The coffee house was at its low point for the morning. Students came in for breakfast as late as ten, and about eleven those who had skipped the morning meal were ready for lunch. Not that the coffee house served much, but the light snacks and sandwiches were more popular than the dining hall's customary fare. There was also something about the atmosphere, especially in the fall, when the athletic trophies reflected the potential reality of Briarpatch sports. Football was the only real game in town, and this promised to be the best season in living memory. The *only* good season in living memory.

The Director of Admissions had done so well in the spring that he had gotten a new job by August. He attributed his success to the innovative telephone campaign he had developed—he would pay students a dollar for every friend they would call from his office and twenty dollars for every one who actually made a visit to campus. This was not actually revolutionary, but his suggestion that the students propose to split the money with their friends was. Others, who thought their effort had gone unappreciated, opined that that the success could be attributed to the previous fall's famous murder. They had promised prospective students a tour of the swimming pool where Dean C. Wooda's body had been found and a visit to the chemistry lab where the murderous pill was concocted; and if the president's office was not occupied, a look inside. Tour guides intimated that chemistry students would learn some very useful skills if they were so lucky as to get into one of the now-crowded introductory classes. There was a rumor that there would be lectures on poison, perhaps with a team-taught biology lab demonstrating various poisons' effects on rats. For every young woman this disgusted, there were two guys who were fascinated. Since Briarpatch was ahead of the national trend in having more coeds enrolling than men, this restored some "gender balance" to the student body. At that thought Stanley Wooda smiled—he was still young enough to remember attractive young women. Then he frowned—there would be more competition for their attention, and worst of all, he was forbidden to date any of them.

More than a few of the curious high school seniors were football players, or had boyfriends who were, and so many had enrolled that the coach, Windy Gale, had won his first three games! He was already talking about the big game against Arcadia Junior College. No Briarpatch team had ever beaten Arcadia, and past Briarpatch coaches would have taken them off the schedule if they could have afforded to travel to a more distant college or if the rivalry had not become so important. But by May Windy had been so confident that he would have the squad of the century that he moved Homecoming to the Arcadia date. The coffee house was decorated for the contest already, even though two games remained to be played before the "big game." One game was considered a shoo-in, since last year's very weak team had almost won, and those players were nowhere as good as this year's starters. The next game looked equally promising: It was an out-of-state team whose coach had spotted Briarpatch's dismal 1995 record.

This college—Occidental East—had acquired its odd name in the usual odd way that small colleges do. It had been founded by an obscure religious sect just before 1890, at a moment when the quarrels over science and religion were at their most contentious. Not unexpectedly, its faculty had rebelled over the teaching of Evolution, but—in the manner common to obscure religious sects—it had done so in its own unique and unpredictable way. The Church members tended to accept Darwin, but the faculty would not—they were willing to teach every philosopher in the Great Books program up to Darwin, but not him or anyone subsequent to him. The solution was to revise the charter, then rename the college, choosing "Occidental" to indicate that the college was in touch with modern "western" civilization. With all attention focused on the quarrel over Evolution, everyone overlooked the fact that another college—one truly located in the Far West—was already named Occidental. When that distant college noticed the existence of a new Occidental, its president suggested that the duplication of names could become troublesome. The problem was resolved by the religious sect founding a new college in New Mexico territory— Occidental West—and adding East to the original name; the church then transferred many of the rebellious faculty west and hired new professors to replace them, men and women carefully selected to assure that they agreed with the trustees' progressive views. Both campuses emphasized study of the Bible, so the split was not as divisive as it might have been, but the challenge of managing two campuses in an era before air travel and air conditioning proved too much; financial crises brought an end to the experiment. Occidental West went under. However, in the perverse way that fate deals with institutions, the crisis was the salvation of Occidental East— in the ensuing years the handful of older faculty members who had refused the opportunity to open the west to traditional values resigned one after another, and a talented president had remade the college in his image, an image that fortunately attracted considerable financial help at a time when stocks were cheap. Occidental East subsequently evolved into a stronghold of liberal arts; in the minds of the current faculty it rivaled Antioch for leadership in progressive education. They resented their many rivals calling them "Accidental East," but there was little they could do about that. Nor about the declining enrollment.

This was not a situation that attracted good athletes. In fact, the faculty wanted to abandon intercollegiate athletics altogether, and perhaps even intramural contests, but the trustees realized the value of being on the sports page Sunday; and of pleasing alumni who could remember fondly their own athletic experiences and using games as excuses for dates. By 1995, however, not only had student attendance at football games declined almost to the vanishing point, but Occidental East had the unhappy reputation of a loser. The trustees, suspecting that there was a connection between attendance at games and the prospect of seeing a close contest, were not happy with acquaintances suggesting that their students were athletically-challenged. In vain the president argued that losing records proved the academic superiority of his new version of OE—how could his coaches compete for talented athletes who were going to state universities on full scholarship? And the trustees' own actions establishing stiff academic standards made it impossible for him to recruit dumb ones. Wouldn't it be better, he argued, to abandon the old-fashioned idea of competition altogether? Couldn't they compete in games based on cooperation?

The trustees, refusing to believe that there were no smart-but-better-than-average-athletes, insisted that a few athletes would bring in tuition and provide some diversity to the student body; also, that the enrollment was already too heavily female—women who went through their first two college years without a date were transferring out. The president had retorted that if adequately-skilled athletes were really smart, they would go to a college with a winning record and lower tuition, and the girls could date each other, but the trustees had truculently ordered him to get find some opponent so hopeless that even his team could beat them; and, furthermore, to schedule the game for homecoming! The luckless coach who had to find such a victim combed the athletic records of every college within two long days drive and had finally decided that Briarpatch might be suitable—its long string of 0-9 and 1-8 seasons also providing the name of one more potential opponent. Windy Burg, however, was reluctant to take on a college from a conference as strong as the one OE competed in, even though OE had finished dead last in recent years. The OE coach, knowing that Briarpatch could not afford to send a football team such a distance, spoke to his Athletic Director, who obtained a trustee's private plane to ferry the team, ten players at a time to the game from the airport at Arcadia. (Middleville's tiny airfield, while suitable for private planes, was judged a tad too short for the trustee's craft.) It was an inducement that Windy Burg could not resist.

The Briarpatch players were excited enough to be playing at OE's historic field, one of the first to be designed at today's regulation width, in front of the largest crowd they had ever seen (Briarpatch crowds of recent years had been even smaller than OE's). To be flown to there, that was heaven itself! Windy Gale had accepted with alacrity, not even insisting on a paper confirmation of a reciprocal game the next season; and now that the OE Athletic Director, having read Briarpatch's surprisingly lopsided scores in the first three games, was trying to find some way of backing out of his oral promise. Windy could only chortle at his good fortune. OE's Athletic Director, having despaired of reaching Windy by phone, had made the error of writing on his college's stationary and then compounded it by baldly saying that it would be bad for his college's reputation to be beaten by Briarpatch! The suggestion that Windy find a reason for avoiding their playing in Middleville made his day—he ordered the letter be framed for a prominent place on the wall of what passed as a reception lounge. He would make all potential recruits wait there before seeing him, and they would have almost nothing else to read. He soon had a second letter that guaranteed that the contest would take place—Windy had obtained it by sending copies of the first letter to OE's trustees and suggesting that he might release it to the press.

One trustee who received a copy of the letter had been among the last great players at OE. He was not amused. As an advisor to a former president of the United States and almost Surgeon General, he had learned how dangerous it was to write letters. He had assumed that everyone at Occidental East had learned from his experience. He had insisted that the home and home agreement be honored.

There were few customers in the coffee house at this time of day. The best known was the chair of the history department, who had ordered the young woman at the cash register to stop cleaning the counter and to open a fresher container of milk for his coffee. He sat by himself, as always, looking through his mail as carefully as if he expected to find a check; however, whenever he found an advertisement offering a financial inducement, he treated it as some potential trap. He carefully tore everything up, then, after reducing it to tiny bits, including the envelopes, he carefully mixed the pieces up and, after glancing about to see if anyone was watching, he scooped the pile off onto the floor and ground it with his shoe. By nature suspicious, he read everything he could find about identity theft and blackmail. From that literature he had learned that thieves often went through trash cans for names and addresses. His own method avoided that danger completely! Standing up, he viewed his handiwork, smiled and strode proudly over to the coffee bar, where he demanded that the attendant brew a fresh batch of coffee and open another new can of condensed milk—the first, being unrefrigerated, was surely sour by now.

The historian had once explained his method of protecting his identity to Donahue, who had listened carefully, then asked, "What's on the average envelope that a thief couldn't get from a telephone book?" It was the last time that the historian took him into his confidence. Henceforth, he dismissed him as simply a "dumb ex-police officer." (His mother objected to the word cop. It was vulgar.)

Moments later Jay was ruefully sweeping up the historian's litter. Although this job was technically below the work associated with his new title, he hated messy public areas and he did not have a large enough staff to move janitors around to crisis locations. The pieces of the letters were now the size and consistency of confetti, which is notoriously difficult to sweep up. Jay was persuaded that the devil's spawn had invented confetti and chewing gum. He wasn't certain what circle of hell the inventors were in, but he was sure it was among the damned who lacked the courage to commit violent crimes, but whose souls were as corrupted as vandals. When Jay looked up, he saw Donahue come in, obviously looking for someone—him. He shook his head discretely to indicate that this was not a good moment. Donahue had started to come over anyway, but once he saw Jay's second nod, toward the historian, he understood; he then got himself a cup of coffee (paid for by the month again, one of Stanley's favors to the student body) and sat down to look at his own mail. Once the historian obtained his coffee, mixed it with condensed milk and the natural sugar that he brought from home, a quarter hour passed. It was another quarter hour before he drained the last drops from his cup and left. Donahue looked around to see who else might be watching, then hopped up and hurried over to Jay.

Before he could ask his question, Jay commented, "I didn't think the creep would ever leave!" Then he signaled Donahue to sit down again.

Donahue did as ordered, then whispered to Jay as he bent under the table to clean up an imaginary spill, "What have you got?" Students wandering in didn't suspect anything.

Jay put a finger over his mouth to indicate that Donahue should keep quiet, then asked, "Remember those letters, receipts, that Mary gave you in the spring?"

"The ones Jenny gave her? That you gave to Jenny?"

As he stood up, he hissed between his teeth, "Don't ask so many questions."

"Yes. I remember," Donahue said.

"I'm Flo's snitch, not yours." This was Jay's way of saying that he had to be careful what he revealed. Donahue had known since spring that Jay reported campus activities and rumors to the president, and that she double-checked the information with the historian. All of Jay's friends understood this and provided him with interesting tidbits that would not harm anyone, but would contribute to building up the president's confidence in her informant.

Donahue looked around, then winked, "Officially." He approved of double-agents. But he knew that some members of the faculty would have condemned as immoral anything short of honestly advertising their loyalties; they also had a weakness for impractical political schemes and hopeless political candidates. Flo Boater had nailed most of them to her flagpole, persuading them that because she was open with them, they should be open with her; as a result, she was building a strong base of supporters who sent her notes about stories and rumors; she tried to recognize these and read them, but was only occasionally successful—most ended up in the trash. There was, not surprising, growing dissatisfaction with not receiving replies from her; the most prominent conspiracy theory that purported to explain this was that someone was sabotaging their efforts to provide information which would lead to more intelligent administrative decisions. As a result, Donahue and his friends had to be careful not to betray their friend's doubtful loyalties.

Jay looked around before returning the wink. He, too, understood the danger he was running by even talking with Donahue

"Yes, I remember them," Donahue said. "They concerned Latin American objects. One receipt listed the darts like the one that Molly had scratched herself on and almost died."

"The same poison that killed Floyd Boater."

Donahue remembered, "Yes, the tests proved that. Curare." He also remembered that Floyd Boater had died from a heart attack, but the symptoms of curare had literally frightened him to death.

Slyly Jay teased, "And what were the other r'ceipts for?"

"More purchases from Latin America."

"And how much was the late Dean Wooda getten?" When Jay saw that Donahue didn't remembered, he prompted, "For the sale."

"I don't remember. For the bow and arrows alone, fifteen thousand dollars. We didn't know it was that much at the time."

"You don't 'member the total?"

Donahue raised his eyes to calculate, while Jay moved around to simulate cleaning a very soiled spot, then he answered, "About a hundred thousand dollars."

"Was that about right?" When Donahue spread his hands as if to say he didn't know, Jay said accusingly, "You're an ant- thropo-gist, you ought to know."

"It's not my area," Donahue said, "I'm really only a Sociologist."

"Make a perfessional guess."

"Okay, it's not inconsistent with what museums pay nowadays." It was a safe guess. Donahue knew that museums were engaging in a bidding war, one that profited criminals and middlemen, i.e., dealers, more than it enlightened their visitors. Not that the visitors weren't enlightened, but Donahue wasn't sure that every museum needed to have an outstanding exhibit from every culture. Or that they needed ten items in storage for every one displayed—many being gifts that would have useful additions to most university collections. But, just like multi-million dollar gifts that could turn around a Briarpatch College around, needy institutions rarely received them. Donors wanted their names associated with well-known institutions.

Jay broke into Donahue's thoughts by asking, "Rare stuff?"

Donahue straightened up suddenly, then asked, "What are you saying?"

Smugly, Jay informed him, "DO, there's more."

Donahue was surprised, "More?" More what?

Donahue was so surprised that he forgot to ask about Miss Purdy. Had he done so, he would have learned that President Boater had sent out a memo to staff not to worry, that women had a right to a private life.

Chapter Seven

Where to meet? That was the problem. Someplace where Jay could pass a package and talk privately. The campus was small. Everyone knew everyone, by sight at least, or so everyone believed. Any public meeting was dangerous, and the coffee house was out of the question. At the beginning of the semester President Boater had passed the word to her informants and Dean Wooda had asked students to "watch out for" Donahue. Originally, that hadn't meant "watch" literally. Rather to be skeptical about anything he said, even in class, but in recent days they had expanded the meaning of the word to include keeping an eye on his movements. This was not a secret for long—no sooner had this request begun to spread around campus than everyone began watching him. Of course, Jay quickly heard of it and informed Donahue. Laughing, Donahue dismissed the matter as "Flo's paranoia." But paranoia is contagious. It infected Jay, too.

This did not mean that Jay lived in fear of being observed. Only that he took prudent steps to avoid arousing suspicion whenever caution was practical and convenient; and being around Donahue was not prudent. He worried more than Donahue, of course, because Jay knew that he could be dismissed on a moment's notice, whereas Donahue was fairly certain of being allowed to finish the academic year. On the other hand, Jay could start a new job at almost any time—good janitors were hard to find. Donahue, without good recommendations, might not find work at all. At best, he would be at another Briarpatch. More likely he would be part of that transient army of adjunct professors, teaching a course here, another there, and always for minimum wages. The academic employment cycle being inflexible, he could not even expect to interview for months, and, if hired, would have to make arrangements to move. This often meant that instructors and professors, who had little control over their employment for months at a time, had more *Angst* about finding a job than other white-collar workers, even to the point of having nightmares about forgetting interviews or showing up at the wrong appointment—and that was *before* starting a job search. Donahue, fortunately, was relatively immune to this. His career had been so irregular that he had learned to say that, "It's futile to worry about such matters," and to believe it. His incurable optimism, in fact, annoyed Mary C. considerably—she fretted over tenure as though the country was in the midst of the Great Depression instead of being in an era of almost unprecedented prosperity. She believed that the Republican Congress's tax cuts would bankrupt the government. Combined with "welfare reform" leaving millions homeless and starving, this would precipitate economic collapse. Briarpatch would have to retrench, starting with people like her. She could not be consoled with the thought that this was her seventh year, with another almost guaranteed—therefore, in principle she already had "virtual tenure." She responded that in her own case, Flo Boater would test the limits of what tenure meant.

Donahue could only sigh. Whenever he would point to the "misery index" being at an all-time low, Mary would retort that the job market for academics was still not good. When he would observe that educated people who were willing to work could do all kinds of jobs, she would almost scream something about not wanting "to flip hamburgers" for the rest of her life. If he asked when she last flipped hamburgers, she would storm away and sulk. She had never flipped hamburgers, but it was "the principle of the thing," and she was frustrated beyond belief that he was so literal and exact. So male!

Thus it was that Jay was more worried than Donahue, though he should not have been. When Donahue suggested meeting in his office, it almost sent Jay into panic: "The *Creep* or Stout might show up any time!" Then, inspired by Donahue's suggestion that as Superintendent of Buildings and Grounds he could go anywhere he wanted on campus, he suggested the Gym.

"Why the Gym? I've hardly been there since the dean died."

"Tell people you're goin' to start swimming again." Jay then grinned. "You need the exercise." And he did.

Donahue liked the idea. The Gym had once been very unattractive, but in anticipation of the increased enrollment, Flo Boater had allowed

Windy Gale to paint the walls and replace the burnt-out lights. The Athletic Director also had a much larger football team, which used the new exercise machines practically day and night. There would be anonymity in numbers. Still, something bothered him, "There'd be a lot of people there, and it would look odd for me to be standing there in my swim suit when you hand me the package."

"I could go to the locker room."

"Could be people there, too."

Frowning, Jay nodded agreement, "Where, then?"

"How about the Music building? At noon." Donahue didn't have to explain that the building was largely closed because of the asbestos problem, nor that, at lunchtime the choir director, the only person other than Jenny to keep an office there, would head off for his usual light repast without bothering to lock the place up.

"Good thought," Jay responded. "I meet Jenny there sumtimes for lunch." Since he and Jenny were an "item," as Jay's generation used to say, it would not be odd to see him go there. "She could ring me when the *odd duck* leaves."

This struck Donahue as strange; he had come to like the choir director and his unusual mannerisms—especially his total detachment from the campus affairs of the day, which seemed a perfectly sane way to get through life. He doubted the director could tell him anything about the college president beyond her name, and perhaps not much more about the president of the United States, and what he knew of the election campaign probably consisted of not having enough time to care, but he was certain that he was dedicated to his choral programs. "Since I drop in to see the 'odd duck' now and then, that's a good cover. Where should we meet?" He wondered idly if the 'odd duck' might know something about Miss Purdy. Sometimes he was surprisingly well informed, though he didn't know it. And he was suspicious of Flo Boater's terse announcement.

"There's a room at the far end," Jay suggested.

"The recital room?"

"How'd you know that?" He knew that Donahue rarely attended musical performances.

Donahue shrugged, "When the windows are open, you can hear the students. I stop and listen. The 'odd duck' told me about the room. Asbestos isn't a problem there."

"Yeah," Jay said. "They thought it was, but it's okay. I checked." The other rooms might be, too, he thought, but he wasn't allowed to go in them.

"The choir's not bad. And the room has good acoustics."

Jay shook his head—apparently even Donahue was capable of surprises. "Jenny and I eat there to get outta her office. Just don't go in any other rooms." He didn't bother to add that the previous Superintendent of Buildings and Grounds had locked them up because they were too toxic to enter under any conditions. That's what he had reported to Flo Boater, and that's what he expected Donahue to know already. "You bring sumthin' from the coffee house. I've already fixed stuff for me and Jenny." In fact, he had packed a quite substantial lunch that morning. All he had to do was call Jenny to tell her they were coming. And to have the package ready, which meant a trip home.

Jenny was late, of course.

Donahue and Jay had almost finished their sandwiches and soft drinks when Jenny finally arrived. A Southern girl, reared in a generation which understood how feminine charm was best displayed, she was fashionably late.

Jay, more of a Yankee, did not waste time before saying, "Show him, Jen."

She sat down, looked over what remained of the lunch, shrugged, then opened her briefcase and retrieved some letters similar to those Donahue had seen the previous spring. She drawled, anticipating with pleasure Donahue's reaction, "These are *very* interesting."

"More receipts?" Donahue asked.

"I suppose. Really just lists of items—archeological stuff, of course, which is what caught my attention—and prices."

Donahue thought a moment, "Where'd you find these?"

She responded, "I've been assigned to the business office temporarily. Financial crisis, they say. The dean wants everyone to help in administrative offices. To replace the secretaries that Wooda is firing."

Donahue was surprised, "I didn't hear about that."

"Just announced, this morning, early. Anyway, Miss Purdy has been gone, and we really need her right now."

"I wondered how they were going to cover that."

"Apparently I am supposed to, though I don't know how well I can do," she explained. "In the Music department we don't count much above 'a one and a two,' but I guess I can sort correspondence and send bills over to the president. She doesn't like that, but I can't sign checks. Anyway, I had just sat down at my new desk when I saw the originals. These are copies—you can see that. They were in a file folder for... and that was the problem—no name. I supposed I was supposed to file them somewhere, but it wasn't clear where they belonged—not even letterheads—and I didn't think anybody else would realize what they meant...."

"Miss Purdy?"

"I don't think so. Came up since she disappeared. I think one of the student assistants just found them somewhere and dropped them on her desk to deal with." She added after a moment, "No name on the file folder, either."

"And you were told to deal with routine matters?"

"Yeah, but this wasn't routine. Too much money involved, and it has more about the archeological collection. Artifacts and all that. Still, who should I ask? Dean Wooda? Not on your life! So, how to get them to you? I thought that if they had waited this long, a few more hours wouldn't matter. So I took them over to the library, persuaded Ms. Gates that it was an emergency..."

"Gates," Donahue said. "I thought she had another job."

"Did," Jay said. "Changed her mind."

"Fell in love," Jenny said. "Now, back to these letters. I risked my job to copy these, so I expect you to pay attention."

Donahue decided not to ask, "Now, who in Middleville could Ms. Gates have fallen in love with?" Assuming it was someone in Middleville. Else, why stay here? "Where are the originals?"

"Back where they belong, in the file folder, waiting for Miss Purdy to return," Jenny said. "I'm not stupid."

Donahue thought for a moment, wondering how many people had handled the originals, then asked her to see if she could prevent too many people from putting their fingerprints on them, just in case they wanted to see if the dean's were there. Then he wondered if they had copies of the dean's fingerprints on file or where they might still find them. "Find a place, out of the way, to keep them."

"In the business office, I hope."

"Yes, let's keep this as honest as possible." This produced the desired effect—smiles.

They all fell silent, passing the copies of the lists around as they finished each one. It did not take long. There were not very many.

It was Jay who spoke first, "Look at the dates!"

Donahue had been thumbing through the documents, "Every year for five, no, six years—up to four years ago."

Jay's math was quicker, "Counten' those from las' spring, seven years."

"Yeah," Donahue said. "That suggests there is another file, or files."

"Somewhere," Jenny agreed. "It's a big office. A lot of paper."

"Maybe that's what Miss Purdy was looking for."

There was a moment of silence before Jay spoke, "Sounds likely."

Looking at Jenny, Donahue asked, "How much money each year?"

"A hundred to two hundred thousand dollars." Jenny had not taken the time to read them carefully, but she knew that a lot of money was involved, and she had a mind for figures. "These are all for sales, aren't they."

Donahue wasn't sure. The occasional totals seemed to suggest that the lists were not "pick and choose what you want to buy" options. An "OK" at the bottom of one page suggested a transaction had been completed. "Let's think about this. If these were purchases, then we'd surely be able to find a record somewhere of the money being spent...."

"Especially if the college wrote the checks, as it must have done! Or did it? Anyway, somebody had to pay for them."

"And," Jay added, " they'd still be 'round here somewhere."

"Unless," Jenny warned, "they were sold."

"Well," Donahue suggested, "for the time being let's assume that these are items he has purchased sometime and was now selling."

"How's that?" Jay asked.

"I see it this way," Donahue responded. "If these were part of a purchase, the cover letters would probably be here. But, if he were trying to peddle them, he'd write separate cover letters and enclose a list with each one. These typewritten lists—which reminds me, are there any typewriters still around that he might have used?"

Jenny looked at Jay, who shook his head, "Lill got rid of 'em all."

Jenny explained, "Replaced them with word processors."

Donahue asked if they had been put in storage.

"Nope," Jay said, "Some junk company wanted 'em."

Donahue wrinkled his nose, then continued, "These lists would probably have been Xeroxed. He would need to have them available to copy, but didn't want anyone to see them. So he stuck them in a file in the finance office. Some place nobody ever looks."

Jenny frowned, "That makes sense, but I didn't see anything about how he paid for the artifacts or got paid. Just that it appears there's a lot of money here."

"Yeah," Jay said, smiling, "Dean Wooda feathered his nest right well."

"I like men who make me laugh," Jenny said to Donahue, and pointed at her friend, "But only Jay Bird would express it like that!"

"What do these mean? That he hid a fortune from Molly in the divorce?"

Jay twisted his face before he observed, "I don't figure so. This b'gan earlier."

At this Jenny took the letters from their hands and began sorting through them, "That's not what is soo exciting!" She was practically dancing, sitting down.

"One point at a time," Donahue said. "Clarify the money first."

"I figure he spent it all," Jay said. Jenny continued to look through the lists for anything specific. As usual, not just for her, but human beings in general, she couldn't find it.

"How?"

"Some of the girls he messed with got new cars."

Donahue admired Jay's inside knowledge, "Not from parents?"

"Nah. I knew they wasn't rich. I jus' didn't know where they got it."

"You sure he paid them off?"

Jay hesitated, "No, but stands to reason… Their boy friends didn't have that kinda cash."

It was Donahue's turn to hesitate, "No way to earn it?"

Jay laughed, "Every few years a girl sells herself. The news spread fast."

Jenny interrupted, "Molly told me once that a parent complained—the girl was charging her son more than other boys. They had to ask her to leave, and she did."

"No drugs?"

"Not 'nough to buy those cars!" Jay laughed.

"Jay'd know," Jenny interjected, "if there was a big-time drug ring here."

"The observant janitor," Donahue commented, with a wink. "But, just when did you learn this?"

"Ah, I getja. Why didn't I tell you before?"

"Yes."

"You mean, other than I was a murder suspect? Or thought I was."

"Yes."

Jay smiled, "They didn't park 'em on campus."

"So nobody knew?"

"Well, I learned it at the alums' meeting. They drink and gossip."

Jenny broke in, "They talk just like he isn't there."

Donahue nodded, then asked Jay, "The meeting right after Commencement?"

"A week or so later."

"I wish I'd known then."

"Well, sorry. I thought that was all over. Nothing but gossip, anyway."

"I suppose I did, too. So don't worry about it."

"Besides, you was already off to your mother's."

"I suppose I was. I don't know any alums, so no point to hanging around. Anyway, I know it now and it might be important yet." He paused before asking, "You remember the names?"

"Of course." Jay had a phenomenal memory for names. "Just didn't put it all together till then." After a moment, he asked, "Is it important?"

Donahue though about this, then sighed, "Not now. It's good to know everything little fact, but this one's probably only good for background right now."

Jenny had still not found what she was looking for, but she looked up long enough to say, "Jay knows everything!"

In his "aw shucks" style, Jay said, "One picks up things."

Donahue, thinking of the clever way that Jay had picked up the incriminating letters right from under Flo Boater's nose in the spring and without her ever learning about it, said, "Literally."

"Janitors pick up things. Good thing, too."

Donahue asked, "So, it seems the late dean was making payoffs."

Jay took one page from Jenny and showed it to Donahue, "He wasn't doing too good on the stock market."

Donahue was surprised, "Oh?" Holding the page, he wondered how he hadn't noticed its contents himself. What had what seemed to be "bought" and "sold" items now appeared to be columns of stocks, the names in a form of short-hand code. He wondered if anyone could trace the sales. No date on the page, not even a year. Maybe it was multiple years. But the losses seemed significant. "Wonder who his broker was," he said, half to himself.

Jay confided, "I heard he asked Stout and one of our 'conomists for advice." They all knew that Stout had money and followed the market carefully.

"And it wasn't good advice?"

Jenny jumped in, "Jay says that for everyone who makes money, there's someone who loses."

"And he was losing," Donahue concluded.

"Let's say the dean wasn't doin' well. Not like he wanted." Jay paused before adding, "He fired the 'conomist."

"What happened to him?"

"He became an *investment counselor*. I believe that's what they called it."

Jenny commented sarcastically, "That figures. For the government?"

"Federal government!" Jay said. He belonged to a generation that knew there were various levels of government.

"Yeah, that's what I meant." Donahue made a mental note to contact him.

Jay did not respond, but he smiled at the thought before answering, "No, with a big company, growing fast. Enron, I think, maybe Fannie something."

"Making lots of money now, I bet," Donahue replied. A private company. He might be more willing to talk than a government employee fearful of being quoted.

"That's what we hear. Quite a turn-around."

"Stout's recommendations were bad, too?" Donahue asked.

Jay shook his head. "He was generally right on. But who'd trust an English teacher for stocks?" Stanley Wooda would surely have bought contrary to Stout's advice. Much safer to trust a real economist.

Donahue smiled to think how Stout would react to being called "a teacher," but all he asked was. "Any idea how money much this involved?"

"Only a guess," Jay answered, "probably a lot." Reading Donahue's eyes, he explained, "Like Jenny said, 'a lot.'"

Jenny was more voluble, "He used to live well. Spent oodles of money. Big house, big cars, big parties. Molly can tell you how hard it was to pay the bills. Debt. Debt. Debt." Her drawl came on very strongly as she concluded, "In the last months, he was practically in pen-u-ry!"

"How about the money he skimmed off the top of the insurance premiums?" Donahue asked. "Wasn't that about $12,000 a month?"

"Yes," Jenny conceded, "but he lost it. You told me that, I think, that the insurance companies recovered their losses from his estate. The money in the secret bank accounts was for more than that."

"Not as much as this," Jay noted.

"So," Donahue queried, "Most likely he was spending everything he got from his salary and embezzlements, then building covering his losses by selling the museum collection?"

Jay nodded sagely, and Jenny, observing him, did the same.

"That's interesting, but since he is dead and there is nothing left for Molly, what difference does it make?"

Jay asked slyly, enjoying the suspense. "Ever wonder where he got the artifacts?"

"South America, of course," Donahue said, "but nothing more specific."

"Ever see them?"

Donahue shook his head, "I'd heard about them, but never laid eyes on them." He paused before adding, "Apparently almost nobody else had, either."

With a deep breath, Jenny promised, "You're going to like this." When she was a teenager, she would have squealed; in middle age she became Katherine Hepburn, but with a Southern accent. She nodded at Jay.

"He paid with college money!" Jay said. "That's our theory."

"With college money?" Donahue retorted. "Impossible. The college hasn't had money for years."

"You check it out," Jay countered, sticking out his lip for emphasis.

Donahue sifted through the lists, looked up and said, "I don't see anything here."

"Then why did we have receipts before?" Jay cocked his head to one side before continuing, "If the college had 'em then, it must have bought the stuff."

"Or been given it," Jenny suggested, "and these are tax write-offs."

"No, I don't think that works," Donahue said. "We looked into that already. He didn't use them on his income taxes."

"Then these things are still around, somewhere?" Jenny asked.

"Seems so," Jay responded. "But where?"

They looked at one another for a moment, then turned their attention back to the lists.

"It's sure an incomplete file, isn't it?" Donahue asked, wishing he had more materials in his hands. "Nothing recent."

Jenny shook her head, no, a bit embarrassed, "That's all I saw."

"Can you look for more?"

"Not easily," she responded. "I don't know my way around hardly."

"This was just on the desk? Can you ask who put it there?"

"I'd rather not. That would call attention to them, and next thing we know, they'd be in Flo Boater's office."

Donahue sighed, "Then we've got a problem." He signaled for quiet in order to collect his thoughts. It was clear that the dean had been paid something, somehow, but the source of the money and the total wasn't clear—no letterheads, no addresses, just lists of items and dollar amounts. At least he thought it was dollars. What if it were some semi-worthless currency? No, there were $ signs. A greater problem was what the dean's papers were doing in the business office. Hidden there? Or did the college actually pay? In some account, perhaps disguised as a legitimate expense?

Jenny pointed at the papers and reminded him, "Jay got you the proof about the poison darts. Those receipts looked a lot like these. Well, sorta like them."

Donahue conceded, "Yes, those cleared up Floyd Boater's death, but they were more specific, more descriptive."

She wasn't going to let Donahue off with that alone, "That was only a few items. You don't plan to build a museum for some bows and arrows!" She pointed at the lists, "There's a lot more here. Just no details, nothing about where and when."

"Where, then, is the rest of the stuff?" Donahue asked. "If these purchases, and they must be, then they must be around somewhere."

Jenny was confused, "You say they must be for purchases, not sales."

Donahue explained, "Records of sales would be too dangerous to keep around. No point in having them unless he had the items to sell. That's the only reason these still exist."

"Maybe the dean just didn't expect to die."

"No, these are for three-four years before he died. He kept them for a reason."

"He was sick, down in South America somewhere."

"Yes, but he recovered. He had plenty of time, and opportunity to destroy them. Unless he planned to use them."

"So," Jay said, "they're still here somewhere?"

"Yes, and there must be records of the money transfers, records of the purchases."

"But you looked for that before," Jenny protested. "And Chief Biggs couldn't find anything."

Donahue nodded, "Maybe the Dean handled it all privately... just put his records in that file where he could refer to it later."

"Why would he do that?" Jenny asked. "Why not in his own files or at home?"

"Maybe to keep Flo from finding out. She was working in his office, and she looked into everything. Certainly he wouldn't have wanted Molly to find them."

"That makes sense," Jay agreed, reluctantly. "His own money... hard to trace."

"Not much to go on here," Donahue agreed. "Chief Biggs can't charge anyone with selling items they bought... legally... or for making lists." He turned to Jay, "There has to be more somewhere. Better descriptions, correspondence. These things had to come from somewhere."

Jenny promised to look, but she didn't even know which file drawer these came from. "They must have been in some file where they didn't belong, and whoever looked in there recognized that and put them where Miss Purdy could put them away correctly."

"Quite a mess," Donahue said.

Jay shrugged, "I can't clean up this campus by myself!"

Donahue was eager to mollify Jenny, "This looks like great stuff, but by itself, it doesn't build a complete case against the late dean. These lists, or whatever they are, seem to indicate that the college bought a museum collection. The trustees could have given permission to sell it—awkward that, we can't ask Flo Boater to check." He paused to see if they agreed with him before he proceeded, "Or the items might have been purchased by the dean, who was using the college name inappropriately as a cover for selling them." When he now saw skeptical looks on their faces, he explained, "Perhaps as a tax dodge, like you said, to avoid paying income taxes." When they indicated that they were understanding, he continued, "Who would have the rest of the records?" When Jay shrugged, Donahue turned to Jenny, "What's your best guess?"

Her answer was a bit sharp, "I've worked in the financial office for one morning and you expect me to know?" With a touch of sarcasm, she added, "You'd do better to ask Stout. I understand he's been up there every day."

Donahue wasn't interested in him—he wasn't likely to cooperate. Besides, Stout was looking for the "money tree" that supposedly existed on every college campus, a marvelous plant that could be plucked whenever the faculty wanted a special project funded. Or Stout was checking into the union, one of his recent interests. But these were vague guesses. "What's he up to? Has he said anything?"

Jay had seen him at work, but he had decided it would have been unwise to be too inquisitive, so he threw the matter back to Donahue, "Hey, you're the detective."

Whereupon Jenny echoed words that were now famous in her circle of friends, "So, go detect!"

Donahue was not willing to allow the conversation to stop at this point. He wondered aloud, "I guess the financial director would know, if we knew where she was."

Jenny dismissed that, "Too new. Barely knows where the bathroom is." That was an exaggeration. In fact, Miss Purdy had already complained that the stalls were too small. Jay had been concerned about this, because he saw no way to correct that problem easily. (Sizeism elsewhere meant that the Briarpatches of America could hire some good people.) The office had once been occupied by the county treasurer. Although not as large as the registrar's office across the hall, there should have been plenty of room for commodious restrooms for both men and women. Although there was a women's restroom in the hall, it was more convenient to use the toilet in a corner of the back room where the vault was located. Slightly more commodious, it was also private, because the staff worried about allowing the public to go back where the vault was left open during working hours. This arrangement had worked well for half-a-century. The public restroom had smaller stalls because previous generations were smaller in size. Miss Purdy did not fit into them well. If she had been a man, she'd have been even more unhappy, since the men's room was on the ground floor and she did not manage stairs well.

"How about the former vice president for financial affairs." Donahue asked

"Hardly lasted a semester," Jay said, to which Jenny added that it had been a decade since any financial officer had lasted more than a year.

Donahue, after turning the papers to an angle to look at them better, "I'd sure like to see the originals. Have some of these turned yellow?"

"Why, yes," Jenny replied. "Didn't I mention that?"

When it became obvious that the lists had been produced over a period of time, on different typewriters, Donahue suggested that the interim vice presidents wouldn't matter anyway. Whoever made the lists out had been at the college for a decade or so. Only the dean's tenure fit that.

"Or Flo Boater," Jenny suggested.

Jay replied cautiously, "I don't think I'd ask her.

Jenny retorted, "She was Dean Wooda's mistress.... Or so they say."

"Coulda been neck deep in it," Jay agreed.

After reflection, Donahue concurred, "You're right. Dean Wooda might not have done all this by himself. This could get complicated."

Jenny replied, "That's right, Flo was into everything."

"And she didn't shrink from murder," Jay added.

"But that's more recent," Donahue said. "That affair began, what, five years ago, four?"

Jay nodded, "'bout then."

"What do we know about financial officers from back then?" Donahue asked, rubbing his thumbs against his forefingers and putting one thumb against his teeth.

Jenny reflected a moment, "Five years ago? Hard to keep them apart. One left… amid rumors. I think that Flo Boater was her successor—as his lover. Do you remember, Jay?"

Jay thought a moment, then said, "I don't follow gossip well. Ask the Creep."

Jenny laughed, "Not hardly!"

Donahue had meanwhile paused to think. When they quieted down enough to look over at him, he mused, "They were partners… in everything?"

Jenny nodded, then asked, "What would Flo have known about this? Didn't the bank accounts come as a surprise to her?"

"She's a sly one," Jay offered. "Maybe pleasure before business?"

Jenny beamed, "I told you Jay had a mean sense of humor."

Donahue nodded, but now he was smacking his lips, "It's not likely he told her, but if she did know…."

Shaking his head, Jay responded, "Flo won't cooperate. If she knows, she'll cover up."

At that Donahue hit his fist into his hand, "If that stupid jury…."

Jenny hurriedly agreed, "You're right. It wasn't your fault she got off. Flo played a full PC defense, and it worked. Just another abused woman."

"That's the way juries are," Jay said. Dragging his wrist limply across his forehead, he uttered the longest sentence Donahue had ever heard from him, "A helpless woman accused by corrupt, incompetent and sexist police."

The tension broken, Donahue laughed, "I'll check into it." Rising to leave, he looked around for a place to deposit his trash. Jay took it from his hand and cautioned, "Be discreet!"

Jenny agreed, "Yes. Discreet. If Flo or Stanley learn where you got your information…."

"I know," Donahue said, "I just say that I figured it out myself. That is, once I figure out how I got hold of these copies in the first place."

"You'll think of something," Jenny said, "Mary will be so proud of you."

That was something Donahue had not considered. He now wondered how disappointed she would be if he couldn't come through. She would surely hear that he was on the case. A case composed of a handful of Xeroxes, conventional wisdom about the late dean's lack of concern for morality or legality, and the looming presence of Flo Boater, who would surely want to cover up any scandal. Briarpatch had seen enough scandal in the past year

And yet, here were new documents, from the finance office. And Miss Purdy had still not been seen. Flo Boater, when asked where the vice president for financial affairs could be contacted, had said that she had no idea. "But don't worry—these things work themselves out."

To which Jenny said to herself, "Yeah, it's not like people are murdered around here all the time."

Chapter Eight

The coffee house was the intellectual center of the campus. It was the place where all and sundry collected. Those who didn't like coffee could buy a variety of an alternate beverages, that is, sodas or soft drinks, the word used depending on which of the surrounding counties one hailed from. But the two students we know best rarely went there. They once preferred the fraternity house, but they were currently suspended for poor grades and failure to pay their dues. "It's no place to hang out, anyway," Jones would say. And Smith would confirm that it was too filthy, even for them. They had moved out last spring without cleaning their room—after Jones's birthday blast the brothers had filled it with wadded wet paper balls; rather than throw the mess out the window—their first idea—they just grabbed their clothes, their electronic equipment, and left without telling anybody. Nobody noticed at first, because all the hall light bulbs had been removed so that inebriated friends could sleep on the floor without being disturbed by people going down the hall to the toilet, but after two weeks the smell was so bad that even the brothers complained. Subsequently, Smith and Jones lived in a dormitory most of the time, in a rented apartment whenever they were told either to quiet down after midnight or move out. They spent some evenings in a local beer hall, where even the billiard table (as they called it) was greasy; but most often they were at parties. For them the coffee house was at best a fall-back home away from home, and they bragged that went there about as often as they visited their parents—not true, but a good joke.

When Jones—whose name was not Jones—was a freshman, he had begun using this *nom de plume* on articles in the student newspaper on those occasions when it was published in order to avoid the unlikely possibility that someone would send a copy to his mother. His fraternity brothers, unable to pronounce his name, much less spell it, began calling him Jones. Smith ended up with his name for the same reasons, and eventually a few befuddled professors, really not able to tell one from the other (or remember if they had ever seen them), had done so as well. After several professors complained to the registrar that her class lists were incorrect, she created an AKA note on their transcripts and all grade notices to prevent future confusions. Soon it was a universal practice to call them Smith and Jones, or Smitty and JJ.

Smith and Jones had once stood out on campus. As freshmen their long hair and scraggly beards had started a style trend, so that by the time they were seniors they were indistinguishable from many of their peers who also didn't play football, didn't play in the band, didn't go out for plays, and didn't take classes in the morning. They had been Goths in high school, but gave it up so as to not appear too conformist. Besides, they weren't sure if Goths could drink beer. Bottom line, though, was that it took too much time to put on the cosmetics every day. Neither had had a date in time out of mind—a situation they blamed on the low quality of women on campus. Smith had once suggested they get haircuts, but Jones had just taken him out for a beer.

Oh, there had been Ellie, but she once said that Smitty had better learn to bunt, because he wasn't going to get to first-base any other way. That is, he hit on girls, but... well, he didn't understand the terminology. Anyway, she wouldn't even go out for coffee with him now. He suspected she was seeing Stan.

Jones asked, "What's Ellie doing now?"

Smith sighed, "She's into something new."

"Something new or someone new?"

"Something, I think."

"What?" Jones almost sat up, he was so interested.

"Oh, I couldn't understand it. All names and theories."

"What names?" Jones had a knack for names.

"She wrote it down for me, so I could look it up. That's what she said."

Jones leaned a bit closer, "Did you?"

"Couldn't find the library."

"Couldn't find the library? It's right over there," Jones said, pointing out the window. "Don't you remember freshman orientation?"

"Orientation? I remember a brunette... or was she more blonde?"

"I remember her! She went out with you, didn't she?"

Smith ignored the question, "Here's what Ellie wrote out." And he handed a note to Jones: "George Lakoff, cognitive something or other. I can't read her handwriting."

Jones snatched it from his friend's hands, "Cognitive Linguistics."

Smith reached out to retrieve the note and study it, "I guess so. Says the guy teaches at Berkeley. That's where she wanted to go, but her parents said no. It would turn her into a jerk."

"So she went to Arcadia."

"Yeah, she said… what did she say? That if she was going to a second-rate place, it might as well be at the bottom."

Jones thought about this for a moment, "Good thing she transferred to Briarpatch. More going on here."

"Yeah," Smith answered as they both lapsed again into silence. The coffee house was actually pretty dull right then. No Lill, no Lily, not even any girls to stare at. They stirred a bit when some sorority girls came in. They knew them from parties. A couple gave a friendly wave, but made no move to join them. Instead, they laughed at some private joke and found a distant table.

The two putative seniors had been sitting there for an hour. There was no lack of coffee, but they had not joined the monthly plan and the cashier was checking IDs. The monthly plan didn't cost the college much, thanks to the many students who came to the coffee house less than they had expected. As is true of so many aspects of life, the idea of hanging out on campus was more appealing than actually doing it. This was a lesson still to be learned, and youth has only one way of learning it—disappointment. Smith and Jones, whose parents were very, very rich, could have paid the more expensive "visitor's rate," but there was the principle of the thing. They wanted examples of suffering to tell their parents so that they could plead for cars; they didn't have much insight into their own motivations, but they knew that their parents could easily have afforded vehicles to replace the ones they had totaled in their freshman year. So there they sat, nursing glasses of water, speculating about the girls who came through, and watching the door. A few girls came in, but only a few were alone, and they had quickly spread out books and launched into composing what appeared to be terribly boring essays. At length the coffee house began to empty out, and Smith and Jones ran out of topics for conversation. Other students could go on for hours about football, but Smith and Jones couldn't remember players' names. As for Xs and Os, that was a mystery that only yokels might care to figure out. They yelled a lot at games, but mostly at the other team's fans. This made for interesting columns in the paper, Jones complaining about the visitors' poor sportsmanship, but it was an inadequate basis for conversation. Classes were equally unpromising, since so far they had missed almost every lecture. That left them nothing to ridicule. They lapsed into silence after grousing, "There aren't even any girls worth watching" (and their standard was pretty low). Hearing some noise from the counter service, Smith looked around, shrugged his shoulders and sagged in his chair before complaining to his friend, "You said she'd be here."

"The Prez hangs out here a lot. 'To talk with students,' she says."

"Then why haven't *I* ever seen her?

"How often do you come here?" Jones knew the answer. They were practically inseparable. They even took the same classes. That made cutting all the easier, they reasoned, since each could rely on the other for notes. But neither took notes worth looking at, and they customarily cut classes together. Not getting a response from Smith, who was trying to decide if the forlorn freshman with fat legs was worth staring at, Jones repeated, "How often do you come here?"

Startled out of his reverie, Smith almost shouted, "Never!" Almost embarrassed, he looked around to see who might be watching, then waved his hand around, drawing attention to the athletic trophies placed here and there amid the Japanese décor, and exclaimed, "Who'd want to come to this dump, anyway? Look at it." Pleased that the chubby girl had looked his way, he gestured at the unwashed tables, worn from overuse and too little janitorial help. Glancing back, he caught her eye, whereupon she hurriedly put down her cup, packed up her books, and left. Turning back to Jones, he gestured at the rest of the place, "Empty. As always." That was not exactly accurate, since there were periods when the coffee house was very lively. However, those times overlapped with happy hour at the bar, and Jones could never pass up a cheap beer.

It did not bother him that the tap at the pool hall served more water in the beer than the coffee house put into its brew.

"True enough, but I've seen her here."

Smith could see that Jones was puzzled as to when he could have been here without him, but he wasn't going to explain.

"And what do you talk about? *With her,* I mean."

"Nothing." Smith said, "What do I have to say to a college president? Except about you know what, and we don't want to mention that."

"No," he agreed uncertainly. "She might talk with the dean of students again."

Smith leaned forward to ask, "You're sure she'll give me an interview anyway? I mean that she'll say anything good?" He hadn't met Flo Boater before or even heard her speak at formal occasions, but from what he gathered from his poorly informed friends, he had reason to believe that they had shared a profound insight with him—they had much in common. He wondered what it could be. It's not as though Lill would be sitting there, with Lily, surrounded by talkative kids. He could relate to her. He was sure of that. After all, he had taken one of her classes. Flunked it, but he had attended several times.

Jones gave him a quizzical look, "You're from the student newspaper, aren't you?"

"Yes," Smith admitted, "but the word is that she wants to close us down." With budget cutting as the excuse. "At least, change our name."

"I hadn't heard that," Jones responded, though he had heard that she was very unhappy about the paper's coverage of the demonstrations last spring. As he heard her quoted, "No news is good news." Probably apocryphal, what his parents would call a "ben trovato," that is, it should have been true. "What would she object to in it?"

"Have you ever read our paper?" Smith asked suspiciously.

"No. What would I learn from a newspaper?"

"But you used to write for it!"

"I quit after the editor insisted that I stick to the facts… He even suggested that the literary magazine might appreciate my efforts at fiction."

Smith looked askance at him, "Did you try the lit rag?"

"Of course, not! I have standards… "

At this, Smith just threw up his hands, "Oh, you're hopeless." For a moment he wished his sister was here. She could do say it so much better.

"Well now, I'm not the one asking around how to meet the president!"

"OK, OK," Smith said, "Then where is she?"

"Dunno. But she'll be back."

"Back? She's been here?"

Jones merely shrugged a reply, then said, "Let's get a cup of coffee and check back later."

Smith yawned and asked, "They serve *coffee* here?" Looking over at the coffee bar, he saw steam rising from a freshly brewed batch and noticed that it smelled pretty good. "Why not?" He then looked over at his friend, "Here or the usual place?"

Jones grinned, "As you always said, who'd want to have coffee here? What? Changed your mind?"

Smith agreed, "You're right. Let's get out of here and come back in an hour. Or two."

"Don't we have class in an hour?" It was odd for Jones to be concerned about this, but he was enjoying Smith's discomfort.

"Sure, but nobody goes. It's just a history class."

"Then we have time for some java."

Smith hesitated, however, "Look's like rain. Let's stay here."

As they stood at the cashier's, their money in hand, Jones asked, "Where do you want to sit? Outside? No rain that I see. But if I go back to that seat, my butt will become permanently attached to it."

After a moment, Smith responded, "Sounds good. Wherever I can overhear some gossip. I've got that column to write."

Jones, who knew his roommate almost better than he knew himself, was surprised at his enterprise. Still, he could not resist a depreciating, "That's your research?" He said that with half a smile, because he was awfully lazy himself, and he knew from his reporting days that listening to gossip requires attention. He had learned that when his stories were due, it was easier to make them up. Might as well, he once explained, not being able to read his own handwriting… when he bothered to write the quotes down.

Smith was as outraged as his energy allowed, "If I can hear them, they're public information… That's what the editor says, and he's in Stout's journalism class, too, and he attends."

"That's how *you* get news?" He had no idea what was in the newspaper now, but he supposed it contained news. "We used to do interviews, that sort of thing."

Smith was firm on this point, "That's old hat, they never tell you anything." Apparently, the newspaper staff had discussed it thoroughly. "If you hear a source talking, it's public, and if it's public, it's news."

"Who ever told you that? Stout?"

"No, Dean Wooda. He taught my journalism class this morning. He was quoting the Creep. That's what my editor says… I was there, but I missed it. Too sleepy, I guess. But my editor made a point of telling me right after class."

Jones was astounded. "The dean teaching? Isn't that unusual?" Almost as unusual as Smith getting up and attending class without him. No point in Smith trying to wake him, of course, but the brotherly thing would have been to sleep in, too.

"He told the instructor that he wouldn't be rehiring him, for next year or something, and he walked right off. Left the dean high and dry without a teacher." It was hearing that—at a party the previous evening—that had persuaded Smith to set the alarm. It could have been really interesting, but even though Stanley Wooda was teaching, it was merely another class, and he dozed through most of it. "I would've told you, but you hadn't come in yet."

"Yeah, I noticed you left early."

"It was after midnight…" Smith explained. "The party was dying out. It was a week night."

"And here I thought you might have gotten laid." He snorted, "That would have been a first."

"Well, Ellie thought it was a good story."

"You're writing about that?"

"No, that's *her* story. She made that clear. *Real* clear."

Jones nodded. Seeing Smith still waiting for an approving word, he flipped his hand at him and said, "Okay, sometimes you have to prepare the way." He stopped to think, "You getting anywhere with her? Anything serious, I mean, not just having a cup of coffee." With another smirk, he sat down at a patio table.

Smith shrugged, "Coffee's good."

Swinging his legs under the table, Jones agreed. He was thinking about how he could refill his cup for free when he looked up at Smith sharply and asked, "The firing. Wasn't that news? I mean there must be an angle Ellie won't see."

"Such as?"

"The story behind the story. Maybe something about the professor's private life."

Smith dismissed the suggestion, "Professors don't have private lives. Anyway, who'd care?"

"Well, write about Stout. He had a role in this?"

"He did? What?"

Jones laughed, "I dunno, but he had a finger in everything."

A sly look came across Smith's face before he sat up straight and responded, "You want me to write about someone who is going to give out grades on my work! Get real!"

It crossed Jones's mind to ask about the missing finance officer, but then he wondered what he would say if Smith asked what, exactly, she did.

Chapter Nine

Smith may not have been able to imagine writing an article that Flo Boater would consider positive, but neither could Donahue. Not after his conversation with Jay and Jenny. He phoned Lill and Lily and arranged to meet them in the woods behind the Gym. Few people came there—everyone had heard of the poison ivy. It was the only place, he suggested, that they could talk undisturbed. Had they gone to the coffee house, as he would have suggested under more normal circumstances, they would have been quickly surrounded by their fans, and the conversation would have deteriorated into witty repartee and wise advice (which were sometimes difficult to tell apart).

Donahue paced back and forth, careful not to venture from the path, and to keep an eye on the path, because the uneven surface could send an unwary walker face down into masses of unfamiliar plants. That earned him a couple swats on the face from low-hanging boughs. A city boy, he wasn't sure which vines were dangerous and which were not. Concentrating on his thoughts and his rotational peregrinations, he was not aware of anybody's approach until Lill came up behind him and announced, "We're here."

Lily added, "You said to hurry."

Apologetically, Lill explained, "It took us a while longer to park than we had expected."

Lily almost exploded at that, "Flo Boater eliminated the parking for motorcycles!"

Because Donahue looked so astonished, Lill explained, "She said it conveyed the wrong image. "

"She also banned pick-ups," Lily added. "At least through Homecoming."

"Wrong image," Lill said, "for prospective students." Her tone suggested that Flo was looking for a kind of student who would have little interest in Briarpatch. Pickups were far and away the most common

121

form of student transportation, though usually they did not move from Monday to Friday. "Is that an invitation for a demonstration or not?" she asked. "And by students who usually never join a picket line!"

Donahue shook his head in disbelief, but he asked only, "Where did you park?"

With a smile, Lill answered, "In the president's reserved space. In front of the administration building." Parking was at a premium there.

Donahue knew that Flo would have to park on the other side of the square; at this time of day, this might involve a walk of at least two hundred yards. She would be furious. Exercise other than deliberately planned was something she avoided. He asked, already knowing the answer, "Isn't that dangerous?"

Lill laughed, "By the time she finds a parking space and walks back, we'll be gone."

He shook his head, "I'll bet she walks faster than that."

This reminded Lily that they could not waste time, "You said to hurry."

Donahue rolled his eyes. There were parking spaces at the Gym. Much closer.

Lill cut his obvious question off, asking, "What do you need?"

He sighed, then said, "Information, most of all."

"You may fire when ready...." Lily intoned, forgetting already the need for speed.

Out of habit, Lill finished the quote, "...Gridley."

Donahue answered, "Battle of Manila Bay, 1898."

"Good job," Lill said. "You are wasted as an anthropologist."

"Sociologist, actually," he reminded her.

But Lily agreed with Lill, "You have the mind of a historian."

Donahue made a wry smile and said, "We already *have* three of them." And looking down the path, he sighed and waved his right hand slightly in that direction, indicating "and *there* one is." So much for a meeting without attracting attention.

The Creep almost smiled as he walked past them. After a few steps he turned to look back at them, stumbled in a slight hole and staggered into the greenery. As he lost his balance he put his hands down. As he stood up, he gave a mild cry, something about poison oak, something about being extremely susceptible to poisonous plants. Although he tripped again, he did not fall down, but with his hands raised above his head, he awkwardly made his way back onto the path, then darted into the Gym to wash every potentially exposed particle of skin.

No one spoke until he was out of sight. Then all three smiled in spite of themselves. Not toothy smiles, but the kind of expression that says, "There is a God."

As Donahue stifled a laugh, Lill picked up the conversation where they had left it, "We have one historian too many."

Echoing the thought, Lily said, "When I'm dean again, I'll have to give some thought to abolishing that department. Future high school coaches can learn to teach something else."

Lill put her hand on Lily's well-muscled arm and smiling said, "Academic freedom, Little Lily, don't forget academic freedom."

Flexing her biceps, Lily caused Lill's hand to spring away, "I'd like to free his academics. Tear off his credentials and feed them to the dogs."

Lill laughed, "Have some feelings for the dogs, Lily." With a glance at the Gym, he added, "So much for secrecy." Then she turned seriously to Donahue, "What can we do?"

"When you were president, were there inquires about your buying Latin American artifacts?"

Lill reflected a moment before answering, "There were some inquiries along that line, but that was so early, I didn't know what was involved. I just said we were not interested."

Excited, Lily added, "That was one of the ways we almost balanced the budget. Not spending money."

"We know from those receipts you 'found,' that somebody, probably the college, was spending a lot of money…" Lill started, and Lily continued, "…for the museum Dean Wooda had planned."

Lill finished the thought, "Ground to be broken 'soon.'"

"Well, that one's on hold," Lily said.

Lill frowned, "Just like the investigation into what money might have been spent. Flo's in no hurry to find out."

"If she finds out," Lily explained, "she'll have to let the trustees know."

"Better to remain ignorant. As for the museum, she claims the cancellation as one of *her* cost-cutting measures."

Donahue squinted slightly, "I heard that Miss Purdy was upset before she disappeared. Anything to that? Maybe she sensed something was wrong, but also that she shouldn't be looking into it?"

"Could be," Lill said, "but that's pure speculation right now."

There was a moment of silence, then Lily spoke up, "Speculation's good. Like speculating about the museum. If she thought we were about to get a museum, she'd have good reason to be concerned. But there's no money for it."

"I never heard about a museum," Donahue said, "except in the distant future. Nothing right away. But I was only here about a month before Dean Wooda drowned... died."

"Only the trustees knew," Lill explained, her voice unusually soft. "Apparently. Though I never heard anything about it."

More expressively, Lily burst out, "There was no point in publicizing it until they had a building."

"That would be several million dollars..."

"....and the college was running a big deficit."

Donahue asked if the trustees had really approved it. It didn't seem logical to spend money on this project, when the interest on the debt was eating the college alive.

Lill explained, "It may have been buried deep in the records. He never gave them copies to study in advance. It was, I suppose, approval in principle, if there was any action. I can't say. I only read the minutes for the last year or two."

Lily laughed, "Me, too, probably less. That is *real* dull reading!"

"Did Floyd Boater know about it?"

"Probably not," Lill guessed. "He relied on the dean. In a pinch, he might have asked the financial officer."

"And a *good* financial officer can bury anything," Lily added. "And with the turn-over in that office, Dean Wooda took an unusually active role in drawing up the budget. No newly-hired vice president would have challenged the dean's instructions. Not over a project that might be years in the future. So we're not talking about a *good* financial officer."

Donahue pondered the matter before asking, "If there was *something* not right, would the financial officer *have* to be involved?"

With a shrug Lill replied, "Perhaps, but maybe not."

Lily agreed, "The college changed financial officers every year…"

"…Or every six months."

"So even they might not have known what was going on?" Donahue was operating on the premise that it was unlikely the dean could have corrupted one financial officer after the other.

"Interesting question," Lill said, "What's this all about?"

"Yes, what's up?" Lily asked.

Donahue waited until two students strolled by, hand in hand, then signaled them to stand closer before he explained, "Dean Wooda was selling artifacts." When their eyebrows went up, he added, "For a lot of money."

"Details?" Lill asked. "Give me details."

Donahue shrugged, "Until minutes ago, I only knew the general situation."

Lily threw up her hands, "We knew that much already. We just didn't know how much."

Donahue explained. "More there than we knew. Several times what was in the bank accounts. Maybe several hundred thou."

Lill looked at him a moment, then said, "Wow."

"Double wow," Lily added. It was not easy to reduce Lily to two words, though it was not unusual for her to use twice as many as Lill. "You sure? How do you know?"

"An inquiry from a supplier, wanting to know why the money hadn't come."

"You? They called you?"

"Jenny gave them my number. They called the finance office. Miss Purdy was not there, of course, so Jenny took the call, told them to talk with me—the anthropologist, she said, who would be in charge of the museum."

"And…?" Lily asked.

"They said that they'd sent the college some expensive items…"

"And…?"

"They wanted to know when they would get paid." He paused, "I don't think they knew the late dean was the purchaser, much less that he was dead. All they wanted was their money."

"They asked you for several hundred thousand dollars?"

"No, they were pretty vague. I got the dollar figure somewhere else, but it sounded like they wanted quite a bit."

Lill paused to think, "What did you tell them?"

"Very little, just that I'd look into it."

"And what did they say? Give you a number to call?"

"No," he laughed. "Said they'd be in contact."

Lily said, "Not to worry. It's unlikely gangsters can find those things. Not even we can."

"If they're gangsters," Donahue answered, "they'll want their money, not the artifacts."

Lill reflected a moment, "They're probably not gangsters. Not if they've waited this long for him to collect on whatever… he'd bought."

"It doesn't sound like it was on the up-and-up," Donahue responded. "Legitimate businesses are not hesitant to leave a phone number."

Lily moved closer to whisper, "We'll be behind you, and Chief Biggs, too, for that matter. Strangers can't show up here without being noticed."

Donahue moved even closer to whisper back, "How did he hide the disappearance of the, uh, items in question?"

Lill reflected before answering, "I doubt that anybody had thought to catalog the acquisitions. No one would know what is missing without pulling together all the purchase orders. And, if I remember correctly, last year you only found only a few short lists of things which had been sold. I was surprised that the bank accounts were for more than what they'd bring."

"You are the anthropologist," Lily observed.

"…and *even you* hadn't seen the collection."

Donahue explained that he was a sociologist, but they dismissed that as a quibble. He was the only person on the faculty who cared whether there was a collection or not, except for Mary, and almost as quickly they dismissed his observation that Mary had been working in the regions the artifacts supposedly came from. Lill concluded her rebuttal by asking, "Who, from the entire faculty, was best qualified to manage the proposed museum?"

The answer was too obvious to bother uttering. Although Donahue denied knowing anything about museums except how to visit them, when he eventually conceded, "I'm only a logical person to...." Lill cut him off, "You are *the* logical person to be in charge of the collection. Jenny was right."

Donahue stepped back and shook his head, "I feel like I should have sensed this coming."

"Maybe that's why Dean Wooda hired *you*," Lill said.

Lily agreed, "Yes, that makes sense."

"What makes sense?" He wasn't sure that the next sentences would be compliments.

"He hired you because you were desperate for a job." Lill's mind worked like a fine calculator.

Lily's was more down to earth, "Middle-aged, second career, inexperienced."

"That's me, all right," he conceded. "I don't know about 'middle aged,'" he said, then caught himself. "But what's the point?"

"A real anthropologist might have pressed for a professional evaluation, stored them safely, and blocked any effort to sell the most valuable items."

Lily added, "And it would have come out that the college had been buying artifacts all along..."

"...despite the financial crisis."

"Then he was selling them."

"And pocketing the cash."

"Moreover, even Old Boater might have asked what happened to the money."

"I bet," Lill added, "that the reason the dean wanted you to swim with him was to size you up. To see if you could be safely 'rolled.' That's the right word, isn't it?"

"You bet it is, Lill," Lily responded, with a friendly punch on her shoulder. "And that's why you were the president, and I the dean. I'd never have thought of that."

Donahue tried to protest that he'd been hired because he was the only sociologist willing to apply for the job, but Lill dismissed that objection, "Lots of people come for a year. The world is full of desperate people. If it hadn't been for the murder… and then Mary… you'd be gone now, too."

As Donahue stared past them, lost in thought, Lill apologized, "We have to run now. See you later, DO." It was an abrupt end to such a serious moment, but he had not expected to have talked this long. She waved vaguely at the Gym, at which they turned to see the historian coming out the door.

Donahue listlessly said, "Bye, girls," and paced back and forth, hands in his pockets, thinking, until he saw the chief coming up the path. He wondered how Biggs knew to find him here, then asked himself, "What happened to the Creep?"

The chief greeted him, "I had a message to drop by."

"From a little bird?"

"You might say so, though his little friend."

"Jenny?" Donahue asked, measuring his steps to the chief's slower pace.

"Yes. You know Jenny's working in the business office?"

"Yes, part-time."

Biggs stopped in order to formulate his words better. "Something's up there. Her boss was really upset."

"Because she told a caller to call me? Is Miss Purdy back?"

"No, don't think so. Something more serious, and that was earlier, before she disappeared. Anyway, Miss Purdy's still gone. People are getting worried."

Donahue thought for a moment, "I get a mysterious call about artifacts and Miss Purdy's nowhere to be found. Or at least she's not here. Been gone a while, I understand." After a moment, he continued, "Can't be a connection. Too soon."

"Too soon for what?"

Donahue waved his hand slightly, "Tell you later. This place isn't as private as it seems. What's on your mind right now?"

"Jenny suggested I talk with you."

Donahue said nothing, but glanced over at the chief, a question in his eyes.

The chief saw the question, "It's really awkward. If I start asking around now, everyone on campus will know within hours that I was investigating the financial office and looking for Miss Purdy. If there really isn't a problem, Jenny might lose her job."

Donahue hesitated, "I'm afraid almost everybody knows already."

"Miss Purdy's disappearance? She's so new, I'm surprised anyone knew her. Or missed her."

"They really didn't." Donahue took a breath, "TBCW."

The chief understood the reference—The Briarpatch College Way. "I don't know why she would just sudden-like go. Upset because the books were in disorder perhaps, or maybe she saw something she didn't like. But Jenny didn't sense any problem. Just that people had been left go, and that was a cost-saving measure, and after Miss Purdy disappeared."

"No indication of foul play?" Donahue asked, unhappily suppressing the urge to tell him what he knew.

"Nothing."

Biggs then fell silent as the historian came down the path, apparently still working at removing every possible trace of poison ivy. A towel, clearly "borrowed" from the Gym, was in his hands, half-damp, half dry, each portion being applied vigorously in turn to his hands, then his neck. His face appeared flushed, almost the same hue seen on the visages of out-of-shape former athletes who had remembered all too well what they could do at age twenty and then tried to surpass.

Once he had passed Donahue whispered, "Looks like we'd better talk later."

Biggs agreed, "Ask around, quietly. Talk with Jenny, and let me know what is going on."

After they parted Donahue wondered how long it would take before Flo Boater knew that he had been talking with the chief... in private. "Minutes," he said to himself, smiling wryly.

Meanwhile, when Lill and Lily exited the woods, they had seen Ellie asleep on a park bench. "We've seen this before," Lill commented.

"Is she all right?"

"We'll check." At that they went over quietly, studied her a moment, then shook her shoulder gently.

"Wha'd want?" emerged from the half-hidden face.

"Ellie, are you okay?" Lill asked.

Ellie slowly sat up, "Sure, why'd you think not?"

Lill sat down beside her, Lily somewhat awkwardly on the other side, the space being too small until Ellie skooched over a bit. "Honey, we're just worried about you passing out like this. It's awfully chilly."

There was the expected indigent reaction, "I wasn't passed out."

At that Lily couldn't hold back, "Ellie, you shouldn't be taking drugs."

Ellie turned to her, "I don't do drugs. Not since junior high, or at least not much. Drugs are for idiots."

"Then why," Lill asked, "do you pass out on park benches."

"I don't sleep. I read all night."

"All night?"

"Sure. That's why I'm better read than Old Stout."

Lill and Lily exchanged glances.

Ellie continued, "He doesn't really understand deconstruction, much less new ideas."

Lill and Lily exchanged another glance.

"Newer ideas?" Lill asked.

"Yeah," Ellie explained as she sat half-way up, "Orientalism, for example. Orientalism is incompatible with the post-modern insistence that the reader is all that matters. Edward Said's arguments suggest that the author is all-important, otherwise it wouldn't matter what the bias is—the reader could figure it out and compensate—whereas if the readers are not competent to do that, as they usually aren't, it becomes essential to know that the author truly understands the culture being written about."

"And Stout doesn't see that?"

"He's like all the other Deconstructionists here. Either the reader is important or the author is, but you can't have it both ways."

Lill paused a moment before saying, "I hadn't thought about that." Lily nodded agreement.

"They're like lemmings, following each other… somewhere… oh, I'm sleepy."

"Donahue says…" Lily started to say, but Ellie cut her off, "Donahue's a fascist."

Lily began to say, "Define fascism," but gave up when Lill waved a finger at her.

"Besides," Ellie continued, "I fall asleep because I'm tired… not because I'm drugged…but I like the feeling of being tired. There's no high like having worked hard. When the brain starts moving slow, you can force it along. You can't do that with drugs, at least not with any I've taken."

Lily thought a moment, "Some drugs speed everything up."

"What's the hurry?" Ellie responded. "Anyway, I'm tired." As she laid back on the bench, she asked, "Can I go back to sleep?"

Also asleep, or nearly so, were Smith and Jones. They were, at least, in their room. It was almost too messy to walk across, but that was enough reason to take a nap before cleaning up. "Say, Smitty," Jones managed to say, "What have you done on buying some grades?"

Smith raised his head enough to respond, "Me? You're the brains of this outfit. At least, you always say so."

"That's why we divide the labor—*I* think of something, *you* do it."

"So *I'm* supposed to find someone who'll arrange it?"

"That's the way it works."

Smith thought a while, "Say, JJ, who'm I supposed to contact? What if I ask the wrong one?"

"Be subtle," Jones replied. "Don't just blurt it out. Be indirect, feel them out. Just like you do with the girls."

Smith thought about that. "Just like you do with the girls." If it's going to turn out that badly, maybe it's not a good idea.

Chapter Ten

Donahue tried to contact Jenny by phone, but failed to make an instant connection. He didn't want to leave a message—"no paper trail" was his motto now. Thinking he might find her at the coffee house, he wandered down there and poured himself a cup. It wasn't much of a treat, but it was at least warm. He started to look at one of the newspapers lying about on the tables, when, to his surprise and pleasure, Mary sat down beside him. She had a cup of coffee and a big grin. "I know something about your hero, Kennedy," she said slyly.

Donahue could only sigh. Here he was, problems piling up on him, and Mary wanted to talk about Kennedy! But what could he say? If he said he didn't want to talk, she would want to know why. And how much should he tell her? Better to talk about Kennedy. It might even be a welcome diversion. He answered, "What?", but he wondered what had brought about this change in her attitude. Cold to warm. Was it just a woman thing? Or specifically Mary?

"You once said that he would have gotten us out of Vietnam."

Cautiously, he answered, "Yes, probably."

"But he's the one who got us in."

He couldn't deny the fact, but he suggested that he hadn't gotten in very deep and he would have gotten out after the election.

"Let me see if I have this straight," she said, mock seriously, "he was ready to let American boys die until after the election of 1964?"

"Not fair," he answered. "He didn't want to appear soft on communism, not after the Berlin Wall, then the Cuban Missile Crisis, with Goldwater as the likely opponent. And there weren't that many there. Mainly trainers."

"So he put re-election above the national good?"

Donahue sighed slightly, then parried, "Communism was on the move."

She smiled as she made a counter thrust, "Eisenhower didn't send in troops. No land war in Asia, that sort of thing."

"Well, Goldwater seemed awfully dangerous, too."

"Do you believe that?" she asked. "Or was it all hype?"

"Some was hype, I guess. By the time I was old enough to know what was going on, he was pretty middle of the road."

"Oh," she asked slyly, knowing the answer, "you *weren't* there?"

He raised his eyebrows. "Do I look *that* old?"

She ignored the question. "How was he going to get out? Just cut and run? Like at the Bay of Pigs?"

This raised his hackles a bit, but he gave the standard answer—"Vietnamization."

"That was Nixon's term."

"Johnson's, I think."

"No, it was Nixon. Abrams had begun to emphasize training, but it was Nixon who changed the strategy, then brought the troops home."

He sighed, "I take your point." He started to say something about Mary hating Nixon, but thought better of it. "Where is your argument going, now that Kennedy has been dead five years by that time?"

"Let me see, now," she started. This was beginning to become familiar. Whenever she had a good argument, she approached it indirectly, and her good arguments were becoming more frequent. "Let me see, now, the Montagnards were our best allies."

"Yes," he said, "they hated the North Vietnamese."

"Wouldn't it be more accurate to say that they disliked *all* Vietnamese?"

He conceded the point, knowing that her next question would concern the logic of Vietnamizing a war in a multi-cultural proto-nation. Indeed, she zinged him, then went on to ask about the role of the Chinese in the cities, and allowing the Vietnamese elite to send their sons to Paris, safely out of danger, where they could protest the American presence.

"Okay," he conceded, "Maybe Kennedy shouldn't have gone in. But he might have gotten out."

"Really," she countered. "After killing Diem, was there any turning back?"

"He didn't kill Diem. The South Vietnamese generals were supposed to kidnap him and send him into exile."

"Really," she continued, her mouth twisted into a wry smile, "the best and brightest we had, Kennedy's brainy buddies, imagined that Diem would not try to get back into power? And the generals would have just trusted him to stay away?" She turned to friendly sarcasm, "What was this, naiveté in the ways of the world. Couldn't Kennedy have asked his girlfriend how her mafia lover would have handled it? Or was he too drugged up to think of that?"

Donahue gave up. Her argument wasn't fair, but she had him. He would liked to have demonstrated a plan for disengagement, but all he could say was that people close to Kennedy were reasonably certain that he had seen the problems there and, therefore, would have gotten out.

"You told me once that truth was so precious that it had to be surrounded by a bodyguard of lies."

"Right. Churchill, I think. I heard it from my mother."

"Sharp lady," Mary snapped. "But what's *your* answer?"

"Okay, that's right. What's your point?"

"In this case," she went on, "any hint of abandoning South Vietnam would have occasioned panic in Saigon. Therefore, his statements of resolute resistance to communism, warnings of the domino effect in Southeast Asia, and boasts of successes in battle hid whatever the truth was. Or, were those statements the truth!? What were those 'close to Kennedy' saying? The truth or Camelot myth or wishful thinking or psychological projection?"

Donahue didn't know which was correct. He knew which one he preferred to believe, but he couldn't prove it. He thought briefly he should have become a historian, then an image of the historian came to him—he was a Kennedy expert. Nuts, maybe, but knowledgeable.

It was Mary's first unquestionable win in an intellectual debate, and she savored it.

For Donahue it was a reminder of how complicated situations often were. Like those right in Briarpatch College.

On the other side of the campus, in the cavernous presidential office bedecked with scaffolding and painting supplies, Flo Boater had been talking with the senior historian. As usual, it was an uncomfortable conversation. Whenever he entered a room, it was as though the air pressure fell, clouds built up, and a dank mist was on the way. The fact that the weather was indeed changing emphasized this, and the longer he was in the room, the stronger the impression became. To make matters worse, even on balmy summer days, whoever shook his hand encountered a cold, wet palm that seemingly lacked the ability to form a grip. Fishlike, some called it, and a few were so unkind as to suggest that his eyes bulged, too. That, however, was pure imagination. They were rather sunken.

At the end of the overly long interview, President Boater extended her hand and said, "Thank you again. Your advice is as welcome as your information."

He extended his hand, made a slight bow (almost a curtsey), and departed. She turned, went to her desk and opened the drawer containing facial tissues.

As soon as her hands were dry, she picked up the phone, dialed and barked into it, "Stanley, come down to my office! Yes. Right away." When the dean appeared a moment later, she said, "Sit down, we've got a problem."

"Yes," he asked.

"I've just been informed that Donahue is onto something."

"Yes, I just saw *the Creep* leave."

Patiently, Flo Boater explained, "He may be a creep, but he's *our* creep! He's very useful."

"You can't trust him! He's ambitious!"

"Ambitious for what?" She had a hard time imagining the historian exercising authority judiciously.

"*You* told *me*. To be dean!"

With a wink, Flo Boater said calmly, "The faculty wouldn't stand for that."

"Oh, I think you could arrange it." Then he relaxed and laughed, "I think he expects you to."

At this she had to laugh as well, "I guess I can't blame him. If I could foist *you* on the faculty, I could probably get away with appointing anyone."

With a pout, Stanley Wooda responded slowly, "That's his reasoning, I hear."

"You hear?" she asked.

"I have my sources, too," Stanley Wooda said. "But that's neither here nor there. Here's the news, He wants to be chair of the Art department."

Flo Boater was stunned, "Still? Why? What are his qualifications?" She paused for a moment, then added, "He's a *historian*. He can't even write." Then, after a moment's reflection, she asked, half to herself, "Why didn't he mention that to me?"

Stanley Wooda agreed, "His qualifications are weak, but there will be an opening for a chair there. It's outside his department, which makes it a step toward promotion."

"How would that work?"

"He believes that if he can demonstrate the capacity to manage a large program, he will be trusted with more important jobs. Perhaps assistant dean at first."

Boater mused, "It might be, if he could take a troubled department and turn it around."

Stanley Wooda had a suggestion, "Art *is* in trouble."

She dismissed this, "All Art departments are in trouble. Everywhere. Question of temperament."

"Everywhere?"

"Well, almost everywhere. Most of the time. Certainly here. Why do you think the chair is leaving?"

At this he shrugged his shoulders, then looked up to ask, "Do you want to do it? Name him a 'super chair?'"

"Maybe, but not just the art department," she said. Her young dean was still reflecting on this when she leaned forward and said, "Theater!"

He wasn't sure, "Theater doesn't have problems. Lill and Lily run it perfectly."

"Just like they did the college administration." She paused before adding, "That's why they are so dangerous." Then, seeing that Stanley Wooda still didn't get it, she added, "They understand management."

Now he saw it, "Ah. You declare the department a mess, undermine their credibility, and let the Creep do the dirty work."

"He won't give them a chance to defend themselves. And we can truthfully say that we had nothing to do with it."

The dean bit his lip, pondered the situation until Flo Boater's eyebrow raised, then he said, "There's a problem. It will look like you are singling them out."

She laughed, "Well, I am." When young Wooda's eyebrows raised, she added, "I've given some thought to this... in more general terms. If we eliminate departments and organize the college on the basis of divisions—in this case, Fine Arts. Our hands would be free to do pretty much as we wanted. This is merely the first step, combining History and Theater, then Art when the chair leaves. Music, too, I guess, though we don't have much of a program. No rush there, but nobody will notice if we do it over the summer."

"Brilliant," he exclaimed. "I'd heard you talk about a Science division, but I knew that would be hard to do."

She responded with a smile, "The fine arts are heart of the liberal arts. Each has a muse."

"Why not literature, too?" he asked.

"Oh, Stanley, you're so impulsive," she laughed. "We'll have to have something to hold over our friend, Max Stout."

"Brilliant," he repeated. "You want me to announce the appointment right away?" When Flo Boater nodded, he continued, "Is that why you called me?"

"No, and actually we need a couple days to set this up. I called you in because we need *to do something* about DO *right away*."

Stanley Wooda, turning slightly pale, asked, "What is he up to?"

Boater said, "The *details* aren't important, but we need to *get rid* of him."

"How rid? *Permanently?*"

"Not so fast!" she said, "I *like* the way your mind works, but not so fast... *yet*." She had in mind the tough guys that he had used once before to intimidate demonstrators, but she didn't think that Donahue would be so easily impressed.

"What's the time frame?"

"Right away."

Smiling at the irony, Stanley Wooda summarized the situation, "Right away, but *not so fast.*"

"You think of something less drastic *than permanently,*" she said sharply. "We don't need another corpse around here until it's unavoidable."

"We can't wait till Mary's tenure hearing?"

"No, that would take months. It's a complicated situation. We can't rush it." They sat silently, thinking. As a result, when Smith and Jones stuck their heads in the room, they were puzzled—the president and dean just sitting there, not saying anything, hardly even noticing them. Normally, they would have resisted Miss Efficiency's efforts—just on principle—to get them to leave. After all, they had just walked past her and opened the door. Now, seeing President Boater wave them away, for once they had the sense to take a hint. Miss E closed the door quietly, allowing Flo Boater to close her eyes and concentrate.

At length Stanley Wooda said slowly, "I think I have an idea." But he leaned back and rubbed his chin rather than express his thoughts. His face was a study in conflicting emotions.

Flo Boater watched him, fascinated and hopeful, somewhat as she would observe tropical fish in a dentist's office, preferring the slow motion drama of the aquarium to the unpleasant experience on the other side of the office door. But at length she became bored and asked, "What are you thinking about?"

He stretched, as if the change in position might clarify his thoughts, "I need to turn it over some more."

"Turn what over?" she asked.

He asked slowly, "What would be reasons for people not to go to the coffee house?"

She shrugged, "Lousy coffee, no food... no music, inconvenient hours, nobody to talk to." She wasn't sure why anyone went. She hardly ever did. "I wouldn't go there if my office was finished." She waved her hand around, "This place is going to be such a mess."

Stanley Wooda said slowly, "In short, no atmosphere. That would do it"

She answered flatly, "I imagine so. But where is this leading?"

"You have curtailed the hours that it is open."

"There will be some evening hours," she said defensively.

"Yes, but nobody knows when they will be."

"Of course, it was too convenient for our enemies to meet here."

"So, why do we keep it open at all?"

"So I can keep my finger on the campus pulse."

Stanley Wooda was a bit surprised at this, since he was her best source about the students' wishes and the Creep kept her informed about everyone else. If she had actually spent as much time there as she boasted of doing, she could indeed say that she had been speaking with everyone who had an opinion, but she didn't. Stanley Wooda wasn't about to argue that; instead, he offered a suggestion. "We could say that if we closed it, we would have money for new ventures."

"Why do we need new money?"

"We've told everyone there is a crisis," he explained. "We can't just 'discover' new funds."

"What would we need new funds for?"

"Remember the faculty exchange that Lill was working on?"

She almost laughed, "Yes, that silly idea about getting new faces on campus while sending our faculty out for experience in the world."

"It was designed to help persuade young faculty to stay."

"Yes, 'To be here and in the world at the same time.' But it would be expensive."

Stanley Wooda agreed, "Yes, but not too expensive. Closing the coffee house would cover it."

"Where would I meet students?" she asked. Then she thought it over more seriously, "I suppose I could make the sacrifice if it paid off big time. What's your idea?"

Stanley Wooda leaned over and whispered to her. When she clapped her hands in satisfaction, they both leaned back, smiling.

He said, "I could start it up again with one phone call."

She was very pleased, "Stanley, you are *full* of good ideas." And she reached across the table to squeeze his hand. Hurriedly, he suggested that they walk over to the coffee house. It was almost time for the doors to be open again, and if she wanted to demonstrate that her policy of administrative openness and access was real, this was a good opportunity. On the way they hardly exchanged a word.

They were hardly seated at a prominent central table before Jones and Smith came in. Jones pushed his friend forward, saying, "There she is. Got here fast! Now's your chance, before they start staring at each other again." That strange tableau in her office was still fresh in his mind.

Smith objected, "She's *with* someone." He was willing to interview her alone, but not with anyone listening. He wanted no quibbling about his quotes.

Jones responded disbelieving, "Don't you know who *that* is?"

"Nah." Smith paid no attention to faces. "Same guy who was in the office. Looks like Stan, but it can't be. He's no older than I am. And he's wearing a tie."

"It *is* Stan. Weren't you there when he announced it? At the demonstration. Remember?"

Smith scratched his head, "I don't remember anything from that day. Except we had a great beer bash."

"Yes, and Stan paid for it."

"He did?" There was a pause. "How'd the charge get on my credit card?"

"On yours?"

"Yeah, my parents had a cat."

"And…"

"They talked to some dean, so it was okay."

"They must have talked with Stan."

"Oh." There was another pause. "Maybe that's why Ellie's not dating him."

"But she is," Jones countered.

"Well, not officially. I think she's going out with me… or will be."

Jones took a deep breath, "Right now concentrate on this interview."

"I think I'm going to regurgulate."

"You can be sick later. Pull yourself together."

Smith hung his head, "I *still* don't know who that is with the president. Okay, I *know* you say it's Stan, but I don't understand why he's there. Or why he's wearing a tie."

"I thought you worked for the newspaper. I *did* get you the job. *Right?*"

"This morning." Smith answered. "But that doesn't mean I know anybody by sight yet."

"That's Dean Wooda., and don't worry about it. Professor Stout says that he is two different people, apparently, which is a good reason for an interview.

"That's Dean Wooda?" Smith said, still unbelieving, "I thought he was dead."

"He is," Jones countered. "That is, the *real* Dean Wooda is dead. That is the new Dean Wooda. The one who's not dead. Not dead yet, I guess."

"What's that mean?" Smith asked, logically.

Jones, unused to getting logic from his friend, answered only, "Nothing, I suppose. It's just that...."

"That what? "

Jones squirmed, "Well, like, men tend to die around President Boater."

"Men? Like me?"

"I suppose *you're* a man," Jones countered, "but not if you're afraid to talk with her." Seeing skepticism on Smith's face, he asked with a smirk, "A five minute talk will be fatal?" It was sarcasm, but it avoided another attack on his friend's manhood.

"Then why don't *you* do it?"

"Why would I want to?" answered Jones logically. "I'm not the one who needs to talk with her. You're the reporter!"

"Why hadn't I heard this before? This *dying!*" Smith responded.

Frustrated, Jones said, "I read about it in *our* paper!"

This had no impact on Smith, "Oh, I thought you never read it. I don't either, of course, just write for it, or will. If I can get this first interview done...." He concluded lamely, "I can't stand news. I don't know how you talked me into this." As he rambled on, he wondered why Jones didn't know all this. They were practically inseparable, which was one reason that neither got to class. When they were freshmen they had declared different majors, and since all the important classes were at nine and ten o'clock, they would have had to attend separately. Once they became roommates, however, and friends, they agreed they would attend all of each other's classes—to be able to help each other study and write papers. However, they could never agree on which class to attend (when they had awakened that early), so they cut them all. Somehow, they were still passing (or almost passing, which at Briarpatch was good enough). Jones had two or three majors, a fact he lorded over his friend, recommending it as a good way to get better grades out of professors who were under pressure to demonstrate their "productivity."

"What's that again about dying?" Smith asked. "I'm too young...."

Jones explained, "That's why she wants to close down the paper."

"Is it? What is?"

"If she does'em in, we'll expose her."

Smith wasn't sure about this. She wasn't a bad looking woman, he supposed, for an old biddy, but he wouldn't want to see her exposed. "I thought she just didn't like what we wrote."

Jones was becoming frustrated. Waving his arms, but keeping his voice low, he asked, "Why would you want to interview her, anyway? If not about that?"

"I'm a journalism major...."

"Since when?" Jones demanded. How could Smitty make such a decision without telling him?

"This morning, I think, or maybe yesterday. But not the kind the dean or Stout wants. I'm going to write opinion columns. Nobody who writes those has to *know* anything."

Jones, who had written for the student paper in his freshman year, was confused again. "What has that to do with the interview?"

"If I don't interview her, I can't misquote her."

Yet more confused, Jones asked, "You want to interview her so you can *mis*quote her?"

"You don't understand modern journalism. According to Professor Stout, if I interview her, I can interpret what she says any way I want.

It's post-modern thought, I think. Besides, if I don't interview her, my editor won't print it."

"Where did you learn this? It doesn't sound like *my* journalism instructor."

"The one who left? Not that you ever listened to *him*."

"Well, it's obvious. Where did you hear that crap?"

"English department. Stout calls it '*deconstruction*'."

Jones was doubtful about this, "Isn't deconstruction only for *literature?*"

Smith excitedly assured him, "No, it's good for *all* forms of communication, that is, all means of asserting power relationships."

"Asserting? Don't you mean *describing*."

"No," Smith said derisively. "It is important to *understand* the world, but it is more important to *change* it. That's not the exact quote, but it's Marx and nobody ever quotes him correctly anyway."

"Where did you learn that?" Jones asked, astonished that Smith could memorize anything that didn't have music.

"Stout. To '*describe*' is only a way of '*understanding*;' to '*assert*' is a way of '*changing*.' Asserting is a use of power. Journalists assert!" he concluded with a fist slamming into an open palm. "It's time we asserated ourselves."

Awed by his friend's newly-found enthusiasm, Jones asked, "Journalism is a *power* relationship?" He had never thought of it that way. He had only used it to interview pretty girls. Well, girls.

Smith was certain about it, "More than that. It's a *sexual* thing— they try to screw us, we screw them." He had learned that, right down to the words, from Stout as well.

"And your editor approves anything you write, as long as you do an interview?"

"Sure, he has real ethics. And Stout oversees everything."

"I thought the dean taught the class now."

"Doesn't matter. Main thing, I have to interview the president." He stopped a moment to shake his head, "Even if she's talking with Stan. That *is* Stan, you say?"

"Well, there she is," Jones said, pointing to the president. "Free. Go talk to her."

"Another time," Smith replied. "She's busy."

"So. Horn in."

"There's dean what's-his-name. I don't want him there."

"It's Stan, and he's leaving."

Smith saved himself by pointing to Jenny and saying, "I don't want another witness around. I can't misquote her if he's there. Besides, she's heard me. I'm sure. Let's get out of here."

Jones observed logically, "She's too far away to hear. Go ahead." He even tried pushing him slightly, but without budging him at all.

Smith tried to change the subject, "Ellie says she won't listen, anyway. The new guy she's reading says so."

Hesitating, Jones asked, "What new guy?"

"Lakoff, you remember. She wrote out the name." After a pause, he added, "She just bought the book, or borrowed it from Mary C. I don't remember which. Something about politics."

"And…" Jones asked.

"He says that people don't act rationally, but emotionally. You can't persuade someone unless you know what buttons to press."

"Buttons?"

"You know, your body is a part of your mind. No such thing as pure reason, whatever that is."

"Did you volunteer to press her buttons?"

Smith stared at him, "How'd you know?"

Jones started to ask what she had said about that, but knew the answer already. Before Jones could say anything, Smith explained, "You have to use the right words, to connect 'deeply' and 'superficially' at the same time. It's our unconscious, I think that's right, that we listen to, when we listen, not to rational arguments, which I think she said don't exist anyway."

Jones thought a moment, "Makes sense. Where does this guy teach?"

"Berkeley."

"Then he must know what he is talking about." After a moment, he asked, "What does Stout think about it?"

Smith looked stunned, "Stout? How would I know? I don't go to class."

"Ellie does, most of the time."

"Some of the time," Smith corrected. "And she thinks Stout is an idiot."

"Well, that's a rational conclusion."

"Ha," Smith retorted. "That's what I said, or something like it. But Ellie, well, she said I was not responding rationally, but emotionally, so I was catching on."

"Were you?"

"I dundo, she started talking about Chombsky and Leftkey, all people I never heard of, then about parenting styles and such stuff, and how that affected the way you reacted to certain words."

"Did you understand her?"

"I guess not. When I asked if she'd like to go make out, she said that she was busy all this week and next."

"And the week after that," Jones asked, knowing that the humor would go over his friend's head.

"Probably. Said she had some reading to do."

Jones raised his eyebrows, the left one higher than the right, then commented, "Maybe you should do something to impress her, like doing this interview."

"She's interested in politics. Not in this."

"Ellie says that everything *is* politics. Except beer. Maybe you should concentrate on beer." He then spoiled the effect by laughing at his own joke.

Smith, after saying that he'd tried that, fell back on the one strategy that always worked with Jones, "The president kinda scares me. I think I'd better have some questions ready before we talk." Indeed, that worked. Jones responded to suggestions that work be put off until tomorrow. Besides, Smith intimated that he would be "buying."

Somewhat later Jones looked at the letter crumpled in his pocket. Officially from Miss Prudence Purdy, it warned him that Briarpatch College expected a check for this semester's tuition. "Who the hell is she?" he asked himself, as he wadded the letter into a ball and let it sail toward a trash basket, missing it by three feet.

Chapter Eleven

Shortly after lunch Mary received a telephone call from Miss Efficiency, asking her to see the president as soon as possible. "What would be a convenient time? Right after lunch?" Mary did not have much to eat at lunch, just her usual mini-veggie half-bagel sandwich, but she instantly developed heartburn. It was a terrible start for what might be the long-postponed discussion of her tenure application, but she came to realize that it might not be what she feared. "Cognitive dissonance," she told herself, knowing that that wasn't quite right. But if Flo Boater were dismissing her, she would probably just have sent a letter, after telling the town hair-dresser. Mary wished that the situation was more promising, that the president was someone else, someone like Lill, but if this was all there was, she would just hope for the best.

Certainly it started well enough. Flo Boater came out from behind her desk to shake Mary's hand and indicated she should sit in one of the comfortable chairs that formed a small circle for more intimate talks with special guests. Flo seated herself nearby, not opposite, and turned her chair more to face Mary before speaking, "I so glad that we could have this chat."

"Always glad to speak with you," Mary responded, nervously.

Flo studied her a moment before speaking again, "I've been giving some thought about your tenure application."

That was not a good start, Mary thought as she uttered a weak, "Yes."

"I think you would be well advised to complete the research project you began in Latin America."

That was a shattering suggestion. Mary had hardly written a word, and this was not a good time in the semester to work on it. "I don't think there's time to do much more before the committee meets." That would be in a matter of weeks.

"I think we could arrange a mutually satisfactory extension."

146

Mary's growing sense of panic was hardly quieted, "For how long?"

"I think you could finish it in a year." She paused to observe Mary's reaction, then continued, "In fact, I've arranged for you to have an extension of your research grant... in Latin America... if you want it. Starting right away." She waited to observe Mary's reaction before continuing, "That would indicate that you are serious about your project." There was an implied threat in her voice.

Hearing this, Mary's effort at calm melted away. "An extension? For the rest of the semester?" Mary had no desire to return to the jungle, but she had calculated quickly that there were approximately three months left in the semester, then she would have maybe three months before the committee had to come to a decision. Could she get a manuscript accepted in that time?

"For a year. Starting in January."

"For a year!"

"Maybe a year and a half. I know it's hard to look for a job in January, and, on the off chance that you don't have a publication by then, if would be unfair to leave you, uh,… unemployed."

"I wouldn't be teaching?"

Flo Boater didn't answer the question, but went on enthusiastically, "It's a great opportunity. With a good publication, you'll be able to compete for the really good jobs in your field."

Mary couldn't keep the disappointment out of her voice, "I really enjoy just teaching Introductory Spanish."

"Nonsense!" the president boomed. "The modern woman, the authentic feminist, won't be satisfied with the run of the mill jobs. We can always get someone without talent and ambition to teach the introductory courses in any department." She stopped to let the words sink in, then went on, "Persons like yourself, on the other hand...."

"Well... I don't know what to say." And she didn't, but she wanted to say NO.

Flo Boater put her hand on Mary's and begged, "Say yes."

Withdrawing her hand, Mary pulled herself together and asked. "One year, starting right away, and you say the grant can be extended?"

Didn't she just say January? To start. How long would that be? Mary's ability to count months had somehow disappeared.

"I made some phone calls," Flo explained. "Laid it on thick. We won't have any problem."

Mary couldn't think of anything to say except the wrong thing, "DO will be awfully disappointed." And she looked toward the windows.

Flo smiled, at first broadly, then, as Mary turned back to her, sympathetically, "DO?"

"He has some plans." She hadn't wanted to say more, but Flo Boater's inquisitive look made an explanation inevitable. "Eventually marriage."

"And.... do you share them? The plans...."

"I'm not sure. But a year is a long time." She paused, then looked up, "Or is it more like… fifteen months?"

The president reached over to pat her hand again, "I imagine that Dean Wooda can find some faculty research funds that would allow him to join you."

Mary didn't want to say that she really didn't want that, either, so she compromised, "That would be expensive." After a moment she asked, "I thought we had no budget for research?"

This did not slow the president for more than two bars, "For a project as promising as yours, I think we can skip the normal budgeting process."

"I don't know."

"He is an anthropologist," Flo offered, encouragingly.

"Actually, only a sociologist."

Flo could not be discouraged. "Practically the same thing."

Mary agreed that Donahue did teach anthropology classes and she almost mentioned his interest in the museum before remembering that this subject was not to be called to the president's attention.

"A year of research would surely be valuable when he comes up for tenure."

"Yes…" she said hesitatingly. No one could disagree with that, though his tenure decision was years away. With a shake of her head, she managed to repeat her question, "How long would this be?"

"Oh, the main grant is for a year, but we can find something to cover the time till it starts." She smiled as she concluded, then reached over and gave Mary's hand a squeeze.

"For DO, too?"

"Then, you'll do it?"

Mary almost said yes, but the thought of mosquitoes and heat caught the word in her throat and held it fast. Shaking her head, she asked, "Can I have a day to think about it?"

The president was obviously disappointed, but agreed, "Yes, of course. A day is no problem."

"It just that," Mary explained, "I'd like to talk to DO. Is that all right?"

Flo Boater smiled sympathetically, "Certainly. We'd want to have you both on the same flight."

"The same flight?" Mary echoed dully.

"For security reasons. It's just safer to travel with a companion."

"Oh, yes," Mary answered, but her mind was not functioning well now.

"There is a flight with connections that leaves in two days."

The speed of the process began to sink in: "You want... I mean, you recommend that we leave that fast? What about my classes? What about DO's?"

"We'll cover them. We always do. Just like when somebody dies."

Mary was not reassured by the comparison. Was it a hint? Was that the alternative?

But Flo gave her no time to dwell on that. Enthusiastically, she exclaimed, "Scholarship doesn't wait. It's a competitive world out there. Briarpatch needs to get some national attention. Besides," she added helpfully, "won't it be cooler down there in the winter?"

"It's near the equator. It's always hot," Mary explained.

"No matter then. Just saves you having to pack for two seasons."

Mary shook her head, "The mountains are very high. I'll have to take warm clothes."

Flo Boater would not be put off, "That's perfect, then, a change of climate whenever you feel like it."

This was beginning to upset Mary to the point she had to change the subject. She blurted out, "I had no idea that DO would be going, too."

Flo Boater took her by the hand, trying to calm her. Although this only heightened Mary's agitation, she kept a firm grip, "I didn't either until you mentioned him. Then I remembered a remark made by the chancellor of the exchange university. They need an anthropologist. When I suggested that I might be able to arrange for one for next year, he became very excited, but I had to make the promise right then in order to get you the grant. They start classes later than we do. I didn't want them to give the very last humanities grant of the year, and perhaps next year, to someone else. I had planned to talk to DO later, but now that you have explained it to me, I see that the only way to proceed is to send you both right away. I'm sure you'd not want to be apart." Seeing Mary's face whitening, she added, "at least for the travel."

"Yes, yes," Mary responded quietly, trying to say what she wanted without explaining. Her words were not quite tumbling over one another as fast as her thoughts, but they still came out more rapidly than she wanted, "I understand, I understand. I appreciate your not wanting to separate us, but I'm not sure that I wanted to be together, either. At least, not so close together." As she got up to depart, she turned to say, "I'll call you in the morning. Or come by."

Flo Boater called after her, "Good luck, and I hope you make the right decision."

As Mary nodded and went through the door, she heard Flo Boater's last words, "We still have a financial crisis. I cannot guarantee anyone...."

Mary had hardly left before Dean Wooda came in. He had been in the secretary's office, sitting close by the door, which had conveniently been left slightly ajar by Miss Efficiency after she had seen Mary into the office. It was a skill that had been necessary for her predecessor, when the late President Boater had visitors, so that she could take notes for Flo Boater to use later to assist him in remembering what had been said; Flo Boater had briefed Miss E on what to do. Today it was useful for Dean Wooda's information. And it was done so skillfully that Miss Efficiency was able to open the door before Mary approached. She had followed the entire conversation, more or less, but the dean, having heard only the concluding words, looked at her notes, then, after seeing they were in shorthand, muttered something about outmoded technology and went into the presidential suite. Miss E sighed as she closed the door behind him. She liked Mary.

Flo Boater, indicating that the dean should join her at the large window overlooking the campus, was proud of herself. She asked the dean, "Did you hear how I handled that?"

Stanley Wooda equivocated, "Brilliantly. I have to hand it to you."

She took this as an opportunity for a short lecture. Half-turning to face him, she said, "Stanley, in this world nobody hands anything to you. You have to reach out and take it." Then she turned back to the view and smiled, "But, Stanley, you already know that."

"I'm learning fast," he admitted. "But I didn't hear the first part of the conversation.

After she recounted it, slightly improved for effect, he nodded, then said, "I didn't know that the exchange university wanted an anthropologist."

"They didn't. I'll really have to talk fast to get them to agree to that part of the deal."

Stanley Wooda beamed with admiration, "Boss, you're incredible!"

"I agree," she said, "but that's enough flattery. Besides, the administration there owes me. I used to be on an obscure education board, the state commission for overseas research and exchanges—SCORE. Not much of a job normally, but since the deans didn't have the time or interest to do much, they let a lowly presidential wife have a significant voice in decisions." At this memory, she made a wry face and let out a sigh. "Anyway, I've put enough money in that obscure university's pockets to ask for small favors. I'll be making them a call now, and I have some papers to write up so that we can get that pair on their plane tomorrow."

"Tomorrow?"

"As soon as we can arrange DO's passport, if that's a problem, and visas. But soon!"

Donahue had been waiting for Mary outside. She emerged with tears in her eyes and tried to walk right past him, but he wouldn't move until she stopped to tell him what happened. She couldn't speak.

Donahue tried in vain to take her in his arms, "What's the problem. You look like you've been crying."

But she warded him off, saying only, "Yes, it's horrible."

"What's happened?" he asked, envisioning yet another corpse on campus.

"Flo Boater wants me to go back to the jungle!"

"How? You can't afford that."

Mary stopped her tears long enough to cry out, "She said that the college would pay for it." After a long sob, she added, "For a full year!"

"A year?" he asked. "I wouldn't see you for a year!"

"Oh, she sobbed, "That's the worst part. She wants you to go, too."

He ignored the implications of that statement to concentrate on the practical problem, "How?"

"An exchange with the university there. I'd do research and you'd teach anthropology."

"That wouldn't be so bad, would it?" he asked.

Mary ignored him, "A year, or longer, without a warm bath! Without a good meal! No wine, no white napkins, without my friends!"

"I'd be there, wouldn't I?"

She continued, almost to herself, "A month I could take. Maybe even another three months. But not a full year!"

"I'd be there."

She looked up at him, surprised, "You'd be at the university. Didn't you know that? I'd be in the field."

"Don't you ever come into town? Wouldn't I ever see you?"

"Maybe every two or three months, if the steamer is running."

Donahue reflected on this, "Maybe the exchange isn't such a good idea."

She grabbed him by the arms, "Can't you do anything to save me!"

His innate chivalry was awakened, though he would have preferred some kind of rescue that led to a happier ending. He didn't see himself ending up with the distressed damsel in any scenario he could imagine. Even so, he promised, "Of course." Immediately, he repented of his rashness, "But what? How?"

Mary ignored his doubts. She brushed her lips across his cheek and ran off, "I'm counting on you."

Donahue, watching her depart, said to himself, "I don't see a way to win this one. If she doesn't go, she may not get tenure. If she goes without me, I may never see her again. If I go down there, too, I won't see much of her. And... what do I tell Chief Biggs about his investigation?"

Dean Wooda went to his office, but could not concentrate. There was something about that story which didn't ring true. Turning to a thick book of state agencies, he looked up a number and called. "This is Dean Wooda of Briarpatch College. I wanted to ask the membership of SCORE."

A voice on the other end reported how pleased she was to hear his voice, "I had heard that you had gotten ill on that investigative trip for us. Mrs. Boater did a fine job as substitute for her husband, who was, of course, your substitute, but it will be good to have a panel again made up of full-time deans."

He responded appropriately, saying that he looked forward to working with her, then hung up quietly. "I bet," he said to himself, "that the university in South America, wherever it is, is similarly confused about who President Boater is... and was. This explains a lot."

Chapter Twelve

As it happened, Flo Boater had difficulties arranging for Donahue and Mary C to be on that airplane. The chancellor of the university explained that at his institution, too, there were "certain procedures" that he had to go through. Once she explained that Briarpatch College would cover the "extra" expenses of a visiting lecturer in anthropology, the chancellor's tone changed, "Oh yes, of course, we will work it out. No problem. And we'll try to make it all as convenient as possible for you. So just relax, I'll call you when we are ready here."

Flo Boater did not relax. She knew that Latin Americans had their own concept of time, at least when it was convenient for them to do so, and that she would get a call, maybe, as some moment inconvenient for her—when the flights were full, when finding replacements would be most difficult, when she had a meeting with trustees or other college presidents or some campus events that required her full attention. With a sigh she put down the telephone, then sighed again and called a trustee who could always be counted upon to advance money generously for worthwhile small projects. She explained the situation, how necessary it was to buy tickets now and sort out the arrangements later. With a few minutes, she put down the receiver and smiled.

Her mood changed after she called Mary and heard that she needed to go home before she left—it was simply out of the question for her to leave her mother for a year without explaining in person. Flo Boater frowned at first, then she brightened—the tickets would be cheaper if bought two weeks ahead of departure. Meanwhile, Mary would be off campus. Ah, if there was only something she could do about Donahue.

Maybe there was. She picked up the phone. Luckily, he was in his shared office and the receiver was passed over to him. "DO, this is Flo Boater. Yes, fine, thank you. I assume that you've talked with Mary. Yes, that's right. Look, we've hit a snag at the other end. It will take me a while to sort it out. Yes, it's still on, but maybe not for months. So just keep teaching your classes as normal and I'll tell you what comes up."

A week passed, then a second. Flo sighed, then rescheduled the flights—one could still do that easily. 1996 was an age of innocence as far as travel went. Security was lax. One could bring bottles, wrapped packages, and even keep one's shoes on. Extra bags were free, and anyone planning on staying a year needed extra bags could carry all he needed, while mailed packages, especially to country districts overseas, might take forever.

These were tumultuous times, everyone agreed, but nothing particularly serious. Certainly not compared to the hot years of the Cold War or Civil rights, and certainly not on the Briarpatch campus. The stock market was rising, so even the miniscule endowment of Briarpatch College was growing swiftly. There were no international crises. Almost no international news made it to Middleville, anyway. Oh, there were scandals in Washington, or whispers of scandals, but the election campaign itself was dull, dull, dull. The World's Series held some promise of excitement, but the defending champion Braves were losing in the playoffs and the revived Yankees were down, too. Most importantly, there was no news about Prudence Purdy. The Finance Office was functioning to the extent that money came in and more went out; the dean's former secretary was put temporarily in charge, with instructions to ask the president about any problem that came up—alas, she only lasted a few days before announcing that she had a new job, as executive secretary to a businessman in Zenith who was looking for someone with experience in finance to replace instantly the woman who had left suddenly to found her own company in competition with his. Jenny, who had been sent back to Music, was now recalled to take temporary charge of the finance office; her classes were assigned to a local piano music teacher.

Most exciting to alums was the victory over Occidental East. They had never imagined *their* football team playing a game out of state, much less winning it. There was some initial difficulty about arranging the airplane flights home, the unhappy sponsor having declared that his responsibility ended with having gotten the "Pricks" to the game, but when the players suggested that they would rearrange the private jet, perhaps carrying it away piece by piece as souvenirs, a compromise was arranged. There was some later unpleasantness about the steering wheel going missing at the end of the last shuttle flight, but after Windy Burg drove personally to Zenith to purchase a replacement (with his own funds), the pilot could escape the misery of Arcadia's lone, ageing motel. OE's coach promised the alums that his team would prevail in '97, it being "unlikely that the Briarpatch players would pass any courses this year." This prompted Windy Gale to check on his players. His best athletes were in the preparatory course for the unofficial honors program. No one, however dull, had ever been known to flunk it. Windy saw to it that they attended.

A more serious concern came in the form of an announcement from Arcadia Junior College that it would indeed convert from a two-year program to a four year degree-granting institution—state funding for this initiative, hitherto unavailable, would almost double the number of faculty while cutting the teaching load. This would mean direct head-to-head competition with Briarpatch for the best students from the region, with Arcadia enjoying a tremendous advantage in having state support. Flo Boater was worried. Already there was an unbridgeable gap in athletic facilities, golf courses and airports; now Briarpatch would face greater competition in tuition charges and the variety of degree programs offered. Briarpath's ability to grant a bachelor's degree had been its most significant advantage over this nearby rival, and that was now gone. President Mankiller was all smiles, but the ones she bestowed on Flora Boater seemed less sincere than those she had given to Flo's late husband.

Middleville observers thought that Luci May Mankiller had taken advantage of the state board of higher education's momentary disarray—caused by the "flagship" university's inability to enroll all qualified students who wanted to attend to first offer advanced level courses, then piggy-back on Zenith University's extension program to offer all four years of classes on campus, and now to parlay the incumbent governor's desperate re-election promises into raising Arcadia's status. At President Mankiller's urging, the local district representative slipped one line in the budget bill at the last moment. Nobody noticed, and, voilá, it was done. Luci May Mankiller did not bring this to public notice until the legislative session was over, so there was no way to correct the action before months had passed; by then it would be too late. Or so she hoped.

The rumor was—probably with some truth to it, though how much was unclear—that this had been a feminist to feminist deal. The governor was male, but an ardent feminist, as was everyone who wanted to be elected. He couldn't balance the budget, but that was the legislature's fault, he said, and he would somehow find the money. He was supported in the deal by the local rep, whose power base rested on her ability to use her father's private wealth to assist fellow legislators in both parties. The college was her pay-back. Rumor was that the college would be renamed for her in the fall. After that rumor spread, no male in the legislature dared challenge Arcadia becoming a four-year institution. Nor any woman. Much less the governor, who was already being indicted for various irregularities connected with campaign contributions. All he needed was one more enemy.

President Boater might have been able to prevent the passage of the amendment, or at least force an open debate on the merits of Arcadia's case (the governor was in favor of private enterprise, which Briarpatch College certainly was, and he would gladly have accepted an honorary degree at Commencement, should he be reelected), but she and her staff were too distracted by the daily demonstrations to follow the legislature's actions, much less to travel to the distant state capital and meet with legislators and state officials. Later, she realized that a protest would simply be ineffective and make Mankiller into a potential Ladykiller, with herself as the affected lady.

Flo Boater decided not to mention her thoughts to Stanley. Ladykiller. That might give him the wrong idea. Worse, he might hold her words back for future use. Nobody could be trusted fully. Well, maybe poor old Floyd, but he was dead now, and even he was likely to say things that he didn't realize should be kept quiet. As for Stanley, he understood politics far too well.

The demonstrations also distracted Professor Stout from his intention to capitalize on what he took to be a "frenzy" over the presidential election. Such was his story. As a matter of fact, there was no excitement. There was not even any interest. The outcome in the state was so predictable that the congressional candidates made efforts to pretend that they had never heard of Clinton or Dole—vote for the man, they said, who could do the most for the district. Most voters believed that would be the incumbent—who was a senior member of the committee that oversaw firearms and tobacco. Except for enthusiastic deer hunters, voter turnout was expected to be less than fifty percent, and it would have been far lower if there had not been so many elderly voters who were persuaded that the act of casting a ballot was more important than voting intelligently. Stout's plan to radicalize the election came to nothing because there was nothing to radicalize. Hence, he turned his attention to the demonstrations. If he could not embarrass Lill and Lily in one way, Dean Wooda explained to the president, Stout would try another. That had a calming effect on Flo Boater, who had feared Stout's statements would be blamed on her; she even smiled when the young dean explained that she could win faculty approval by defending "academic freedom" and "freedom of speech." Provoking violence, mild violence, of course, would be easy, and the blame could easily be shoved onto Lill for not controlling her people.

The first step was for Stanley Wooda to suggest—indirectly and slyly, by warning what not to do, knowing that Stout would do exactly that—that Stout arrange for the fall demonstration to have as its central theme a demand to name Lill president again. Stout wasn't sure about the suggestion at first, but when he was assured by the dean that the plan had Flo Boater's full approval, since it would make Lill look like a schemer, and an ineffective schemer at that, he changed his mind. If Lill fell into the trap, if she accepted the leadership of the protest, she would look foolish when most of the protesters ceased to appear. When the dean assured Stout that his cooperation would be appropriately rewarded, he agreed to present the idea to the Anarchist Assembly, a newly formed volunteer body of ten people somehow representing the entire student body. Stout was momentarily disconcerted by only recognizing one name—Ellie's. She was highly articulate when not in a state of incomprehensibility, and he sensed that she did not respect him. But he had good luck with the Student Assembly. There his proposal met with such general acclamation that Stout was able to step back, observe his handiwork briefly with satisfaction, and then slip away. Unfortunately for him, the Student Assembly's attention span was very brief—the elected officers turned their attention to the biennial revision of the Student Government Constitution, hoping to find some formulation that would guarantee them sufficient funds to be effective.

The next hitch had come when he had tried to locate the Anarchist Assembly. It announced its presence by graffiti on campus walls—much to Jay's annoyance—but rarely met as scheduled or where announced. After all, they were anarchists. If Jay could not locate them, imagine the poor professor's difficulties! For other quasi-political groups this secrecy would have presented difficulties, because they wanted to recruit more members; but the Anarchist Assembly grew largely by person to person recruitment. They pasted their posters over those of other groups, so that the usually dependable "check the doors" process of locating members of organizations was invalidated. Their meetings were usually called on the spot (since everyone was present anyway) to discuss pro-active policies. (Pro-active was a new term that year— at least at Briarpatch—indicating that one was in the mainstream of academic and revolutionary thought. It was supposed to mean taking action before a situation became a crisis, but at Briarpatch it meant to create a crisis.) These meetings generally took place at a quiet corner of the coffee house or a local bar, where they could implement "direct action" against the "Establishment" by finding ingenuous ways of not paying for their beverages; afterward, they contacted those students who habitually turned out for any demonstration at any time, and then those known to support Lill and Lily. At Stout's suggestion, they began to prepare signs for the demonstrators to carry. He left the content of the placards to the students' vivid imagination. By the time the demonstrators were gathering on the green, the Anarchist Assembly had half a hundred signs reading, SINK BOATER; TWO DOWN, ONE TO GO; POWER TO THE PEOPLE; LOWER TUITION, HIGHER PAY; BOATER, FLOAT AWAY; FEWER EXAMS, HIGHER GRADES. Now to hope for good weather. Rain washed demonstrations away quickly.

Donahue heard the chants begin only as he passed Old Main. The original building had been remodeled many times but none had managed to correct its most basic flaws—heating and wiring. The bedraggled, castle-like structure was state of the art design in 1856, but 1936, the year of the last major renovation, had not been a good year for a fund drive—the architects had consequently eliminated "frills" that later generations came to see as "necessities." Old Main had contained the administration offices until the county donated the court house, and past presidents had been very proud of the Virginia Creeper vines that covered its façade. It was, they said, one of the college's connections to ivy. The ivy was impressive at a distance, but if it was pseudo-ivy, it was at least safe, unlike the ivy in the grove by the Gym—much like the professors whose offices were there, the cynics said, doing little good, but no harm. It made Donahue pause a moment, to reflect on whether it would be better to flee the college or to love it. He decided that, for the moment, he had taken Briarpatch for better or for worse. Whether it would be a lifetime commitment... that depended on Mary. And perhaps on students indicating that he was making a difference in their lives—and so far only a few had spoken up.

The demonstrators' chants always reflected the more popular themes on their signs. This was the way that the more radical students "imposed" their values on the "pseudo-liberated phony protests" of "hegemonic autonomy." Most of the demonstrators did not worry what their signs said—if they couldn't understand themselves, nobody else would do better. In this matter they trusted Jones, because anyone who could use big words had to be smart. Moreover, the point was to make Flo Boater squirm! None suspected that the plot was deeper than even Stout could imagine—he thought it was designed only to entrap Lill and Lily, but he was blindly putting his own neck in the noose. It would also discredit the protestors.

Donahue, realizing that he was too far away to see well, walked over to a slight hillock—created decades ago of the remains of an ancient hall that fell victim to time and fire, covered over by dirt that reluctantly allowed odd tufts of grass to grow on it. Donahue, watching, smacked his lips, then covered his mouth with tented fingers. There was a part of him that wanted to join the protest, another part that wanted to laugh at the "demands," and the dominant part that remembered being on police duty for demonstrations. He frowned at the memory. Although usually demonstrators were polite, well-behaved and even friendly, he remembered better the times that he had to wash his uniform to remove the spittle. He relaxed as the protestors formed into a line that soon doubled back on itself and eventually, as more young people joined, made a continuous column that resembled a loose engine belt— discipline was a good sign. As Donahue watched silently, the historian silently sidled up to him and stared at the chanting marchers; Donahue noticed him, but neither spoke. What should he say, anyway?

Donahue recognized the leaders, and when the historian asked who they were, he told him, "Jones and Smith," and with a deadpan expression suggested that they were history majors. The historian was appalled—he thought he knew all his majors. After all, there weren't that many, and none had hair that long. But, unsure whether Donahue was serious, mistaken or joking, he made no response.

Unexpectedly a group of counter demonstrators appeared from the left—tough-looking kids. The two lines almost collided as the newcomers demanded a share of the sidewalk. There was easily room for one line going right and another left, but not for a third one, then it counter-marching. Donahue spotted Professor Stout trying to persuade the counter-protestors to march in a different area, but his efforts did little more than cause the lines to knot up around him, creating a traffic jam right in front of the small central entrance to the administration building.

The historian observed that he understood now why the signs were so lunatic—that it was Stout's show, not Lill's. Donahue grunted agreement, but he was not going to provide his companion anything quotable to take to Flo Boater. Thinking of that, he wondered if she were watching. He saw no movement in the windows of the president's office.

When the counter demonstrators raised their signs, STICK TO STANLEY, STAN'S OUR MAN, STAN CAN ROW THE BOAT AWAY, it began to look tense. The knot began to throb, moving back and forth as the two sides pushed. Clearly, Stout's numbers should have prevailed easily, with Smith and Jones urging the anarchists to work together, but the more determined toughs were holding their own. As the shouting grew loud enough to drown out the chants, Chief Biggs appeared. He sized up the situation swiftly and swung into action.

His immediate problem was to get the crowd's attention. He could hardly be seen, much less heard, so he climbed onto a bench and shouted for quiet. He didn't have a bull-horn. In fact, although the demonstrations were a predictable affair, he never thought to bring one. He didn't even know if he had one that worked. The last time he had used one had been at a high school football game riot, years ago, and it had been ineffective. The visiting team was never rescheduled, and the bullhorn had since sat quietly in an equipment closet that was so seldom opened that it might as well be locked with the key lost; in fact, that might be the situation. The best Biggs could do now was shout, "Break it up! No violence here today. We want to keep it all peaceful." He was ignored by those who could hear him, and most of the crowd had gotten his message only through body language. A somewhat bulky cop nearing retirement doesn't inspire much respect, especially when he doesn't even have a billy-club.

Professor Stout was trying to lead a chant that would drown the chief out and perhaps drive him off. He was hampered in this by his efforts to push his supporters against the other demonstrators in a way that would encourage them to shove back. The crunch was now so great that Donahue could not press through to join the chief.

At that moment Dean Wooda appeared beside the chief and joined him on the bench. He raised his hands for quiet, smiled broadly and announced in a deep, melodious voice, "My friends. I have a proposal we can all agree on. *Free beer at the Student Center* for Happy Hour!" The marching stopped, those closest having heard him and passed the word. He repeated his message, and as the crowd cheered, he added, "*Free beer* for everyone over twenty-one. At the coffee house." And when a few boos were heard, he laughed, "No checking IDs!" There was wild cheering, and the crowd departed, some more hastily than others, toward the student center. Stout, left alone, slipped off as quietly as he could.

"That was quick thinking," the chief said, "For a moment I really thought I was in trouble."

"One has only to understand the student mind," Stanley Wooda explained.

"And the law's," the chief agreed. "I guess it would not do for me to drift by the coffee house."

The dean smiled, "I'd appreciate it if you were busy elsewhere till six or so."

The chief thought for a moment, "I don't believe you have a liquor license."

"Not that I know of," the dean responded. "But there'll be a real riot if there's no beer at there, or you try to stop it."

Biggs smiled back, "It's probably dereliction of duty, but I suppose I can arrange to go back to the office, to be ready in case I'm called."

"*Great* to do business with you, sir," Stanley Wooda said, shaking his hand. He would have left, but the chief held him for a question: "Since when did the coffee house serve beer? Where'd it come from?" The dean merely smiled at the chief's next comment, "That was really short notice," obtained the release of his hand, and departed.

Donahue came over to the chief, "That was a close-run business!"

Biggs shook his head from side to side, indicating agreement. He then asked, rhetorically, if the dean had kept a stock of beer on ice just for a moment like this. "Or was this a set-up?"

Donahue couldn't think of any other explanation. Their exchanged glances indicated that there was more to this near riot than met the eye. After a sigh, he said, "That young man is going places."

Biggs, shaking his head, agreed, "And he knows it."

As they left Donahue said, "I've got some information you ought to know. Two bits of information, in fact." Seeing a question on the chief's face, he added, "Nothing on Miss Purdy."

"Too bad," the chief responded. After a moment's thought, he asked, "Official information... or background?"

"Let's say background."

Biggs was satisfied with that, "Okay, what does Deep Throat have to say?"

"First, the late Dean Wooda seems to have doctored the books."

"Oh?"

"He appears he was buying museum pieces with college funds, selling them, and pocketing the money."

Biggs stuck his hands in his pockets and shook his head, "Is that dean going to return to life every semester?'"

"Pardon?" Donahue wondered if he had missed something.

"Each time that we're about to put him to rest, he seems to come right back."

"*He's alive again*, you say?" Donahue jested.

"*Dead again*, I bet you wish."

Donahue nodded agreement, "I don't think we'll ever get over him. I don't know how he was manipulating the college funds, but it's pretty clear something was going on."

Biggs asked the logical question, "Was anyone else involved?" That is, could the dean have pulled off an embezzlement without the financial office noticing?

"Probably not. Not over a period of time, at least. But there was constant turnover in that office," Donahue said. When the chief gave him a quizzical look, he suggested, "Some think Flo Boater knew."

This interested Biggs, "Any proof of that?"

"Not yet."

Biggs couldn't do anything with mere conjectures, even from an inside source, especially not against Flo Boater and when the source was anonymous. "Flo worked in the dean's office, and her husband's, but that's not proof."

"Miss Purdy?"

"Going missing is suspicious, but it's not a crime. In fact," he said with a slight smile, "being missing, well, I worry more that the usual suspects doing her in than about her being their accomplice."

"Really?"

"No, of course not. It just seems that bodies turn up wherever Flo Boater is. Here we have a non-body." When Donahue gave him a smile in return, he added, "It's not as though we're dealing with gangsters here."

Donahue remained mute, wondering how much to tell him.

The chief, taking this for agreement, said, "When you have more than suspicions, contact me again."

"And in the meantime?"

"In the meantime, I will stay well out of Flo Boater's way and you should do the same."

"Why? You took her on twice before."

The chief's eyebrows and lips tightened, "And I lost each time. Next time… well, I may not lose my job, but there'd be a state investigation at the least. No, I'm not even going to look into this until there is more to go on."

Donahue protested, "But I can't do this on my own. I've no authority."

"Right enough," Biggs agreed, "But right now I've got to stay on the right side of Dean Wooda or I'll have a student riot on my hands."

"Should I drop it?"

Biggs answered with a question, "Who stands to benefit if you persist and succeed?"

"There's Lill and Lily. They could become acting-president and dean again."

"And everyone would benefit from that."

Donahue nodded, "Of course, and there's Mary, and probably me."

Biggs was a bit surprised at this, "I thought you had it all worked out with Flo Boater?"

"We did, but…."

"But…?"

"Flo Boater is trying to send Mary back to Latin America. And me, too."

Bigg was mystified, "I heard Mary talk about her last trip. She wasn't happy. Why would she go back?"

"To finish her research and write the paper."

"Does she want to go?"

"No."

"How?" Biggs asked, almost stuttering, "How could Flo Boater make her?"

"Tenure."

Biggs understood, "No paper, no tenure."

"That's the idea."

"Why hadn't I heard?"

Donahue shrugged, "We've been busy, Mary's been out of town."

Biggs didn't understand one part, "How do you fit it?"

"Unless I go, she can't." Donahue then explained how the grant program worked, and how Flo Boater had made all the arrangements without asking them. When Biggs asked why they had to go along with the plan, Donahue said, "It appears to be Mary's only chance to keep her job."

"This sounds like it's tied to the first problem. Flo realizes that the only way she can remain president is to get rid of her enemies. That is—you."

Donahue agreed, "You're right, I think. This is just a way to get us off campus."

"Let me frame this differently," Biggs said, "In spite of Flo's underhanded methods, is it a legit offer? Does it advance your careers?"

"Ordinarily, it would be great opportunity... for both of us. For me, especially, to get an exchange position at my age, with my little experience. But so much depends on Flo Boater's good will. One telephone call from her...."

"So, your career is in the hands of Flo Boater."

"No one in his right mind would trust that woman long."

Biggs noticed that they had almost reached the edge of campus. Nice timing. The end of the walk coincided with the end of the conversation "Then I think you've answered your question."

"Your advice, then," Donahue asked without spirit, "is to hang in there?"

"More like, think about it overnight."

"What do you think of my going away? Or should I stay and see if Deep Throat has anything significant?"

Biggs wouldn't commit himself to such an important decision, "Either way, you have my blessing, son."

Donahue persisted, "But not your backing?"

Remaining uncommitted, Biggs said only, "A man's gotta do what a man's gotta do. I want to work until I can retire." After a pause he added, "As for Latin America, I can't help you much on that kind of decision."

The demonstrators had meanwhile hurried to the coffee house, impatiently waiting for WOODA, WOODA, WOODA, who waved his hands appreciatively when he came up, keys in hand. He had obviously ordered the building closed so that the beer kegs could be brought in and set up without having to contend with students who had no interest in the demonstration. It would have been very awkward if the words had spread prematurely that there was free beer on campus!

As soon as students ceased to pat the dean on the shoulder, Flo Boater congratulated him, "You handled that nicely."

Stanley Wooda offered one of his broadest smiles, "Thank you, President Boater."

She led him slightly to one side and said, "Stanley, I think it's time you called me Flo."

Stanley Wooda hesitated, "Yes..."

"It makes us sound more like a team."

Stanley Wooda was more decisive now, "Yes."

"It could sound like even more." Her suggestive tone was unmistakable.

A bit shaken at this, Stanley Wooda could only stammer, "Yes, President Boater."

"It's *Flo*, Stanley. *Flo*," she crooned.

"Yes, Flo."

As Donahue reached the central sidewalk again, Stout accosted him, "That was interesting, wasn't it?"

"Yeah," Donahue said cautiously, "it was."

"Good to see Democracy in action!"

"Is that what it was?"

"Certainly, anybody could see that!" Looking askance at Donahue, he asked, "Have you voted yet?"

Donahue hardly knew what to say, "It isn't election day yet."

"No, but it's important to vote ahead. Absentee ballot. In case something comes up."

"What difference will that make, except on local issues, and it's too early for the *Moderate* to print the candidates' statements?"

Stout dismissed that, "Local issues are unimportant. We have to make sure the national vote turns out right."

"Right? Do you know how I'll vote?" Donahue could not resist a smile.

Stout thought for a moment, "I guess you're right. It's better if conservatives wait till the last minute, just in case something comes up that will change your mind." He then patted Donahue on the arm and began to turn away.

But Donahue hand reached out to stop him, "Do you mean that liberals would never change their minds?"

Stout laughed, "Steady on, old fellow, people with the right principles know which candidates to vote for."

Chapter Thirteen

Donahue had been looking for the choir director for two weeks, but their schedules had not coincided. It was "one thing after another," a phrase that was becoming the unofficial college motto, but at last he heard that rehearsals were being held in the president's office again. Donahue was surprised that this practice had survived Lill's demotion, but when he saw that the room was under serious renovation, he understood. Flo Boater would not be spending her time here. Moreover, it was an excellent space for music lessons. The acoustics in the former courtroom were excellent, especially with much of the furniture covered by large cloth and plastic sheets.

"Why not use the rehearsal room in the Music building?" he asked Miss Efficiency.

"It's being used for a meeting of the Personnel and Promotion Committee," she responded. "A joint meeting with the committee on Finances and Grants. They are discussing the financial crisis and ways to spend the insurance money when it comes in."

"Oh," was all that Donahue could say in return.

Miss Efficiency allowed him to wait just outside the door until the lesson reached a natural break, and as the handful of students in the ensemble hurried out in search of water, he approached the director and said, "Hi, can I have a moment."

The choir director actually recognized him, "Well, hello. I didn't expect to see you again so soon."

"It hasn't been long, has it?"

"Really well done," the director gushed, "the way you solved the last murder."

"You heard of it?" Donahue was surprised.

"Actually, it was my wife who heard," he admitted. "I never have time for news. But I still think it was *great*!"

169

Donahue was surprised to learn that he was married—he had heard he had many female admirers. He couldn't imagine, the college community being small, that he hadn't heard of her; certainly he should have heard of a marriage, if that had happened recently. But to ask would have been a distraction from the purpose of his visit. Therefore, he only replied, "I appreciate your saying so." Still, he could not help wondering how any woman could put up with his working hours; they must be as impossible as his were when he was a cop.

Then the real cause of the jubilation became clear, "Can you imagine? Today I had two candidates for music scholarships say *Yes*," and he took Donahue's hand to pump it enthusiastically, "just because they had *heard* about the scandals!"

"It didn't drive them away?"

"Oh, no. People *love* scandals. I told them that both murders were solved *right in this room!* They were charmed. They asked if we practiced here all the time!"

"In fact, they *were* solved here," Donahue said.

This news was completely lost on the choir director, who was off in his own world, "*Two* scholarships accepted in *one* day! And both have *great* voices!"

"Is that unusual?" Donahue asked.

The director turned deadly serious, "Do you have any idea, any idea of the kind of competition we have for good voices?"

"I guess I don't." Who ever thought about it? Donahue certainly never did.

"The Athletic Director... what's his name?"

"Windy Gale."

The choir director was dismissive, "He has *no* idea what *real* competition is." Turning in a circle and dramatically stopping to face Donahue, he exclaimed, "There are *many* more cornerbacks than there are coronet players, and *more* coronet players than *good* baritones." Then he put his hand on his face and supported that elbow with the other hand, muttering, "Whatever cornerbacks are." Then he brightened and said, "Don't let me get *started* on bassos!"

Donahue had no intention of that, "I'll tell Windy."

The director missed the mildly ironic tone, "Yes, yes, but that *can't* be why *you're* here."

Smiling now, and appreciating this fellow's ability to charm an audience of any size, Donahue said, "You are right. *I'm* here for some help."

"Again," the director teased.

"Yes, of course... again."

The director turned in a circle, made a slight bow, and asked effusively, "How *may* I be of assistance?"

"I believe the Music building has been used for general storage?"

"Oh, my goodness, *yes*. You *can't imagine* what *junk* they have *foisted* upon us."

"I'm interested in Latin American artifacts."

The director was repulsed, "The feathers and *stuff?* The *animal* skins?" Apparently he had seen it.

"Bows and Arrows," Donahue said. A reminder of how Floyd Boater died might jog a memory.

"Oh, yes, though I haven't seen those. They move it in, they move it out."

"Materials for a museum?"

"We never took that excuse *seriously*. At least not the *first* time."

"The first time?" There was a second time?

"We expected they would take over the building for *their museum*."

"Museum?" asked Donahue, puzzled.

"They were talking about, oh, all sorts of things. Exhibit cases, how many they'd need. Useless stuff, what would go where. Had to be for *a museum*."

"You heard the dean talk about those plans?"

"Yes, I'm pretty sure it was the dean. He acted as though I wasn't even *there*."

"Who was he talking with? President Boater?"

"No, somebody I didn't recognize. Maybe the guy who fixes all the buildings. I think he left... No, I'm sure he left. I asked him about getting the rehearsal room back, and he said that it was '*low priority*'.

Can you imagine! *Music* low priority! I was so glad when I heard he quit."

Donahue made a mental note to check the man's name, but erased it when the choir director continued, "I wasn't happy to hear that he was in an automobile accident.... A deer came through his windshield. Killed him instantly." He paused, "I wanted him to leave, but I wouldn't wish that on anybody." After a moment, almost with a sob, he continued, "His successor wouldn't change the ruling, and now we have this *new* guy... Jay, I think... who says he's been told to leave well enough alone. Otherwise, nice enough."

Silent for a few moments, Donahue, wondering if Jay could have actually said that and how it had come about that the rehearsal room was available again, allowed the choir director to compose himself before asking, "You said they were planning a museum?"

"Must have been. They, they were acquiring so many... *things*."

"Things?"

"I don't really know what, didn't care."

"No musical instruments?" Donahue asked.

"No, nothing interesting. I'd have noticed musical instruments!"

"Furniture, clothes?"

"Costumes maybe, but it was all boxed up, and I didn't look." After a pause, he added, "Nobody was allowed to look."

"You said feathers, clothing."

"Oh, I looked a bit, but most of it was taped shut."

Donahue thought for a moment, before asking, "How much material was there?"

"Oh, boxes and boxes. The dean filled several rooms with them, then locked the rooms so that even I couldn't go in." At that he became terribly incensed, "Can you imagine how dangerous that it. What if I'd smelled smoke? I couldn't have gone in to check. By the time the fire department got there, it would be too late. And if it was nothing, I'd be reprimanded for causing an unnecessary panic."

"I can understand."

"Then he closed that whole area off. 'Asbestos danger,' he said." The implication was that the danger was minimal.

Donahue decided not to try to resolve that matter at this moment. He stuck to the subject, "No labels on the boxes?"

"All in Spanish or Portuguese, and I don't know those languages."

"But most choirs sing in Spanish. Surely yours do." If Donahue had attended any concerts, he might have known.

"Oh, I can *pronounce* those languages well enough. For *musical* purposes. But not well enough to read *labels* on boxes."

Donahue, wondering how hard addresses could be to read, asked, "Any big items?

"Mostly small ones, but lots of them. That's when I began to worry."

"Worry, how?"

"Like I said, that they'd take over the Music building as the museum. They were looking over the rooms, talking about displays." He stopped before complaining further, "They didn't even *talk* about the mold!" After a pause, he added, "Or the *asbestos*, whatever that is."

"Who was *they?*" Donahue inquired.

Unobserved, a small thin man crept within a few yards of the pair. He had come in to see President Boater and, Miss Efficiency being on break, had gone right to the door. Stopping just out of sight "to learn if anyone was inside," he heard familiar voices and leaned his head around the door frame to see. Donahue and the director, expecting students to return any moment, paid no attention as he slipped inside the room and took his place behind a painter's partition only scant feet away from them. He smiled as he heard the director say, "Dean Wooda and Flo Boater." He didn't know the context, but he could make one up.

"Where are all those boxes now?" Donahue asked.

"Ah, ha," the historian said, almost saying it aloud. This was better than anything he could have invented.

"They weren't there *long*. Only a year or two."

"Then what happened?"

"A moving van came and carried *everything* away. Or most of it." Obviously, the director lost interest after that. His building was safe. Except for the mold and asbestos.

"A moving van?" Donahue knew he could trace that.

"More like a pick-up, I guess. Or, what do they call that truck now, *a mini-van?*"

Donahue was disappointed, but tried to not show it, "Know where they took it? Did they say anything?"

"Didn't know, didn't *care*. I was just happy to have my building back...or a couple rooms... *temporarily*."

"Temporarily?"

"Within a few months *another* van came. Brought more *junk*."

"To be stored there?" Donahue had not imagined that there had been so many artifacts.

"Yes. But only temporarily. Then it disappeared *too*. At least I think it did."

"Temporarily?"

"Yes. *More* came in."

Donahue was losing track, "Then it went out, too?"

"Yes. But then *another* came in. In and out, in and out, and I'm *never* allowed to look."

"You're sure about the number of deliveries?"

"No, of course not. But it seemed like a lot."

Donahue sighed, then asked, "How long did this last?"

"Till Lill became president."

Donahue was surprised that the choir director remembered Lill's name, but he was learning that this man was full of surprises; he probably surprised himself all the time, and his wife, too. Donahue shook his head at the thought and asked, "In the fall, then, last year. What happened to the last shipment?"

"That last one just sat there. Not moving at all." After a moment he added, "Of course, I'm not allowed to look."

"Interesting, very interesting," Donahue said. Then, shaking hands with the surprised director enthusiastically, he said, "Thank you very much. This has been very, very helpful." There was a time when the other cops joked that he was trying to become Sergeant Friday; that persona was gone.

"Very *glad*, very *pleased* to have helped. Can I tell the prospective students that another murder has been solved right here?"

Donahue smiled, "Well, a mystery has been solved perhaps. But nobody has been killed."

"You sure?" His voice was filled with disappointment.

"Oh, we have a missing person…"

"That's hopeful!" Then, "Oh, I didn't mean that *that* way."

"I didn't take it so. But I don't think we have another murder."

"Too bad, too bad," the director said. Then brightening up, he asked, or should I say, "Yet." Donahue smiled and began to leave, when the director called to him, "Oh, by the way, you haven't heard of anything *strange* happening with the computer?"

Donahue said that he hadn't and asked, "What makes you think there's a computer problem?"

"Nothing really, I guess. But when I wanted to look up some back grades, to see who qualified for the honors society in Music, I found two names I didn't know. I'm *sure* I know everyone who was in the choir, but *these* were new to me."

Donahue asked who the students were. The response was strange, "I didn't recognize them, but the registrar said that they were *Smith and Jones*. That made no sense to me. I didn't have *anyone* in the choir named *Smith and Jones*. Or by those other names."

Promising to look into it, Donahue took his leave. When the students began coming back from their break, the historian slipped out from his hiding place and watched Donahue go toward the stairs, stopping quickly, however, when he saw Jenny run over to Donahue at the landing, he slipped back inside Miss E's office, straining to hear. This proved to be no problem.

Jenny was almost frantic. "DO, There's a fearful fuss in the office."

"The Financial Office?"

"Yes, Miss Purdy is on a tear!"

"She's back?"

"Yes. Right down the hall. Hadn't you heard?"

"Where'd she been?"

"She didn't say. Just showed up and began digging through records."

"What records?"

"She won't tell anybody."

"Not even you?" he asked. "You were doing her job."

"Only sort of! I was a sub. I'd filled in while she was gone, as you know, then she came back and sent me away. Then she called me back to fill in, to help out, then gave us this long list of things to do while she tore into the records. First she tells us to just stay out of her way, then that we've neglected everything, then changes the way we've been doing things. She's just been out of control." She gasped for breath, then continued, "It's really complicated. I call you, she comes back, then… it's just so complicated. I barely managed to slip out for a minute. Gone to the bathroom, I told her. 'There is one just right there,' she said, 'next to the vault,' but I explained that I preferred the one in the corridor. That bought me some time to call you, but I saw you coming out President Boater's office. So I hurried right after you. I was so afraid you'd start down the stairs, because I didn't want to call out your name." She took a breath, then concluded, "Anyway, I have to get back inside in a hurry, but I wanted you to know that something was up."

"Should I go talk with her?"

"No, I don't think she wants to be interrupted. Not right now. You'd better wait."

"Did she see the lists?"

"I don't think so. I hid the file in last year's library expenses. To keep more fingerprints off, just like you suggested."

"What's she doing that so strange? I mean specifically. You look all shook up."

Jenny gave a strong shake of her head. "She has been saying to herself, 'Can't trust anybody. Gotta do it myself.' So I thought I'd better speak to you, or somebody." With a shiver, she concluded, "It's scary in there."

"Any idea what she means?"

"No. She's got files strewn all over the place. It's like she's gone insane. I've never seen anybody so angry. Not even Jay, before he hit the dean, and I really didn't see that."

"That's good," Donahue said. "It's not personal. Go back and help her however you can. Do routine work, so that she can concentrate on whatever she's doing."

"Professor Stout has been nosing about, too. That has made her even more nervous."

Donahue hesitated at this, then he said, "No point in you worrying about anything further. We know she's not happy with something, something in the past, and that probably means the late dean and perhaps Flo Boater. Stout may be a bother, but he's not a problem. You shouldn't be in any danger, but if you get really uncomfortable, find some excuse to go home."

"Headache," Jenny said, then nodded and hurried down the corridor, muttering that Miss Purdy would ask why she had been gone so long. Donahue watched her till she went back into the office, then went down the stairs. He was wondering why the financial officer wouldn't trust anybody, and might even see Jenny as... a spy? Her connection to Jay, perhaps? Of course, if Miss Purdy suspected Boater and Wooda, she couldn't confide in them. But there had to be somebody who was a close friend, someone she could ask about what was going on. She wouldn't have suspected Boater and Wooda unless she had heard about the events of the past year or so. Then he saw Molly.

The historian was following, but too far away to hear anything, so he took up a discreet position where he could observe. He could, at least, report on Donahue's activities, all of which had to be of great interest to Flo Boater.

Molly had been on her way home. It took a few minutes for her to answer his questions, because she wouldn't talk until she knew what the problem was. As it happened, because Molly and Prudence Purdy were about the same age, a while back, during the summer, on one of the weekends she could not visit Sal, Molly had been eager to have some pleasant company for supper and watching TV. The television shows were only mediocre, but Miss Purdy was an excellent cook. They had hit it off.

No, she didn't know why Miss Purdy had been missing; but she hadn't taken it seriously. "I learned quite a bit about Miss Purdy's life, more than Miss Purdy had learned of mine." She made that comment with a smile. Not a wicked one, but it was an ironic comment on the vice president's personality. Prudence Purdy was a trained accountant, with an MBA from a prestigious university. No family. Her parents had died young. When about her present age, in fact. She had formerly worked for a church organization, checking the books of perhaps twenty regional churches and the headquarters. That was all fine, but she had grown very disturbed with the practices of the missionaries abroad. Some of them were making "gifts" to local politicians and policemen that were not in their budgets. "Any way, she had complained and, when it was explained that they had to allow some discretion to the men and women in the field, that without a bribe here and there… she had quit. Right was right, and that was wrong." Unfortunately, she had resigned before having a new job in hand, or even in sight, and when the bills began to pile up, she knew that she either had to take the first job available or go into debt. So when she saw the ad for a financial manager at Briarpatch College, she applied immediately.

"Interesting," Donahue said.

"I never saw a woman so honest," Molly replied. "That's why I never told her about Sal."

Donahue had spoken to Lill several times about the investigation, always discretely. It was one of those situations, well-known only to those who have experienced it, that whatever individuals might be talking about, their enemies believed they were conspiring against them. It was best to avoid meeting publicly… which made their infrequent sightings even more suspicious.

It was on one of these occasions, in the theater, drinking some of Lily's excellent coffee, that Lill asked how his romance with Mary was going.

He hesitated before answering, "Not well."

Lily asked the obvious question, "Why don't you just give up?"

Lill quieted her with a sharp look, then said, "It's none of our business, really, but you're both our friends…." The question was there, but unasked.

He thought a moment. It's like this. During the summer I was at my sisters, reading to one of her girls. A children's book. No, more grade school to middle school. *Wyatt Earp, the OK Corral and the Law of the West.*"

"Great title," Lill observed.

"Yeah," Donahue laughed, "it seemed like the perfect gift for an ex-cop to give." He laughed again, "My sister didn't appreciate it much."

"Anyway…" Lill prompted.

"Ah, anyway… Well, there was a passage about Wyatt abandoning his wife, his common-law wife, for an actress.…"

Lily broke in here, "I don't see where that's getting us to Mary!"

"Oh, it does," he laughed. "His wife was a nice woman. Probably just what he needed—cooked, did laundry, put up with him.…"

"Oh, I see," Lily responded, "the perfect little woman."

Donahue could have made a joke, but all he said was, "Yes, but Wyatt found her dull." At that he fell silent.

It was Lill who finally spoke, "And Mary isn't dull."

"No," Donahue finally said. "She's worth fighting for… even if she's the one I'm fighting with."

Chapter Fourteen

Flo Boater looked at her watch, said to herself, "That idiot should be finished now," and climbed the stairs to her office. The choir was indeed gone, but there was Miss Efficiency pointing inside, mouthing the words, "You've got company."

Ten minutes later Flo Boater shook hands with the historian as he departed, "Thank you very much. I am greatly in your debt." Then, as soon as she wiped her hands, she picked up the telephone, dialed quickly and said tersely, "Stanley, I need you."

Stanley Wooda was there within a minute, "Yes, President Boater, er, Flo."

"I have a job for you," she announced.

"An urgent job?" There was something in her voice.

"Very."

"More urgent than the demonstrators? I have a meeting with them scheduled…" He looked at his watch, "in ten minutes."

"I thought you took care of them."

"Those, yes. This is a new group."

She had no patience for this. "We always have demonstrators here. Tell them something. Make them happy."

Stanley Wooda offered suggestively, "A longer spring break perhaps?"

She snapped back, "Sure, why not?"

"That won't take but a moment, then. How else can I help?"

"DO is onto something."

"Oh," he said. She sounded serious. "What?"

"You know, I imagine," she asked, "that there is a roomful of Latin American artifacts in the Music building."

"Yes?" he ventured cautiously, implying that he needed more direction than that.

"All boxed up."

"Yes," he said, suspiciously. This was news to him.

"I want you to find someplace else to store them. Someplace that no one will think of."

This must be important, but how important? Not wanting to ask that question directly, Stanley Wooda fished for more information, "You want... them.... *hidden*?"

"Yes!" she boomed, "*Well* hidden."

"For how long?"

"A few weeks at least. Until we can arrange to sell them."

"Do you have a place in mind?" he queried. This sounded close to participation in criminal behavior, and it sounded like Donahue was close to exposing it. Not that the dean was above bending the rules, but he preferred to think out the situation and all the possible permutations—he had vowed never do anything without a plan. Yet here he was, with no plan and no clear idea of what he was getting into. Yet, he argued with himself, he couldn't defy her, not in her present mood. Stanley Wooda felt suddenly cold and warm simultaneously. He realized that he was extremely nervous, and for the first time he could remember, anxiety was making him sweat.

"Get Jay Bird to help. He knows where everything on campus is. Everything except this junk. Yes, I said junk. Expensive junk, but junk. I wish we had gotten rid of it long ago. But I didn't know how. More important, Jay would know where nothing is, that is, a place that isn't being used. If there's a hiding place on campus or off, he'll think of it."

"An *excellent* idea," he said, happy to pass off the responsibility to somebody else. Anybody else.

"Give him a key to everything except our offices, or he can't get in."

"He can't get in?"

"I didn't want anyone snooping around, not even Jay. He has keys to everything except the Music building and the offices on this floor." She paused before adding, "Also, this conversation didn't take place! You understand that. It didn't happen." She paused a moment, then added, "Don't tell him what's in the boxes, just say, uh, 'old stuff from the, uh, Athletic department.'"

Stanley nodded cautiously. It took an additional second to ask himself if the campus phone system automatically made a record of all calls, then realized that he didn't know. In a firm voice, he said, "You called me about the spring break. We never discussed anything else."

After a moment's hesitation, she spoke, "I'm glad that we're in agreement on that."

He paused only a moment, then asked, "Do we have a master key? Otherwise, I'll have to tell Miss E to give him the Music building keys and every place else he may want to put that… uh, stuff. Don't we have one master key he can use? That would be better than making her suspicious."

"Of course. The more important a person, the fewer keys they need. But a master key would open our offices, too. M.E. will give *you* the keys you'll need, and you can give them to Jay, and he can drop them in the return box over here—right through the door—when he's finished; and have him turn in all the rest of his keys, too. She won't be suspicious at all."

"All his keys?"

"We'll sort it out later which ones he needs. Now, run along and don't bother me with details again."

As he put down the receiver, he let out a long breath. "What the hell is going on?" He paused for a moment, asking himself, "Why'd she call? She was right across the hall?" Then he sighed, "The less I know, the better." Looking about his office as if something might inspire a better plan, he was barely able to refrain from wringing his wet hands, which he wryly realized would come close to a Peter Lorre imitation. "I'll get right on it." He was very glad that he had not worn a white coat today. He almost had. White went well with his complexion.

Stanley Wooda slipped out of the office, muttering that he'd have to get to the students later. Miss Efficiency had the keys ready, as promised, giving them to him with a wry smile that said, "Don't lose the key ring, we'd have to replace every lock in on campus." As he walked hurriedly by a large mirror in the hall, he ruefully saw himself—bent over slightly, the beginning of a little stomach pouch, and his hair in a bowl cut—and was unhappily aware that he was once more imitating Peter Lorre. He had not finished contemplating the unfairness of nature, transforming handsome people into caricatures of themselves, when he ran right into Jay Bird, who was coming up to collect the trash. It was a very convenient coincidence, which made the dean purr, "Marvelous. You are always Johnny on the spot."

There was something about the performance that the Acting Building and Grounds superintendent found unattractive. But all he could think to say, without getting himself into trouble, was, "My name's Jay, not Johnny."

"No matter. I need you now. Let's go." He took Jay by his sleeve and pulled him along, down the stairs. Jay tried to protest, to explain that there was a shortage of janitorial staff and that unless he emptied the trash, it might be two or three days before the president's office was cleaned, and Flo Boater liked her office spick and span. No, she *demanded* clean. But Stanley Wooda was not to be put off. Saying, "I'll explain later," he led Jay out the door and across the campus to the Music building, taking only a slightly circuitous route to avoid arousing suspicion. There he gave him the keys, told him what to do, and said to do it immediately.

Jay stood there several moments, looking at the keys, glancing at the departing dean, and wondering what to do. With a shrug he entered the building, went to the first of the locked rooms, found the right key after only a few tries, and went in.

Flo Boater was meanwhile giving instructions to Miss Efficiency, "Get DO Donahue over here. On the double." After a moment's pause, she added, "Who's my next appointment. Okay. Send her in the moment she arrives. If DO shows up, have him wait."

She then sat at her desk to look through the mail, most of which she threw away, unread, including a thick sheaf of notes from faculty committees that Miss Efficiency had carefully sorted and annotated. At length Mary C. entered, nervous but not cowed.

Flo Boater stood up, came around the desk and took her by the hands before speaking, sincerely, woman to woman, "Mary, I need to know right away what your decision is. Sorry to rush you, but the university insists on knowing today. Will you take the research offer or not?"

Mary hesitantly freed herself, turned her back on the president and walked to the window. After a moment, she turned and said, "I really need another day to think. I really need the time."

"I can't do that," Flo said, then after watching Mary sink into one of the large chairs, she said, "The problem isn't really you, but Donahue. He won't go without you."

Mary's voice quavered, "I don't want to rush into this."

The president sat down opposite her and looked her full in the face, "If you don't go, I can't promise tenure. Simple as that. And the university wants an answer now for both of you." Mary tried to turn away, but Flo reached over to catch one arm, then said forcefully, "This means both your futures! I don't care whether you get married or not, but both of your careers depend on seizing this opportunity!"

Mary, looking up at the president, was about to cry. "Both our careers?" she sniffed.

"Yes. Do you imagine that we would give Donahue tenure unless he publishes?" It wasn't *DO* any more. Just *Donahue*.

Mary sniffled, "It doesn't seem fair. Hardly anyone else publishes. And he would be teaching down there, not doing research."

Flo Boater was in her element now, totally in charge, "Oh, he would find some way to do some research. He always does." She walked away a few steps, then waved her hand as if speaking to an invisible audience, "Anthropologists can do research in a cantina, drinking cool beers."

Mary answered more rationally than was necessary, "He's a sociologist. Anyway, cold beer doesn't exist there." That was probably not true, since he would be in a big city, but all Mary could think about was the countryside.

Flo Boater wasn't about to be distracted, "Donahue is different. Non-traditional." She then turned back to Mary, ready to apply some flattery. "As are you." Seeing Mary perk up slightly, she moved to rationality, "We are hoping that the financial situation will turn around soon. That will allow us to *tighten up* on faculty standards." She made a dramatic gesture that caused Mary to flinch, continuing, "In the past we couldn't demand much of the faculty because we couldn't *pay* enough to attract the most highly qualified candidates. But now we can see our way to raising *salaries...* "She paused before finishing the thought, "and *standards*.! No more promotions without *good* publications." Seeing Mary's hesitation, she added, "Everything is changing. We're going to divisions rather than departments. That will give us the flexibility to raise standards, and we will need people like you to make it work." She extended both hands to Mary and invited her to stand, then finished her oration, "So, you and DO, whatever your other plans, *have* to seize this opportunity!"

Mary replied only, "I don't know what to say."

Taking her by the shoulders, Flo Boater ventured a guess, "Even if you don't love him..." and when Mary shook her hands off, she continued, "You don't want to hurt him." Not seeing a reaction, she pressed on, "Do you?"

At this Mary came out of her stupor, "No, of course not."

"Then you'll go!"

"I suppose so...."

"Great! Great news. Now go tell DO. And tell him that I've already got the tickets ordered, and paid for."

Hardly listening now, Mary spoke automatically, "Yes, thank you, President Boater." She then accepted Flo's outstretched hand and allowed herself to be escorted out of the office. She had hardly left the secretary's office when Dean Wooda entered quickly.

Flo Boater was proud of herself, "OK, Stanley, I did my part of the job."

"And I mine," he reported. "The artifacts are out of the Music building. Or soon will be."

"Where did..." she started to ask, "No, don't tell me. I want to be able to say I don't know."

Stanley Wooda, wishing he could say the same thing, answered anyway, "They are still on campus, but out of sight. Jay could have moved them farther away with a van, but that would have attracted attention. I'll have them completely gone within twenty-four hours."

"Remember, be careful with them," she advised. "We may want to sell them later."

Stanley Wooda almost made a smart reply before he caught himself, "Wouldn't it be safer just to dispose of them?"

She answered calmly, "Yes, if Donahue were to stay around. But with him gone, we can sell them at our leisure. After all, we've had them a long time, and they *are* worth a lot of money."

"How much?" he inquired. He was always interested in large sums of money.

Putting a finger to her forehead, she said, "Enough to cover our relatively modest concepts of wealth. Even yours."

Stanley Wooda admitted, "That's a lot."

This made her laugh, "Let's just say it would cover our salaries next year."

"Even with the raises you suggested to the trustees?"

She laughed again. "Even with the raises."

Stanley Wooda remained suspicious, "But it all depends on Donahue leaving?"

At this she became more serious. She indicated he should sit for a longer conversation, but he issued a soft but still stern warning before she sat down herself, "You'd better see that he gets on that plane."

Donahue was sitting outside the coffee house. The doors were closed, with a sign indicating the new shorter hours posted prominently, with an apologetic explanation taped to the glass that budgetary cuts had eliminated half the staff hours, etc., etc. At least Donahue had a place to sit. If Jay had not just lost another two janitors, he would undoubtedly have put the outdoor tables and chairs away to prevent vandalism. Already unhappy students had rediscovered spray paint graffiti, something that had almost vanished from campus during the past year.

He greeted Molly and Jenny as they came up. Molly looked at the sign and indicated she would go back to Old Main. At least there she could plug in the coffeemaker (which had survived, well-hidden, despite efforts by the previous Boater administration to forbid use of any appliance that might cause the ancient wiring system to fail). Jenny declined the invitation to accompany her. She wanted to talk with Donahue.

"It's worse than ever," Jenny said after taking a seat. "Miss Purdy has sent us all home."

"All home?"

"She doesn't want anyone in the finance office with her until she's finished. She's even shooed Stout off, but he said that he would be back."

Donahue made her sit. This had the desired calming effect. Once she was composed again, he asked, "Finished with what?"

"She won't say. But she's treating us all, like… criminals."

"You?" Donahue asked, momentarily unbelieving. But then he remembered that Miss Purdy didn't know Jenny as well as he did.

"She called the last vice-president an idiot."

"That's no surprise," Donahue said. "He was."

"What?" Jenny responded.

"It took him months to figure out financial situation, then he kept quiet about it even when Lill was president. When Lill fired him for general incompetence and began the search for a replacement, only then did he tell her there were problems." He stopped to think, "He wouldn't say what, but he told Lill to look very carefully at the candidates—to look at their ethics as well as their competency."

"That was sporting, at least."

"Yes, Lill thought maybe she had made a mistake, that… well… but it was too far along to turn around. Then the coup came. Lill couldn't finish the selection process, but Flo didn't want to start the search over, so she ended up with Lill's top choice." He laughed about this, "Lill left a list of candidates, marking the best ones low."

Reflecting on this, Jenny agreed, "That's right. I remember. Lill said she would be a sharp one." Lill meant the new vice-president.

"Apparently she's onto something. There had been a lot of *unusual* bookkeeping practices—if the faculty suspicions are right."

"Where is all this going to lead?" Jenny asked. "Will she blame me?"

Donahue assured her, "If she had suspected you were involved, you'd never have been allowed to set foot in the office. You told me earlier that she was upset before she disappeared, and she called you back to work when she realized that her secretaries had been let go. No, her suspicions must rest higher up, and earlier."

"Flo Boater?"

"Probably, but maybe back in her husband's administration."

"The dean? The late dean?"

"Who else?"

"What should I do, then?" Comforted, her accent began to come back.

"Right now, stay out of her way," Donahue suggested. "Try to get some sleep."

"Should I tell Jay?"

"I imagine that Jay already knows, but it might help if you would tell him what you've seen."

"OK, then. I'll look for Jay, then go home and get some sleep. My nerves are frazzled. I can barely stand. This has been the longest day of my life."

"Sleep will help."

"I don't know if I can fall asleep, I'm so worried."

"You stand a better chance of sleeping than Flo Boater," he said with a smile, "if she ever hears of this."

Flo Boater, however, was relaxing at home. A glass of wine and a satisfying memory of how cleverly she had gotten the choir director out of the Music building. How nice, too, to leave work whenever she felt like it. Miss Efficiency could take care of any problem that arose. And Miss Purdy was back. The chief's suspicions of foul play could be laid to rest. All was good in the world. At least in that central part where Briarpatch College stood. Maybe she'd have two glasses of wine. Maybe three, if Stanley were here… Ah well, something has to be saved for tomorrow.

Chapter Fifteen

It was late in the afternoon. Donahue was sitting outside the coffee house, supposedly reading mail, but actually watching for Lill and Lily. It was warmer than he liked, but bearable; Cloudy and a brisk breeze—that's what the weather forecast promised—wrong, as usual. When he saw them coming, he jumped up and asked why they had left a message for him to meet them here, a message with no indication of why they had called.

"We want to know what's going on," Lill said, without waiting to sit.

Lily was right behind her, "Jay brought a lot of junk into the theater a little while ago."

"All he told us was to 'store it,'" Lill said, not happy about being kept in the dark.

"'Label it as props,' he said, 'and stick in a corner.'" Lily then sat down and smiled slyly, "We did as ordered, but we needed a lot of corners. There were quite a few boxes."

"Did you?" Donahue asked, then explained, "Hide them, I mean." He had no doubt that they had done as instructed, but he was too excited to just nod sagely.

"Of course," she answered, again with a smile. "Whatever Dean Wooda orders and our new chair*man* instructs. We always comply." The implication was that she was willing to pretend that Jay would not have asked anything that the administration had not ordered, and if there was a misunderstanding…. Well, that was the way things worked out sometimes. There was also a strong hint that the chair's masculinity was in doubt. Not that he was gay. That would not have bothered Lill. Just that he wasn't quite, you know, a *man.*

Donahue was suspicious, but he understood what she insinuated, "The *Creep* is involved? *He's* your new chair?" This was not a good turn of events.

189

"I don't think he knows what it is all about," Lill answered, "but he *is* eager to please the dean."

"How long has he been chair?"

"Hardly any time," she answered, "but it seems like weeks. He wants to change everything."

"Why haven't I heard?"

"DO, we've been busy, and, face it, people are afraid to talk with you."

Donahue stopped to think, "You've always complained about the job. What difference will it make?"

Lily jumped in, "He want to change the play. Now! After we've paid for the script and costumes, and we've assigned the players their parts."

"And you went along?" Donahue asked.

"What choice do we have?"

"Also in hiding the stuff Jay brought?"

"Well, no. He just showed up as Jay was unloading," Lill explained. "We hadn't heard him coming, or seen him. He was just suddenly there."

Lily agreed, "We always go along with Jay's requests."

Lill was emphatic, "He always knows what he's doing…"

"…even if we can't figure it out."

"And the Creep knew about this?" Donahue wanted to make sure he understood.

Lill saw what he was driving at, "Now that you mention it, I don't think he did."

"No. You are right," Lily said. "When Jay left, the historian said… What did he say, Lill, do you remember?"

"He said that we'd better learn to do whatever the dean wants, because he'd see to it. I think I just assumed that the Creep knew about it. Then he left, too, looking pretty proud of himself."

Lily agreed, that the Creep had no idea the materials were coming into the theater. "When he saw the situation, he put two and two together."

After a moment's reflection, Donahue asked, "Did you look at the boxes? Look into any?"

"Not really, most of it was all packed up," Lill said. But Lily had investigated the packages more closely, "Some looked like it came from a used clothing store."

"Yes?" Donahue asked.

"There was some interesting stuff there," Lill conceded, admitting that she had looked at the packages that Lily had partially opened.

Lily added, "You'd think you were in..."

"....a mall specialty store. The kind that sell 'exotic' clothing." Lill was less expert in this than Lily, who quickly corrected her, "Good costumes for a Latin American play."

This sparked Donahue's interest, "It's probably the museum artifacts."

"Really?" Lill said. "I thought that..."

"...Dean Wooda had sold it all."

Donahue explained that the dean was dead before he could dispose of the last shipment or shipments. Thus, although many valuable items were gone, there still could be sufficient materials to make some fine displays. "Anyway, he hadn't expected to die, and his plans seemed to be working flawlessly. With so many records destroyed, who knows what he still had?"

Lill was thinking rapidly now, but she spoke slowly, "Yeah, makes sense."

"Yes," Lily ventured, then turned to her friend, "Lill, you cancelled the last orders. I remember that. That suggests he was still buying and selling."

"I'd forgotten about it..."

"...but once we talked about it, the old memory began to work again."

Lill nodded agreement, "It didn't make sense for the college to buy such things in the middle of a financial crisis. We already had a collection, somewhere, I thought, but I didn't see the point in adding to it when we didn't have any place to display it."

"He was selling the collection," Donahue said, "probably to cover personal expenses."

Lill was perplexed, "I had no idea. I'd forgotten about it, but early on we got an invoice for a number of items, so I asked the business manager, that is, the vice president for financial affairs, Miss Purdy's predecessor, to find out…."

Lily interrupted, "The title's bigger than the person, usually, so we used to call that officer the VP for FA. But that was earlier. I was thinking of renaming the office…."

Lill threw her a dirty look, then finished her sentence "…when the order had been placed."

Lily interrupted again, "In Miss Purdy's case, I think the title was smaller than she was."

Lill persevered, refraining from noting that Lily was larger than the VP for FA, "The business manager had no record of any purchase, so he called the import company, but said that whoever was on the other end hung up. I tried to call myself, but got no answer, so I told him to return the invoice with a note canceling the purchase."

"Oh, I wish you'd kept it," Donahue said.

"Yeah, I was still new," Lill admitted, "and he said it was just a crank letter."

"Did he keep a copy of the letter?"

"For a few weeks, yeah, then he cleaned out his office. He had a 'pending business' tray where he kept letters that didn't need to be filed permanently. He might have sent that over to Flo Boater, in that period of transition."

Lily broke in, "You remember how chaotic everything was at that time."

Lill gave her friend another sharp glance, then continuing, "I remember hearing that Miss Purdy was unhappy that there were so many gaps in the correspondence."

"Yeah," Lily said, "and she was told not to talk with you about it."

"No computer record?" Donahue asked.

"DO, do you remember where you're working? This is 1996, and Miss Purdy has inherited a program years behind the times. It had been set up by the dean before we had any computers."

"Oh, if he were only here!" Donahue burst out.

"Yes, I'd be ready to strangle him, too," Lill agreed.

This prompted Lily to explain unnecessarily that the dean was already dead, that they couldn't kill him again.

Lill was still disturbed. What kind of personal expenses could Dean C. Wooda have had? Expenses so high that he had to divert money from the college archeological collection to his private account? How could he keep the scam from coming to light? And why were the artifacts suddenly appearing in their building?

"Flo Boater is hiding evidence," Donahue concluded. "They are here only temporarily, till *she* can decide what to do with them!" He paused briefly, "At least, that's my guess."

Then Lill understood, "She was involved! Had to have been."

"Someone must have heard I was asking about the artifacts. Perhaps the choir director mentioned it to someone, and it got back to Flo," Donahue said, but he warned that her interest in the artifacts doesn't prove that she had agreed to selling them."

"No," Lill said decisively, "but if she's trying to hide the stuff, she *was* involved somehow."

"They were lovers," Lily interjected. "*cherche la femme.*"

Lill ignored this, "But why did she wait until now to get rid of it?"

The answer was simple, Donahue said, "With all the demonstrations, she didn't want a scandal. Maybe someone phoned her about it."

At that Lill asked, "Someone phoned?"

"Too complicated to explain now. But what if her enemies—you— had gotten wind of it? It was safest just to hide it. There was a lot of stuff to move, which suggests that, well, even now there's some left. More than Jay could move at one time. There must have been quite a collection at one time."

Lily agreed, "It seemed safer for her to just lie low."

This did not satisfy Lill, she wanted to know why Flo Boater had changed her mind now. "Why not just put them into proper storage? Who would look? Even if they were labeled as museum items, no one would bother to inventory them. Not without her permission. And she could sell them off piecemeal without anyone knowing." Looking around at the others, she concluded with a crucial question, "Does she need money, too?"

Listening to her carefully and nodding, Donahue thought a moment before answering, "It's a small town. People might ask." He thought a moment, "She's probably in a hurry now, before Miss Purdy starts looking into it. It might be that it's not the stuff we know about that worry her, but another scandal coming out, maybe one even she isn't aware of. Even if she knew about the dean's activities in general, it would be in character for him not to tell her the details. As long as the people on the other end of this process still think the business has only hit a snag, there's a scandal waiting to break."

Lily saw what Donahue was trying to say, "Are you suggesting that Woody had contacts for a regular supply of artifacts, perhaps illegal artifacts? And purchasers, too?"

"Absolutely," Lill agreed. "Also, it stands to reason that the supplier would not have been happy with my refusal to pay. He may have contacted Flo directly, maybe right at that time, then just waited till Lily and I were out. There could be blackmail involved, or strong-arm tactics. She can't stop the demands from coming."

Donahue asked, "Or maybe the supplier only contacted her quite recently?"

"Could be." Lill stopped to think. "Probably. That makes more sense than believing she just left them in the Music building to be discovered by accident."

"How did she know where they were?" he asked.

"Oh," Lill responded, "If any of us had known for sure that the collection existed, we could have reduced the list of possible hiding places down to a few, then checked on them."

"If we had the keys."

"Yes," Lill said, "she had the keys. And now she's got to decide what to do with them, and with the supplier?"

"Why doesn't she just pay?" Lily asked, "and have them delivered somewhere else?"

"Well, my guess is that Miss Purdy is on the lookout now for something like that. She wouldn't write a check for anything suspicious, and she'd catch it if Flo wrote a check."

"Why not just pay privately?"

"My guess," Donahue ventured, "is that she doesn't have the money. Or she'd have to pay import duties and taxes on them. The college doesn't have to pay for buying and selling such items, at least the state tax. That's in our charter. It also shields her from charges of dealing in illegal artifacts. Not completely, but somewhat."

"Why doesn't she stop?" Lily asked. "Just return the stuff she's already got?"

"Probably just greedy. If there's a profit, why not make it herself?" Lill suggested. "Or the seller doesn't want the stuff back, just the money."

"I bet," Donahue said, after a short pause, "that the dean was in debt."

"To whom?" Lill asked. "And what difference does that make?"

"He was probably just churning money, holding off payments to one creditor until he could sell something. He may have ordered more items just to put off paying for what had already been delivered, or he may not have been fully paid for whatever he had sold."

"Do you think so?"

"Happens all the time. Guys get into hock with loan sharks."

"Loan sharks?"

"Who else would make a loan to buy illegal imports?"

Lill thought for a moment before repeating, "Why didn't Flo just stop it."

Lily jumped in, "I bet they were gangsters putting muscle on her!"

It was Donahue's turn to think. "I doubt she was afraid. They might have approached her, but probably more like a business proposition. Otherwise, they wouldn't have waited this long. Like you said earlier—real gangsters would have been collecting already."

"So she saw it as a way to generate some money?" Lily asked. Seeing Donahue's left eyebrow rise, she followed up with, "And why were they still on campus?"

Donahue laughed, "The simplest explanation is probably the best. Flo knew how to buy them, but she may not have known how to sell them."

"Ah," Lill said. "The sellers contacted her, but not the buyers."

"Actually, that's how this came to my attention—a seller contacted me, wanting to know when we would pay him; that's why I think they might have phoned her earlier. This time they had wanted Miss Purdy, but she wasn't around."

Lily summed up her thoughts, "Hmm...."

They stood quietly for a moment, lost in thought.

Lill at last rubbed her face in frustration, "What does Flo do with this stuff, if she can't sell it?" She continued on to answer her own question, "She can keep it indefinitely if nobody knows enough about them to ask questions. But there are two people on campus who know enough about South America and native artifacts to do exactly that—to ask questions."

Donahue thought a moment before asking, "Maybe that's why she wants Mary and me out of the country?"

Lill was uncertain, "You are sure she asked Jay to hide it?"

"Wooda did," Donahue said, "and Wooda does nothing without her approval."

Still puzzled, Lily asked, "Why in the theater?"

He was not sure, but it might have been the only place they could think of, at least the only place where they could expect cooperation from the new chair. Every other building was crowded, even the top floor of the science building now that the enrollment had increased.

This made sense to Lily, "Sure, the Creep would do anything." But, if that was Flo Boater's reasoning, she would have been better advised to check the situation with her own eyes than to rely on the historian's own self-serving assurances that he had everything in hand.

Donahue swept this reasoning under the rug, "Too busy right now, more importantly, she trusts Jay."

"Why?" Lill asked. Jay was an old friend.

Lily hit her palm with her hand, "Jay's playing both sides. Isn't that it?"

Lill disagreed, "Jay's a straight-shooter."

"I don't know now," Lily retorted.

Donahue almost stepped in between them. "In a sense, you may both be right. Flo *thinks* Jay's on *her* side."

Lill agreed, "But *we* know he's not."

Concerned, Lily asked, "What if she finds out?"

Clearing his throat, Donahue observed dryly, "She's killed before."

"Or at least tried to," Lill agreed.

Lily didn't understand, "You're saying Dean Wooda's death was an accident?"

Lill sighed before trying to explain, "You don't kill your lovers."

But Lily had none of that, "Happens all the time."

"When you *really* want to kill them," Lill joked, "but that doesn't fit here." She looked Lily right in the eye, "Flo's husband died of fright, and the death of her lover was less than a well-planned affair."

"I guess that if you *really* kill them," Lily laughed, "you *enjoy* it! At least at the moment."

Even Donahue was forced to smile, but his opinion of Flo Boater could hardly have been more dour, "Her affair with the dean may have been cold-blooded anyway."

"You're probably right," Lill agreed, "but the heart is hard to figure. I think there was a time when she was in love with him."

"She had *meant* to kill her husband, at least," Lily objected. "If she took up with Woody, it was because she was disgusted with Floater."

"That was intended to make her lover president," Lill objected, as if that was a justification.

"No, Lill, your reasoning is off," Donahue commented, "She did that so he would make *her* dean." He paused for a moment, "And it may have started off as a mid-life crisis."

Lill persisted, "Motivation. That was always the weak part of the case. The district attorney couldn't demonstrate reasons the jury would buy."

Lily intervened, "How could she guarantee that *C.* Wooda would name *her* dean? *See?* The Creep wanted the job, too."

They mused about this for a moment. Then Lily half-snapped her fingers, "She had the proof that Wooda had been embezzling funds."

"Selling the artifacts!" Lill exclaimed. "That had to be it."

"No," Donahue said. "They were in on the murder plot together, too. The whole insurance scheme. He had to do what she wanted."

"Exactly right on both points," Lill said. "He had to make her dean. No choice in the matter."

Lily's mind raced ahead, "Once she was dean she could get rid of him. Use the artifacts as a threat to get him to resign, or to move on to another job. All quiet and respectable.... But only after a suitable period, after she had proved she was up to the job of being dean."

Nodding in agreement, Lill said, "And then, on his recommendation, she could become president herself."

"And now she *is* president," Donahue summarized. "It's plausible. Not much evidence to back it up, but it's plausible."

Lill's eyes narrowed as she saw a possible explanation, "Now she has to get *rid* of the *evidence*."

Lily suspected the worst, "And *anyone* who *suspects*."

"Or just hide it better," Donahue suggested.

Suddenly amused, Lily joked, "DO, don't eat any of her cookies."

Donahue caught the moment, "I'd worry more if I were the young Dean Wooda."

"He's a slick one all right," Lill said. "He'll do anything to get ahead. And the Creep is just waiting for him to fail to live up to Flo's expectations. Maybe Stout, too."

Lily knew what Flo Boater was capable of, but she was less sure of her partner, "Is Wooda up to murder?"

"I hope we don't find out," Donahue said.

"Should we tell Chief Biggs?" Lill asked.

Donahue hesitated, "We really don't have much to go on yet. Suppositions and guesses. Not enough for him to get a search warrant." Then he hugged them and started to leave, but after two or three steps he hesitated and turned back, "Do either of you have a camera?"

"Of course," Lily said. "An instant camera. We take lots of pictures at each stage of a production."

Lill explained, "That's so we can show actors what they look like. Otherwise, they just don't believe they look like they do. Also, at the end of the run we can discuss what worked and what didn't."

"Can you take pictures of the boxes? As many as you can. And if you find any papers, make copies of them. Put the originals back in place. Very carefully, so we can identify the contexts later on. But get me the copies and photos as quickly as you can."

When they promised to act immediately, Donahue thanked them and started to leave.

"Oh, DO," Lill asked. "Where was Miss Purdy those weeks?"

"She won't say. She just says, 'I'll tell you later. I'm busy now.'"

As Donahue disappeared out the door, Lill and Lily looked at one another questioningly. Then as they stood up to go, Lill observed, "DO is one sharp man."

Lily added seductively, "And nice looking, too."

They had not gotten two steps before Mary came sailing through the doors.

Lill whispered, "Here comes your competition."

Lily ruefully retorted, "Against her, nobody is competition." Then they both said, "Hello, Mary."

Mary managed to say "Hi…" then hesitated, before asking, "Have you seen DO?"

Lill pointed out the other door, "He just left."

Mary started to hurry that way, but Lily quickly grabbed her by the arm and asked, "What's the problem, honey?" When Lily had a hold on you, you don't go anywhere.

Mary slowly freed herself from the gentle but firm grip, "I've got to talk with him. We are supposed to go to Latin America... together… right away."

"What's the problem, then?" Lily asked, "Sounds pretty good to me."

"I thought that was way in the future," Lill interjected.

"I did, too, but now Flo Boater says we have to leave right away. For a year!" Mary said, almost sobbing. "That's a condition of employment!"

"She said that?"

"In so many words, yes."

"What do you mean?"

"We will both have to publish to get tenure," Mary explained, "and Flo Boater has arranged for us to go to Latin America to do the research. At least, I'll do research and DO will teach."

Lill looked at Lily and said, "This is the way she is getting rid of DO!"

Mary agreed, "We either leave immediately or lose our jobs."

After a moment's reflection, Lill exclaimed, "There's no danger, then!"

Mary didn't understand, "What do you mean?"

But Lill didn't explain, and Lily, who grasped what Lill probably meant, said only, "We'll explain later."

Lill excused them, saying as she left, "You find DO, tell him what Flo said and have him get in contact with us right away."

Flo Boater called her dean as soon as she heard of the new activity in the finance office, "Stanley, when did fatso come back?"

"Miss Purdy, you mean? Well, I don't know really. This morning, I guess."

"Her office is right down the hall. Don't you ever check?"

He thought for a moment, that she could have gone down the hall, too, but all he said was, "Not every day." As the silence on the end of the line grew longer, he asked, "Do you know where she was?"

"No idea, Stanley, no idea."

"But you told us not to worry."

"That was public relations, Stanley. Think about it. It could have been a state-wide scandal, and chances were that it was nothing. As it was. But I have no idea where she was."

Chapter Sixteen

It was four in the morning when the light went on in the president's office. Flo Boater was distraught. She looked for a place to put her coat, distressed that painters' coverings were everywhere and she could not find a place without drops of semi-dry paint. At last, she just threw it on top of what had the vague shape of a file cabinet and hoped that the smell of paint did not mean that she had just made a mistake.

Flo Boater uncovered her desk and chair, found the telephone, lifted the receiver and dialed. Impatiently, she drummed her fingers on the desk. After what seemed like an eternity, she began speaking, "Chief Biggs. I need you to come over *right away*." There was a pause, then, "The Vice-President for Financial Affairs. She's *dead...*, at least I think so. *Yes*, I suspect murder... No, *I don't know* who did it. *Yes*, in her office. No, the building is open, or will be. I'll block the side door open. You can come right in. No. Nothing's been disturbed." She put her finger on the receiver, clicked it until she got a dial tone again, then dialed, "Mr. Bird, are you awake? I'm at my office. Yes, this is President Boater. I need you here. Yes, right away. OK, I'll see that the side door is open." She repeated the process, "Stanley, Can you come to my office right away? Yes, *now*. No, I can't talk about it on the phone." Perturbed at the answer, she continued, "*I don't care* who you have with you. *Come now*! OK. Fifteen minutes."

After returning from having placed a trashcan to keep the side door open downstairs—"Damn, left my keys upstairs!"—she paced back and forth, rubbing her hands together, trying to collect her thoughts, and had just wandered out to her secretary's office when she heard footsteps in the hall. Someone going down the stairs, then another coming straight to her door. She saw Stanley enter and, without further thought, said, "Thank *goodness*, you're here!" Then she asked how he had gotten there so quickly.

"I was in my office," he said, "I've been sleeping there. All I had to do was get dressed."

"What?" She was dumbfounded.

"To get my work done. Remember, I fired the secretaries. All except yours."

"You were right across the hall?"

"Yes."

"But I phoned your apartment."

"All calls are forwarded automatically. It's actually more private here. No landlady, no night watchman."

Flo Boater wasn't happy about that, the vision of him with a young woman. (She hoped it was a woman, but nowadays, who could know?). Too distracted to think about that now, she waved it off and led him into her office, "Good idea, good idea," she mumbled, "but not important now. Do you know what has happened?"

"No. Is there a crisis?"

She almost screamed, "The VP for FA is *dead!*" Many administrators talk in initials, and the more important they imagine themselves, the more initials they use. Flo Boater considered herself very important or, at least, on the way to becoming very important.

Stanley Wooda collapsed into a chair. "The VP for FA. No! We just finished one search! Now we'll have to start all over again." Throwing off the painters' covers, he leaned back in one of the new comfortable VIP chairs in what his boss called the PC (Power Circle) in the ES (executive suite), then spun it slowly. "Who can do her job?"

"That's *not* the point, Stanley! She's *dead* and Chief Biggs could think *we* did it."

"*What*! I might be involved?" That thought woke him up.

"You *do* have an alibi for tonight, don't you?"

Stanley Wooda decided to lie, "No... I was working late. In my office. I told you that I'm sleeping there now. When I got tired, I just laid down and dozed off."

She twisted her mouth in disgust. "And whose footsteps just went down the stairs."

"Oh, her. Okay, I have an alibi for the last ten minutes. We had barely... uh, when you called. I was asleep before then."

"And how did she get in?"

"She phoned."

"That's an alibi?"

"I'm sure the phone company has a record of every phone call ever made nowadays. But I'd rather not involve…." He stood up, somewhat uncertainly, but he staggered back down into the depths of the power chair when she rushed over toward him.

Angrily, Flo Boater lit into him, "So, you were *sleeping* in the very building where the *murder* occurred! Right down the hall! And nobody saw you?" He started to mention the visitor, but she cut him off, "You didn't speak to anybody before that?"

Stanley Wooda was a bit confused by it all, "I don't even know when I fell asleep. I certainly didn't know the VP for FA had been killed."

Unbelieving, she persisted, "You didn't hear anything? There was only a restroom between your office and hers! Miss Purdy must have made some noise!"

"I was dead until you phoned," he said, wishing immediately that he had made a better choice of words. "I heard something slam, I guess, a while ago, but there are lots of strange noises in this old building." He managed to get onto his feet, but almost instantly wished that he had not, as he had to backpedal to keep her from smashing into him.

Exasperated that he managed to get a chair between them, she turned and yelled at no one in particular, "Another dead dean!" Then she turned to the high wall of the former courtroom to moan, "Oh, God!" She then proceeded to excoriate every male of her acquaintance over the past two decades for their shortcomings—mental, moral and physical. She was a Medea without children to sacrifice, except Stanley Wooda, who just might have to do.

Stanley Wooda tried to make sense of her statements, "How was Miss Purdy murdered?"

This brought her suddenly out of her tirade. She started to shout at him again, then stuttered and stopped, "I don't know. Just lots of blood there. And it looked like a body had been dragged out."

"Who discovered it?"

"I did."

"You?" He approached close enough to grab her by the wrists. This was not an easy operation, because she was a powerful woman and powerfully excited. But the dynamics of the "conversation" had changed. He was now in control, and she made no effort to bring out of his grip.

She explained, "I was going to get some financial records..."

He ignored her smile, asking instead, "The museum files?" It was not a question.

"Exactly," she replied, serious again. "And there was the blood, on the floor, with papers scattered all over the place."

"The museum files."

"I suppose so. What else?"

"So what did you do?" Seeing that she was calm now, he let her wrists go.

"The logical thing," she said, turning toward a chair and trying to decide whether to sit or not. "I picked up the papers, put them in the folder, found some records from last semester in a file drawer and dumped them out, then put the files in that drawer."

Stanley Wooda admired her style, "Cool head. Good planning." We certainly wouldn't want anyone's attention drawn to those files, if that's what they were.

"Then I came in here and called the police. The station, I don't know who it was, not Chief Biggs, said he'd send someone immediately. I think he's arriving now." Indeed, there was the sound of a car coming up the sidewalk, then the sound of its door slamming, followed by the central door on the first floor rattling.

Stanley Wooda asked, "Gotta be the cops. Shouldn't we go open the door?"

Flo Boater stopped him, "We need to talk first. He'll find the side door open."

He had only one question, "I know *I* didn't do it? You didn't either? For sure?"

She was angry at the suggestion, "Stanley. Only *fools* use brute force!"

"But you thought *I* might have killed her!" He was more upset at being considered a potential fool than a possible murderer. After all, he had recruited his bully boys for the demonstrations; that should prove that he was a man who was ready to act when others just stood around and talked.

She beat a quick retreat from that suggestion, "No, of course not, not deliberately, at least." She turned involuntarily when she heard more pounding on the door, but she stopped him from going down to open up. "Stanley, I didn't mean it that way."

That was hardly better. He tried to push past, saying, "I didn't do it accidentally, either! I don't do anything *accidentally*." But as she held him, pleading with her eyes, he relented. Then he asked, "What were *you* doing in her office in the middle of the night."

She released him and turned half away. "Stanley, listen. I couldn't sleep knowing that those records might be in the financial office," then turning toward him, explained, "and the historian had called to say that Miss Purdy was upset about something. I put two and two together."

"You knew where they were?"

"Not until today. The Creep told me. I thought she might find them tomorrow."

He seized her hands again, afraid that she was becoming too excited. "I could have *found* those files and *destroyed* them, if you'd told me to, and what to get. I had a key and could have gone in when nobody was in the office."

"You should have figured it out. Didn't you hear that she was going through old records?"

"Not really. I thought she was just taking care of the backlog."

Her nod indicated that she had thought of that, but, "It had to be more than that. She even sent her staff home. So I didn't think we could wait. I stayed in my office until I thought everyone had left, then slipped over, started to unlock the door... but found it slightly open. I went in, saw...blood. My first thought was that you had gone in yourself, gotten caught, and hit her in an effort to escape."

They then heard the sound of pounding on the side door.

Stanley Wooda ignored the noise, "You thought I would panic?"

She freed her hands, turned away and said, "I'm sorry, Stanley. I know you better than that."

Stanley Wooda stood, shaking his head. He ignored the sounds of more pounding, now even louder. Lifting his head slightly, he said, "I *am* a smoother operator than that." He started toward the secretary's office to go downstairs, but turned once more to explain, "I'd have told her that I had wanted to talk with her. How attractive she was, and how attracted I was. That sort of thing."

"Stanley, she's gay!"

This didn't bother him at all, "Even Lesbians enjoy flattery. Besides, she might be bi-sexual." What he didn't say was that, if Miss Purdy was lesbian, Flo Boater might just be able to pull off the sweet talk better than he. Nor did he say that his boss probably didn't know a lesbian from a thespian. But, thinking of Lill and Lilly, he smiled to himself— "Maybe they are the same thing."

Flo Boater was now so engaged in this conversation that she almost didn't hear the renewed pounding. He broke in to ask, "Shouldn't we open the door?"

"Stanley, I blocked it open. Whoever you were with probably just ran out and let the door lock automatically. It's more important now to get our stories straight." Right then she heard the sound of glass shattering. "So, we say that we were both working late, that you fell asleep and I heard some noise. Okay."

He agreed, "Sound good. But why was Miss Purdy working late? Maybe she was meeting some coed?"

She took a breath. Yes, the remark was a distraction, and a stupid one, but now she was calmer. After all, there wasn't even a body. There wasn't anything to do except wait for the police. After taking another breath, she turned to him, "Stanley, don't even think that. Miss Purdy probably didn't even *know* she was lesbian, *if* she really was. She was practically a nun! And besides, never complicate a story." After a moment she added, "And just what makes you think you could seduce her?"

Her relaxing caused him to relax, too. He smirked, "That just makes the challenge more interesting! Men like me like challenges."

"So, you'd have talked your way into her confidence?"

"It's never failed yet." Religious types, as he summed up Prudence Purdy, were just challenges. But once they took the bait, they were hooked for good. Reflecting on past successes, he allowed himself a confident smile.

There was a sound of footsteps on the stairs. Dean Wooda went to the secretary's door and opened it to prevent damage to yet another of the building's locks.

Flo Boater followed him out, and, looking over his shoulder, recognized her Superintendent of Buildings and Grounds. Hurrying into the hall, she gasped, "Jay, thank goodness, you're here. I didn't expect you so quickly. But that's all the better."

Stanley Wooda was baffled, "You called Jay?" He preferred to keep conspiracies small. Turning to Jay, he asked, "Why didn't you use a key?"

Flo Boater answered the question, "I decided that too many people had access to the building, so I called all the keys in."

"But I gave him a ring full of keys. Yesterday. At your instructions."

Jay looked from one to the other, "I dropped them in the box at your office, like you said. And my other keys, too. So I didn't have them no more."

She pushed Stanley back into the office, "He didn't have a key to this building."

Stanley was too busy thinking to process that thought, "I thought you blocked the door open."

"I did, your …"

Stanley Wooda didn't let her finish the sentence, "Where are the police? I thought I heard them."

"The officer?" Jay asked.

"Yes, the policeman."

"He's still at the main door. I don't think he heard the glass break."

Flo Boater exclaimed, "He must've heard you beating on the door! He'll be here in a minute."

Jay looked at her suspiciously, "I reckon he thought I was 'nother cop, or he'd have come tried the side door." Surely she could have figured that out herself, or there'd have been a policeman upstairs by now.

The president threw up her hands and said, "Okay, that gives us a few minutes. Jay, it's an emergency. Those museum materials. You've got to get rid of them immediately. Where are they?"

Stanley Wooda intervened here, "They're in the Theater building."

"Right where Lill and Lily could find them! You've got to move them, move them right now!"

When Jay looked at her quizzically and asked where to, she made her wishes clear, "I don't care where or how. I don't want to know. But get them out of the Theater before classes start tomorrow."

"Yes, ma'am!" Jay said, and, after asking how he could get into "the place I hid them," he waited for her to retrieve the keys from the drop box, then left hurriedly.

The dean was totally confused. His first question was, naturally, the one that concerned him most, "Can you trust him?" He would ask later what was going on and whether they could get away with it or not.

"He didn't ask any questions," she responded, as if that was a sufficient clarification. Then, seeing that her dean had not yet grasped what she meant, she looked around, wondering if someone might heard her in the empty building, then led him into her office, shut the door, and explained, "He was arrested the last time a dean was hit over the head. He'll understand how quickly people jump to conclusions... the wrong conclusions."

"If you say so, but I'd..."

Flo Boater interrupted him, telling him to find the coffee pot.

He did that quickly, but shrugged, "It's off. It's been off for hours."

Ignoring his comment, she muttered, "Coffee, I've got to have some coffee." When her dean merely shrugged, she started to make a pot herself, but succeeded only in spilling the grounds on the oak floor, then knocking over the water when she bent down. "Just my damn luck. Canvas everywhere and I hit the only bare spot around. I hope it doesn't stain."

Stanley Wooda went into the secretary's room. There, in the small refrigerator hidden behind some potted plants, he found a container of cold coffee. "She isn't named Miss Efficiency for no reason," he said aloud while pouring a cup. As he put the cup in the microwave, he asked, "Hot, I assume."

"Hot, cold," she said, having uncovered a chair and collapsed into it. "As long as it's coffee."

Stanley Wooda took a preliminary taste, made a wry face and suggested, "Cream will help."

But she only muttered, "Black, Black Coffee."

As Stanley Wooda handed her the cup, he said, "I hope this helps fast. I think I hear Chief Biggs."

Chapter Seventeen

The coffee house opened that morning at its usual hour to the usual small crowd, but within minutes more students appeared. The usual handful of instructors were there before classes, complaining that senior professors should teach at least a few of the early classes; some were looking at lecture notes, others gossiping, but by 9 AM more had appeared, more animated than the early arrivals. Mary had been among them, then had phoned Donahue, but failed to reach him. She fretted a few minutes, then called another number and left a message, "Chief, this is Mary. Can you meet me at the coffee house?" To her surprise, Donahue appeared first. For a change, she was very pleased to see him come through the door. He seemed a bit frazzled, almost as much as she was.

He hurried over to greet her, "I'm here. How did you hear what happened?"

"The campus is buzzing. But not much is known other than that Miss Purdy is probably dead. She was working late. There is blood in her office and signs of a struggle. And the glass on the side door was smashed."

"It's barely past nine," he responded. "How did everyone hear? It hasn't made the radio yet, and I thought almost nobody came onto campus before nine." Except for people like me, he thought, and I think of morning as the end of the night patrol—a good time for classes. "Only half my students showed up for my 8 o'clock, so I gave a pop quiz and told them I would repeat it in two days. By the time I got to my office, it seemed everyone knew. The chief told me to come over here."

"They seem to wake up early for a murder! The cafeteria is packed, too. Never saw anything like it. Not even Boater's death, which was more like an accident. This was violence. It's scary."

Donahue tried to reassure her, "I hope that you aren't worried."

"That could have been one of us. Flo Boater won't stop till we are gone!"

So absorbed in one another were they that neither noticed the historian make his way through the crowd and sit down not far away. He grinned as he heard Donahue say, "We can't leave now." And the grin widened when Mary answered, "Why not? I was up all night packing." He turned half-way away, to be an inconspicuous as possible, and he was more than half-hidden by students in between.

It was apparent to Donahue that Mary was exhausted, not quite all there. But she was deadly serious when she asked, "Do you know how hard it is to pack a year's clothes into one suitcase and a small bag?"

Donahue knew, "Yes, I just did it myself."

"Fortunately," she said, "I hadn't fully unpacked yet, just put my stuff in a drawer, so most of it would have been ready if it all didn't need washing. It took me all night, every moment that I wasn't crying."

"You don't have to go," he whispered.

Mary responded with a breaking voice, "I don't?"

"We've got to stay here till this is over. We have to protect Lill, Lily and Jenny."

"You think they are in danger?"

"You said it yourself, Flo Boater will stop at nothing. If somebody killed the vice president, she might try to blame them. If she doesn't, Stout will." He saw no reason to explain that they had been seen near the scene of the crime, near the time it occurred. She had enough to worry about.

Wiping away tears, she sobbed, "I understand. At least, I think I do. Lill and Lily were president and dean. They might have wanted to cover something up." She corrected herself hurriedly, "But they couldn't be dishonest!"

"But you're right. That would be the story—that they had something to hide."

"But it's not right!"

"Flo Boater could spin it to the press," he explained. "To divert attention from herself."

There was one point she didn't understand, "I see that. But why Jenny?"

Her voice had weakened so much that Donahue could barely hear her, frustrating the more distant historian. Worse for him, Donahue spoke softly out of sympathy, "Because she works in the financial office, because Miss Purdy was angry with the staff, and because she is their friend."

"And our friend," she added.

Donahue agreed, "Friends don't leave when friends are in trouble."

"This might cost you a chance at tenure."

"I can always become a cop again," he quipped. Then he asked seriously, "You could learn to like a cop, couldn't you?"

She ignored the question, "What about my career?"

"This college doesn't pay much anyway," he responded. "Marry me, move to a big city, and you'll find a better job."

She decided to be as practical as he was, raising her voice as she spoke, "All the cities offer is adjunct positions. A part-time class here, another there. The pay is lousy, and you're always driving from one campus to another. It's a terrible existence."

Donahue wouldn't be put off, "Take a chance! Life is full of chances!"

Almost angry, she responded, "The competition for language positions is fierce. I'd never get a regular job. And once you're an adjunct...."

"Then let's stay here and see what happens."

She was willing to compromise, "I'll go this far. I won't get on the airplane."

"And...."

"No promises beyond that!"

"What will you tell Flo Boater?"

She responded brightly, "That I've stayed to talk you into coming with me!"

Donahue laughed, "I think she'll buy that!" Taking her hands, he asked, "How come a woman as smart as you won't marry me?"

Pulling her hands back, she answered good humouredly, "You figure that one out yourself, detective."

"Okay," he agreed. "I'll call the airline now. Cancellations are easy. You get some sleep, then call me when you wake up."

As she stood up to leave, she responded, "And you do whatever it is that detectives do."

Getting up, as well, he saluted and said, "Right away" It was a gesture she had used once, and he believed she would remember it. Fondly.

Watching her leave, he failed to notice the historian slipping away in the opposite direction.

It was only moments later that Chief Biggs came through the door and indicated with a toss of his head that Donahue should follow him. He led him toward the administration building, explaining that he needed Donahue present during the second round of questioning. He needed to go over everything with Flo Boater while her memory was fresh, and he needed a witness—his tape recorder wasn't working.

Donahue was eager to assist, in fact. He had missed the first session, in the wee hours of the morning, having gone to Miss Purdy's apartment at the chief's request and, not finding her, had awakened all her neighbors to ask if they knew where she had been. He was happy that none had wanted to see his badge, but none was pleased to have been awakened at that hour. He had then gotten Miss Efficiency out of bed, though she put aside his apologies with the comment that it was almost time for her to walk her pets anyway. She had provided from memory all the information she had about Prudence Purdy—Miss Purdy had not listed any contacts except those related to her education and former employment. From the state police—who had been alerted to his involvement in the case—he obtained the license number and make of her car and determined that it was not anywhere around her apartment or the campus. He asked the state police to put out a bulletin. Then he had gone to teach his class.

The chief had done what he could to collect physical evidence, then had called the officer in charge at the state police. By 8 AM a forensic expert had arrived—record time, he had said, for the drive from Zenith. He worked over the scene quickly, taking photos and prints, and declared, "It looks like half the campus has been through here." Jenny had told him that he was probably right—every student came in to pay the bills and staff picked up their checks here. Unhappily, he had no prints to match with the many he had lifted, except Miss Purdy's, which he found at her place later. He did smile when he noted that there had been a successful effort to wipe prints off the small table and the nearest file cabinets. More blood was on the floor there than in the center of the room, and that was where it had been smeared. Not very much anywhere, but still very suspicious! And there was the broken side door. "Whoever did that wanted into the building awfully bad."

Lie detector tests…. Not yet. Better narrow down the list of suspects first. DNA would confirm if the blood was indeed Miss Purdy's. Surely there were strands of hair or toothbrushes in her apartment.

The message from the chief to go to the coffee house had seemed urgent enough that Donahue had left a steaming cup of coffee in his office; fortunately, having already had four cups, he was still "wired," ready to take on the world. Even Flo Boater.

It was difficult to quite literally "take a back seat" after that, but that was where the limited seating in the president's office put him. The normally capacious room was crammed with the decorators' apparatus—the high ceilings required enough scaffolding to satisfy Michelangelo. Donahue looked around, wondering what this was costing—there was more than before. And where the money was coming from?

Biggs opened the questioning quietly, "So, once again, how was it that you went into the business office?"

"As I said earlier," Flo Boater explained in a voice so soft he could barely hear, "I couldn't sleep, so I went to my office to work."

Skeptically, he asked "You often go to work at 3 AM?"

"Since my late husband died, I can't sleep well."

Biggs, who remained skeptical, spoke sympathetically, "So, when you can't sleep, you work?"

Through the approach of tears, she replied, "Yes, don't you?"

Biggs was not greatly impressed, "Police work is different. Don't you usually take work home?"

"Usually, yes, but I hadn't read yesterday's mail."

His eyes betrayed a suspicion this was a fairy tale, but all he said was, "Okay, so you came onto campus… entered the building."

"Yes."

Biggs thought for a moment before proceeding, "The building was locked?"

"Yes, I have a key."

"Did you meet anyone?"

"Just some students. Hurrying back from some pub."

This was odd, Biggs thought. 3 AM? No beer joint in town stayed open that late on a weekday. But how would she know that? He asked, "Recognize them?"

"How would I recognize students?" she responded, more acidly than necessary. "I don't teach classes." The tearful mode being too difficult to resume, she had given up on the effort. She was not about to admit that she needed glasses. "Besides, I only saw them for an instant."

"How many were there?"

"Two, most likely."

"Most likely?"

"Two, I'm pretty sure." She shifted her position in her chair, "Look, if I'd known what I saw upstairs, I'd have paid more attention."

The chief nodded, then asked, "Why a pub, did you think?"

"They went into the restroom, the men's room downstairs."

"Why weren't you suspicious, about their being in the building?"

"We haven't been very good about locking up. Until recently, that is. I remember saying, to myself, of course, that we'd have to be more consistent in the future. Locking up, that is."

"Common to leave it open?"

"Only when the dean of students is still working. But she is very good about locking up when she leaves."

He made a note to ask about that, then said, "Okay, you went to your office."

"No, I didn't get that far." Seeing Biggs's quizzical look, she continued, "Something, I don't know what, didn't seem right. It was awfully late for them to be here."

"They were in the building? The students."

"Yes, of course." She gave him an addition snort to indicate her distain for his inability to listen carefully. "I waited on the stairs until I heard them leave."

"Then you investigated?"

"Yes. After I locked the building, I checked the offices on both floors. I saw the door of the finance office open."

"You turned on the lights?"

"The hall lights you mean?" she asked. "I suppose I should have. But I didn't."

"No, the office lights."

"Not really. There was a small light already on."

"You didn't turn on the office lights?" Biggs's eyebrow rose involuntarily.

"And let the entire campus know that I was there?" Clearly, she saw no reason to explain why that would have been bad.

The chief realized that the finance office faced toward town, not the campus, but he didn't want the interview to get sidetracked. "Weren't you a bit frightened?" When she didn't answer, he continued, "A woman alone, in a dark building that had unknown people in it."

"You might be confusing me with some ordinary woman. I can take care of myself."

Biggs muttered, half to himself, "I'm sure you can."

"When I saw that the door was half open, I looked in. I saw what I told you. Then I called the police station."

"You saw the door half-open when the hall was dark?"

"Certainly, there was a small light in the office. I could see that easily."

After a moment's thought, Biggs asked, "When did you call Dean Wooda?"

She tried to resume the tears, without much success, "At that same time, or right afterward. I don't remember the details. I was too upset."

"And he came right over."

"It turned out that he was in his office. He had worked late and fallen asleep. He keeps a couch in there."

The chief sighed, "Yes, that's what he said."

Flo Boater sighed, too, "Is that all? Can I go?"

"Not quite yet," the chief responded. "A few more questions…Was there anything in the office worth stealing?"

"You mean money?" It was her turn to stop and think. "Perhaps, but we don't deal much in cash, and the checks are kept in the vault. It was closed."

"Did the vice president have any enemies?"

Boater rejected this idea, "I don't think she had been here long enough to make enemies."

"Good point," he admitted. "So you think we can eliminate robbery and hatred as motives?"

"I can't imagine," she said innocently, "why anyone would commit this horrible crime."

The chief was always suspicious of Flo Boater. He looked at her closely as he asked, "You made these calls from the finance office?"

Once this would have intimidated her, but she was now experienced in interrogation techniques. She responded coolly, "No, I came right over here, to my office. I was too distraught to remain in there any longer. Besides, the killer, the culprit, whatever he is, might still be around."

"And Dean Wooda joined you right away."

"Yes. He had clearly been asleep."

"Fallen asleep at work."

She was not fully responsive on this point, "You said you had checked that with him."

"Do you have any reason to think he was involved… in any way?"

Her response was totally logical, "If he could fall asleep after doing what I saw, he would be the most cold-blooded man in the history of crime."

Biggs persisted, "He couldn't have heard something?"

"Perhaps, but probably not. This is a big building."

"But not many people come there at night?"

She answered, "Jay, I suppose, now and then. Dean of Students office downstairs, they have night time emergencies. Students… there's a lot going on." She paused before continuing, "We can't afford a night watchman any more. But I can't imagine what Jay would have against the vice president."

Biggs said ironically, "Not at all like hitting Dean Wooda over the head—the *late* Dean Wooda."

She pulled her shoulders square and smiled, "A very different situation. Not likely to be repeated."

Biggs gave a quiet smile himself, "No, not likely."

"When can we get back into that office? The college is a business, you know."

"It's a weekend soon, so you'll be able to work there Monday or Tuesday."

"You mean we can't clean it up until then?"

"No, you can do that pretty soon. I'll let you know when, but I want to keep the room closed for a while. You know, so I can imagine what it looked like without a lot of people around." Standing up, he said, "Well, thank you for your assistance, President Boater. You have been *most* helpful."

With a sickly sweet smile, she responded, "It's always a *pleasure* to help you, Chief Biggs."

The chief returned the smile and walked out; in fact, he almost waltzed out, Donahue behind him. He disliked Flo Boater, but he was beginning to enjoy annoying her. He was hardly out of sight before Jay slipped into her office. He was obviously agitated.

She asked, "What is going on, Jay?"

"I'm not completely sure. They won't let me clean up."

"It is a crime scene," she explained.

"It's a mess. Why didn't you tell me that last night?"

She sighed, "Oh, last night was… it was such a… I was just so upset. I couldn't remember what I had said to anybody."

He must have felt some pity, because all he said now was, "I'm told the body's gone, but blood's there and papers are scattered all over, and the door is sealed."

Flo Boater took this in calmly, "That's right. I hope that you will be able to clean it up soon."

Jay thought a moment before asking, "When can I get in there?"

"This afternoon, I suspect."

"Good," he replied. "I'll tidy it up, then give you a call."

She was very pleased and said so, "That would be good. Thank you, Jay." A moment later she called out to him. When he returned she asked if "that little business" was taken care of. It was, he assured her.

As soon as he had left, she turned to her next appointment, wondering only momentarily what Jay might have thought about seeing Jenny sitting in the secretary's office, awaiting her turn—she knew they were romantically involved, but that couldn't be very important at their ages. Flo Boater would not have thought of calling Jenny, but Miss Efficiency had known that she was the right person right now—she had been working in the financial affairs office. As soon as they were both seated, Flo Boater leaned forward and stated, "Jen, I need you to take over for Miss Purdy for a few days."

"Again?"

"Yes, again."

Jenny was appalled, "I really don't know anything about finances!"

"That's not a problem. I'll hire a temp in a few days, then start a search, but right now we need someone to answer the phone and open the mail. Just like you did before. We have to have the checks deposited in the bank promptly."

After reflecting on this a moment, Jenny agreed, "Okay, I can do that."

"We don't want to create a cash flow problem," the president said. "Just take money in, but don't write any checks."

Jenny shrugged her shoulders, no longer suspicious, "I couldn't anyway. The bank only recognizes the vice president's signature."

Flo Boater corrected her, "And mine, and Dean Wooda's. So that's covered. You just check on the mail and the phone calls."

"Sure. No problem," Jenny drawled as she stood up. But she had a strange feeling that more was going on than she knew. She turned as she reached the door, "The office is closed. Where should we work?"

"Oh, use the dean's office. He never has much to do anyway."

"You sure?"

"I'm always sure, Jen… But you have a point. It would be easier to be across the hall, in the Registrar's office."

Flo Boater ordered coffee, and as soon as Miss Efficiency had brought it, she tried to read the local paper. It was yesterday's edition, of course, and contained nothing of interest. She started to put in carefully in the trash, but couldn't find the container; at last she stood up, looked around at the painters' mess and just threw it on the floor. After trying to pace back and forth from her desk to the window, she saw Lill and Lily coming down the way. Faster than she knew herself capable of moving, she was out the door, down the stairs, down the hall, and out the front entrance, "You two! Come over here."

Lill and Lily stopped, looked at one another and shrugged their shoulders, but they complied. The president came all the way up to them before saying anything. Only when she had fully confronted them, face to face, and caught her breath somewhat, did she say, "I've heard that you have been less than cooperative with your new chair."

They made no response other than a quiet shrug of the shoulders. This annoyed Flo Boater more than any other answer could have, "I won't tolerate that. If you can't learn to get along here, you'll have to find someplace else to make trouble." She then marched off, heading toward the coffee house, leaving the leather twins looking at one another.

"What was that all about?" Lily asked Lill.

"I suspect it had something to do with your putting the Creep's car on blocks so that he couldn't drive home last night."

"Oh, surely he wouldn't hold that against me."

"That and offering him a ride home on your motorcycle."

Lily laughed, "He'd never been on a hog before. He was scared pissless."

"Oh? You didn't mention that."

"It took me half an hour to clean the machine up." She laughed so hard she slapped her thighs, "Had to go to the car wash!"

Lill laughed at her memory of their having seen the Creep's car parked outside the administration building late at night, and of Lily having fetched four blocks of wood and a jack out of the garage and driving off, but she hadn't known that Lily was still there when the Creep had returned from whatever he was doing to see his tires stacked on top of the vehicle. Lily had apparently "just come by" at the right moment to offer him a lift. "What was he doing there?" she asked.

"I think he was spying on the dean."

"You did all that yourself? You weren't gone very long." Lill, somewhat worried about Lily's plans, had looked at the clock when she heard her come home. She had been worried that the night patrol might catch her. Only one patrol car, but all they needed was an arrest for malicious mischief. That would make Flo Boater's day!

"No," Lily replied, "Smith and Jones came by and lent a hand."

"Oh," Lill said, surprised that they would literally stoop to such work. "Pretty early, wasn't it?"

"Not for them, in a sense—it was actually the end of their usual day."

"Nice of them."

Lily laughed, "They wanted to know if this would count as extra credit."

"And you said?" Lill prodded.

"I said that if they'd do some work—like taking the mid-term exam and turning in papers—I could think about extra credit."

"And they still helped you?"

"Sure. They'd wanted it as a substitute, but they're optimists. Maybe I'd forget."

"Also not too bright," Lill suggested. "If the patrol car had come by, they'd have run and the officer would have ignored you."

Lily almost blushed at this, "I thought of that, too." She paused for a moment before adding, "They aren't even taking a class from me!"

In the meanwhile Donahue and Biggs had gone to the Diner. The buzz of conversation provided them all the privacy anyone could wish, and they were away from the prying eyes of everyone except one businessman who would bring his paperwork here where he could be certain of not being interrupted by phone calls or visitors. It was the perfect time to compare ideas, especially to reflect on why the finance office would have been broken into. Money, of course. But what kind of money? There would not have been much cash on hand, and whatever there was would have been locked away.

Donahue summarized his understanding of the situation, "The insurance money is not going to be the windfall everyone expects. First we have to pay off the debt—and the payments for some dormitories are due soon. Second, we have to rewire all the instructional buildings. Do you know that until last year we couldn't even have coffee makers in the secretaries' offices because the fuses for the entire building might blow out? That also limited the number of computers we could use there. Now everyone wants coffee machines and computers. Then we have the deferred maintenance—roofs, painting, new mattresses in the dorms, a new kitchen for the cafeteria, maybe an entirely new cafeteria that will attract the students back. Right there is fifteen million or more, and the settlement would be only ten. Maybe not quite that."

"What about the dean's secret bank accounts?" Biggs asked.

"That looks like a lot of money if you are thinking about the average professor's salary, but compared to the insurance settlements, it is chicken feed. There could be more out there, of course."

"There could?"

"The trustees have only been able to check the regional banks. He could have had any number of accounts, say off-shore. There is some evidence for that."

"Evidence?" the chief inquired.

"Bank transfers. But those were only right after he opened the accounts. Later withdrawals were in cash. Perhaps he realized that the money could be traced too easily the way he was operating."

"Maybe that's what we should be looking into," Biggs suggested. "Follow the money. That will lead us to the crime."

"Blood money," Donahue said, causing Biggs's eyebrows to rise slightly. He liked the black humor, but he would have enjoyed it more if there hadn't been a body potentially involved. A very big body. And a smeared blood trail. And no fingerprints.

Chapter Eighteen

The next morning Flo Boater looked around her cluttered office, grimaced, then cleared away some of the painters' supplies so that she could get to her desk—the painters had apparently been back, but Miss E had sent them to work somewhere else for a while. Where? She didn't care enough to ask. Picking up the phone, she called her young dean and summoned him for a "chat." It would have been easier to cross the hall to his office, but she understood the symbolic importance of meeting on "her" ground. Besides, she didn't want to talk about architects and painters, but a more important subject. Important matters cannot be discussed in unimportant quarters, and no place seemed less important than Dean Wooda's office. Moreover, it held memories that she would just as soon forget, and every important issue brought the late dean to mind.

She started to say to herself, "Mohammed must come to the mountain," when she remembered that she had seen an extra two pounds on the scale that morning. Besides, Stout had told her that it was no longer acceptable to say "Mohammed." What the hell was she supposed to say? She couldn't remember. At that moment her youthful and slim dean scurried in, interrupting that thread of thought.

When they were seated, her "power chair" slightly higher than the one she assigned him, she leaned forward to proclaim, "We can't let this crisis go on. The trustees won't stand for it."

He shrugged his shoulders, "There are no leads, at least none that Biggs will tell us about. What can we do?"

"I assume that *neither* of *us* are involved," she said, staring at him. "I know *I am not.*"

He was slightly embarrassed, having wondered if she were, but after last night he wasn't sure of anything. Still, he assured her that he was not involved and added that he could, if necessary, provide a witness as to… well, as an alibi. She had suspected this, but found it reassuring to hear it personally. Neither had a theory, but both were worried. Flo Boater asked about student radicals trashing the place, but Stanley Wooda dismissed that, saying that protestors were unlikely to turn to crime. "Burn the building down, perhaps, or occupy it. That was Sixties' stuff, so they might copy that. But nothing small time like stealing petty cash." This was no consolation—she had to have something to tell the trustees.

"What can the trustees do?" Stanley Wooda asked, trying to adjust to his knees being uncomfortably high. "Firing us would ignite a firestorm of media speculation."

"They could suspend us both. Like they did my husband. And the interim president would find out what we've been doing."

"I doubt that," he responded. "They'd appoint some idiot, maybe one of their retired businessmen. And, with Miss Purdy gone, who could suggest where the problems are?"

Flo Boater disagreed, "Our trustees may not be great shakes in educational matters, but they know how to read books."

"Books? I doubt it."

"Financial records," she responded, a bit sharper than she intended. This was not a moment for levity.

Stanley Wooda nevertheless made light of the matter, "Do you think? You've been able to keep them away from the details before."

"Stanley," she responded, "I don't keep the details from them. I give them details—more than they can digest—just not all of them. It's the big picture I worry about."

He wrinkled his brow, "How does that work? I think you've lost me."

Flo Boater explained her theory about handling trustees, "I've found that the only way to deal with them is to throw so much information on their plates, at the last minute, that they can't read it all—they'll go right to the executive summary. Then schedule a lot of big receptions, with no chairs, so that they can't talk with anybody very long."

Stanley Wooda admired her style, "That's a great plan."

Flo appreciated the praise, but recognized that it was excessive, "It's not much of a plan. Everybody does it." She added ironically, "At large universities, the deans treat the president like a trustee."

He liked that strategy, "Keep *him* in the dark, too!" He very carefully said "*him*." More women were becoming college presidents, but the public (and Flo Boater) still thought they were rarities.

"It works," she admitted.

"Sounds like my kind of place." He was already thinking of the next job. Bigger and better.

Flo Boater put her hand on his shoulder, "Stanley, you are going to go places. But remember this, small fish swim fastest in the wake of big fish." She frowned again, remembering those two pounds.

He gulped before finding the right words, "And right now, you are the big fish."

"Not a flattering image," she admitted, "but, yes, if I can get the hooks out of my mouth."

"Huh?"

"First of all," she explained, "I won't be able to distract the trustees very long." At that she stood up and walked to the window, gazing out on the campus and wondering to herself whether she liked the college as much as she disliked the problems associated with it.

Stanley Wooda stood up and followed her, then asked skeptically, "What if they call on me for information?" He wondered if he was being offered as a sacrificial lamb, but the look her face assured him that he would be kept on, at least for a while. Probably for long enough.

She gave him half a hug, which, surprisingly, he did not resist. "Stanley, I know you are smart. You know you are smart. But look at it from the viewpoint of a retired businessman. To him you're still a kid. After all, technically you haven't even graduated yet!"

"Yeah," he agreed, trying gently to escape her grasp, "if they remove you, they'd probably fire me, too. Guilt by association."

She gave him a mean glance, removed her arm and took a few steps away in order to think better, "Secondly, in the minds of the media, I am tied to past accidental deaths on campus."

"They know you've been found innocent," he protested.

She said patiently, "Yes, but I'm good copy. Stories about me will attract readers. The trustees are nervous about negative publicity."

"So what do we do?"

"First of all, we have to make sure that they won't call Lill and Lily back."

Horrified, he asked, "The trustees *wouldn't* do that, would they?"

Flo Boater wasn't sure, "Lill almost balanced the budget; she knows *almost* everything about this place, and what she doesn't, Lily probably does. More importantly, there were no murders while they ran the college."

"How will you stop them?"

"I've been on the phone with key trustees, suggesting that the Leather Lesbians might have been in the financial office that night."

"That's a great name for them, it really works with the trustees."

"What's even better—they invented it themselves. As a joke." She made a forced laugh, "The joke turned out to be on them."

He thought a second, "You said they might have been in that office last night. You know something I don't? You always tell me not to complicate matters."

"I know that they were outside the building about 2AM."

"How do you know that? You weren't here that early."

She smiled, "I have my sources."

Stanley Wooda shrugged, then pose another question, "What if the trustees appoint an outsider? Temporarily."

"We can't have that. It might be temporary for the outsider, but it would probably be permanent for us."

"Why? Why *us*?"

"Clean slate," she explained. "The trustees are leaning toward starting over fresh anyway. An acting president would push for it, hoping to be named himself, and even if that didn't work, the trustees would get the idea that new leadership might be a good idea. No more embarrassing headlines. No more sick jokes at the Country Club or Rotary."

"The Creep would surely give them all the gossip they would need," he agreed, "to seal our fate."

"He would, wouldn't he? Unless we make it…." she said, languidly, before turning part way around toward the windows, "Thought I heard a noise…"

"Nervous," Stanley Wooda thought to himself.

"It's nothing," she said, turning back.

"That's one scary guy," Stanley Wooda agreed. "Sweaty palms, the works."

Flo Boater gave him a sideways glance, "He's *your* worst nightmare."

"Mine?"

"He wants *your* job."

Stanley Wooda smiled wanly, "Oh, yeah, I know that."

"Did you know?" she asked, innocently, "That he was spying on you last night?"

"Spying?"

"Oh, yes. He called me last night to say that his car had been vandalized."

"Vandalized?"

"Well, not quite. More like a prank. Someone took the wheels off, and he couldn't put them back on alone. That was the reason I came into the building then, rather than just get up early in the morning. I was already here."

"You talked with him then?"

"No. He had gone home. But I saw his car, with the wheels piled on top of it."

Stanley Wooda thought quickly, "Why do you think he was spying on me?"

"Easy," she replied. "The hour. I wasn't in the building, but you were."

"So was Miss Purdy."

She laughed, "You think he wants *her* job?"

He paused for a moment to think, "You're probably right. Do you think he saw anything?"

She laughed again, "If he did, he didn't tell me."

"So," he responded, "why should I worry?"

"He's probably in contact with the trustees, too." She smiled when she saw that she had scored a hit. The dean knew that they all wondered if he was mature enough for the job.

Stanley Wooda rubbed his hands together nervously, "Why is it that faculty all think they would be good deans? They can barely teach classes."

Flo Boater yawned, enjoying the moment, and, looking again over the campus, observed philosophically, "Classes get boring eventually. For many of them. And, if it's not too much to the point, they have reason to think that they can do as well as a graduating senior." She paused, "Or one who won't graduating soon." At that, she smiled.

"I'm doing a *good* job!" he insisted.

She leaned toward him to explain, "They've seen a lot of incompetent deans, and nobody ever notices what parts of the job the deans do well."

Pouting, he said, "They only notice when you screw up!" He crossed his arms and turned away from her to stare at the campus.

She explained patiently, reaching over to touch his arm, "Stanley, that's why you need a lower profile. If they don't know what you are doing, they won't know when you screw up!"

He turned back toward her, thereby sloughing off her hand, and complained, "But if I keep a low profile, I'll never get anywhere in this profession!"

She sighed before explaining, "That's the paradox. It's the deer hunting scenario. If you stand out, show your racks, you get shot down. If you don't, the does don't notice you."

"How do we deal with the historian? You already made him teacher of the year."

"Stanley, *you* did that. *You* manipulated the student vote."

"On *your* instructions," he insisted. Seeing that she was not going to respond, he asked, "Okay, what do we do?"

Flo Boater, not as concerned about the *we* as he was, suggested a tactic: "Talk with him. Agree with him. Flatter him."

"In short, tell him what a great job he's doing in the Theater department."

"Even if he hasn't done anything yet." Seeing him look up, she added, "Especially if he hasn't done anything yet."

"What else?" It was one of the few times in his life that he didn't have a plan.

"Confide in him, confess how you dislike the long hours, the committee meetings, the student protests."

"But I love all that stuff!" he countered. And he believed he did, though he was very good at avoiding it all. Committee meetings were boring. Besides, it's that why they took minutes, and it only took him minutes to dispose of most committee recommendations. He was learning the job from Flo Boater.

"He doesn't know that, and, in fact, you're supposed to hate that part of the job."

"You mean, make him think I can trust him with... with my innermost thoughts."

"Exactly," she said, "and drop hints that *you will need some help...* soon."

This intrigued him, "Make him see that we can advance his career faster than the trustees can." He saw the potential. He also saw a way to avoid attending committee meetings personally.

"Yes, and emphasize how much the trustees appreciate loyalty."

He hesitated at this, "That could be a bit tricky."

"Make him see, indirectly, how much the trustees appreciate inside information, especially information that makes everyone look good."

He sought to clarify the instructions, adding, "They don't want bad news." Good news would be harder to find.

"No, never, or only the kind they can resolve quickly." She thought a moment, then added, "Information that usually gets to them through me. They don't like people who don't follow the chain of command, especially if it's nothing they can do anything about."

"Are you sure? I thought some had close contacts with individual faculty."

"There are those exceptions, but for anyone else they have lives and businesses of their own. They know the limits of their time and energy."

"But he's surely one of those."

"I don't think so; it's possible, but not likely." She thought that trustees could speak with Stout easily—he understood the stock market. But nobody liked to talk with the historian.

"Then why not just cut off his communication with them?" Stanley Wooda was always practical, though he immediately saw the problem with his suggestion—how to stop the Creep from just picking up the telephone and asking that the conversation be kept confidential. Any effort to keep him from calling would work against them—the trustees would smell a cover-up from the get-go.

But this was not what Flo Boater meant. Her plan was more subtle, "He can be our *backdoor*. The way to get *our* side of the story to them."

He was struck by this idea. "Without it appearing self-serving." He paused before adding, "Clever."

"That way everyone is happy." She beamed a self-satisfied smile.

Also smiling now, he suggested, "Let me carry this one step further. He doesn't like Lill and Lily." He didn't elaborate. He saw that her mind was racing in the same direction.

"Right. They are competition for the job he wants. They resent his becoming chair of their department. I understand they have been making life difficult for him."

"How?"

"Among other annoyances, they switched the name plates on the restrooms. Nobody else noticed. Just went into the usual place. But he went into the 'men's room' and couldn't find the urinal. Then two women came out of the stalls. Then there was his car."

"What's the connection there?"

"Lily. She just 'happened by' and gave him a ride home. It was more of a ride than he wanted. That's why he woke me up."

Stanley Wooda smiled, "I can see why he dislikes them!" Then he asked, "He's hardly been chair any time at all. They worked that fast?"

"Yes. And he wants revenge!"

"So *he* will happily undermine *their* position for us"

"With the proper encouragement, and some inside information we can provide."

The dean agreed, "I think I'd better talk with him right away."

As she escorted him toward the door, she added, "There is one other thing, Stanley."

"Yes?"

"We've got to get Chief Biggs off our backs."

"I can offer the historian a better deal, but the chief is incorruptible!"

"Perhaps you can bring him around," she suggested, "for the good of the college and the community."

He doubted this would work, but rather than say so, he suggested, "Why don't you talk to him? You're the president."

She hesitated before responding, "Let's say that Chief Biggs doesn't trust me. But his honesty is something we can play on. He knows he has no evidence against us."

"Because we didn't do it."

"No," she explained. "Because you can appeal to his sense of honor to lay off the college... and us."

He was doubtful, but he agreed, "I don't know. I'll give it a try, but I don't see it working."

She was very careful in her instructions: "He's probably on campus with Donahue. Don't speak to them together. And ask Donahue to come see me here." She then repeated the orders, worried that Stanley might improvise a plan on his own.

"Biggs won't trust you, and neither will Donahue."

"No, that's true. But Biggs will follow the law."

"And DO?"

"Donahue's different, so we handle him differently. Cops are different than chiefs. They know that the law and rules sometimes get in the way of justice."

"So, what's the strategy?"

"He is concerned about Mary, so we work on that... Trust me," she said, seeing that he was skeptical. "This is where the woman's touch is truer." She turned him around and pushed him gently off, "Now, scoot. Call me when you find them."

As soon as he was gone, she summoned Miss Efficiency and told her to find out where Jay was working tomorrow. Being asked what it concerned, she said only that she had a special job for him. She did not explain that she did not want Stanley Wooda to know about it, but saying that this was "confidential" was sufficient warning. She then asked her to arrange a meeting with Mary C, and to ask the dean to join them.

Chapter Nineteen

It was the next morning that Mary appeared in the president's office. Stanley Wooda, who had arrived before her, stood up, but it was Flo Boater, feigning a combination of happiness and surprise, who went over to her and said, "Why Mary, I thought you'd be on the plane by now."

"DO cancelled his reservation," she explained after they had all sat down. "He said he had to stay to help Chief Biggs, and I thought you'd want me to stay to, to persuade him to come along as quickly as the matter, whatever it was, was resolved."

"The murder," Flo Boater said dryly.

It was Mary's turn to feign surprise, "Was it really *murder*? DO thought it might be an *accident*." Mary was adjusting to the political poker game, and she surprised herself in having some skill at it, and some pride in that developing skill.

"That's a pleasant surprise!" the president exclaimed, then added. "Are you sure it wouldn't work better then for you to go ahead? DO would surely join you quickly."

"I really don't want to go back quite so soon, anyway."

"You don't?" Flo Boater was disappointed, though she knew that Mary had no enthusiasm for South America at this moment. Too bad she couldn't arrange for Mary to go to one of the cities—world class comfort for those with dollars, and the dollars went a long way.

"Not really."

"Not even with your tenure decision hanging on it?" If at first you don't succeed, try, try again.

"I've really had enough jungle life for a while." When Flo Boater looked crossly at her, she explained. "After all, I've just gotten back. When I unpacked my bags, everything was mildew and mold." After a pause, she added, "And I need to replace those clothes." What she wanted to say was that she missed the classroom, but she knew that Flo Boater would never understand that.

Flo Boater took her by the arm and led her toward the door, "Then what you had better do... right now... is throw away those things, buy some new clothes. Charge them to the college. No, you won't find clothes in Middleville. Go to Zenith. Give Miss E the receipts. I'll find the money somewhere... Relax a bit. Pack quietly. Remember, research is God's gift to intelligent folks. And you'll have a great time with DO."

As Mary reached the door, she released herself and said, "I'm really *not interested* in marriage yet."

This did not slow the president at all, who tried to grasp her elbow again, "If you are *not* married, you'll have an even *better* time." She glanced over to Stanley Wooda, indicating with her eyebrows that he should stay out of this.

Fighting off the grip, Mary retorted, "Oh?"

Flo Boater ceased her efforts to get "the upper hand" and explained, "He'll be on his best behavior. Besides, I understand you won't see him that often."

"Every month or two," she said.

Smiling the president advised her, "That's as often any woman needs to see a man. Now run along and get ready." She then pushed her gently on, and Mary, quite willing to see the interview ended, went. But not to pack.

Flo Boater turned to her dean, "See what we're up against?" He didn't have anything to say. He wasn't even sure why she had wanted him present, except perhaps as a witness in case it should become a "she said/she said" situation. He had other problems to deal with, like Smith and Jones wanting an interview.

She dismissed her dean, giving a sigh as she watched him stroll away, then rang Miss Efficiency, "Mary needs some clothes. Create a budget line for it. Yes, that should be Miss Purdy's job, but she's not available now." Another sigh. She should have just walked out to her reception room; the order might have seemed less... less... whatever. Putting down the receiver, she looked with disgust at the mess the painters had made. This would not have happened if Jay had been in charge. But he had not been. She wondered if that was because the interior designer had insisted on total control or because she herself was having doubts as to whose side Jay was on? Should she give him access to her office? Or even a key to the building? She then told Miss Efficiency, "I'll be back in an hour," and walked as briskly as she could to the Gym. She knew that Windy Gale was out of his office, and it would be a good place to meet Jay, who was scheduled to clean up there—Miss E had checked on his whereabouts and then left him a message to meet her in the Athletic Director's office. Just as well to meet there—Windy was doing whatever Athletic Directors did and wouldn't be there, and she couldn't stand to be in her office any more; moreover, she wanted to speak to Jay privately.

As usual, Flo Boater occupied her time waiting by going through Windy's correspondence. As usual, he had not locked his desk. As a result, she was fully absorbed in trying to make sense of the letters and bills when Jay knocked on the door. Flo Boater wasn't sure how long he had been there, listening, but she was unperturbed—she hadn't said anything, and it was probably just her nerves. Was she becoming paranoid? No, of course not. She opened the door, signaled him to come over, indicated that he should sit, and then closed the door—but not before checking to see if anyone else were in a position to "hear" their conversation.

He sat and explained, "I was told to report."

That wasn't exactly how she had expected her secretary to instruct him, but she ignored it, "I am glad you could come in. Do you know where Donahue is?"

Jay knew, "He's with Chief Biggs over at the Theater."

"What's over there?"

"He might be looking for them boxes I moved out of the Music building."

"Oh, my God!" she exclaimed.

"They look *awful* happy."

"What could it be?" she wondered. Then she asked, "The artifacts? Did they find them there?"

Jay was slightly miffed at the suggestion he had failed to carry out orders, "No. I don't think so."

"What else could it be?" she asked, half to herself.

"I think it has something to do with them jungle treasures. They think those are the link between you and the financial corpse."

"Those *are* the artifacts!" she snapped. "I told you to move them!"

"Oh," Jay said. "It still doesn't matter. They're gone already. The chief is more looking for Miss Purdy, anyway. DO, too."

She stopped to think for a moment, then gasped, "They think *I* killed her?" She looked around the room before concentrating on Jay again and asking, "Have they found her body?"

"Hard to say," he said, scratching his head in search of a better idea. "No body, I think, but that's what it looked like." Seeing her going pale, he hurriedly added, "Now, I don't say it does. They weren't talking loud." And, as she stood up and walked back to the window, he stood up and followed her. He didn't like her, but he did not enjoy seeing any human being suffer, "Don't take it for more 'an it's worth. But DO was at the Music building earlier, then to the Theater, and now they're both asking around."

"*You're sure* it's all safely hidden now?" Flo Boater asked.

"It's safe. I put it....." He got no further than this before she put her hand over his mouth and said, "Don't tell me. Don't tell me. I've got to be able to say I don't know."

"I *haven't* told you," Jay retorted, "or *anybody else here.*"

"Well, don't. And I'll not forget it. Also, let me know if you see Donahue. I've got to see him. Have him call me."

Jay hesitated a moment, then said, "I think he and Biggs were on their way to the *financial* office… again."

"Oh, my God," she blurted out. "I've got to get there first."

As she flew out a side door of the Gym, going through the ivy-filled woods, she almost ran into a student wearing a sweatshirt emblazoned with JJ. He was with a young woman, but she still was still startled; she almost reached for her glasses, but quickly abandoned that idea. Wondering briefly where she had seen him—it wasn't Jones, she was sure of that—she forgot to tell him—loudly—to watch where he was going. She had to get to the administration building, and it was all the way across campus.

Smith's conversation with Ellie was purely business. When she had phoned, he had thrown on his roommate's sweatshirt and hurried to meet her. He never thought to wonder why she might be romantically inclined so early in the morning—and so he was very disappointed to find that she wasn't. She wanted to talk about how the newspaper would cover the story of the murder.

Chapter Twenty

Jenny had been about to enter the coffee house when she saw Flo Boater hurrying toward her. "Wow. Is she all ret up!" Flo was not a graceful walker. She had kept her figure by dieting, not by exercise. That was apparent within moments—she could not keep up her initial pace, but would not give up her effort at speed. The resulting alternation between spurts and gasps made even the passing students stand aside and gape. Fascinated, Jenny only reluctantly went inside to avoid meeting her. She was still watching through the windows when Jay came up and stood beside her. She touched his arm, but did not move her eyes away until the president was far away; wondering if Flo Boater would collapse before reaching the administration building and its long flights of marble stairs up to the second floor, she asked, "Jay, what's going on?"

"She wants them records about them arti-facts," he said, "From the fi-nance office."

"Can she do that? Isn't it closed off as a crime scene?"

"It won't matter. They aren't there any more."

"They aren't? The records are gone?"

"I thought they'd be safer with the arti-facts."

Jenny was amused, "Where were they?"

"In the file drawer that the mess on the floor came from." Most people would have found this incomprehensible, but Jenny understood that he meant the spilled papers were not the ones Miss Purdy had been studying.

"Those weren't important, were they?" she asked. "The ones in the drawer."

"Miss Purdy had them out," he said. "Had to be a reason."

"Oh, I see. The ones on the floor were a distraction."

"Someone wanted us to think... they was important."

"You sure they weren't?"

237

"Receipts from the sody-pop machines? Not likely to get anyone excited."

"When did you see them?"

"When I went in to clean up."

"They were just lying there?"

"The chief left 'em on the table. Not important."

Jenny suddenly understood, "So you looked in the soft drink file..."

"And found the real stuff, the museum sales."

She thought for a minute, then asked, "Why didn't you give them to Donahue?"

"No time. Mighta got caught."

"So you just took them away?"

"Didn't want the murderer to come back for them. I put them with the *arti*-facts."

"Why there?"

"Nearby. Safe."

Her eyebrows furrowed at this, "The artifacts are still on campus? Can you tell me where they are? Donahue is looking for the artifacts."

"I can't say. I promised President Boater I wouldn't tell anybody, not even her."

Disappointed, Jenny pouted, "So you won't help save Mary, and Lill and Lily?"

With a wink, he reassured her, "I have a feeling it'll all work out. I don't think there's anything particularly new in them."

She wasn't sure, "How will it work out?"

"Some of that I'd seen before."

"Duplicates?"

"Pretty sure. Of those we found last year. I've got a good mem'ry for things like that."

"Shouldn't DO have seen them anyway?"

He shrugged his shoulders, "He'd've recognized 'em. DO's a smart guy... for a professor."

"Right you are," she admitted. "And you, too." With that she gave him a kiss on the cheek. As soon as he had left, she went to the public phone to call Donahue. Jay had made the promise, but she could do what she wanted, as long as the trail didn't lead back to him. Donahue, however, was not around. She had half-dialed Chief Biggs before she realized that he could not make a promise of secrecy; and, moreover, she was out of quarters. She hung up, but unable to keep the secret entirely to herself, she stopped one of her students, borrowed a coin, and called Molly.

When she put down the receiver, she was disconcerted to see that the historian was seated several tables away, watching her.

Dean Wooda, the late Dean Wooda, would have been amused. He would probably have laughed at the ineptness of his namesake, the new Dean Wooda, who had no idea what to do now. When young Wooda saw Flo Boater reaching the top of the stairs, half-ready to collapse and fall back down, he didn't move until she called out to him, "Stan, give me a hand."

Puffing, she allowed him to put an arm around her waist and guide her into Miss E's office. Collapsing into a chair, she squeaked out, "Chief Biggs is coming… hurry."

The dean stood there, wondering what that meant, and said, "Why?"

As her breath returned and the color left her face, Flo Boater went through a succession of emotions. First, what did he mean, "Why?" Wasn't it obvious? Second, what would the chief be looking for if he searched the room? The files apparently in Miss Purdy's hands when she was beaten to a bloody pulp? Or had she been that badly injured? And hadn't she hidden that file? Was the chief smart enough to…. No, impossible. Anyway, whoever committed the assault… Who could have done it? She hadn't, and Stanley, no, he couldn't have, either; and certainly not Jay—he didn't even have a key. Or did he? Earlier? No, put that idea away. When he clean up? Therefore, third, the assault might not have had anything to do with the artifacts. Gangsters? Probably not. The file… And wasn't that Stanley's arm around her again?

In the end the chief never appeared, nor did Donahue. If Flo Boater had not been so exhausted, one dream might have come true. But she had to settle with a nightmare not appearing.

The next day the president asked Jay what had happened.

"Oh, they heard that Miss Purdy had been seen."

Her brow furrowed. She should have heard. Staring at him closely, she asked, "Had she been?"

"Oh, no. Probably a prank phone call."

"And…" she asked.

"They decided to interview her neighbors again."

"I thought you said they were going to her office."

"Seems they thought she had a travel diary. Where she'd been. That sort of thing."

"Did she?"

"Yes, but the patrolman left it where he saw it. No evidence of foul play yet."

"They'd forgotten that? Or what?"

"I guess. But you'd said it wasn't important—that she'd not disappeared. They went to the chief's office to look at it again."

She gave him a pensive look, "And what did they find."

"Nothing. Nothing before. Nothing now."

"So nobody knows where she went?"

"It's like she vanished."

But Flo Boater already knew that… Vanished, leaving a trail of blood.

Flo Boater was equally mystified to discover that the file she had put in the soft drink receipt drawer was missing; when she looked for the one that she had originally gone into the office that night to look for, it was gone, too. Was it the same file?

Chapter Twenty-One

The next day did not go as Donahue anticipated. He had expected a partial repetition of yesterday—quiet inquiries sandwiched between classes. However, at breakfast Chief Biggs asked him to drive up to Zenith to talk privately and unofficially with some bankers, to ask about ways the late dean might have concealed money. He used the Diner phone to ask Mary to substitute for him, to talk about her experiences in Latin America, and drove the chief's ageing private car the two hours to the metropolis. The meeting with the bankers went well—the chief had arranged it for mid-morning, so there was no rush, and the presidents had been very cooperative once he had explained that he had no interest in going through *their* records. "Not that you had anything to hide," he explained with a laugh before they could protest, "but I don't want to disturb the normal flow of business." He then added that there was always a potential for somebody to ask why investigators were there and, getting no answer, would jump to a wrong one. "Therefore, if we cooperate with one another, we can do this quickly and quietly, and to mutual benefit."

The bankers agreed, though they were a bit concerned about his initial laugh. In fact, they agreed that they would search through their records themselves, so that he would not need to open a single book himself. "Come back in three or four hours."

Donahue breathed as quiet a sigh of relief as possible. "What did I know about bank books anyway?" He was glad that the bankers weren't sure of that. He then shook hands with each of them and left, noting as he exited the room that their heads had quickly gone together and a buzz of low conversation had begun. "The chief was right," he thought. "A personal visit is more effective than a phone call." He had not thought much about that before. As a detective he always did interviews in person. But he had been on the night shift. After midnight was a poor time to call people—though they were usually home, they were rarely in a good mood.

The business had gone so quickly, in fact, that Donahue discovered that he would be able to attend an alumni luncheon at a prominent hotel. Months before, thinking that he would probably not know anybody at the gathering, he had sent back a "sorry, can't do it" to the organizer. Now, feeling slightly hungry and having time to kill, he made a quick call over to the hotel desk, located the organizer and received a warm renewal of the invitation.

The crowd was not large and, as he feared, he didn't recognize anyone. Not surprising, he thought. The small college he had attended as a freshman had once been even smaller, and he had only been there for a year; moreover, the president, who was supposed to speak, had not arrived yet—she was, he heard, addressing a group of Zenith University women on "the glass ceiling in American Higher Education." Donahue had smiled at that, thinking that somehow she had broken through— an accomplishment, if the alumni magazine pictures were accurate, for such a tiny woman. As he walked around the room he noted that most alums were senior to him, and some very senior. He wondered if school loyalty increased the farther away one was from the celebration of Commencement, and marveled that the older ones could actually name their Commencement speaker and even remember a few of *his* comments—all the speakers had been male. Maybe there had been a glass ceiling there, too. Donahue felt a bit awkward, because he wasn't even a proper alum, but he had held a Stout fellowship for half a year— the memory of which caused him to wonder if there was a connection to Briarpatch's Stout. Gratitude for its having made possible his first step into college—even if it had largely been a misstep—had caused him mail an occasional small check back for the scholarship fund. That and having played football for one season—more accurately, having practiced with the team that fall—made him more closely tied to this small college than to the large university he had attended in his thirties.

By chance, there was another recipient of the Stout fellowship there and, thus, they had a common bond that was a good excuse to start up a conversation. She had held it for four years, half a decade after he had left, and as soon as she had finished her Ph.D. in history, she had found herself in a very crowded job market. She had applied for the Peace Corps and a Fulbright grant, and, while waiting, had accepted a part-time job at Arcadia College. Not enough money to live on, but the daytime job at the hamburger joint provided the rest.

Donahue asked, "Why daytime?"

"The classes are in the evening. I can prepare lectures or write in the morning. They need me there for the lunch rush, and I can eat cheaply. Though I doubt I'll ever want another hamburger after this job is over. Good, though, especially for the price," she added hurriedly. "Right after the supper rush, I'm off. Teach till nine. Then the rest of the day is mine."

"Not much of it left," Donahue commented. He asked about weekends. She was, after all, attractive, single and apparently unattached—no ring. "Family," she said, "right in Arcadia. That was one of the attractions of the job." But she was a bit vague on the details and Donahue left it that way. He did ask about the Peace Corps. He knew that the Fulbright Commission understood about academic calendars—he had inquired about a grant himself, but had lost interest once he got the job at Briarpatch. But he had heard that the Peace Corps sometimes sent invitations at the most awkward moments. Their training program ran year-around, not from semester to semester.

She explained that her chair was very understanding. Initially, he had been reluctant to make a promise to allow her to leave if a Peace Corps invitation came, but ultimately he had said that if the "worst-case scenario" suddenly appeared, he would handle it somehow. First, he explained, it probably wouldn't happen. Now, if she had taught business or science, or anything practical, the Peace Corps would have already snapped her up. Second, there were some retired history teachers in the community who might be persuaded to jump in an emergency. Third, in order to persuade the outside world that Arcadia really should be a four year school, President Mankiller wanted as many Ph.D. titles on the staff as possible, and there were no similarly qualified applicants for the part time job.

She declined to talk about President Mankiller, saying that it was too soon to make a judgment. Only that the next year would be interesting. Changing from a traditional junior college clientele to an experimental college, cutting edge, had never been tried before. She was more eager to exchange ideas about teaching. "Classes were a challenge," she said. "Not at all like being a graduate assistant at the university." Not all the students were working full-time, but enough of them were that she couldn't assign the reading "that one can at a college like Briarpatch." Her tone indicated honest appraisal, not irony, and that was a refreshing change from the usual outsider's way of describing his place of employment.

"My students are bright enough," she said, "and more important, they are *motivated*." She was most impressed by the veterans. "Oh, they can't write worth a darn, but they are old enough to care and some of them have seen the world. One had been in Somalia!" He had some very interesting things to say, she said, but she did not say what they were.

It didn't matter much to Donahue now, anyway. If what she said was somewhat garbled, a bit nervous maybe, so was he. It was impossible not to think of Mary and to compare the two women. They were very different in many ways, but also very similar. Certainly very serious about their work, well-dressed but not excessively so, and modest in their use of make-up and lipstick. Practical in their short haircuts and fingernails. Good-looking, but not so much that photographers would hurry to take her picture. But who was? Certainly not Mary. One of the new people in science, he remembered, was stunning, but she had a husband trying to get started at a distant university and, therefore, was not available. Obviously, looks weren't everything, and everyone in the two-profession track was struggling just to get along. They chatted about the problem created if one job was fast track and the other slow. That was okay, they agreed, but today all the tracks seemed slower. Too many people looking for too few jobs. Two of those few jobs were even harder to land, especially at the same university. Not that it was her problem—everyone assumed she would want to leave, and nobody wanted to do another search right away.

"How had you gotten off work?" he had asked, which reminded her that she had brought some students to see a museum—some had hardly gotten out of Arcadia before—and now the lunch hour was over. She had promised to meet them at twelve-thirty. She wasn't sure that they would all make it, since some had expressed an interest in investigating more fully the wider range of fast food places available in Zenith, "but I still have to run." Shaking hands and excusing herself, she went to the organizer, thanked her for the luncheon—which hadn't actually started yet—and hurriedly left after a wave to Donahue.

He realized with a start that he hadn't gotten her name.

Chapter Twenty-Two

Later, back in Middleville, Donahue couldn't even remember what he had eaten for lunch. The conversations with fellow alums, had been pleasant—he could imagine some mystic bond with them, and he thought he recognized some faculty names, though he had not been on that campus long enough to know whether they were good or not. Worse, he could not remember the names of the professors whose classes he had attended. Although he had long considered those whose classes to be among the best he'd ever had, that might have been the result of time blurring his memory; he had not been a good student, and his judgment might have been equally bad. The pep talk for finding potential freshmen, the description of the scholarship opportunities—especially the Stout fellowship, the organizer emphasized, looking straight at him with a smile—and the importance of even a small annual contribution, because foundations and government programs gave great weight to having a high percentage of alumni demonstrating a commitment to the college. He wrote a small check before he left, ignoring protests that he didn't have to do that right away, saying that anything he put off, he forgot.

He put off calling Arcadia College.

There was much to think about. He met Chief Biggs in the station house, who said they needed to confer with Jay. "I think he's at the coffee house." On their way over there they talked about general problems concerning the apparent act of violence, especially the time sequence. Jay was not pleased to see them. That is, he was not pleased to be seen with them. But he cooperated fully. He was certain that Miss Purdy had been working in her office earlier in the evening. Alone, he believed, though he could not be certain. No, there were not many keys to the building—the president, the academic dean, the dean of students and her small staff, the registrar, the vice-president for finance (Miss Purdy), Miss Efficiency. "And yourself," Biggs asked.

"Now 'n then b'fore the crime," Jay said.

"Now and then?" the chief asked.

"The d'rector of buildens und grounds gotta git in to clean up."

"But not the day of the break-in?" Biggs asked skeptically.

"I had a key earlier that day, but I turned it back in."

"Why don't you have keys of your own?"

"President Boater don't trust nobody." Jay, having been reared to respect earned authority, tried to give everyone the right title. Besides, they might be listening. "I'll probably get one 'ventually."

"Strange," Biggs commented. He remembered that Jay's grammar got worse when he was nervous. Why was he nervous now? The chief put a finger alongside his nose, a gesture that Donahue recognized as a warning that something was not quite right.

Without seeming to do anything special, Donahue returned the signal. Then he commented, "Lots of strange things go on around here." When Jay looked over at him, he explained, "Like the locked rooms in the Music building."

Jay's eyebrows went up, but he didn't say anything.

Satisfied that he wasn't going to get information volunteered, Biggs returned to his earlier line of questioning, "Who had keys to the finance office?"

"Miss Purdy, of course," Jay answered. "And the dean and president."

"That narrows down the list of suspects," Biggs said. "Assuming that she kept the hall door locked. But it was open when Flo Boater went in. Or so she says."

Donahue nodded and so did Jay. At length Biggs said, "We'd better take another look at the crime scene. Especially at those papers on the floor." With that, he thanked Jay and they left.

On the short walk Donahue asked, "What's up with Jay?"

"Hard to say, but I imagine he'll tell us when he's ready."

Donahue shrugged in agreement, then asked, "So you think Miss Purdy died from hitting her head while falling?"

"Don't know, but that would explain why there was no murder weapon. If she's dead, it wasn't murder in the classical sense."

"Someone pushed her? Threw her down?"

"Hard to say. Rug was moved. We could see she hit the floor there. Some drops of blood. A chip from a tooth, too. On the other side of the table a body was apparently dragged a short ways, but no signs of a struggle other than the papers, which she probably just dropped. We'd know better if we could find the body."

"It's a bit odd," Donahue said, "blood in two places."

"Very odd. And not much of it. Bothersome."

"And the door was open. No effort to hide whatever happened. No blood down the hall or on the stairs."

"If Flo Boater is telling the truth, and I think she is, for once, she found the door ajar. The killer ran out so fast that he didn't even shut it. I think Flo Boater was as surprised as anybody."

"Sounds like panic."

"Yes, not premeditated."

"Not a situation for carrying away a body."

"I wouldn't want to try it," the chief responded with a hint of a smile. "And there is no trail of blood drops. Just blood in those two places."

"You think she's dead?"

"No, but we had better assume she is. My rear end will be in a sling if her body turns up and I didn't take this seriously enough."

"Wooda was right down the hall. Couldn't he have done it?"

"Could have," the chief said. "But his computer entries suggest that he worked late in the evening till he fell asleep. So he says. If he was smart enough not to sign out on his last program, he is sharper than I think." When Donahue chuckled, he added, "Besides, although hunches aren't supposed to be police practice, I think he'd have thought of a better alibi than going to sleep." He stopped at a bench and indicated that he wanted to sit there a moment and think.

Donahue joined him, "If Flo Boater didn't do it, and Stanley Wooda didn't; and we know that Lill and Lily wouldn't do it, who did kill the VP for FA?" He smiled at his use of administrative jargon.

Biggs, after giving him a half-smile, responded, "You forgot Jenny. She could have been asked to work late. She says she didn't and I believe her—it was awfully late—but we've still got to check. But I'm sure that

Jay didn't do it, either. Nor you or Mary, not that there was any reason for you to be there. At least I hope not."

Donahue laughed, "No. None of *us*. You are *sure* Flo couldn't have done it?"

"Not certain, but it's too clumsy. Not her style."

"Wooda maybe? He's pretty sure of himself, and very ambitious."

"He's a talker. But not very muscular. A dancer, I understand, but no upper body strength. I don't see him confronting the vice-president." It wasn't that Stanley Wooda was a weakling, but Miss Purdy was a very big woman. It was unlikely that he could have assaulted her without getting the worse of the engagement, and if somehow he had managed to kill her, it is unlikely he could have gotten her body downstairs without leaving blood on the stairs; he certainly did not appear exhausted when they first talked with him.

"Jay? You're sure about him?" Donahue asked. Neither man doubted that he would have found a way to have moved a whale, if he had been so inclined, but Biggs had to think for a moment about this before responding, "He hit one academic dean over the head, one who deserved hitting. But I can't see a motive this time, and I can't imagine him doing it again... Still, he could probably get into any room he wanted to."

"Even without keys?"

"We are talking about Jay," Donahue reminded him.

"Then who?"

"I dunno. Let's go over it all again. Maybe something will show up."

They went on to the Administration building, letting themselves in with a key they had obtained from President Boater. Earlier they had asked for the president's and dean's keys, so the crime scene specialists from the state capital could enter and leave as they chose and to guarantee that neither could disturb the scene until the experts had finished. After they had left, the chief returned all the keys except the ones to the Administration building and the Finance office. He was pleased to see that Jay had cleaned the place up. He had not looked forward to trying to work around the blood stains. He did not close the door behind them, but left it ajar and then opened a window to admit some new air into the room.

It was late Friday afternoon. The weekend had already begun, so the building was very quiet.

This was the situation when two slim figures appeared in the doorway and quietly observed the investigators at work—actually, though, all the chief and Donahue were doing was standing there, away from the areas marked off with tape, looking first at one place, pointing, talking about the women's restroom and its open window, the half-open window right below in the men's room, glancing inside the private toilet near the vault.

Jones pointed to the chief and Donahue, whispering, "There they are."

Smith was hesitant, "I don't know that this is a good idea."

"You are the one who suggested we write a story for the paper."

"That was then," Smith countered. "This is now." No point in bringing Ellie into the conversation, he thought, but if she had not encouraged him, he wouldn't have come along this far.

Jones pulled his friend over to the table he had indicated, then cleared his throat and introduced himself, "Chief Biggs, Professor Donahue." When they looked up, he continued, "We've got something to say about Miss Purdy, the vice president."

Their announcement caused both men to jump slightly. Neither had expected anyone to be in the building. But both relaxed when they saw only the two rather shaggy students, the only two students they would ever imagine having the nerve to enter a seemingly empty building that contained a crime scene. Still, neither made a move or said anything until Jones cleared his throat nervously.

"Yes," Biggs said cautiously, indicating that the boys should come over to a table and sit down. There was little chance evidence would be disturbed there.

They took places opposite the chief, who suggested that Donahue keep looking around, then Jones and Smith looked around as if worried that their friends would see them. Or someone else.

"We've heard about a murder," Smith said after some coaxing by his friend.

Looking the boys over carefully, Biggs asked, "You've heard about a murder?"

Smith hesitated, but when Jones nudged him, he began to talk, "I'm a reporter on the student newspaper, the *Penprick*, and I want an interview."

Biggs thought for a moment, then asked what kind of questions he had in mind.

"Well, for example, what did the murder scene look like?"

Biggs glanced over at Donahue before answering, "I'm not certain that I can say much right now. It is a crime scene. Maybe tomorrow you can look at it yourself. With the rest of the press." Actually, they could see most of it already, but they couldn't be expected to know what they were seeing.

Jones broke in, "My friend really needs an exclusive."

"Why is that?" Biggs asked.

"This is his best chance to make a name in journalism. It's not every day that something like this happens at Briarpatch."

Biggs glanced over at Donahue, then turned to Jones and smiled, "Son, we've had two murders here in the past year. Isn't that enough?"

Smith broke in here, "I wasn't on the newspaper then."

"I was," Jones said, "but I've made my reputation." He carefully refrained from indicating what that reputation was. He was enjoying himself. Smith was not.

At this Biggs relented. "You've been in the Finance office yourselves?" They didn't answer, so he suggested, "Perhaps to pay your tuition?"

"Oh, yes," Smith said. "We've been here before." In fact, he explained, he and Jones were the only students at Briarpatch who did not qualify for any scholarship or grant and, therefore, had to pay full tuition; that is, Jones had a scholarship, but lost it, and he himself never had any of the "regressive talents that were being rewarded by the Establishment." He relaxed somewhat when he saw that the chief was looking at them with new appreciation.

"What's your view on violence?" the chief asked.

"We're against it," they said almost simultaneously.

"We're here for Truth and Justice," Smith added. "You know, the American way."

Jones rolled his eyes, then explained that, "Some aspects of life are too important to be impeded by the commission of crimes that should be remissioned. Anyway, we believe in the life of the mind, not the death of whatever she was." This statement was sufficiently vague and sincere that Donahue was moved to whisper to the chief that it was unlikely either one could have carried Miss Purdy downstairs and that together they stood even less chance of doing so.

Reassured, Biggs told him that there were relatively few clues—some blood on the floor, some papers scattered around, the hall door left open, both doors of the small toilet locked from the inside, the men and women's restrooms having open windows, the broken glass on one side entrance to the building. Smith jotted down three or four words as notes.

Biggs, no longer certain that he had made a good decision in saying anything at all, told the boys only that the vice president was missing and that his entire force was currently looking for her, and that several state policemen were on the case as well. He had contacted the state police at the capital to send down a forensic expert.

"Don't you have an expert of your own?" Jones asked. "A *factotum* of special skills."

The chief explained that he did, but the man lacked experience, and this was not a case…" He almost said "for a beginner," but he saw Smith's pen move into position for a direct quote and decided that it was better to rephrase his words to, "This was a case that required the most expert criminologist in the state."

"No body, though?"

"No, no body." He didn't inform them that the criminologist had already been over the scene and found nothing useful to the investigation.

Smith floundered around in unconnected questions, asking about the late president, rumors about stolen money (it was the "financial office," he noted), the potential whereabouts of Miss Purdy, and the impact this would have on higher education. Biggs disclaimed knowledge of any of those matters. Smith thought hard to come up with new questions until Jones finally asked, "Why do you think this was murder?"

The chief answered this one seriously, "I am not certain that it is murder, but given what we see at the scene, we have to treat it as a potential homicide."

Smith tried to phrase the question differently, but got the same answer. When he faltered in the next attempt, Jones nudged him again. This started him off in a new direction, "For example, I know it wasn't murder."

Suddenly interested, Donahue leaned forward, "What was it then?"

"Huh, I dunno."

"Son," the chief said, "You seem to know more than you're saying... a lot more."

Jones tried to take back Smith's statement, "It's a long story." And he tried to leave, pulling Smith behind him.

Donahue, however, was in a position to block their path. He laid a hand on Jones's shoulder, indicated that they should both sit back down, and said, "The chief will take the time to listen."

Jones made himself the pair's spokesman, "My friend here wanted to write about the rumor that grades were for sale. What did President Boater know? That sort of thing."

Smith was embarrassed, "But I couldn't get an interview."

"She's in the coffee house every day," Donahue observed from over their shoulders. Catching the students' eyes when they turned to look at him, he pointed, "And her secretary works right down the way. You could make an appointment."

Smith hedged, "Well, our schedules never meshed." Glancing up at the police chief's stare, he explained, "She's a morning person."

Jones explained, "And Smitty's a nocturnalist."

"A what?" the chief asked."

Jones sighed, "He doesn't get up before noon."

This reminded Donahue of something, "Say, aren't you both in my Beginning Anthropology class?"

Smith admitted that he was, but "It's at 11. I can't make it all the time." Jones added that "Smitty dropped in now and then, but not often. He's kinda busy. You know, an omnivore for knowledge."

"And *your* excuse?" he asked Jones, interested in hearing the story he would invent.

"I can pass it by reading the textbook. No reason to attend... unless there's an exam."   Donahue threw up his hands. He didn't use a text, only a series of paperback readings and handouts. He paid for the handouts himself, since he had no budget for photocopying. Disgusted, he walked away and looked for anything that might be out of place.

As the boys sighed, Biggs asked, "Can we get back to your story?"

After a pause Jones said cautiously, "We just came by to see what was going on."

This made no sense at all to Biggs, who suggested, "Maybe you had better start at the beginning."

Smith now warmed to the subject. His shyness was evaporating. "Okay. In the beginning I needed a story. But there wasn't anything to write about."

Jones agreed with this, "How can you do an interview unless you know most of what you want already."

"Yeah, Professor Stout says to go prepared," Smith explained, "in case they try to feed you a line of bullshit."

"So when we were leaving the president's office—she wasn't in we heard the uproar in the financial office."

"Now when was this?" the chief asked.

"Afternoon sometime," Jones said.

"Yeah, afternoon," Smith agreed.

"And what the uproar about?" Biggs asked.

"Don't know," Jones replied, "but Miss Purdy could be heard yelling clear down the hall. A real harpy-fest."

"So we decided to find out what it was all about." Smith said. It was a lie, and he knew that Biggs knew it was a lie—they had intended to go there all along—but, hell, it was only a little lie. Nothing that people don't tell all the time. And nobody could get hurt by it.

"Did you?" Biggs added.

"No, she wouldn't speak to us."

"Practically threw us out of the office."

"When was this?" Biggs asked suspiciously.

"Like I said, in the afternoon."

"Which afternoon?"

"The afternoon we went in there."

This didn't satisfy the chief. "Is this story going somewhere?"

Wearily, Smith explained, "Yeah, I was writing this story, see?"

Jones hurriedly added, "I was helping."

"And we decided to find out what the hullaballoo was all about."

"So we went back after dark."

"Aha," Biggs said, "now we're getting somewhere." He glanced over to Donahue, caught his eye and gave a signal to join them.

As the boys brightened up, happy to be taken seriously, the chief apologized for what he had to do now, which was to read them their rights (actually only to "tell" them). The apology was unnecessary. Smith and Jones were well-informed and ready to talk.

Biggs, after summarizing for Donahue what had been said, asked the boys, "What were you looking for? To speak to the vice president again?"

"Honestly," Jones admitted, "we had no idea that she'd still be in the office."

"Nobody misses supper," Smith explained, seemingly unaware that supper had been hours earlier.

Jones was more to the point, "And almost nobody works late."

"You wanted to know about grades for sale?" Donahue asked.

"No, no," Smith assured them. "About the rumor. There's a difference. Besides we had other questions."

"When did you go back?" Biggs asked. He wasn't willing to get side-tracked again.

"Let's see," Jones said to himself, scratching his chin, "We had a couple of beers at the Pub." That was a new beer hall just off the square that had just opened to serve the larger number of students now on campus. There was nothing English about it. The barkeepers barely spoke English.

"That was about ten." Smith added.

"Then Smitty tried to write for a while. Didn't get much done, though."

"You and that damn computer game," Smith countered. "Who can concentrate with all that noise?"

"He finally gave up. Dunno exactly when."

Smith did, "I heard the bells at midnight."

"Then we talked a bit."

Biggs interrupted, "Is this going somewhere?"

Jones impatiently indicated that it was. "We were walking down on the square, hoping to get another beer, but the Pub was closed, when we saw some lights in the administration building. The light went out in Stan's office, but somebody was still moving around in the Finance office."

"What did you see?"

"Not much. It was on the second floor."

Smith decided to add his bit: "It wasn't a big light, either, you see."

"Sorta like a lamp."

"Sorta secretive, like," Smith explained.

"So we decided to see what was going on."

Biggs reflected on this while the boys watched him expectantly. At length, he asked, "What did you expect to find?"

"Well, we didn't expect to see her there. The main light had gone off a few minutes before."

"The main light went out, so you thought she had left?"

Without warning Jones jumped to a new subject, "We wanted to know how the president was stealing money." He had forgotten completely that Biggs was still thinking about the mysterious light.

Smith seconded Jones, "Yeah, *stealing* money."

Biggs was suspicious, "You *knew* she was stealing money."

Suddenly realizing that he had entered a dangerous zone, Smith retreated slightly, "No, not really. But there were all those stories about… about… you know, the rumors." He looked to Jones for help.

"You remember all those artifacts?" Jones asked.

"Yeah," Smith interrupted, "The artiwhats that the dean bought." He took a breath before continuing, "That poisoned ball that killed Floater."

"Yes," the chief and Donahue responded slowly, simultaneously. Indeed, everyone was aware how Flo Boater's husband had died. Just as everyone suspected she had been involved.

Smith exclaimed, "There must have been some money there. It's got to be in the finance office! A record of it, we mean." He was trialing off with, "We're not interested in the money itself," when Jones came to his rescue, "After all, where *is* all the money from that museum stuff?"

Biggs and Donahue exchanged knowing glances.

Jones then unexpectedly changed the subject. "Professor Stout says that everyone in power is stealing. Property steals from labor, power from the powerless. That's us, he says. Everyone steals."

"Everyone?" Biggs asked, incredulous.

"It's part of the capitalist system, see," Jones explained. "Property is theft."

Donahue held his head in his hands—of all the political philosophers whose ideas had lived past their time, it had to be Proudhon's which survived at Briarpatch.

"What do you call it, Jonesy? The Establishment. Well, we're going to disestablishmentarize it." He was proud to have gotten the word out.

"Disestablishmentarianism?" Donahue asked.

"Yeah, that or something like it," Smith explained. "Like a street gang. Old Boater's stolen our turf. We want it back."

"You want it back? Briarpatch College?"

Smith just shrugged, "Whatever. Jonesy says it's the principles that matter, the facts are only details."

"So, if she's a part of the system," Jones explained, "she's got to be stealing."

"Yeah," Smith said, warming again to the subject. "Miss Purdy had to be part of it, too."

"Why else," Jones continued logically, "would she be working that late, when nobody would be around to ask what she was doing?"

Donahue and Biggs exchanged glances.

"The only question was, *how?*" Jones continued.

"We thought it'd be easy to figure out."

"How?" Biggs asked.

"Well," Smith started to say, "Jimmy can…." It seemed like he was about to say "…any lock," when Jones cut him off, saying, "It stands to reason she would leave whatever she was working on in plain sight. So we wouldn't be breaking and entering, just sort of entering, like investigating reporters do. If we found something, no one would care that… well, no one would care. They never do on TV."

Smith took over again, "Staying there so late, that was suspicious! We couldn't just ring the buzzer. There isn't any buzzer."

"Besides, the light went out. She must have left."

"The main light, you mean?" It was Biggs's last question for a moment, it opening the locks to the boys' dammed-up memories.

"Yeah, the little light was left on. Like she forgot it."

"That would make it easier for us to see."

"Yeah, we didn't have flashlights or nothing."

"But we didn't want to turn on the big lights, like we'd have to."

Biggs, though confused as to who was stealing what, and what the boys envisioned her doing, decided to let them talk. But he finally interrupted, "So you broke into the administration building."

"It wasn't quite 'breaking in,'" Jones said defensively.

"No, the door wasn't locked," Smith added.

"It wasn't locked?" Biggs couldn't believe that, though that was what Flo had said.

"Well, I suppose it was supposed to be locked," Jones admitted.

"But Jay left it unlocked while he moved some stuff from a truck."

"When was that?" Biggs asked.

"About six, supper time."

Donahue interjected now, "Interesting!" A long time from six to three, he suggested.

The boys thought so, too.

"You know Jay?" Biggs inquired.

"Everybody knows Jay," Smith said.

"And Jay knows everybody," Jones adding, not mentioning that not everyone was happy about that. He remembered all too vividly his sports car being filled with campus trash day after day until he finally ceased to empty his ashtray on the street. That was back when he had a sports car, and when he could afford to smoke.

Biggs returned to the topic, "What did you do then?"

"We took refuge in the men's room until he left."

"On the first floor?"

"That's the only one."

The chief calculated, "If that was about six..."

Jones snapped the answer back quickly, "Jay was there maybe thirty minutes, then he went upstairs."

"To return some keys?"

"I suppose. Could be. We heard him leave maybe thirty minutes later."

"You sure it was him?"

"We were ensconced in the men's room, hiding out, so we couldn't see. But who else was there?"

Biggs continued to calculate aloud, "You said you were drinking beer till ten, writing till midnight, the murder—the presumed murder—occurred about two, maybe three." He stopped there, "You've lost me."

Jones hurried to explain. "It wasn't a murder. Not at seven."

"We came back," Smith admitted.

"We weren't going to sit there all night." Jones didn't want them to think he was an idiot. Imagine sitting in the men's room from six till three in the morning. One hour was bad enough.

Smith explained further, "Besides, Dean Wooda was still in his office. He would have had to take a leak sometime and seen us. So we left."

Interesting, Biggs thought and cast a glance toward Donahue, who nodded that Smith was right. Stanley Wooda didn't have a working toilet in his office. The renovations in his office had started with new wiring, new heating and new plumbing. Somehow the boys knew that.

"We left a window part way open so we could get back in." Smith explained.

"Didn't you think that would be noticed?" Biggs added. "Why not just unlocked?" This was on the side of the building facing the square, so there were people around. Still, there were trees there, and trees meant shadows.

"Lots of windows on campus are left open," Smith answered. "We didn't think we could get any leverage if we closed it. The old paint sticks pretty bad."

"It was just barely open," Jones added, "just enough to get a screwdriver under."

"Wouldn't that be suspicious?"

"Nah, the smell made it seem logical."

"Then you went out for a couple of beers?" Biggs asked.

"Probably more like five or six," Jones said. Smith nodded agreement.

"You can prove this?"

Jones laughed, "The barkeep will remember us."

Smith concurred, "Boy, will he! We didn't pay for the last two."

"You should have heard him," Jones said, "Dinner, Dinner." I think he wanted our money, but I was fiducially embarrassed." He hesitated a second before explaining, "I was broke."

"So we split," Smith said.

"Okay," Biggs said. "Then you came back about, what, two?" When they nodded, he asked, "How did you get into the building?"

Smith spoke up, "We came through the restroom window."

Then Jones happily admitted, "That was harder than we expected."

"Five feet off the ground," Smith snickered, and Jones, giggling, explained why it was funny, "We weren't exactly sober...."

"You mean the men's restroom?" Biggs suggested. He realized that the boys had gotten confused again. He studied their eyes for signs of drug use. Nothing unusual, he decided, and they weren't even wearing their habitual dark glasses.

"Yeah," Smith said, "We unlocked it earlier. That was easier than jimmying...." His voice trailed off.

Biggs gave him a quizzical look, but didn't ask.

Jones hurriedly explained, "We knew that there wouldn't be anyone to check it." After the briefest of pauses, he rattled on, "The budget crisis—the janitors are always let go first. You know how it is in capitalism. Always the proletariat first."

"The night watchmen, too" Smith said, interrupting, to which Jones added, "And they had already started on secretaries and faculty, so we knew that nobody would notice for a day or two."

"Damn capitalists," Jones added. "Never pay their bills."

The chief sighed, then asked, "Anybody else around?" The tone of his voice indicated that he understood there wouldn't be a night watchman.

"It was dark. Nobody was on the street." Jones explained, and Smith added that this was, after all, Middleville, and by then it was very late.

"Was anyone in the building?" Biggs queried, refining his earlier question.

"The dean's lights were off, too," Smith offered, "and we couldn't see any movement in the Finance office."

"There was still that little light in the Financial Affairs office," Jones added. "Silly name isn't it? Affairs!" When neither Biggs nor Donahue laughed, he continued. "We saw that from outside, but it might just've been left on. That happens all over the place. Not usually there, but we didn't think anyone was there. After all, the door was locked."

"But was there!" Smith said. "Wow!"

"Slow down, slow down," Biggs pleaded. And once they did, he asked, "Now, how did you get into the Finance office? You just said it was locked." Donahue leaned forward to give emphasis to the question.

The boys responded to the gesture. "Through the toilet, the private john," Jones admitted. He knew that his parents' lawyer would have told him to shut up, but he had sense enough to realize that no jury (should it come to that) would buy any story that got him into a locked building at 3 AM and then into an office where money might be found. Besides, he couldn't think of a story. Might as well tell the truth.

"The one you hid in?" Biggs asked.

This time Smith answered, "No, the Finance office bathroom."

Jones explained, "Not a bathroom, just a toilet. It had two doors, one to the office."

"One to the hall," Smith clarified.

"Slower, slower," Biggs said. "You're losing me."

"Me, too," Donahue admitted.

"I'll start at the beginning," Jones said. "When we cased the joint, we saw that we could tape the hall lock open. Learned that in history class. Watergate, you see. Once we got into the Inner Sanctum, we had it made."

The chief asked, "You mean, the office?"

"Yeah, from the Sanctum Sanctorum we could get into the office."

"They were more concerned with privacy," Smith explained.

Jones, seeing that the chief didn't understand, explained, "Having privacy in the toilet was more important than worrying about someone getting into the office."

"I don't understand," Biggs interjected before they could get started on one of their usual roundabout explanations that often made professors wish that the pair skipped class every day.

"The hall door was always locked," Smith explained, "and never used, so nobody ever checked it."

"Hardly nobody came in from the hall," Jones added, "so we knew that once we taped that door unlocked, it would remain accessible all night. Maybe for weeks."

"Nobody ever used that toilet?" the chief asked.

"It was right next to the women's room."

"No sign on it," Smith added. "Everyone thought it was a janitor's closet."

"How'd you get in then?"

"From the finance office, like I said. The women there use it."

"They let you in?"

"Of course not," Smith explained. "It's not a public toilet."

Jones, seeing Biggs was losing patience, clarified the statement, "I slipped in from her office, opened the outside door, put the tape on. When I came back out, Miss Purdy yelled at me."

"Boy, was she angry," Smith confirmed.

"But she never checked. And the Sanctum only unlocked on the inside anyway."

Biggs shook his head at the ingenuity of these burglars. For less effort they could become straight A students. But he confined his comments to, "Okay, then what?"

"We opened the door real quiet."

"Into the office?" Donahue asked.

"Yeah. Real quiet," Smith replied.

Jones gave him a sharp glance—this was his story now. "We didn't want Dean Wooda to hear. He sometimes works all night," Jones said, "and his office is on the same side of the building; if we took pictures for the paper, he might see the flashes."

"How?" Donahue asked.

"Reflection in the trees," Jones explained. He was the photographer of the two.

"We was very, very quiet, Smith continued, "but when we came into the office we heard noises...."

"Yeah, like pigs snorting," Jones clarified. He wasn't a farm boy, but he knew that pigs only went "oink, oink" in children's stories.

"Nobody heard us, 'cause we didn't come in the main door."

"And, like Smitty said, we were *real* quiet, existentially inaudible."

"And when we looked around the corner of the file drawers, there she was!"

"There she was all right," Jones added. "Making out with Professor Stout!"

Awed, Smith said, "I didn't think people that old could still do it."

"It was pretty gruesome," Jones agreed. "Practically unimaginable."

"Then what happened," Biggs asked, reflecting on the ages involved—Stout being in his late thirties and Miss Purdy in her forties, or the other way around. It may not have been a pretty sight, but only youths could believe them too old for romance or desire.

"She looked up, then came right after us!" Smith exclaimed. Apparently, this had been a frightening experience indeed.

"And you ran?" Biggs asked, trying to imagine the scene.

Jones shook his head vigorously up and down, his long hair keeping time, "You bet we did!"

Smith confirmed this, "Yeah, ran like hell."

"Out through the toilet?"

"Of course," Jones explained, there being no other way to retreat. "Through it, into the hall...."

"Then?" the chief asked. "Into the men's room?"

"Na," Jones said, "that's downstairs.

"Women's room. We opened the window."

"We thought someone was coming in the door, right behind us."

"Then what did you do?"

"We went out the window." He then added, "*Sauez qui peut*, if you pardon my French."

The chief shook his head, "That's a long jump in the dark."

Jones agreed, "It would have been a hell of a fall, but we grabbed onto the tree."

"And… what did the two… uh, lovers… do?"

Smith had to think about this. Finally Jones said, "They really didn't try to chase us. I guess they were…. Well, they just weren't in a good position to run."

Biggs smiled at this, but did not want to detract the boys from their story, "Where did the noise come from, from whoever was chasing you?"

Smith thought a moment, "Probably just our imagination. JJ was whispering, 'Jump, jump!' I don't know why he whispered. It didn't make no how difference then."

The chief barely managed to change his laugh into a question, "Where did the blood in the office come from."

"Dunno," they both said. "None there that we saw."

"No ideas?" Biggs asked.

They looked toward the heavens, as if hoping that a thought would come to them, and eventually Jones offered, "I may have heard a crash."

"Yeah," Smith agreed. "Now that you mention it. A big crash."

"Yeah," Jones said, "That's probably what we thought, why we thought someone was coming after us."

"When?" Biggs asked. "When you in the restroom?"

Smith had to think about this. "Afterward" he thought, while they were trying to open the window. Maybe while they were in the hall. But maybe while they were still in the office. Or slamming the toilet door and locking it.

Jones agreed, adding that he was too busy falling down himself to think about it.

Biggs mulled over this, "Very interesting story... But it has some flaws."

"Such as?" Jones inquired.

"The toilet was locked, both doors, from the inside."

The boys looked at one another, then Smith said, "It must have been the... uh, the door locked automatically."

"The one to the hall," Jones added. Talking was improving his memory.

"Why do you think so," Donahue continued.

"Smitty locked the door to the office so that she'd have to go around, through the other door," Jones said. "I'd forgotten about that. That's why it was locked. And I'd already pulled the tape off the other lock when we went in. It just clicked into place."

Smith added, "I thought she was right behind us, so as soon as Jonesy got through, I slammed the door, so nobody couldn't follow us."

"I don't understand," Biggs said.

"We'd locked the hall door from the inside, so we'd have privacy, just in case," Jones said.

"So, when I slammed it, it locked. But good. Then we got the hell out of there."

"We moved pretty fast," Jones explained. This was not something he did often.

"Still," Smith said, "when we fell down, I thought she might have caught us."

"Yeah, I fell down on the floor. Really slick."

"Me, too," Smith said. "Damn marble,"

Donahue remarked that Flo Boater had insisted that the new floors be polished and kept very clean. Everyone complained that they were too slick.

"I think she fell down, too," Jones said, "or she'd have had us."

"Miss Purdy, you mean."

"Who else? Not Stout. He was on the bottom."

Nodding thoughtfully, Biggs turned to the boys, "Didn't you think to look to see if she was hurt?"

"Her?" Jones asked, incredulously, "She's bigger than either of us."

"Both of us," Smith corrected. "Hell, I just wanted out of there."

"Didn't you worry about her recognizing you?" Biggs asked.

Jones shook his head negatively, "At first I wasn't even thinking."

"Later," Smith said, "we reasoned that our part of the room was dark."

"All they had on was a reading light. And they were right under it."

"So her eyes wouldn't have been adjusted...."

"Besides, she was busy."

"You didn't hit her?" Biggs asked.

"Never!" Jones was adamant about this.

"Never even came close," Smith confirmed.

"Close to hitting her?" Donahue asked.

"Never close to her in any sense," Jones insisted. "Propinquity, that just woulda sucked."

"I just wanted the hell out," Smith said.

"And you never thought to check on her, after she fell?"

"I wasn't sure she fell," Smith said. "I wasn't thinking right then."

"Would *you* have?" Jones asked, meaning "stopped to check." He had strong opinions about the behavior of human beings, and it was none too favorable.

"Would anybody?" Smith shared Jones's views of people.

Jones's final comment was the clincher, "I don't think I could've lifted her in any case, and Stout was there somewhere. Still underneath maybe."

"Yeah," said Smith. "He might have recognized us if he could have gotten up. Then we'd never have gotten the story printed."

"You sure it was Professor Stout?"

"You bet." Smith boasted. "We'd know him anywhere. I just never expected to see him there!"

"Still can't believe it," Jones confirmed, "but seeing is believ'ng. No clothes on.

"Not a stitch," Smith added. "I think. But, hey, everything was going down fast."

Donahue thought a moment, "You said you had a camera."

They understood the implications of the question. After looking at one another, Jones said, "I forgot to take a picture."

"No, you didn't," Smith corrected. "You took one. But I forgot all about that. Where's the camera? D'you lose it?"

After a moment Jones remembered dropping it, then said, "Hey, that's it over there!" He pointed to a nearby desk. A camera sat there, its back open.

Donahue and Biggs exchanged glances. They had wondered about the camera earlier, no film, no fingerprints.

Biggs pointed to the hall and said, "You boys go out there and wait." As they went out and found two chairs, he said to Donahue, "It all seems to fit."

"Breaking and entering, but no murder," Donahue agreed, "not even assault or an intent to steal. Just a stupid accident."

Biggs smiled, "But at last we have witnesses."

"Not ones the State's Attorney would want to put on the stand, but they made life a lot easier for us."

Donahue nodded in agreement.

Jones watched the two adults carefully, trying to lip-read without any success. Finally, he asked Smith, "Are we in for it?"

"In for it? No way. A slap on the wrist. But what a story! I might get national attention for this!"

"National attention?" Jones asked.

"My fifteen minutes of fame" Smith boasted. "When I graduate, editors will know how far I will go for a story. This will make my career!"

Jones was less thrilled, "Think I'll get my camera back? My parents paid a lot for it."

Chapter Twenty-Three

The next stop was at Miss Purdy's apartment building. Bigg's visit had hardly seemed necessary when she first failed to show up for work, since a patrolman had checked it out, then President Boater had assured him that there was no real disappearance. He had been skeptical, but without a formal complaint…. Since then the forensic specialist had gone over the apartment, and Donahue had interviewed the neighbors. He hadn't expected to see her there—few murder victims are taken home by their assailants *after* the deed is done. Now it wasn't important. What is the point of once again looking for addresses of friends and relatives? If she were well, she would show up eventually, and even if the boys' story surely had been more imagination than fact, murder was no longer a consideration. "It would be different," he said to Donahue, "if any one was suspected of any type of crime—other than breaking and entering—but every indication points to Miss Purdy looking for evidence of a crime herself."

"Complicated," Donahue responded, "by what seems to be Flo Boater's interest in that very evidence."

Biggs gave him a sideways glance. He didn't know about the artifacts and records.

Donahue hurried to say, "As for being caught up in some kind of crime of passion, it wasn't rape, probably, given the position of the…." At that he stopped, the door being opened by the landlady.

Miss Purdy was not there, which was no surprise, but a neighbor who worked a night shift said that she had told her that she was going away, and that she might not be back. "Yes," she said, "she seemed to have been injured." It was hard to tell, because she had a kerchief pulled around her lower face, but she seemed to have a "gigantic headache." She had two suitcases and her cat and did not say when or if she would be back. No, the neighbor didn't read the newspaper or listen to the radio. And, yes, she was hard of hearing. She hadn't even known that she had returned from her earlier absence.

Professor Stout was at home and apparently expecting them. He had not slept well, that was clear at the first glance, and, though his packing was still incomplete, the half-empty suitcases on the dining room table suggested that he, too, had intended to flee the city, or had so intended until he thought better of it. He invited the chief and his colleague in, offered them coffee, which they accepted because it was already started. (Stout was famous for his excellent knowledge of all sorts of beverages, including a taste for coffee so refined that when he went to the coffeehouse, it was not for coffee; and he avoided the Diner altogether.) Normally, Biggs would have declined, but since this was as much a courtesy call as an investigative matter, why not enjoy it?

Stout was always entertaining, if you didn't take him seriously, and Biggs never did. He could listen without even cracking a smile, and whenever Stout got too outrageous, he would just take another sip of the excellent coffee. Truly excellent coffee, too, and real cream. It was harder for Donahue, so he left the talking to Biggs.

Stout had his story prepared. He had been "courting" the lady for some time, but she was too embarrassed to go to his place and there was no privacy at hers, and the relationship hadn't gone that far anyway…. "Anyway, she was working late, so when I saw the light on in her office—I was just taking a late walk around the square. I often do that when I want to think—I phoned her, at home first, then the office, to see if anything was amiss."

"Light? What kind of light?"

"The room lights. The whole place was lit up, and someone was in there."

"Go ahead."

"Miss Purdy came down to let me in, told me she was looking for expenditures for the museum that were not in the budget—and, well, one thing led to another. But it wasn't what one might think, though I was surprised at how forward she was."

"The lights," the chief interrupted. "What lights were on?"

"Interesting you should ask. There was only that small lamp. The overhead lights were off."

"Didn't that tell you something?"

He shrugged, "Only that, maybe, she didn't want people to see us together."

"See you?"

"Somebody on the square might notice. It would be a clear view above the trees. Big windows, you know. Former courthouse."

The chief sighed before asking, "Then what happened?"

"Nothing really. We just sat at the table…"

"Close together?

"Well, we had to both see by the light, and it would have been awkward to look at the papers upside-down." He talked on and on, how they both had their clothes on and were just sitting at the table, looking at some papers she had found. Nothing untoward.

"What about the noise?" Biggs asked.

"What noise?"

"The boys who broke in on you. They heard noises."

"The boys heard noises?"

"Yes, the boys heard noises, and investigated."

"I don't remember noises, but Prudence, that is Miss Purdy, had said something about the building being as bad as a dormitory—music, people coming and going. You sure they weren't imagining things? Young people often do."

"No," Biggs responded. "The boys sounded pretty convincing."

"Uh," he started, "What did they see?"

"What," Biggs countered, "do you imagine they saw?"

This made him stop to think. He didn't remember anything unusual. Maybe when he kissed her on the throat. That must have been it. She did have a "strong reaction." After that, she had essentially attacked him, pushing him against the file case and trying to strip his shirt off. Maybe he had made some protests. He couldn't remember. But he could show them the torn button if they wished.

The main point was that "when she saw something, maybe the boys, she pushed me aside and started after them. But when she tried to open the toilet door, it was locked. She turned, slipped on the floor and went down." She made a tremendous "thud," but wasn't hurt.

"No blood?"

"Oh, maybe a bit. She said she could have chipped a tooth. I couldn't really see. It was dark over there."

"I understand. What happened next?"

"By the time I reached her, she was already getting up, but was extremely frightened and angry. She came right at me, hitting me, yelling that her reputation was ruined—I don't know why—and that everyone would laugh at her and such nonsense." He had tried to hold her away from him, but she was just too strong, backed him right into the file cabinets. So he slapped her.

Donahue's eyebrows went up. Stout using force! It was hardly in character. At least not his public character.

Stout shrugged. "Unavoidable," he said. "She had panicked, and I had calmed her down." She was bleeding from her nose, though. "Only a bit. Not much, but saying something about chipped teeth. Certainly not from my little slap, though something might have happened when she fell between the file cabinets a moment later, while trying to pick up the papers. Cut her lip, for sure, but teeth! Not likely. Blood smears? Maybe from my helping her pick herself up. She did fall over, you understand, twice."

"It looked like she was dragged."

"Dragged? Not at all. It wasn't easy to get her up, of course. So it may have looked that way. She kept flailing and turning over."

"Fighting back?"

"No. I'd say just scared and panicked. Nothing serious." After he helped her up, she pushed him aside, saying something about "people seeing us together and talking." No, she didn't want to wash her face in the restroom. Her private toilet was locked, and she wouldn't go in anywhere else. "'Just get me out of there,' she had said. And once I got her downstairs, she left."

"How?"

"Oh, by the side door. Everybody uses that door."

"Did she break the glass?"

"Don't know, don't think so." Himself? "I just went home. Didn't think much about it, except to soak my clothes in cold water, to get the blood out, until I met the Creep's mother on my morning walk and learned that Miss Purdy had been murdered." He paused to look for sympathy, but found little.

"What about the camera?"

"The camera. Oh, that. Yes, I took out the film while she was resting on a chair. Fingerprints? Yes, she told me to wipe up every surface, so that nobody would know we were together. I took out the film—her instructions—and exposed it. Threw the film away later."

"You left the door open? The office door."

"Yes, I suppose so. Once I got her into the hall, all I could think about was getting her downstairs."

"What next?"

"I heard somebody come in downstairs. From the head of the stairs I saw Flo Boater coming up, so we went down the other way. Flo climbs stairs fairly slowly. We didn't have to rush. Not that we could have."

"Awkward to explain, I imagine, your being there."

"Yes, it would have been," he said, almost with a blush.

"Then what did you do?"

"I rushed home and started to pack. Pure panic. But, fortunately, I realized that flight would have been foolish. So what if blood were found in the office? There wouldn't be much and it didn't mean anything. First, I knew that she was alive. Second, I hadn't done anything, and, third, who would know *I* had been there? I hadn't seen anyone, and whoever had been there probably hadn't seen me; and even if someone had recognized me, they would probably not say anything. Next, I couldn't have gotten all my fingerprints, but I had been in the office so often recently that it wouldn't prove anything. And lastly, where would I go? I had no 'home,' so I decided that it was best to say nothing until I was asked." He looked quizzically at the chief, then started in again, "I knew that she was not dead and that she would turn up eventually; moreover, she would probably make up some explanation that failed to mention me; and, if I was asked, I would just 'confess' the truth. That was the 'moral' way to handle it. 'Situational ethics' and all that."

"Was the side door blocked open?"

"Not the door we went through. Not many people use that one."

Biggs thought a moment. "What about the papers on the floor?"

"Nothing I know anything about," Stout said. "She had some file in her hands when I came in. She was going to show the contents to me, but I didn't get a chance to see much. Actually, I didn't know why wanted to show them to me, but she must have thought them important. After all, she invited me to her office late at night. I thought she had found something. You could have... well, I was really *floored* when she kissed me. Nothing more to it than that."

"Came as a surprise?"

"Yes. Shouldn't have I guess, the lights being off, that sort of thing. But she acted so normal up till then."

"Why did you wipe away your fingerprints?"

"Wipe away my fingerprints?"

"Yes, your fingerprints."

Stout thought for a moment. "I did clean up a bit, like she asked me to. Nothing to hide. Then I saw some blood." He paused, "I guess that's when I got the blood on me. Cleaning up."

"I thought you slapped her."

"I guess, yes, I did. Necessary, you know. Hysterical... Women, you understand. Prone to that sort of thing."

Biggs didn't understand, but all he asked was, "Didn't that cause bleeding?"

He thought a moment, "I doubt it. It was dark, you see. Just the little light on the desk."

"Not too dark to clean off your fingerprints."

Stout puffed up, "I explained that, just putting things in order again. And there was that light there."

"And where was Miss Purdy at that time?"

"Just sitting there. Then she stood up and sort of fainted, right next to the file cabinets. I think she wanted to keep me from looking at the papers. Then stood up too fast, or bent over too quickly. Anyway, I got up and helped...." At this he laughed, "Pulled her some, I guess. That must be the smeared blood. She's a big woman."

"I thought she slipped and fell."

Stout thought a moment, "It's hard to remember. It all happened so fast. And it was confusing. She had been yelling at somebody, or about somebody. And it was dark, only the small light until I turned the overheads on. Oh, later, to see if I'd cleaned up everything." After a pause he added, "I can hardly put it all together now." After another pause, he continued, "Now, if you had asked me right after the event...." At that he smiled.

"Flo Boater said the overhead lights were off."

"Oh, she's right. They were. I turned them off... automatic reaction... when we left. Didn't even think about it. After all, what difference did it make?"

"The small light was left on?"

"I guess so. Once the overheads were on, I didn't think about it again. Anyway, I couldn't have left her standing there alone to go back and turn it off. She might have fainted again."

An image ran through Biggs's mind—the crumpled rug, the bloody streaks. And he thought, "A story this bizarre has to be true, or largely so." He decided to change the subject. "Before all this started, did you find out anything about the money?" If Miss Purdy was alive, he could check with her, to see if her story matched his. Not that it made much difference. She was probably alive, and he doubted that she would press charges, or that there were any charges at all to press. The money, however, was a different matter. And maybe the boys, for illegal entry.

"No. Nothing. I still believe that the administration has money that no one can find—like perhaps an advance payment on the insurance. We could use that for projects we need to do. But that old maid's obsession with obscure sales was not going to locate it. I'm talking about hundreds of thousands of dollars, and all she could think about was a few tens of thousand for a few years."

Donahue winced at the term "old maid" being used so cavalierly by a person who was ready to employ seduction to get what he wanted—information. A roué, he thought, was usually willing to make a pretense at providing romance. But it took a certain winning personality to carry that off, and Stout had always seemed less likely to whisper amorous phrases that would remain long in the memory than to issue denunciations of capitalist exploitations. Some women go for that, too, he mused, but probably not a VP for FA.

Later, Donahue asked, "Did you believe him?"

Biggs laughed, "How could he *make up* a story like that?"

"How about Miss Purdy *assaulting* him?"

"Oh, I have some doubts about that."

"Me, too."

"My guess is that she showed him the documents, but refused to allow him to have them."

"My guess, too. What reason couldn't achieve, perhaps seduction could."

"Well put," the chief agreed, "but apparently he wasn't ready for the passion he aroused."

"Once he started, he couldn't back off."

"I kinda wish I'd been there to see it… Stout no longer in control of events!"

"Do you suppose," Donahue asked, "if right at the end, he tried to grab the papers from her?"

Biggs thought for a moment, "I think only Miss Purdy could tell us that, and I doubt she will. They ended up on the floor and he never had a chance to pick them up."

"Not even when cleaning up?"

"I'll bet he was too panicked by then to think about the papers. The intruders, then her falling down, the blood, her crying, wanting to get out of there."

There was a long moment of silence, finally broken when Donahue asked, "Chief, What do you intend to do now?"

"Nothing" was his answer. "Unless Miss Purdy wants to press charges for attempted rape or assault, and I doubt she will." Moreover, he couldn't even use Stout's own statements against him—he had not thought it necessary to give a Miranda warning. And even if he repeated them under oath, what did they prove?

"The boys?"

"Okay, they shouldn't have been there. But we don't need to drag Miss Purdy's reputation through the media mud."

Saturday morning early Donahue was at Flo Boater's door. When she appeared, apologizing that the maid never came until lunchtime, he said that it didn't matter—he didn't have time to come in. She looked puzzled as handed her a small manila package, for which she thanked him perfunctory, then asked what it was.

"The financial records you had been looking for," he replied, "and a few photos." Then, with the faintest tip of an imaginary hat, or a salute, he turned to leave.

"Wait," she called. "Have you found Miss Purdy?"

"No," he replied, "Not yet." He hesitated a moment before adding, "But we are fairly sure that she is not dead." Then he was gone.

Flo Boater sat down, put her head in her hands. "What the hell," she asked herself, "is going on?" Then she sighed, "At least she's not dead. Just injured or something. Assault? Must have been. But I didn't do it. Who then?" After a half-hour of thinking, she saw the papers on the desk where she had dropped them. Reluctantly, she picked them up and began to read.

It took Flo Boater about an hour to work through the lists and make sense of them. There were gaps, but the outline of the late dean's activities were clear enough. Nothing that implicated her, thank goodness! Nothing here, at least. But was there more? Had to be. Dared she ask? If she did, would Donahue tell her?

And the photos of the boxes, some of them opened. The labels could be read, though a magnifying glass would help, but there was no doubt what the contents were—the artifacts, at least some of them. She had no doubt that it would not take anyone very long to match photos to items in the invoices. "Where'd they get the photos? I thought that stuff was safely hidden."

Unsure of her next step, she called Stanley Wooda and told him to hurry over. Under the present circumstances, she was afraid to say anything over the telephone.

Their conversation ran in a great loop—what to do with the lists? She would have liked to analyze them, to see how much of a scandal she had to deal with, but that required more time than she had; and she didn't even know where the items were. Moreover, right now she wanted to concentrate on the "missing persons" investigation. Was she a suspect again? Did her possessing these records serve to exonerate or implicate her? Who would believe that Donahue had just handed them to her? Were his fingerprints on the bag? And did it make any difference? If he gave the records to her and she didn't turn them over to the lawyers? Lastly, where was that damned bag? In the trash.

"In the trash!" Stanley Wooda had exclaimed.

"Actually a shredder. It was an automatic reflex," she said. "Everything goes into the trash."

"But a shredder?" he protested.

"I'm starting to shred everything I can. It's much safer."

"Well," he commented, "it probably doesn't matter. It would be damned hard, even if his fingerprints were on the bag, to prove that the bag was connected in any way to the records."

"You are right," she conceded. "There were no witnesses."

"Did he make copies?"

"Wouldn't you have?" she snapped back.

That was the sticking point. If copies existed, they couldn't take any chances. Their only course of action was to deliver the records to the college attorney. Stanley Wooda pointed out that now they might have to find some way of displaying the artifacts, the ones that hadn't been sold.

"That could be very embarrassing. It's out of the question," she stated. "Besides, we're going to have to pay that buyer, whoever he is. We can't have him calling around, asking for his money."

"No, that's not what I mean" he suggested. "A museum might be the only way out, even if all we have left is junk. Tell the board that in order to offer students more experience with non-western cultures, with alternatives to our so-called modern civilization, we need a museum to display the materials *that have been donated*."

"Donated?"

"Yes, by the late dean."

"But that wasn't in his will, or written down anywhere I know of."

"Tell them that *his nephew* knew it." He then pointed to himself.

"You're not his nephew!"

"No, but they don't know that. All we need is some funds to build a museum. Then buy whatever we need to fill the gaps in the collection."

"We don't have that kind of money! Or are you thinking they'll endorse a capital campaign?" She was sarcastic. "It takes three to four years for that"

"That might string Donahue along. Keep him off our backs."

"Not very likely," she said, "unless, unless...." She then paused to think, "Unless we tell him that we already have a building."

"What building?" he asked, genuinely puzzled.

"The Music building, of course." Seeing amazement spread across his face, she asked, "You didn't believe that nonsense about mold did you? Sure, there was some mold, and asbestos, but it's no *Little Shop of Horrors*. The point was that Woody needed storage space. Private space. So he made up those stories. The Superintendent of Buildings and Grounds went along... I don't know what Woody paid him, if anything, but people like him come cheap."

"Woody," he gasped. "Dean Wooda. It was all a scam? You mean that he never had any interest in multi-cultural studies?"

"God," she complained, "you sound like Stout!"

"Why did he make all those plans, tell everybody about it?"

"Think about it, Stanley," she said. "Would he have hired anyone as inexperienced as Donahue if he had been serious about starting a museum? DO's not even an anthropologist."

Stanley Wooda was silent for a minute, then he walked over to the window, pulled back the curtain and looked out at the perfect lawn before speaking. "This can still work out. Tell Donahue that he can be director when he comes back from Latin America."

"You mean, to have him here forever?"

"No," he explained smoothly. "This is just temporary. We can find a reason to change our minds later."

When Lill and Lily heard the story, Lill asked her friend, "You still believe Miss Purdy was a lesbian?"

"Well, she had me fooled."

"Maybe life is just more complex than we think."

Chapter Twenty-Four

In the late afternoon Donahue and Biggs were seated in the coffee house. They had taken a table at a discreet distance from everyone and the background noise, complete with juke box, assured them of privacy. Students celebrating the 22-21 win over Arcadia Junior College had mostly gone to the Pub, but the enthusiasm of those in the coffee house made Donahue wish he had seen the game. Homecoming and all that, but he didn't know enough former students…. Anyway, he had wanted to help wrap the investigation up.

"I'm glad to have this over with," Donahue said. "Nice of you not to embarrass the kids."

Biggs shrugged, "The district attorney can take their statements in private. The *Moderate* editor will cooperate. No publicity."

"He won't print a story?'

"Oh, there'll be a story. He'd have to, or the big city papers would, eventually. But he'll stress Miss Purdy's decision to leave."

"A rather sudden decision."

Biggs smiled, "People do that."

"For the boys. No jail time?" Donahue hoped.

"Guilty plea to breaking and entering, perhaps negligent indifference. No previous trouble. Probably only probation. We don't need to use jail space for fools."

"Young fools," Donahue corrected.

"They probably watch too much television," Biggs suggested. "People break into all sorts of places, and nothing ever happens to them. It's another of Hollywood's misleading messages."

Donahue shook his head, "Do you believe their story about coming in through a window?"

Biggs almost laughed, "I know how Jimmy got his nickname. He's probably been into every building on campus. But he's never stolen anything that I know of."

279

Donahue thought for a moment, "They'll have a police record."

"Probation, no jail time. They're lucky they didn't enroll in the university up to Zenith. The experience may keep them honest till they graduate."

"If they ever do."

As they mused over this, Biggs asked where the artifacts were now. They weren't in the Theater. Earlier he had been sure they were in the locked rooms, but without a warrant he hadn't dared enter them. It had been less than an hour that he had looked again. The rooms were unlocked and empty.

"Oh, Jay moved everything to a safer place. He's just cleaning the rooms up now."

"Where would that be?"

"You remember that Jay was in the administration building between six and seven?"

"I had wondered about that."

"The artifacts."

"Empty rooms on the third floor? I checked up there, to see if the 'murderer' was hiding there. The rooms were packed, but dust was on everything. Nothing new there."

"Better than that. He was moving the boxes into the storage area behind Flo Boater's office."

Biggs was stunned. What a perfect hiding place. No one would suspect looking there, and Flo could say with a perfectly straight face that she had no idea where the materials were. Biggs wasn't clear how Jay had gotten into the presidential office, since Flo Boater had called in all the keys necessary for cleaning and repairs, including his, but Donahue explained that the painters had needed access, so she had given them the keys to the main door and her office. Jay was there when they finished the day's work, and since he was the Superintendent of Buildings and Grounds, they assumed he was the proper person to give them to. He simply kept the keys until his work was done before dropping them into the box at the president's office.

"And she wasn't suspicious?" Biggs asked.

"No, she even gave him the keys again so that he could get the boxes out of the theater. She didn't know they were already in her own office."

"Then he just calmly returned the keys the next day?"

"That's the way he did it."

"Now," the chief said, "I'm a bit confused. Why'd he move the stuff out of the theatre?"

"The Creep had seen it. He figured it wasn't safe there any more, so he got Lill and Lily to help him move it away."

Biggs laughed, "He's a clever bastard."

Donahue chuckled that the move had the additional advantage in, should the matter become public, it would make Flo Boater's situation very suspicious indeed. How could she not have known that it was all there? The number of boxes was, after all, considerable. Only someone who knew her well would understand.

Biggs had thought of this, too, and more. He wanted to know how Jay had been able to move all those boxes in an hour.

Donahue explained, "First, he didn't move them all that fast. They were all in the theater, but that was totally unsatisfactory after the historian saw them—he wasn't above some crude blackmail. So Jay got Lill and Lily to help him load the stuff. They met at the administration building and got everything into a downstairs storage room. He was worried about Lill and Lily's being involved further, just in case there was real trouble, so he asked Lily to drive the truck back to the service building while he moved the stuff upstairs."

"What about Lill?"

"He said that couldn't load the freight elevator alone, then run upstairs to upload, it, then run downstairs, so he asked Lill to load, while he went upstairs and unloaded. Once he had the boxes upstairs, he told her to leave. Dean Wooda was in the building. He could make up an excuse, but she couldn't."

"That makes sense," Biggs commented. He then scratched his chin, "I didn't know there was a freight elevator."

"Hardly anyone does," Donahue explained. "It was really old, and very small. Nobody but Jay could make it work. Good enough to get the boxes one at a time to the second floor, then all he had to do was get them into the president's office."

"So what the boys heard about six-thirty was Lily leaving?"

"That's right. And they heard Lill leave about seven, and Jay went upstairs."

"I thought Wooda was there all that while," Biggs asked. "Wouldn't he have heard? I can't imagine that elevator not making noise. Probably a lot of noise, if it hasn't been used much."

"It was more like a dumb waiter, at the end of the building, and originally they could unload into it directly from wagons."

"An outside door? I don't remember one"

"Long ago. It was bricked in, but the lift could still be reached from inside."

"Then he carried everything by hand into the room behind the secretary's office?"

"Not quite. Once he got the boxes upstairs, he used a dolly. It was in the room with the dumb waiter. They used it mainly for paper supplies, that sort of thing."

"The dolly must have made noise, too. Those are marble floors."

"Sure," Donahue said, "but Jay said that Wooda had 'company.' So there was music and maybe something to relax them."

"That early? I thought his visitor came in the wee hours."

"Technically, Stanley said he was working—doing research on 'student interests,' but I bet his guest had come in earlier. That's why the side door had been unlocked when Flo Boater first came in, so he wouldn't have to hang around to let the young wo... whoever it was, in. Flo didn't think anything about it because the Dean of Students occasionally worked into the supper hour, and she would have to go upstairs to consult the Registrar, who stayed late whenever the dean asked her to. So the door being open, and some noise at that time wouldn't have been unusual. Consequently, Stanley Wooda wasn't listening for anything except a knock on the door, and with no night watchmen, Jay didn't worry about being heard. But it took a long time to move the boxes into the president's office, and when the dean or his company moved around, or Miss Purdy did, he had to wait until it was quiet again. Someone came in about two. He wasn't sure where they went."

"Stout."

"Probably, maybe Stanley's visitor. There was still a light in Miss Purdy's office at that time. Jay was worried that she would just step out and see him, but when she didn't, he just kept working. He had to move the furniture and the painters' coverings, then put them all back. He was really 'whipped' by two-thirty, when he left."

"Who broke the glass in the door then?"

"Jay. Flo Boater called him first. He had dropped the keys into the box, so he either had to wait or break the glass."

Biggs smiled, "Jay is never one to stand around and wait."

"No, he thought it was a real emergency. And there was your patrolman banging on the main door. He still can't imagine why he didn't follow him right on up."

Biggs nodded, smiling, imagining the situation and wondering if he had sufficient grounds to search for illegal substances in the dean's office. His thoughts were interrupted by Donahue saying that Jay had reported seeing a young woman leave the building just before he got there. "He was miffed by not having caught the door before it closed. He tried to get the attention of whoever was inside, but Flo didn't come downstairs again to open up."

Biggs smiled again, "I'll bet that's why he responded so quickly when she called him. He hadn't even gotten undressed."

"I don't remember either of them saying that."

"They didn't, in so many words." Suggesting that it wasn't important anyway, he slipped into a daydream, trying to imagine how Stanley Wooda was able to function during the day.

"When you do make a public announcement?" Donahue asked, breaking into the chief's reverie. "That would let everyone breathe easier."

Sighing, Biggs agreed, "I guess I'd better do that now. Before we have rumors of a serial murderer being loose on campus."

Donahue smiled, "Don't we?"

Biggs laughed, "Yes, but I can't prove it, and she had nothing to do with *this* incident."

"Not danger to the public, either," Donahue offered, and upon Biggs giving him a quizzical look, explained, "The killer only strikes deans and presidents."

Biggs laughed again and said that, moreover, one suspect had been dead for more than a year and the other had no more obvious victims ahead of her. Not as far as we know. He had hardly finished his thought before he looked up to see Flo Boater come through the door, look around and start in their direction. He stood up to say hello.

She was suspiciously friendly, "I was really hoping to find you here, DO. I've been looking all over for you." Turning to Biggs, she said frostily, "And you, too, Chief. Do you mind if we go to my office? Easier to talk there."

The chief shrugged and said, "Not at all, but I've got to check with the office."

"Will that take long?" she sniffed.

"No," he responded. "You two go ahead. I'll join you in a few minutes."

On the walk Flo asked, "DO... You don't mind if I call you DO?"

"Whatever you would like, President Boater."

"First of all, I want to thank you for bringing me those records. The college attorney will certainly find them useful in clearing up the late dean's... affairs." She stumbled at the last, aware too late of its double meaning.

"Not at all," he responded. "That was the right thing to do."

Curious, she asked, "How did you come by them?"

He evaded the question, leaving her to jump to the conclusion that they had been in the finance office and that, with no vice president who would know what to do with them, that he had delivered them to her. It was unclear whether Biggs knew about them and whether or not he had made copies as potential evidence.

"DO, this is a bit awkward." She paused before continuing, "This is the situation." There she paused again before taking a deep breath and continuing, "I remember how nicely you cleaned up that last misunderstanding."

"You mean your being accused of murdering Dean Wooda?" he asked.

Taken aback by the sharpness of his comment, she blurred out an awkward response, "Well, yes… to put it bluntly."

Donahue then took the edge off his comment, "But we know you didn't do it."

"No, of course, I didn't," she said. "I didn't kill my husband, either."

After a long, uncomfortable pause, Donahue added, "And certainly not the Vice President for Financial Affairs."

"No," she responded, somewhat confused. "Not her either. She's not dead, anyway, apparently."

"Then how can I help you, President Boater?"

"First of all," she purred, "I want to thank you for those documents. That should aid me greatly in resolving the *problem* of the missing artifacts."

"No thanks necessary," he said. "I was only doing what was best for the college."

"Yes, of course," she conceded. "You always do." She bit her lip to keep it straight, then continued, "I have another *small* request." This was the approach she had used so successfully when she was sixteen. It had never failed with her late husband and the more elderly trustees.

"How may I be of service," he inquired, a bit stiffly.

She tried to take his arm, unsuccessfully, then said, "It's this way. It's embarrassing… for me …and for the college… to have all this bad publicity… and speculation."

"Speculation? By whom? Chief Biggs?"

She dismissed that angrily, "By the press! I don't care what Chief Biggs thinks, but the press reaches potential students, donors, and the trustees." She took another deep breath before continuing more quietly, "Those vultures never miss an opportunity to run down our poor little college."

"I thought the problem was that they ignored us."

"When things are good, they do," she snapped. "But the moment we have trouble, they are all over us."

He spread his hands helplessly, then asked, "How can I help?"

Returning to her seductive tone, she purred, "Do you think, would it be possible... to persuade Chief Biggs to, well, to...."

"To wrap up the investigation quickly?"

Delighted with the suggestion, she exclaimed "Why, yes. My very thoughts. Elegantly expressed." After a moment she added, "No scandals, no scandals of any kind."

He hesitated, then said, "I think I might have some influence."

"Excellent, excellent," she exclaimed, clapping her hands and touching his in thanks.

Donahue did not join in the celebration and quickly his serious mien transmitted itself to her. As she waited expectantly, he said, "I have a request of my own."

"Oh," she said, cynically, stopping to face him. "A *quid pro quo?*"

"No, just a request."

"Let me hear it," she said dryly. "If it's reasonable, I might be able to do something for you. You *have* earned it."

"Not for me, necessarily."

Suspiciously, she asked, "You are sure you can persuade Biggs?"

"I think so," he said. "If I put my mind to it."

She shrugged and, proceeding into the building, said, "Name your price."

"My *request* or *requests*, I think there are three of importance, might seem rather high." He wanted to make it clear that this was not extortion. Seeing that she was in a mood to negotiate, he asked, "Interested?"

"If you can deliver, nothing is too high," she said, then added quickly, "Other than my resignation!"

"That never crossed my mind," he assured her.

As they entered her office, she touched his arm again, then confided, "A resignation would make the college look too bad. It would be a confession of sorts."

"Besides," he said, taking a chair, "I'm sure you are *innocent.*"

"You are!?" She was stunned. "I thought you were just saying that." She slumped back into her power chair.

"You are probably innocent of *any* wrongdoing."

She hardly knew what to say. After all, she had been at the scene of the crime at a very suspicious hour. "You really believe me?"

"Yes, I'm almost certain you are innocent."

"But the others..." she pleaded.

"If it's a matter of persuading *others*, the price of that, my *requests*, that is, is high."

"How high?" She was suspicious again.

"Tenure for Mary." When she nodded agreement, he added, "Without going to Latin America." This time the nod came more slowly, but it came. Then he told her the third request, "Lastly, canceling the exchange you arranged for me."

She pretended to be surprised, "But the *opportunity!*"

"I'll make my own opportunities," he said. Then he asked, "Agreed?" She thought for a moment, then said she could manage that, too.

They stared at one another across the desk until she asked, "Not tenure?" She could not imagine anyone passing up an opportunity for advancement. Her belief that all wisdom could be found in *The Godfather* series had made her cynical. She never quite grasped why Michael had joined the army.

Donahue kept firm eye contact as he responded, "I'm not eligible yet."

Boater wouldn't accept this as final. She tried to tempt him, "I can arrange it."

"I'd rather earn it."

With a deep breath, she gave up, "Whatever you say."

"Wait," Donahue said. He had realized that she was ready to pay more than he had asked, so he plunged ahead, "One more request...."

Flo took a deep breath, half out of satisfaction in knowing that Donahue was human, too, and half out of trepidation over what he might want. She said, cynically, "A *last* request?"

"Yes," he said. "But it's a hard one for you."

When she indicated that she was steeled for the ordeal to come, he said, "Make Lill chair of the theater department again."

"Never!" she snapped.

Starting to stand up, Donahue shrugged and said, "I guess justice will just have to take its course."

She jumped up to stop him, "That could take forever!"

"I'm in no hurry," he said laconically and tried to move toward the door.

But she was in his way, "Okay. Stop. *Stop.*" And when he managed to hold her hands off him long enough to get past, she shouted, "Come back. *Whatever you want.* Just get this *nightmare* over."

He turned to her, "Put it in writing."

Depressed, she repeated, "In writing."

"Now," he said, indicating they should sit down again. "Signed and dated."

Flo Boater asked one more time, "No publicity?" Then she sought out some official stationary and sat with the pen poised for action. Then nothing happened. "Writer's block," she said, "This will take a minute." At that moment Miss Efficiency knocked, then said that Chief Biggs was waiting. Flo Boater thought only a moment, then said to Donahue, "You go talk with him while I think."

Donahue could only wonder what was going on. Why was Miss E working so late on a Saturday?

Chapter Twenty-Five

"Right away," Donahue said as walked out to where Biggs was waiting. They then went out into the hall.

For a moment she watched them through the open door, speaking in apparently quiet voices, then leave. She frowned before turning to her task. When she was finished, she read the letters again, then when asked her secretary to bring Donahue back in.

Donahue came in alone, sat down, then nodded to indicate that the chief had agreed.

"You're sure he's agreed?" she asked, doubtfully.

"He doesn't know the details. But he trusts me."

"He trusts you?"

"If the letters are what they should be, it will be okay."

With a sigh, she handed them over, "Here, read them."

Donahue asked, "Shall we ask Chief Biggs to sign the letters as a witness?"

Ruefully, she agreed, but not without asking, "You are sure he will call his investigation off?"

"Absolutely," he assured her.

Biggs looked through the letters, asked her if that was indeed her signature, and when she nodded, he signed and dated them. He took the letters out to Miss Efficiency, saying, "We might as well make photo-copies now, then I can deliver the originals." Once the letters were back in his hands, he mimicked a salute to the president, "I'll see that you get a copy of my final report to the state police." With that he sauntered off, apparently feeling pretty good.

As Flo Boater stood up, she asked Donahue, "When will he make an announcement?"

Donahue had apparently asked about this already, "It will be on the radio first, in the newspapers tomorrow morning, that the investigation

289

is over. Biggs will call Miss Purdy's leaving town a personal decision. Nothing about missing money."

"Or the broken door?"

"No, nothing."

"Leaving town? That's the story."

"Yes, she's already gone."

"And the scandal?"

"No, why hurt her chances for another job?"

Her mood changed instantly. "That sounds *just fine...*" she said seductively. "I don't know how to thank you enough."

To Donahue this was just inappropriate enough to be classic Flo Boater. It must have worked for her in the past. But he felt just like Pericles accosted by Cimon's sister. His response however, avoided suggesting that she was too old to influence men in this way, "Just carry out the promises in those letters."

"Then," she said, "Thank you!" With that she extended her hand.

Donahue, to his own surprise accepting the handshake, managed to come up with a platitude, "I am so glad that we could work this all out." Then he excused himself, "I think I'd better go tell Mary. She will be pleased to have this behind her." With that he left.

"Not nearly as I am!" she exulted to herself. She then literally danced around the place, imagining what a splendid ball she would have for her inauguration. What a shame that she would have to wait a "decent interval" before she could cut loose. She hadn't danced much since she and Floyd were courting. Afterward, Floyd and she became too busy, and after he became president at Briarpatch, they learned that two aged trustees insisted on maintaining the ancient No Smoking, No Drinking, No Dancing and No Work on Sunday of the college's past. Out loud, she said to herself, "Well, those crones are gone and so are their rules!"

She went out to Miss Efficiency and told her to inform the trustees that rumors about a burglary in the administration building were not true, and that Miss Purdy, who had been out of town, had decided to leave for personal reasons.

Her morning coffee was interrupted by a loud knocking on the front door.

She was very displeased at the interruption—Sunday morning was her favorite time, a few hours for total relaxation. For a moment she wondered if she could just ignore the noise, then she discerned Stanley Wooda's voice. Reluctantly, she got up and let her dean in.

"Thank goodness I've found you," he gasped. "You weren't answering your phone."

"I didn't want to be interrupted on Sunday morning."

"I hope I'm not too late."

"Too late for what?" she asked as he sat down opposite her.

"To stop you from making another deal with DO. Biggs has gotten two students to confess!"

"Confess? To what?"

"That the vice president wasn't killed. She was only injured slightly in an accident. It was their fault for breaking in on her and Professor Stout."

"Stout?" she asked unbelievingly. "And Miss Purdy?"

"Yes," he exclaimed. "They were making love on the floor of the office when the boys sneaked in. She fell trying to catch them. Slipped on the floor."

"No," she said, "one of the rugs probably slipped. I'd warned her about those. But she didn't like the marble and wouldn't buy anything big enough to put furniture on."

"Did you give her money for rugs?" Stanley Wooda asked unbelievingly.

"Of course not! That's why she had only small rugs." There was a budgetary crisis, she wanted to remind him.

"The boys didn't say anything about that."

"Who were these boys?" she asked.

"Smith and Jones."

"Those scamps," she exclaimed. "You can't trust anything they say."

"The chief believes them, and so does Donahue."

"Donahue!" she cried out. "Did Donahue know about this?"

"Oh, yes. He heard them confess."

"What's going to happen to those hippies?"

"Nothing. The chief wants to keep it all quiet... to protect Miss Purdy."

She collapsed into a chair, "Damn, damn, damn, damn." With each damn, she pounded her fist on the arm. At last she just put her hands in her face and wished she could weep. But she was too angry.

"What's the matter?" Stanley Wooda asked, very concerned that his worst fears were true. And they were. As he listened, horrified, to how she had written letters giving Mary tenure and making Lill head of the theater department. He buried his head in his hands, muttering, "We could have bargained one silence for another."

"We had them right here," she said, pointing to her palm. "And we could have insisted...." She started to stand, but couldn't. "I could have insisted that they go to Latin America."

All that could be heard for some time was her muttering "damn" and him mumbling "Donahue."

Having exhausted all the damns at her command, she stood up and shouted, "That bastard has done it again! One of these days I'm going to kill him."

To which Stanley Wooda responded quietly, "Only if you beat me to it!"

Donahue wasn't worrying. He had a dinner date with Mary, to go to the Diner, then to the college choir's concert. Molly would be the lead soloist.

That evening Flo Boater called the parents of Smith and Jones, both fathers now trustees on the college board, and explained how she had managed to keep their sons out of public embarrassment. And, though they had made a serious lapse in judgment, they were fine young men who would be a credit to their family and to Briarpatch College.

She concluded by expressing a hope that funds might be collected to turn the Music building into a small anthropology museum, with offices and classrooms for the professors who would manage it.

Chapter Twenty-Six

On Monday Donahue and Biggs arrived at the coffee house toward noon, looking for Mary and Jenny, Lill and Lily. None of them were there yet. They knew that Lill and Lily would have had their breakfast and coffee already in the little kitchenette in the theater building, and then have taken care of the paperwork associated with managing the theater program; rehearsals were in the evening and classes consisted of listening to student efforts to deliver plausible persuasive speeches. Mary would have gone for her run and gone to her classes as soon as she had showered and dressed. Jenny? Who knew? She ran on Southern time. As a result, Donahue and Biggs had never really expected that any of them, except Lill, would be there exactly at the time agreed upon. The place was almost deserted. Students who had gotten up for breakfast were probably in class, 11 AM being a favorite hour for both faculty and students; a few students were undoubtedly still in bed, exhausted by the celebration of the football victory. The chief suggested they take a seat, but it was only moments before the caffeine called to him. He was disappointed—it smelled better than it tasted, but Donahue thought it was not as bad as usual. They then lapsed into silence.

Donahue was the first to speak, "So it's all wound up now?"

"More or less. There are some loose ends, but it's not my responsibility to tie them up."

"Have you reached Miss Purdy?"

"Yes," he laughed. "Her disappearance was a business trip, to speak to trustees and various endowments."

"What? Then why didn't Flo Boater know?"

"She couldn't say. She had sent her a note, with all the details."

It was Donahue's turn to laugh, "Flo Boater never reads notes."

293

The chief smiled, then added, "And what she had learned on the trip worried her so much that when she got back, she just ripped into the old records."

"Had she told anyone of her suspicions?"

"No," the chief said. "She was completely loyal to the president. Tight lips."

Donahue pondered that for a moment before asking, "The boys? What becomes of them?"

"The District Attorney will recommend probation and community service."

Donahue was intrigued, "What kind of community service." He tried to imagine getting them anywhere on time.

Laughing, Biggs said that they would have to put in one hundred hours under Jay's supervision. "Next summer Smith and Jones may pick up as much trash in two or three weeks as they scattered across this campus in three years!"

Donahue had to smile at the mental image. "Yes," he told himself, "and they will show up on time, too, if I know Jay." After a moment, he asked, "What did the boys say about buying grades?"

"Oh, not much. Only that they had heard rumors, and that they had no idea how their names had gotten on the choir grade lists."

"Oh?"

"Lots of foul-ups in the Registrar's office, they said. They can't be responsible for other people's incompetence."

Donahue pondered this a while, "That's a reasonable defense. They could get quite a few people to confirm it."

"That's what I understand," the chief responded. "Anyway, without those grades, they are back on academic probation."

"No Honors program for them."

"Surprisingly, you are wrong there. Stout has waved all requirements for them."

Donahue had to laugh, "Sounds like a story behind the story there." Changing the subject, he asked, "What about the financial records? Can the State's Attorney tie them to Flo Boater?"

"More or less, he says, but his experience with her in the past makes him cautious."

Donahue agreed with that, "Her lawyer did make him look foolish in the last trial."

"There's no proof, he says, that she intended to profit personally. Just to avoid involving the college in another scandal. If she pays the outstanding bills, she could come out looking like a saint, and the State's Attorney, well, rather lacking in sympathy. In any case, we sort of promised to keep her name out of this."

This bothered Donahue, who wanted to argue the point, "Her husband must have signed the papers, or the dean, and she must have known all about it. She probably even accompanied Dean Wooda to look over the Music building as a possible museum." Donahue still thought like a cop, not like a lawyer. He could almost imagine Mary saying that. But he could see who was guilty long before he could prove it.

Biggs disagreed, "She could make the late President Boater look like a trusting dupe who signed anything that Dean Wooda put in front of him. She would come across as the loyal wife protecting her husband's memory."

"And her relationship with the dean? Is she going to deny that, too? For all we know, they wanted the Music Building as a love nest."

"Pure speculation, she'll say, idle gossip by her enemies."

Donahue smiled at this, "Among which you would be prominent."

"Yes."

"Lill and Lily, too." Then he added, "And Mary."

"It's a good thing you got those promises in writing."

Donahue asked, "Even so, don't you think she'll try to back out?"

"You and I both saw her sign them. Miss E made copies and now Mary, Lill and Lill have the papers in their hands."

"Can't she claim this was extortion?"

"You didn't ask for anything personally. At least, nothing of importance. And you didn't quite lie to her. So... in this case, the situation is reversed. If she tries to get rid of you all, it will look like a personal vendetta."

"But what about moving the artifacts around, trying to hide them?

Biggs agreed, "To you and me, yes, that is proof of criminal intent. But we are policemen, and we know what she has done in the past. The State's Attorney says that Jay would not make a good witness because he was never told why he was supposed to hide the boxes, and it would be his word against Stanley Wooda's and Flo Boater's. He's seen what she can do with a jury, and I would like to have Jay right where he is, where he can keep an eye on her."

"She doesn't suspect?"

"She's suspicious of everyone, but when the Creep reported that Jay had refused to tell Jenny where the boxes were, and hadn't even told us about breaking the door, she was persuaded of his loyalty. She was very impressed by his ingenuity in hiding them right behind her office, and of putting more of the records with them. She apparently hasn't checked them yet, but she rewarded him by making him permanent head of Buildings and Grounds."

Donahue found this analysis compelling, but he still had a question, "If she thinks she has safely bought him off, what about Jay's relationship with Jenny?"

Biggs dismissed this with a laugh, "She doesn't think of anyone in Music as being smart enough to be dangerous."

"That's Jay's reasoning?" Donahue asked.

"Yes. He's my best source."

"But she's still smart enough to manage the Finance office temporarily?"

"Yup. Ironic, isn't it?"

"This is like a spy novel," Donahue observed. "Double agents in the enemy camp."

"It might make the future interesting," Biggs conceded, "if we don't give them away."

"Maybe less interesting. I always enjoyed talking with Jay, and now... I can't."

Biggs concurred, "Yes, if you talk with him too often, Flo Boater will get suspicious."

With a wry smile, Donahue said, "I guess I had better get used to feeding him useful information to pass on."

"If you have anything useful. But you don't have to. You are back to being an ordinary professor now."

"You are right about that. Not likely that I'll ever again learn anything worth passing on."

"One other thing. Something really good," Biggs added.

"What? What could top all this good news?"

"Remember those thugs at the demonstration?"

"Who could forget them?"

"You've seen worse, surely?"

"Better, too. Crowds weren't my favorite duty."

"Well, you'll not have to worry about them again."

Donahue slapped his thigh, "I'll be damned. How'd you do that?"

"Easier than I thought. I went to the Gym this morning."

"Where they hang out, lifting weights?"

"That's right," the chief said, "and I asked their names."

"I bet they were reluctant to give them."

"Oh yes, but I reminded them that Briarpatch was a small place and I'd find out soon enough."

"True. I didn't know any of them, but somebody would have."

"I warned them that if they made any mischief again, as they did earlier, I'd call their mothers."

"That did it?"

"Sure did," the chief said. As Donahue patted the older man on the shoulder and was commenting about how little power women are reputed to have, they heard a familiar laugh. Biggs looked up and pointed, "Hey, look who's coming!"

It was Jenny, Mary, Lill and Lily, all in a holiday spirit.

Lill cried out, "Hi guys, time to celebrate!"

Lily added, "But not here! We need suds!"

Mary agreed, "I'll say! Lunch and suds!" She gave Donahue a hug and whispered, "Thanks for saving me from a year of warm beer!"

Donahue, delighted, answered, "My pleasure!" It was. All the more for being so unusual and unexpected.

Biggs waved for attention and announced, "I know just the place! Just let me take off my badge!" As he did, he announced, "I'm off duty now."

As he led them toward the square, Lily cried out, "He's taking us to the Campus Crawl!" The traditional watering house for successful alums, it was too pricey for today's undergraduates and most faculty members. "Imported beer, on tap!"

Mary turned to ask, "Isn't it too early?"

But Lily responded, "This is an up-to-date college town now. Twenty-four hour pubs!" Not exactly, but it was open during the day, 10AM to 10 PM. Barbeque on weekends. Happy hour four to six. "Lunch specials, too, I'm told."

Lill added, "With Internet!"

"That's news to me," Mary said. "And I'm not sure I like it."

"Hell, Mary," Lily cracked. "We don't have it on campus. But it might save that place."

"Fill it with people too young to drink, you mean," Mary retorted. "All playing games."

"Too young to drink legally maybe," Lily suggested, "but just right for the Internet. What do you think, chief? About their drinking."

"Ha. Not my problem," he responded. "Not right now. I'm off duty."

Their laughter was still audible as Flo Boater and Stanley Wooda were about to enter the administration building. The president looked around for the celebrants, but couldn't see anyone. Digging in a purse for some rarely-used glasses, she complained to her dean, "Listen to that! Drunken students at this time of day."

Stanley Wooda, cautiously not telling her what he could see, took out a small pad, "I'll make a note to take care of it."

She snapped, "Your notepad had better have a lot of pages. You've got a lot of work to do." She began ticking off items on her fingers, the dean taking notes, stumbling up the stairs, until she finally ran out of ideas, fingers, and steps. Finally, he whistled, "A long list, but I can handle it. But what a mess! The newspapers will soon be trying to figure out how all the scandals fit together. How do we explain our moving the artifacts around and trying to hide the financial records?"

As she opened the door to her office, she explained, "We don't. It will all blow over."

"I don't know." What he was really thinking about was his political career. How could he be sure this wouldn't come up at the worst possible time?

She consoled him, "It could be worse. If Jay Bird hadn't hidden them in my back office, it would really have been suspicious."

"In your office! Here? Is that where they were?"

"Yes. He said that I was never in there, and moreover, no one would ever think to look for them in such an obviously inappropriate place." After a pause, she added, "And what a proof that we weren't hiding anything! It makes me look so innocent."

Stanley Wooda said with admiration, "Clever." But he wasn't so sure. He didn't like the "me" in her conclusion.

"We might even be able to put the blame for the misunderstandings on the former chair of the theater department."

"The Creep?"

Flo Boater nodded, "He's the perfect fall guy. No friends." With that, she slumped into her chair and slumped back.

"The vice president's accident?" he asked, "Did she really slip on a rug? Nobody will believe that story. Who has rugs nowadays?"

She looked upward as if in search of divine guidance, then bit her lip, made a loud smack and suggested, "Let's say, 'A deplorable accident caused by the immaturity of two naive young boys.' Maybe some will believe the story of their checking the strange light late at night. The trustees did."

He looked up at her, "I like your calling them *boys*. Makes the point better than *students*."

"Does, doesn't it? So, in the end no one really at fault, except perhaps a workaholic too tired to watch where she was going." She then added, "And we say this only if asked. Volunteer *nothing*!"

"How about saying the boys had seen the broken glass in the door and were investigating?" "Good idea, Stanley, but we'll have to insinuate that rather than say it. Some reporter might check."

"I'll take care of that."

She leaned forward to touch her dean on the arm, "No point in mentioning Stout either, is there?"

He was enthusiastic, "That could get us off completely!" He began to spin a story about the tireless president working day and night, concerned about a subordinate's effort to keep up with her. "And we can hold the real story over his head!"

But Flo Boater was not satisfied with such a small triumph. Her mind was already racing ahead, even faster than the dean's, who was very impressed with her next question, "How do we spin her accident into something positive?"

"Perhaps we should have a conference on encouraging relaxation." Seeing her quizzical look, he explained, "Faculty and administrators need more time to think and reflect."

"Administrators maybe. Faculty already have summers."

He studied his pen briefly, his eyes betraying some doubt. "Are you sure you want to antagonize the faculty? They're a bit touchy about their work load."

Nodding, she briefly considered shortening the semester, which might reduce the strain of caring for the now-enlarged student body. Then she imagined what Lill and Lily might make of "watering down of academic content;" she was physically jolted at the thought of water, bringing up, as it were, an image of the late dean floating in the swimming pool—though she had never witnessed that tragedy personally. Then, remembering some long-ago speech of her late husband's, she smiled and asked, "The creative aspect of golf?"

The dean calmly agreed, "Properly phrased, it might get us national publicity."

She almost laughed, "We could use some *positive* publicity."

With impeccable timing, the historian came through the door. In his hands were two morning newspapers that they recognized as the *Arcadian Woodman* and *The Zenith Apex*. Flo Boater never failed to smile when she saw the first paper, knowing that the only woodman of any importance in Arcadian history was torn to pieces by his own hounds. Her smile deepened at the thought that anyone would bother to read such provincial newspapers—she subscribed, but she rarely looked through them. However, there was something about the historian's demeanor that made her smile change to a frown. The way he handed the papers to them seemed to suggest that it was the *Woodman* who was doing the shredding today. She took the paper in her hands, read, crumpled it up, then handed it back to him. The historian, appalled by her clenched teeth, stepped unsteadily backward.

Stanley Wooda, meanwhile read aloud the *Apex's* headline: "*Scandal-wracked Administration Back in office. Podunk Outraged.*" He ran his eyes swiftly down the columns. It was all there—the presumed financial scandal, the investigative break-in, the accident, the president's suspicious arrival at the scene, the artifacts and the suspicion of murder. And no mention of any exonerating facts. The story started with Smith's byline and ended with the police chief looking for the missing body.

"What happened to Max Stout?" the dean cried out. "How was he left out?"

The historian thought a second before speaking, "Smith and Jones are English majors… The omission will guarantee passing grades this semester."

There seemed to be minimal connection between the headline and the story. Only two sources were cited. The first was an unfortunately phrased quote from "a senior historian" to the effect that the college was "doomed to suffer from the mistaken policies of the previous Boater administration." Smith had meant Lill's presidency, but the editor who had rewritten his contribution could only remember Floyd Boater's years in office.

"I never said that!" the historian explained. "I told him 'no comment.'"

Stanley Wooda gave him a pitiful look, "In context, the question must have… it must have sounded like a confirmation of his question."

The second source, a "community" member, was the rewrite editor's great-aunt, now living in Arcadia and sharing that community's views of the rival college; moreover, years ago Briarpatch College had torn down the house in which she had been born—that was an insult she would never forgive, though many years ago the family had sold the surrounding pasture and farmland for a housing tract. Long abandoned, the rambling old farmstead was a fire hazard that the late Dean Wooda had acquired cheaply, saying that the property was essential to the college's future (he had carefully said "property," which only she could think meant the structure) and paying for it with a modest bequest intended to help the college expand the campus into the surrounding decaying neighborhood; he had used it as a fraternity house for a while and then, when the joists began to come apart from the stresses of overcrowded dancing, sent in the wreckers. The old lady was furious that the site became a gravel-covered parking lot. Moreover, even though she had moved away from Middleville when she married, she still considered herself an "expert" on the college relationship with the community. Whenever she visited friends, especially the mother of the history department chair, she caught up on news that she then passed on, filtered through her hatred of the Boater administration, to her ageing friends, who, out of a combination of politeness, ignorance and memories of past affronts, vigorously agreed with her.

Flo Boater said grimly, to the shaken historian, "We won't forget this." The poor man, misunderstanding what she meant, was about to lose control of his lower extremities when she continued, "You are the only one we have been able to count on, you and Jay." She took him by the hand and led him to a chair, into which he sank gratefully. She bent down beside him, finally lowering herself awkwardly onto one knee to look him in his ashen face, "Can you speak to the faculty about these libels, explain that they are part of a vicious campaign, not against me, but against the college?"

Stanley Wooda moved close to add, "Rednecks attacking intellectuals. That sort of thing."

She aided the historian to his feet and added, "We *would* be grateful."

The poor man could only nod his agreement and hasten away. He had even forgotten to ask about the chairmanship of the Theater department. He had only seen the headlines before hurrying to bring the papers to them. How could he know that he and his mother would be named in the articles?

Stanley Wooda had by now wound up for his own tirade, "This is *intolerable*! *Accusing* us of, of, of, *nothing*. They don't have anything but the *old scandals*! How can they keep bringing that museum business up!?"

Flo Boater hit the table with her hand, hard, "This is all the fault of that *bastard*, Dean Wooda, and my *idiot* husband."

"Your husband knew?"

"No. *That's* why he was an idiot! He had no head for details, so he just left everything up to that *crook*, his dean."

Stanley Wooda hardly knew how to frame his question, so he kept the language as neutral as he could, "I understood you worked *closely* with the late dean." He was careful with the word *closely*, so as not to imply that he knew how close the relationship was.

Her eyes narrowed at the question, but she resisted the impulse to snap at him. "That was the only way to keep track of what he was doing," she explained. "Just like I was doing with Max."

Stanley Wooda was taken aback at this, "Stout? You and Stout?"

"Don't be silly, Stanley. No sensible woman would have an affair with Max Stout! I meant I let him think he was important."

At this he recovered enough to ask, "What would you do to the dean, if he were still alive?"

"Stanley, I'm only speaking *figuratively*." She paused for a deep breath, then continued, "Only figuratively, but you take note, if the late Dean Wooda came back to life again, right now, right here in this room, I wouldn't care if he was your uncle or your aunt's tailor, or not related at all—*that dean would be dead again!*"

Later, after the historian had left a message with Miss E, asking about the chairmanship of the Fine Arts division, Flo Boater called Stanley Wooda in, "What should we do about this? He was counting on it, you know, as a step toward becoming dean."

"Yeah, my job."

"Probably, but maybe somewhere else."

"I can't imagine his leaving his mother."

"Hmm, good point. Maybe her health isn't so good now. But either way he needs to enhance his Vita."

Stanley Wooda thought a minute, "How about faculty secretary?"

"Faculty Secretary? Why would he want that?"

"He has complained that Ms. Gates doesn't quote him correctly."

"Well, she does, and she's had that job forever. She wouldn't want to give it up. It's her main claim to faculty status."

"Buy her off."

"With what?" she asked.

"You know, we've been talking about an internet center. Well, we could put it in the library."

"It's not in the budget."

"Flo, you've told me many times that there's always money for what we need."

She thought a second, then said, "Okay, that would make her happy... but why would the Creep want the job?"

"I'll hint that he could make the minutes say whatever he thought he heard...." He then gave Flo a wide smile, "It's a deconstructionist argument. Stout will understand."

She smiled back. Poor Stout, he loses in every respect.

As Mary and Donahue were crossing the campus later that afternoon, talking animatedly about the recent adventure, they saw the choir director coming the opposite direction. Mary tugged at Donahue's sleeve, indicating that she would like to chat with him. The choir director waved and stopped to talk.

"Nice concert," Donahue started to say. But the choir director spoke up first, "I was hoping to see you," he said to Mary. "Rehearsals are Wednesdays, as usual."

"Yes," she said. "I plan to be there."

"You've been missed."

"It's been complicated," she explained.

"Um, um," he continued, slightly embarrassed, "we have a problem... a serious problem."

"What? And how can I help?" she asked.

"We are desperately short of male voices. And Miss Purdy has left."

She shook her head, unable to help. After a moment, Donahue spoke up, "Would a baritone help?"

They stared at him. In his first year he hadn't even attended a concert, and now he only attended to see Mary, "Can you sing?" the director asked.

"I could once." It had been years, but he had no reason to imagine that his voice had vanished. After all, he didn't smoke.

The choir director hugged him. Mary *considered* doing the same.

Chapter Twenty-Seven

Life returned to normal at Briarpatch College. Normal except for the unusual number of "searches" for new hires that began immediately after the first insurance payments were made on the lives of the late president, Floyd Boater, and academic dean, C. Wooda. Optimism was high, despite realistic warnings that the best applicants sent out dozens of letters, some perhaps not realizing that Briarpatch was not Sweet Briar, others just so concerned about being unemployed that they applied for every opening available. No one knew why these job ads were called "searches," since it was the applicants who did most of the searching. Perhaps it referred to the task of sorting through many essentially identical applications, with very similar and very fashionable dissertation titles, with largely identical letters of recommendation (always in the top 5%), to find the ideal candidate—who undoubtedly was going to be hired at some more prestigious college where the search committee appreciated more fully esoteric dissertation topics, and which paid better salaries. But few complained. At long last, the faculty would receive raises equal to the increase in the cost of living, and departments could fill gaps created by "temporarily" not replacing retirees and those who quit or simply never showed up at the beginning of a semester. There was also a search for someone to help Stanley Wooda, or, more likely, Flora Boater, in dealing with correspondence. Flora Boater had discovered how dangerous it was to discard faculty notes and throw letters away without reading them. It seemed logical to hire someone to read these materials first, someone who could be blamed if a problem arose. In a normal college Miss Efficiency could have performed those tasks, but she was too competent—she would have noticed if good ideas were not acted on. It was better to hire someone more likely to be less efficient and less confident of being in any way important. An assistant dean seemed to fit the bill exactly. A low salary would ward off all but the least qualified people.

Donahue was not sure why he had been put on the committee. He wasn't even sure that President Boater wanted an assistant dean. Yes, her young dean was absent from campus quite a bit—speeches and state political events—but she had been giving some of his work to the historian and Stout. Maybe that was it… they were not quite what she wanted, or she didn't want them to know too much about what was going on.

Anyway, the committee was stacked. Stout was chair. He had selected two young feminists from his department—one good looking, one not so much—and… maybe Donahue was to provide the appearance of balance. You know, two males, two females, three liberals, one conservative. That was about the way it always went, unless it was four liberals…. And guess who was selected to call the references? Modern women did not do secretarial work.

Donahue sighed, picked up his copies of the applications, looked at the first one, and reached for the telephone. Then he stopped. Why call the people suggested by the applicant? At least, why call them first? They were undoubtedly going to say good things. Maybe he should get some background, to learn what questions to ask. He remembered that he knew one person at that college. That is, he had met him at a conference a few weeks ago, before he knew there would be a search. Digging around in his desk, he came up with a card. Strange, he thought, that he had kept it. He himself didn't even have a card and probably wouldn't have thought to hand it out.

The voice on the other end was familiar, but his name was not immediately recognized. Then, "Oh, yes, Donahue. I remember now. What can I do for you?"

Donahue explained, then asked if he could speak in confidence, that it might be embarrassing if it got around that the candidate was applying for a job at Briarpatch. He meant to say that the candidate might be embarrassed if it was known that he was on the market, but it came out as though he might be embarrassed by having it known that he was stooping so low as to think of working in Middleville.

"No problem," the voice responded. After hearing the name, the voice said, "I don't think I'm the right person to speak to, but I know who is." And he then gave a name and, after a pause, a telephone number.

Donahue dialed, explained his mission, and waited for a response.

"I, uh, don't think he is really what you want for a dean." Silence followed.

"Could you elaborate? Just why wouldn't we want him?"

There was a pause. "Well, it's a woman problem."

"A woman problem? Do you mean affairs… or discrimination… or something else?" His cop instincts began to kick in. Was he a wife beater? No, the voice had suggested something more sordid. Nothing evil, just sordid.

"To tell the truth, his wife drove a cab."

"Drove a cab?"

"Yes. She was bored, so she got a job."

"Having a job isn't unusual, not nowadays."

"No, but driving a cab is so… so déclassé."

Donahue pondered this a moment, "Is that why he was let go?" There was nothing in the application about why the candidate was looking for a new job, but there was always a reason. Might as well ask.

"No, no, of course not." There was a pause, then, "They divorced within a year in any case. No children, thank God, but she left town and he stayed on."

"Oh," Donahue answered, wondering where this was going.

"It was, well, he married a student."

"An undergraduate? Someone he met in a class?"

"No, we don't allow our deans to teach classes here, and he tried to defend himself by saying that she was a 'non-traditional' student and almost his age, and it had been almost two years, but… around here we just don't do that kind of thing."

"Faculty don't sleep with students?" Donahue hoped that his smile did not make itself too obviously into his question.

There was a note of resentment in the response, "Of course, but one just doesn't marry one. It would set a bad precedent. Don't you see the difference?"

Donahue ignored the question, "And that caused him to be fired?"

There was a pause, with obvious reflection going on at the other end of the line. "No, not really. The board fired the president and the new president has given notice to everyone associated with his predecessor."

"Had he done okay as dean until then?"

There was another pause, "Probably about as well as the circumstances allowed. The president gave him no authority to make decisions. He had to take every matter upstairs, that is, down the hall. He was just a messenger boy."

Donahue resisted the urge to saying something about shooting the messenger, then expressed thanks for having assisted him so much. As he hung up the receiver, he thought that the candidate was indeed dead. The two feminists on the committee would approve of nothing he had heard. Imagine a woman so oppressed that she would take a job as a cabbie!

Otherwise, the candidate seemed perfect for the job—no backbone, no complaining, and an embarrassing past. The perfect fall guy. Maybe he did stand a chance.

Forthcoming:

Is the Dean Dead Yet?
#4 in the Briarpatch College Series

Mentioned in the text:

William Urban, *Wyatt Earp, the OK Corral and the Law of the American West*. New York: Rosen Press, 2003.